—That's how this works, Grace. I rob you, then I ride away. Someone will be along soon enough to help you.

—Take me with you.

—Why would I do that?

Grace stepped forward and grabbed the reins of my horse to keep me from leaving.

—So I can tell your story. Everyone says you don't exist. I can make sure you get the recognition you deserve.

I have to give her credit. She knew exactly what I wanted, before I knew myself. If I'd had more time, logic would have prevailed and I would have left Grace Trumbull on the road to Columbia. But I didn't.

—Come on, then.

She closed her carpetbag haphazardly and handed it to me. I looped it on my saddle horn, held my hand out, and helped her up behind me.

Jehu's voice managed to rise above the rushing water and ricochet off the mountain walls.

—You're going to regret this.

He was right, of course.

By Melissa Lenhardt

SAWBONES SERIES

Sawbones

Blood Oath

Badlands

JACK MCBRIDE MYSTERIES

Stillwater

The Fisher King

Heresy

HERESY

MELISSA LENHARDT

www.redhookbooks.com

Author photograph by Amy Freshwater
Cover design by Crystal Ben
Cover photographs by Shutterstock

Redhook Books/Orbit
Hachette Book Group
1290 Avenue of the Americas
New York, NY 10104
hachettebookgroup.com

First Edition: October 2018

Redhook is an imprint of Orbit, a division of Hachette Book Group.
The Redhook name and logo are trademarks of Hachette Book Group, Inc.

Library of Congress Cataloging-in-Publication Data:

Names: Lenhardt, Melissa, author.
Title: Heresy / Melissa Lenhardt.
Description: First edition. | New York, NY : Redhook Books/Orbit, 2018.
Identifiers: LCCN 2018019893| ISBN 9780316435352 (trade paperback) | ISBN 9780316435338 (ebook)
Subjects: | BISAC: FICTION / Historical. | FICTION / Action & Adventure. | FICTION / Westerns. | GSAFD: Adventure fiction. | Western stories.
Classification: LCC PS3612.E529 H47 2018 | DDC 813/.6—dc23
LC record available at https://lccn.loc.gov/2018019893

ISBNs: 978-0-316-43535-2 (trade paperback), 978-0-316-43533-8 (ebook)

Printed in the United States of America

LSC-C

10 9 8 7 6 5 4 3 2 1

For Jenny,
without whose support and encouragement
this book would never have happened

HERESY RANCH

TIMBERLINE

ORO CITY

COLORADO

·1877·

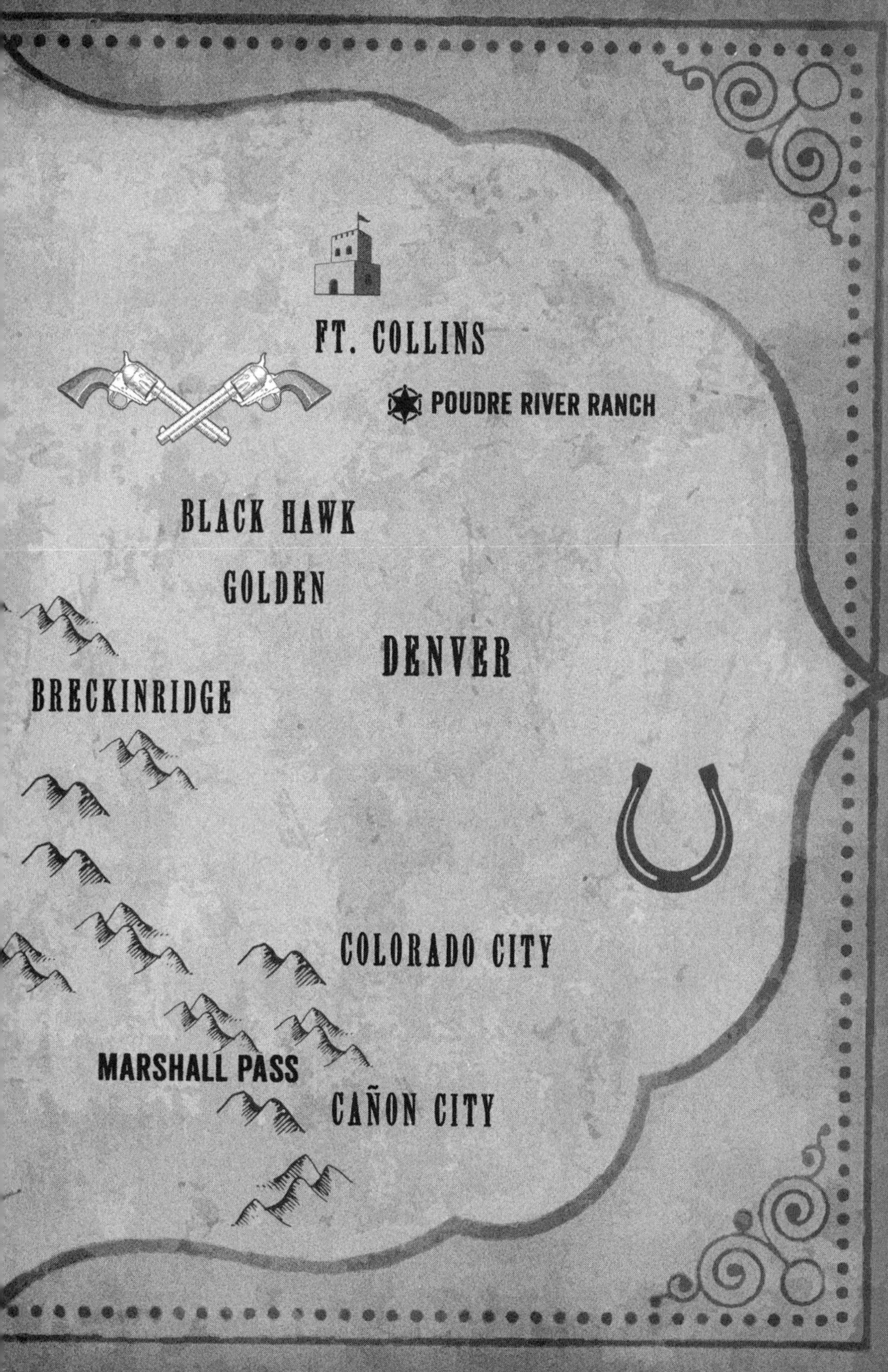
FT. COLLINS
POUDRE RIVER RANCH
BLACK HAWK
GOLDEN
DENVER
BRECKINRIDGE
COLORADO CITY
MARSHALL PASS
CAÑON CITY

"Men have been faithful about noting every heroic act of their half of the race, and now it should be the duty, as well as the pleasure, of women to make for future generations a record of the heroic deeds of the other half."

—*Susan B. Anthony*

Introduction

Dr. Stephanie Bailey
Professor of Western American History
University of Colorado Boulder

This story starts, like so many others, in an attic.

One thing I've learned as a historian is that stories, especially ones about the forgotten, are rarely told in a straight line. It would be wonderful if, in the process of cleaning out the house of a dearly departed elderly relative, an heir disgruntled with the enormous task of sifting through decades of memories discovered a treasure trove of correspondence, journals, and newspaper articles bundled together in order, with extant copies of letters both to and from to give clarity to the story. That rarely happens, most often because the heirs either don't understand the importance of the brittle bundle of letters bound by a faded red ribbon, or they don't care. They may keep the letters with the intention of reading them, but shove them in the back of a drawer for the next generation to discover, and wonder at whose faint scrawl covered pages and pages of a dry, cracked leather journal. Or, more often, they toss them, and one more person is lost to history.

Being a historian who focuses on women in American history, I have a vast network of friends and colleagues who love history, who see it slipping through our hands as our society moves ever faster away from our heritage and into the digital age. These estate agents, antiques dealers, amateur historians, collectors, and librarians want to see our history preserved as much as I do. When they come across something that might be of particular interest to me, they give me a call, or sometimes an unexpected package arrives at my door. The latter is how I came to be in possession of *Margaret Parker; or, Saints and Outlaws: A Tale of the Old West.*

A friend of mine with a penchant for antique books, first editions, and obscure literature found the penny dreadful at the Round Top Texas Antique Fair. The antiques vendor told her it had been found in the attic of a Galveston mansion that was being turned into a bed-and-breakfast. She knew what it was, and how valuable it might be, despite being only a fragment of the whole story, the moment she saw it. She paid $150 for the brittle, yellowed pages with print so faded in places as to be unreadable. When she got home and did some research, she realized that its publisher had been a penny dreadful writer himself, and had made his fortune by writing an Old West blooder loosely based on real events. She could find no reference to *Saints and Outlaws* online. On the off chance this one might also be based on actual events, she copied the pages and sent them to me.

Penny dreadfuls, also known as penny horribles, penny bloods, penny awfuls, and blooders, were popular in Victorian England, having their heyday in the 1860s and 1870s. With roots in Gothic novels, these sensational serials offered outlandish tales of adventure, villainy, horror, and romance. Printed on cheap paper and sold for a penny apiece, they weren't made to last, which is why so few copies exist. This particular dreadful was published in 1890, at the tail end of the penny dreadful glory days, and published in the States, which never had the same appetite for the outlandish as the British Victorians.

I read the incomplete blooder and almost immediately dismissed it as total fiction. *Saints and Outlaws* is the story of a young female adventurer traveling through Colorado who gets caught up in a stagecoach robbery. The robbers kidnap her, for no reason other than that the author needed a kidnapping in the first few pages, it seems, and our heroine soon discovers they are women disguised as men. The adventurer joins the gang, and over the five surviving chapters, the gang is portrayed as Robin Hoods of the Old West, master con artists, lovers, and, finally, revenge-seeking horsemen of the apocalypse. It was entertaining, and I longed for the complete blooder, but the story and characters bore no resemblance to any historical figures I'd come across in my study of the Old West. I filed it away, moved on, and forgot about it.

It wasn't until five years later that I came across an essay about Opal Steele Driscoll, a prostitute turned miner's wife turned society lady, and the throwaway mention that she played the accordion. It was such an unusual quirk that it reminded me of the penny dreadful I'd been sent years earlier. I pulled it out and discovered that there had indeed been an accordion-playing prostitute in the penny dreadful. The essay stated that Opal Steele Driscoll had claimed to run with the Spooner Gang, but she was a notorious liar, and her claims were dismissed.

You may think this is a very thin connection, and you're right. But the idea that this fictional female gang might be based on truth had firmly planted itself in my imagination, and no respectable women's historian would ignore such a possibility. Bigger histories have been uncovered from less. I put the word out to my fellow historians to be on the lookout for anything related to a group of female outlaws, and decided to start the search with the penny dreadful's eponymous outlaw. Margaret Parker was too normal a name for the heroine of such an outlandish adventure story. The census records for 1870 and 1880 turned up no good matches, but that isn't surprising. Emigration was constant, and Margaret Parker could have lived in Colorado for nine years and not been included on the census, so I turned to newspapers and found her obituary.

I will elide the details of the next five years (my editor says no one's interested; they want to read the story). Research takes time, and when it's a side project it takes even longer. It's been ten years since I received the unexpected package from my friend, and I think I've finally pieced together the story of Margaret Parker, Hattie LaCour, and their gang through a journal, an oral history, a detective's case file, newspaper accounts of the time, telegrams, and specialty histories of towns, prostitutes, and the suffrage movement. You'll also note that while the journal and oral history are similar enough that you know there were three women experiencing the same events at the same time, the "official" accounts tell a quite different story. It's up to you, the reader, to decide which is more likely—that the same story told by three women sixty years apart would tell strikingly similar false stories, or that the newspapers at the time told the truth. The whole endeavor was eye-opening in a way I never expected, and I'm forever thankful to my friend who saw a brittle antique blooder about the Old West and thought of me.

Margaret Parker and Hattie LaCour were real, they existed, and they were magnificent.

Dr. Stephanie Bailey
University of Colorado
December 15, 2017

PART ONE

THE LEGEND OF HATTIE LACOUR

1

WPA Slave Narrative Collection

Second interview with Henrietta Lee,
by Grace Williams

Saturday, September 5, 1936

Henrietta Lee is a ninety-two-year-old former slave from New Orleans. She was interviewed in July by Gerald Coleman and told him the story of her life in slavery, of her service in the Buffalo Soldier regiment disguised as a man, and of being discovered and discharged. Having completed his brief, Coleman ended the interview. I transcribed his notes, noted her parting comment, "The story is jus' gettin' good." Curiosity got the best of me, and I returned to finish her story. Below is a word-for-word transcription of my multiple interviews with Mrs. Lee. —Grace Williams

"I didn't expect anyone to come back to talk to me. Got the impression Mr. Coleman wanted to be doing anything but talking to an old slave. Oh, I'm sho Mr. Coleman is a busy man. Everybody's busy these days, driving cars, staying out until all hours. Nobody knows how to sit silent with yourself anymore. If they're not going, they're listening to the radio. Lots of racket these days. I miss the silence of the mountains, I'll tell you that.

"You want to know about my life after the army, huh? This for the project? Come on, girl. I can spot a liar a mile away and blindfolded. You're getting something out of this. Screenwriter, huh?"

Mrs. Lee laughs for a long while, so long that tears start to come down her wrinkled face.

"No, no. I'm not laughing at you. I'm laughing at the damn perfection of it. Sixty years on, and I'm right back where I was in 1877."

Her laughter dies off.

"Except I'm alone now.

"You know, it's funny, I was a slave for twenty-one of my ninety-two years, just a drop of time when you think of it. But that's still all anyone wants to talk about. As if I didn't exist in the seventy-one years between then and now. Why do you think that is? Times are changing and they want to remember? But why do they want to remember? To do better in the future, or to remind themselves of the good ole days? It can always get worse. Every time we get a bit of progress, things get worse. One step forward, a dozen steps back.

"Between you and me, most of the stuff I told Coleman were lies. What he wonta 'ear, how he wonta 'ear it, chile. If I told what really happened to me? The beatings? The midnight visits from the master? Hell, he wouldn't believe me. He wanted all benevolent masters and sweet-as-sugar mistresses with happy slaves smiling as we picked the cotton, so that's what I gave him. I never picked a boll of cotton in my life. You really think the government is going to keep honest accounts of what was done to us? It's up to us to keep our oral history passed down between the black folks. We won't forget, and maybe someday our real story will be told.

"Nah, that's going to be lost like so many other stories have been lost. Or changed. Because the white men are writing the history, child. They aren't going to show themselves in anything other than a heroic light. Uh-huh. You know what I'm saying is right. You want a truth, I'll give you a truth, Grace Williams.

"I knew a Grace once. Back in Colorado. Did I like her? At times. You like everybody all the time? Your husband? Child, you are a liar. But don't worry, everything I'll tell you will be the God's honest truth. You heard of the Parker Gang? Didn't think so. The Spooner Gang? *Tsk*, that damn movie. Not a word of it was true, though Gary Cooper is a pretty good likeness of him. Jed was handsome, and knew it. He could just look at a woman and she'd drop her bloomers. Not me, no. I wasn't the one with a relationship with him. That was Garet. Margaret Parker, was her Christian name. A British lady, and a duchess. Had the prettiest voice of anyone I've ever known, though she tried to hide it most of the time. Weren't a lot of British ladies in the West and even fewer British lady bandits. Yes, I said bandits. *Outlaw* is probably a better word. I'm getting there, don't worry. Are you going to listen, or are you going to ask questions? That's what I thought.

"As to Garet and Spooner, not sure when she and Jed started up, if it was before Garet's husband died or after. But it wasn't too long after, I know that. Jed and his gang used our ranch as a hideout when they'd done a job, the Poudre River ranch at first, then the one in the Hole, Heresy Ranch we called it, after Thomas died and Garet's place was stolen by the colonel.

"Did I work for Margaret Parker? Hell no. We were friends. Guess it was fate, me ending up hiding in her barn in 1869. I was on the run, you see. After the army found me out for a woman, I couldn't very well disguise myself as a man and go join somewhere else. That was done a lot in those days. But there were only a few regiments I could go to, being a Negro. I didn't much like pretending to be a man anyways. I had freedoms women didn't, but clothes couldn't change the color of my skin. I liked the men I served with and they liked me. So I became a camp follower. Laundresses, we were called. It was pretty much what it sounds like, but a lot of us also serviced the men in other ways.

"It was a good living for a while. Until a cracker couldn't get his johnson to work one night and decided it was my fault. I wasn't a little woman, not like I am now, but he was big as a bull. Didn't have much of a chance. He tied my hands up on the center tent pole, took his belt off, and tore my back up good. Guess it reminded him of days gone by. He didn't have equipment problems after that. Left me a bloody mess, tied to the pole. You OK there, Mrs. Williams? This too much for you?

"Took me a few weeks to heal up. The other laundresses, they took care of me. Mainly a woman named Sue. She'd lost her sister to some violence some years back, she never said what or how, but I suspect it was at the hands of a man. We didn't get along, generally. I took too much business from her. But she looked past everything to make me better. Women do that, you know. Take care of each other when the chips are down. The good women do, anyways.

"When I was able to get around and my lashes had stopped seeping, I took my revenge. Sue, she knew what I was going to do. We never talked about it, but one morning I found a big Bowie knife hidden under my pillow. You know what a Bowie knife is? Named after Jim Bowie, hero of the Alamo. Big knife, blade about yay long. This one wasn't much to look at. Yellow bone handle wrapped with a leather cord, to give it grip, you know. Had to change that cord out after. Soaked through with blood. Damn right I killed a white man. Slit his throat. Quite a mess. Never killed that way again. What do you think Mr. Coleman would've done if I'd told him that?" *Laughs.*

"I stole his coat and his horse and rode like hell. Blew the horse. That was before I knew how to manage one so that it could last for miles. Went on foot after that. Hid in the foothills for a few days, eating berries, drinking from rivers. The man I killed was just a private, but I figured they'd go after me for obvious reasons. You let one nigger get away with it…

"It was fall, and the nights were getting cold. Too cold for the cracker's duster I'd stolen to be much help. I couldn't risk a fire even if I had a soapstone to light it. One night I came across this horse ranch, big barn out back. I snuck in and slept in a stall. The horse didn't mind overmuch. But I've always had a way with animals. Not like Garet and Jehu, mind you, but I held my own.

"Anyways. Told myself I'd wake up before dawn, maybe steal a chicken and be on my way. Nah…didn't even occur to me, if you want to know the truth. Horse thieves were barely a step above niggers who killed white men. You know, I've never been afraid of dying. Still aren't. It was the after that always terrified me. No, hell doesn't worry me. I've repented, been washed in the blood of the Lamb. I imagine Peter'll let me in easy enough. No, the *after*. When my soul has departed but my body's still there. I've seen what they do to black bodies, even today. You? So you aren't stupid. Good. Good. That mind of yours, that's what'll keep you alive and out of trouble. Remember that.

"Lord help me, there was something about that barn. Comforting like. The smell of hay and horse. And manure. The warmth. I was woken the next morning by a young, smock-faced boy. Or so I thought. He didn't yell or scream or run to the house and get his boss. Garet and her husband, Thomas, as it turned out. He saw the dried blood on the front of my dress and asked me if I was hurt. He snuck me some food from the house, a little whisky, a clean dress. Then the sheriff came. The boy hid me in a haystack.

"Find me? I'm here, aren't I? Garet did, though. She looked at the clean dress I was wearing, hers, and looked me in the eye. She had beautiful eyes, Garet. Ice blue. Dark hair. She was more handsome than pretty, had a horsey face if you want to know the truth, but there was something about her that drew you in. She knew who I was. Couldn't have been many strange Negro women in the foothills around the Cache la Poudre. 'Did you kill him?' she asked. 'Yes, ma'am.' 'Why?' 'He took my dignity.' She nodded once, and told me to come inside.

"She treated me with respect, like an equal, from the start. She didn't order me around. It was always please and thank you and asking me for my opinion. I didn't trust her at the beginning. Besides Sue at the end, I wasn't used to kindness from a white woman. I thought for sure Garet would reveal herself to be like everyone else in time. But she never did.

"I loved that woman, I really did. She was like a sister to me. We fought like sisters, too. But when it came down to it, we took care of each other. We all did. Margaret, though. I sure miss that woman. Her life was cut too short, and that's a fact.

"October 1877. That summer before was…I don't know. Maybe I shouldn't tell you. You aren't going to believe me. No one does, and there's no one left to back me up, neither. You're going to go back to your writers' project office and talk about the crazy auntie who says she was an outlaw. They're going to write me off as a senile old woman. You see, this may really be the last chance for our story to be told. Grace tried, but the best she managed was a penny dreadful that bore little resemblance to the truth. Dorcas Connolly never said a word about it. Oh yeah. I paid attention to her over the years. That accordion-playing whore Opal never came within a mile of outlawing, but she told so many lies about her exploits that no one will believe a word from a woman who lived then if it doesn't follow the lies they all decided on. What lies? Hell, girl, anything you see on the silver screen, for one. Anything you read, anything you hear. The story of the West is one big lie they call a myth because it sounds better. The biggest lie is that men did all the settling. Sure, women were outnumbered, but we were there. Hell, they couldn't've settled the West without women, but do we get any credit? Have we ever gotten to be the hero of the story? Hell, no. And a black woman? Shit.

"So, you can see why I'm hesitant. This isn't a short story, and I'm not going to be able to tell it all in one day. But if you're willing to humor an old woman, to be patient when I get too tired to go on and to really listen, then I'll tell you my story. You are? That's fine, then. But you have to promise me one thing: don't give this story to anyone until I'm dead. Well, that's sweet of you to say so, but I'm ninety-two years old, best as I can tell, and I'm tired, Grace Williams. So tired. It won't be long now, and I'm ready. Child, am I ready. Sure, I can talk a little longer today if you'll refill my tea for me. Kitchen's straight through to the back. Get yourself one too while you're back there.

"Thank you. There's nothing better than a glass of tea on a porch, is there?"

Mrs. Lee pauses for a long moment, gathering her thoughts.

"I can't tell you about the summer of 1877 until I tell you how we got there, the course our lives took to us being outlaws. It all started a few years before, when Thomas died of consumption. January 1872, it was. Things went OK for a while. Me, Garet, and Jehu ran the ranch. We had a little Chinese cook, too, Julie. She was one of the women who found her way to us, worked for a while, then moved on. And of course Joan and Stella were there by the time Thomas died.

"We had a neighbor, rich fellow called Colonel Louis Connolly. At first, after Thomas died, the colonel was very helpful.

His was a cattle ranch, we broke and sold wild horses. Garet was a hand with a horse, I can tell you that. Quiet them right down. Didn't realize she was better at it than Thomas until he was bedridden. We weren't any sort of competition for Connolly, in fact we kept him in horses, and he was very helpful, like I said. Well, he was just laying the groundwork to buy her out when running a ranch got to be too much for the little lady. That never happened, though. We thrived.

"About six months after Thomas died, Garet bought the three hundred and forty acres between her and Connolly's ranch from a widow whose husband was kicked in the head by his mule. Took us up to almost seven hundred acres of prime river bottomland. Chafed Connolly something fierce. He'd put an offer in for the ranch, but the widow's husband had made her swear not to sell to "that bastard Connolly." The widow told Garet what the offer was, and asked her to offer for one dollar more. They could say in honesty that she paid more. The colonel found out what the selling price was and was incensed. We didn't know that until later. It boiled down to him hating being bested by a woman, but I think a part of him admired Garet's shrewdness. That's why he tried to marry her at first. She was young and had a lot of spirit, Garet did, and a great wit. Men, and a fair few women, fell under her spell pretty easy, and the colonel was no different.

"He came to the ranch one night all gussied up, and I knew exactly which way the wind was blowing. Garet did, too. You should have seen how still she went when Connolly walked in the door with that bunch of wildflowers in his hand. This old man—he was a good twenty years older than Garet, but he looked thirty or more with his leathery face and silver hair. He had a nice, full head a hair, I'll give him that. The sisters and I went into the other room while he made his offer for her hand in marriage, but you better believe we listened in. It wasn't a bad proposal, and most women would have been flattered and jumped at the chance. Not Garet. But she told him she needed time to think about it.

"She and I stayed up all night, talking about it. Combining the ranches into one operation did make a sort of sense. Like I said, they complemented each other. But we both knew that as soon as she said yes to Connolly, she would be giving up control of the ranch. There was no telling what would have become of the rest of us, but we damn sure wouldn't have been moved into the big house. That was what decided her, the worry about what would happen to us, and where would the women who searched us out for a safe place to stay go? No way the colonel or Dorcas would have agreed to being a halfway house to a bunch of whores and runaway wives.

"Garet didn't want to remarry. Why would she when she had Spooner to satisfy her now and then? Garet got a taste of freedom, you see. What it was like to be her own boss, to be able to run the ranch without having to pretend like its success was all down to her husband. What woman in her right mind would give that up? Especially since she had Jehu, me, and the sisters helping her out? If things had gone differently, I think Garet would have amassed her own business empire.

"Anyways. She turned down Connolly, very politely. She knew she needed his help—he was a powerful man in the territory—if we were going to survive, and that one good word from the colonel and the banks would play.

"Garet was a nice woman. One of the best. How else to explain how she took all of us in, treated us like family? Like equals. That was the difference. The colonel didn't see anyone as his equal, just as people to dominate and control. I guess that was Garet's big mistake, always wanting to see the best in people. She didn't realize how vain the colonel was, that he wouldn't forgive her for the rejection. I expect his sister, Dorcas, riled him up about the audacity of Garet rejecting him. Garet always liked Dorcas, but I saw through her. Hell yeah, she treated me like a slave. Called me *nigger* to my face.

"After Garet rejected his marriage proposal, the next offer Connolly made was for the ranch and it was about half of what the ranch was worth. When Garet told Jed about Connolly's offer he laughed and told her she could get a better take by robbing Connolly's Denver bank.

"You better believe she filed that away. We weren't totally broke, but money was tight. She'd spent most of her savings on the widow's ranch, and had kept more horses back to breed than usual, so our sales were pretty low, and nearly all of that went to pay off a loan Thomas had taken out two years before. Garet was confident that we would pull in a good herd the next spring, and when the bankers saw the numbers for a full year with Garet in charge, they'd see her as a good bet.

"Jehu started back driving freight to bring in some money and Spooner left—he hated the cold and couldn't abide the Colorado winters. Jed helped out a little before he left, but it'd been a while since their last job and he wasn't flush. Garet didn't want his charity anyways. Said taking his money now, when it wasn't for trading horses, or for putting up the gang between jobs, made her feel like a whore taking money from a john.

"We made it through the winter. It was all down to Jehu's driving and Stella and Joan's canning skills. We rounded up another herd of horses that next June, '73 it was. Spent the summer breaking them. My God, Garet was a hand. She broke two horses a day, sometimes three. Broke her arm when one threw her. Doctor put a cast on, and as soon as he'd driven away, she was back up on that horse.

"There were nights where Garet fell asleep at the dinner table. We all worked hard, don't get me wrong. I tended all the livestock and helped with the horses. The sisters planted the garden and took care of the house. Jehu helped Garet with the horses, but he'd be gone hauling some. That little bit of steady income helped. But Garet nearly killed herself.

"Despite the hardships, and the fear that hung over everything we did, I count that as one of the best summers of my life. We were happy. We had high hopes, let me tell you. It was the best herd we'd ever had. We pulled ten of the best mares for breeding aside, that gave us twenty-five broodmares all told, and had our stud mount them. We wanted to eventually get to where we were a breeding farm, not just rounding up mustangs. We were counting on the money from selling those horses to get us through the next winter, and to leave us some to put aside, as well.

"I'm fine. Haven't you ever seen an old woman cry before? Haven't thought about this all in a long time. I couldn't, you see. It was too perfect, that summer. Thinking about how hopeful we were, well, it just breaks my heart. No. No, that's not right. It makes me angry. Still. Sixty years later. We weren't hurting anyone. Just women minding their own business, being a family, running our business, contributing to the settling of the West, by God, just as much as the men did. But they couldn't stand it that we didn't need them.

"He was called Colonel Connolly, but the highest rank he held in the Mexican War was lieutenant. He called himself *colonel* when he commanded a territory militia during the war. He took to the title, and had a good relationship with the army because of his past service. Provided them with livestock and such for their forts. When he asked one of his army cronies to requisition Garet's herd of horses, they agreed.

"They took our horses, every last one, as well as our hay, feed, wagons, goats, and chickens. They took our fucking chickens, said it was all in service of the army, that they were stretched thin in the northern forts because so much of the supplies were being routed south for the campaign against the Comanche. Must not have been in too dire straits since they didn't take anything from anyone else. They gave us pennies on the dollar for our property and said that we would probably see the money in the spring, seeing as how bureaucracy took time. We knew we would never see that money.

"We didn't expect the colonel to stand up for us, but the other smaller ranchers we did. Turned out, they didn't like that a ranch run by a bunch of women was more successful than they were. No help to be found there, though the wives had the grace to look abashed at their husbands' behavior.

"Margaret went to the banks to ask for money to tide us over, but Connolly got to them so no one would loan Garet money. Not sure many of them would have lent to a woman anyways. More than one of them suggested she should return to her natural place, in the home. When she got back from Denver, a letter from Connolly was waiting with a final offer on the ranch, the lowest price yet.

"I didn't know Garet had that kind of rage in her. Did she take the offer? Hell yeah, she took it. She didn't have a choice. We had no money and no horses. The only thing of value we had was the land. If she was going to lose her dream, she was going to take every cent she could from the bastard that stole it. He delivered the money and five horses. Nags, they were. We rode off with nothing but the clothes on our backs and what we could shove in saddlebags and tie onto the back of the extra horse.

"Lots of people will tell you the first daylight bank robbery in Colorado was Butch Cassidy in Telluride in '89, but that's a lie. It was Margaret Parker robbing the Bank of the Rockies on November 19, 1873. Even then, her first job, men were trying to write her out of history. In the end they succeeded, too. Despite Garet's best efforts.

"You come back tomorrow, Grace Williams, and I'll tell you about Grace Trumbull. Kidnapping her was the beginning of the end of us. We didn't know it at the time, of course. She was there for the summer of '77. She was supposed to be our witness, to tell the story of the last days of the Parker Gang. Like I said, she tried, but she failed. Guess it falls on me now. Soon enough, it'll fall on you."

ROCKY MOUNTAIN NEWS

TUESDAY, NOVEMBER 25, 1873

BANK OF THE ROCKIES ROBBED IN BROAD DAYLIGHT

On November 19, John Powell closed the safe and walked out the front door of the Bank of the Rockies, thinking of the dinner his mother would have waiting at home. That is the last thing he remembers until the next morning when he woke up on the floor of the bank, tied to a chair. It was dark outside, but he could see snow falling in the streets. It was midnight by the time he was able to free himself and walk to the sheriff's office through bouts of dizziness and nausea to report that the bank had been robbed.

The safe had been cleaned out and papers had been burned in a metal trash can. Upon questioning, Powell couldn't remember anything between the time he turned to lock the door of the bank and when he woke a few hours later. Sheriff Brandon Smith sent the young man home to recover and, as of this printing, John Powell still does not remember what happened.

The bank hasn't disclosed how much the thieves got away with, but it must have been considerable. There was a hole in the wall of the bank manager's office that hadn't been there before bank owner Colonel Connolly visited to survey the damage.

ROCKY MOUNTAIN NEWS

TUESDAY, NOVEMBER 25, 1873

ALFRED GERNSBECK KILLED

WOMAN WHO REPORTED IT DISAPPEARED

Alfred Gernsbeck, editor of the *Colorado Tribune*, was murdered in an alley behind Porter's Millinery on the same night as the Bank of the Rockies robbery. Gernsbeck was found with a bullet to his head, missing his coat and hat, but still in possession of his pocket watch and wallet. It is a strange fiend indeed who will kill a respectable man for a coat and leave the more valuable items on the victim's person.

An unidentified woman heard the gunshot and alerted men standing on the street. When the men and the sheriff attempted to find the woman later, as a possible witness, they could not locate her. The businessmen who investigated weren't surprised; the woman was terrified and running away from the danger.

Mr. Gernsbeck leaves a wife, Altoona Gernsbeck, four children and a newspaper with a dwindling readership.

2

Margaret Parker's Journal

Events of Wednesday, May 23, 1877
Written Friday, September 28, 1877
Heresy Ranch
Timberline, Colorado

I should have known Grace Trumbull was trouble when she stared down the barrel of my gun with an expression of complete and utter delight. Of course, it's easy now, in hindsight, to see it. But at the moment I almost laughed at her audacity at being at the business end of my gun.

—Are you holding us up, Mrs. Butler? Really?

—I am.

—You're that female gang.

Grace turned to the man standing beside her.

—You said they were a myth. Yet here they are, robbing you.

—Be quiet, you silly woman.

Benjamin Adamson, God rest his soul, held his shaking hands aloft, and sweat ran down his face, but his voice was gruff. I wondered if he was more afraid of the gun held to his head, or more angry at the fact that a woman held the gun.

—No need to be testy. No one's going to get hurt as long as you all do what you're told, Benjamin.

His face turned a mottled red at my use of his Christian name, which answered my question.

A shot splintered the stagecoach. Grace Trumbull flinched, and I saw her smile fade at the realization that she wasn't living in a penny dreadful, and that there were real bullets in our guns. The guard, I think his name was Toddy, froze, his eyes wide. Blood bloomed where a sliver of splintered wood scratched his cheek, and it slowly trickled down into his beard.

—I tole you not to move.

Hattie leveled her rifle from the back of her blaze-faced black horse. She wore a Union soldier's coat and kepi with a turkey feather sticking out of the band. The hat sat at a jaunty angle over her close-cropped kinky hair. A thick cigar smoldered in the corner of her mouth.

—Toss your gun down. Slow like.

—We got a gun on each of you.

Joan and Stella stood back-to-back, with a gun trained on the driver and one on Adamson. A breeze rustled their blonde hair, which fell down around their shoulders and made them both look five years younger than they were, which had come in handy since we left Cañon City. The doll at Joan's feet had helped convince our traveling companions they were two young daughters on their way to Columbia to join their mining father. Joan's fresh-faced beauty had distracted Adamson and Grace Trumbull from the gun hidden beneath the doll's dress.

—And don't think 'cause we're young we don't know how to use them, Joan said.

Jehu, as the driver and man in charge, tossed the guard's rifle down.

—And your pistols, I said. Jehu did as told.

We moved quickly, giving ourselves about five minutes for the holdup, the road between Cañon City and Columbia being busy with traffic to and from the gold mines tucked into every gulch and pass in the mountains ahead of us. Everyone knew her job: Stella gathered the guns, Joan went around the bend in the road to retrieve the getaway horses Hattie'd left out of sight, and, with a rifle held steady on him, I told the driver and guard to bring down the strongbox.

We had to yell for our voices to be heard over the river rushing twenty-five feet below the wagon track. Hattie sat on her horse in front of the coach, blocking the draft horses from moving forward and holding the driver and guard accountable with her Spencer. Stella stood between the mountain wall and the coach, both guns trained on the teamsters unloading the strongbox, while I held my gun on Grace and Adamson. Four guns for four people. Good odds, I'd say.

—You rode in the stage with us for hours, making conversation, knowing this is how it would end, Grace Trumbull said.

It had been one of Hattie's more brilliant ideas. Buy as many places on the stage as we could to decrease the number of people we had to guard. Gain the passengers' trust so they would be easier to manipulate when the time came. We'd luckily lost a passenger at the Gunnison stop, which left us with Grace Trumbull, a Chicagoan traveling through the West with an eye to writing a book about her adventures, and Benjamin Adamson, a lawyer on his way to Columbia to deliver the payroll to the Connolly Mine Company. He hadn't told us that, of course, only saying he was going to Columbia to deliver papers to his boss, but he was the reason we were on this particular coach. Or the Connolly payroll was, I should say.

Grace took us outlaws in, one after the other, and shook her head.

—I would have never supposed. I thought you were a war widow.

I looked at her from behind the tightly woven tulle of the black veil that covered half of my face and said maybe I was.

She said she doubted it and proceeded to tell me about how buying three seats on the coach increased our odds, gave us fewer people to deal with.

—I suppose me being a woman helped as well.

I dipped my head, impressed with the adventurer's discernment.

—It did. Thank you.

—And your consumption? Is that a ruse, as well, Mrs. Butler? Grace Trumbull asked.

I shrugged, watching the men pulling down the strongbox communicating with significant looks.

—I needed a reason for the stage to stop at our assigned spot, and having a fit seemed to be easiest.

—Less talking. You two hurry up, Hattie said.

Grace studied me, a small smile playing on her lips, ignoring Hattie.

—Is Emily Butler your real name?

—Real enough.

—Does your gang have a name?

—We're a myth, remember?

Since the spring of '75 we had four holdups to our name, not counting the first bank I robbed in Denver, and still there was no word in the papers about the female outlaws and their exploits. If the press's determined ignorance of our existence hadn't given us a good cover to keep on stealing, I'd have been offended at the slight.

I turned my gaze to Adamson.

—So I've always wondered: Will you pay them—I jerked my head in the direction of the teamsters who had the box on the ground now—to say it was the Spooner Gang that robbed you, or will you all just agree? A gentleman's agreement to not let the rest of the world know you've been bested by a bunch of women?

—You haven't bested me yet.

I looked at the gun in my hand and pointed it back at Adamson.

—You have a gun trained on you, Ben, and, as my young associate said, we know how to use them.

—We practice our shooting every day, though when it comes to killin', I am partial to blades. Big ones, little ones. Don't matter, Stella said.

—You've never killed anyone before, Adamson said.

—Oh, so you have heard of us, I said.

—I've heard of you, Grace said.

I turned my gaze to the adventurer, knowing Stella had Adamson well covered. I partly hoped he would go for me so I could shoot him. My trigger finger was itchy.

I'd liked Grace Trumbull from the moment I met her, which just goes to show I'd gotten soft and complacent with all our success. She talked too much and had an alarming affinity for the ridiculous tall tales Henry Pope spun about the West in his penny dreadfuls, but she was uncommonly intelligent otherwise, as evidenced by the way she'd pretty much deduced our holdup plan from the moment I pulled out my gun. Between Cañon City and the first team change I'd spent an enthralling thirty minutes listening to Grace and Adamson argue about education and women's suffrage, an argument Grace won. Made quite a fool of Adamson, which made me like her even more.

With wide, disbelieving eyes I opened my mouth and clicked my tongue at the lawyer.

—What do you think of that, Ben? Grace has heard of me from as far away as Chicago.

—Us, Stella said.

—What?

—She's heard of *us* from as far away as Chicago.

—Yes, us. Of course.

—Three minutes, Hattie said.

—Give me the key, Ben.

Adamson inhaled deeply, his face mottled from anger.

—I will not.

Stella stepped up behind the lawyer and hit him in the back of the head with the butt of her gun. Adamson yelled and dropped to his knees. Stella pressed the gun to the back of his head. Joan had returned with the horses, astride her own. She handed the extra reins to Hattie and kicked her horse forward to pin the driver and guard against the stagecoach. It was Joan's first heist, and she was showing herself to be a natural. She'd been pestering me for months to allow her to go with us. I'd finally relented, surprising everyone. When Hattie and Stella had asked me why, I'd told them that adding Joan would allow us to do bigger jobs. The truth was, I'd decided this would be our last.

—I don't like the way you looked at my sister, Stella said.

—I didn't like it much, either. You think you have the right to leer at young girls because they're sitting in front of you? Grace said.

—She was flirting with me.

Stella hit him again, this time drawing blood on his temple. Grace gasped and turned white at the sight. She clutched her throat and swallowed. Stella pressed her Colt to the back of Adamson's head, her eyes blazing with a fever I knew only too well.

—Can I shoot him?

—Of course not.

—No, no. I'm sorry. Don't kill me, Adamson said.

—Wasn't going to kill you. Just make you wish I had for the rest of your life.

I shook my head at Stella in warning.

The front of Adamson's pants darkened. Grace looked away from his shame, and I almost felt sorry for him. I stepped forward and held my hand out. Adamson dug into his vest pocket and handed me the key.

—Thank you.

Hattie pulled irons from her saddlebag and tossed them at Grace's feet.

—Come on, woman. We ain't got all day.

I told Grace to put the irons on Adamson. The clerk didn't look up, but put his hands behind his back. After Grace clamped them on, she looked at me expectantly, her eyes shining with excitement.

—Now, Grace, I'm going to open that strongbox. You aren't going to give us any trouble, are you?

—No. Of course not.

—Humor me and move back a few steps.

She did as told.

—And keep your hands up. You boys, too, I said to Toddy and Jehu.

—Ain't no boy, Jehu said.

Stella had mounted her own horse, and she tossed me an empty saddlebag. Our horses jerked their heads up but didn't move. They'd done this before, and I'd trained them well. I opened the strongbox and filled the saddlebag with greenbacks and coins.

—You know you ain't just stealing from the mine owner, Toddy said. You're stealing from a lot of hardworking men.

—Hardworking men who will drink and gamble and whore away their pay. While their California widows starve with the children.

I closed the bulging saddlebag and threw it over my shoulder, enjoying the heft of a good haul.

—Besides, they should have kept their claim instead of selling it to this bastard's boss. It's always better to be your own boss than to rely on someone else to provide.

Hattie motioned to the guard and driver.

—Unhitch the team.

Joan moved her horse away, releasing the men.

—I ain't taking orders from no jumped-up slave, Jehu said.

I'd expected one of the men to challenge us, but not Jehu. Everyone looked at Hattie, wondering what she'd do.

When we finally unmasked ourselves as the fairer sex, men were so shocked at being robbed by women they'd comply easy enough. When we were challenged, they mostly went Hattie's way, and she'd done a fine job of keeping her temper in check. Until the Columbia robbery. From Hattie's expression, she hadn't expected the challenge to come from this quarter, either.

Hattie got down off her horse with a slow deliberation we didn't really have time for—our five minutes had come and gone, but I knew better than to go against Hattie LaCour when she was angry—and handed the reins of our getaway horses to Joan. She holstered her rifle, and Joan and Stella pulled theirs back out and leveled them at the men. Hattie stood in front of the men with her hands behind her back, and I saw in Toddy's eyes that he thought that was their chance, despite the four guns pointing in their direction.

I cocked the lever of Toddy's own Spencer and put it up on my shoulder. He stopped moving.

Hattie LaCour blew cigar smoke in the driver's face.

—What's your name, little man?

—I ain't got to tell you nothing.

—That's true enough. Why would you? I'm just some jumped-up nigger, and a woman to boot. It'd be a downright insult to your manhood to do the courtesy of telling me your name.

Quicker than the eye could notice, Hattie's knife was out of the scabbard at the small of her back and the blade was between his legs. His eyes bulged with surprise, then narrowed in anger.

—Everybody wants to sass the nigger woman. Nobody ever sass…

She looked my way.

—Emily?

I nodded.

—Ole Emily over there. Everyone treats her with the utmost respect, even when she humiliates them with her words. She got some mouth on her, that Emily. She ain't ever made a man piss himself before, so I suspect we might need to start looking over our shoulders. We always known there was a limit, that you men wouldn't let us get away with this forever. So if the Pinkertons gonna come after us, might as well give them a real reason to chase us.

—For God's sake, tell her your name, Grace Trumbull said.

—Don't do it, Toddy said.

—He talks big without a knife on his pecker, Stella said.

—My name's Jehu. I'll unhitch the team. Take that goddamn knife off me.

Jehu was short and wiry, with strong arms from driving horses for a living. His hands were small for a man's, but rough and scarred, with leather dust tattooed into the creases of his knuckles.

—Nope. Not now. I want you to get down on your knees and kiss my boots.

—That's enough, I said.

—What? You gonna let this cracker insult me?

—You're taking this too far, Jehu said.

—Oh, I could take it farther. I haven't killed a white man in a good long while. I've been itching to, I gotta admit.

—We're out of time. You've made your point. Unhitch the team, Jehu. Toddy, help him.

Jehu stepped away from Hattie and with the guard's help unhitched the team. Hattie shoved the knife back into its scabbard. I tied my saddlebags onto my horse, checked the cinch, and returned to the carriage. I pulled Grace Trumbull's carpetbag out of the stage and started rifling through it.

She stepped forward.

—Wait a minute. There's nothing of value in there.

I pulled out a Peacemaker.

—I figured you for the derringer type, Grace. This is a big gun for a little lady like you. Expecting to be robbed at gunpoint?

—If I were, you'd think I would have had it in the cabin with me.

—True.

I put the gun in the back of the waistband of my skirt and pulled out what I had been looking for: a leather-bound journal. During one of her soliloquies she'd let drop about her travel journal for future publication. I'd known immediately the journal was worth stealing. I would need a good book to read in my retirement.

—Not that, please. That's months of work.

I rifled through the pages, noting that a good bit of it was blank.

—You can start your new one with a retelling of your first holdup.

Hattie, Joan, and Stella were on their horses. Hattie scowled at Jehu as he unhitched the team. I pulled two sets of irons from her saddlebag and put Grace's journal and gun in it. I squeezed Hattie's leg, felt energy thrumming through her. I glanced at the driver.

—Good job, but don't take it too far.

Hattie jerked her chin down in acknowledgment.

The driver and guard finished unhooking the four-horse team. I motioned for Grace to come close. She did, with a wary expression on her face, her eyes on the irons.

—These aren't for you. They're for them. Lock the driver and guard together.

I mounted my gray horse, and my gang rode off around the bend. Old Blue danced around in excitement for the getaway she knew was coming.

—Wait. You can't just leave us here, Grace said.

—That's how this works, Grace. I rob you, then I ride away. Someone will be along soon enough to help you.

—Take me with you.

—Why would I do that?

Grace stepped forward and grabbed the reins of my horse to keep me from leaving.

—So I can tell your story. Everyone says you don't exist. I can make sure you get the recognition you deserve.

I have to give her credit. She knew exactly what I wanted before I knew myself. If I'd had more time, logic would have prevailed and I would have left Grace Trumbull on the road to Columbia. But I didn't.

—Come on, then.

She closed her carpetbag haphazardly and handed it to me. I looped it on my saddle horn, held my hand out, and helped her up behind me.

Jehu's voice managed to rise above the rushing water and ricochet off the mountain walls.

—You're going to regret this.

He was right, of course.

3

WPA Slave Narrative Collection

Interview with Henrietta Lee

Sunday, September 6, 1936

Well, look who came back. It's a good thing I'm an early riser, Grace Williams, or you might have caught me without my tignon. Worn one for years. Your auntie wore one? All the best aunties wear one.

"Now, I'm not sure how much I'll be able to tell you today. I didn't get much rest last night. Talking to you yesterday brought up all those old memories. I sit on this porch every day, watch the world go by, and remember. But it's a different kind of remembering when you're telling a story. In my mind I can replay the same things over and over, the best parts, I guess you could call them. But if I'm going to tell this story right and true, I have to give you the bad parts, too. Parts where I don't come out so shiny or innocent.

"Let me see that notebook. How are you getting this down? Those symbols don't look like they mean anything to me, but I guess I have to trust you. Suppose this story is going to be like all the others, filtered through someone else. Some of the truth will be lost. Oh no, I don't mean you'll do it on purpose, but there's probably a lot of shifting between what happened sixty years ago, my memories now, my words to you, your shorthand,

and then to true words. Right now there's no story, so I guess whatever you get down will be better than nothing.

"Where'd I leave off? Grace Trumbull. Right. Thinking on it last night, I need to back up a little more before we get to Grace, but we'll get to her today, don't you fret.

"After the colonel stole Garet's ranch and she robbed his bank, we went up to Cheyenne for the winter. It was big enough town we could blend in. Jehu drove freight. I got on as a cook at a hotel. Garet did some nursing for one of the doctors. Mostly watching over people at night. Joan was too young to work, so she and Stella stayed in the little house we rented, took care of it. We got along fine that winter of '73 to '74, but none of us were very happy. I hated cooking, being ordered around by people. Course I'm good at cooking, but that doesn't mean I like it. Garet was a good nurse, but she couldn't stand being cooped up inside like that. That woman could get by with less sleep than anyone I've ever known. Four, five hours. When she had free time during the day, she sweet-talked the livery man into letting her exercise horses, brush them, feed them. Didn't take him too long to realize who she was. Her reputation as a horsewoman was that good. They spent a lot of time talking horseflesh and racing. That wasn't Garet's line, but she'd learned a lot about it from her grandfather. That livery man picked her brain something fierce. He was a gambling man and wanted to make his fortune with the horses. Men bet on anything back then. Probably hasn't changed, I don't know. Jehu wasn't ever much of a gambler.

"The man, I can't remember his name, got kicked in the leg by a draft horse. Bones sticking out of it from all angles. Garet said blood was spurting everywhere. She saved his life, stopping the blood and sending for the doctor. Course, the man lost the lower part of his leg. He was out for a couple of months and asked Garet to run the livery for him in the meantime. So she did. He appreciated her keeping his business afloat, appreciated her running it so good he was making a tidy profit, even during the slow winter, but he sure didn't appreciate the fact that other men poked fun at him about it. So when he got a stick to hobble around on, Garet was back to nursing.

"We could have stayed there, had an OK life. We'd made some friends. Garet even thought about opening her own livery to compete with the men. There was a woman there who was going to give her a loan, but Jed showed up and told us he knew just where we could stake a claim that no rich rancher would ever try to steal. None of us liked living in town overmuch, so we followed him to Timberline, his hideout on the Western Slope.

"Brown's Hole was hell to get to. It was a box canyon that was part of three states, so the law didn't tend to look too hard for it. Jurisdiction was a booger to figure out. Jed Spooner found the town the year before when he was on the run from the Cheyenne bank holdup. He offered the town money if they'd let them hide out there when needed. Jed kept that town afloat for a few years, until the pressure got too much and he and his gang split up for a spell, went down to Mexico. Those Texas Rangers turned him into a cold-blooded killer. Another story ole Hollywood gets wrong.

"The men were gone and the town was too remote to have much in the way of business. Those settlers were sold a bill of goods by the land promoters, and that's a fact. Course, everyone lied to settlers. Nothing new. I suppose Timberline was worse off because they were almost trapped in that canyon. There was only one way in and out, and it was treacherous.

"Someone needed to take care of the town, so we did it. I always knew Garet wanted to pull another job. Saw it in her eyes every time Spooner and his boys would get into the bottle and start bragging. She knew she could do it better, and we did.

"We had a good run, too. Two years. Six jobs. Over fifty grand. You better believe it, 'cause it's a fact.

"You know what, nah. I'm not going to tell you this story if you're going to sit there and say you don't believe this and I'm lying about that. We are too early in the proceedings for that. Hell, it isn't any wonder women's stories don't get told. Anything out of the ordinary is written off as fanciful, or an overactive imagination. Like it never once occurs to people that women are just as capable as men, more capable in most cases 'cause we're not all caught up in being men, and all that means.

"If you're going to have that attitude about everything I tell you, if you're going to interrupt me with that, you better get on up and leave right now. I have no time for it. Good.

"Jehu was what you might call our forward scout. He would keep his ears peeled for gossip about goings-on, listen to when payrolls were typically delivered and how. Gauging which mines were most successful, where the booms were, so we could hit the mine office. If we were hitting a bank or an office, Garet and I would move to the town, separately, and get jobs there. Well, I got a job. Garet would pretend to be rich British woman looking for investments or on a jaunt in the West like that Bird woman. You never heard of her? She was a little sensation back then. Wrote a book about her time in the Rocky Mountains. I read it. Not terrible. People didn't think it too strange when Garet pretended to be the same.

"The first stage we held up in the spring of '75 was up in Wyoming. Wore masks for that one because we knew men wouldn't comply with women, especially since there was only three of us, me, Garet, and Stella. Jehu was the driver and he had a signal for us. If he wore a red kerchief around his neck, then there were too many guns in the stage. If he wore a blue one, we weren't outnumbered. It went pretty smooth, but the odds made me nervous, all the same. There were five men and two women, all told, with only three of us. We knew Jehu wouldn't try to take us, but you just didn't know with the others. Went fine, though. We never stole from the passengers, only the businesses.

"We wanted to rob another stage in the mountains because we could disappear before anyone could get to the next town to call for help. We had horses trained in mountain riding. There wasn't a posse in Colorado that could track us, and we knew it. When Jehu finally got a route that carried a Connolly payroll, I suggested we be bolder still. Purchase tickets on the stage to decrease the number of passengers we had to guard. It was Joan's first job, so we had three people in a six-person coach. We lucked out even more when one of the passengers got off and his seat wasn't taken. We were afraid if I rode in the stage someone might get suspicious, a black woman traveling alone wasn't a common sight. I met the stage on the road at the appointed spot, and Garet had already had the stage stop and had everyone guarded.

"Went off without a hitch, and on the ride up to the cabin where we were going to change horses, I was having visions of doing more regular jobs, maybe going farther afield, doing some jobs in Utah, Wyoming. Hell, maybe even Arizona Territory. There's nothing like the rush of outlawing, let me tell you. Nothing.

"I didn't know that was the last job we would do when Garet rode up with Grace Trumbull riding double, but I guess I should have known. You can't kidnap someone, bring them into your family, and expect for everything to keep going on as it was.

"Losing her ranch on the Poudre changed Garet. In lots of ways, but I think she saw injustice everywhere, even where it might not actually be. She saw the fact that the exploits of a female gang were being ignored, swept under the rug, as one more wrong against women. Hell, I saw it as a free ticket to do what we were doing as long as we could.

"I don't think Garet wanted to brag about what we'd done, but she wanted us to get credit. Sounds like a contradiction, but it wasn't. Not really. Garet saw in Grace an outsider who could write about us, objectively I guess. But Garet had a motivation I didn't know anything about, and wouldn't for a few more weeks. It was the most selfish thing she ever did, bringing Grace Trumbull along, and for a bit I hated her for it. Grace, not Garet. Garet had done too much for me, for others, to hold a grudge. I'll be honest, my loyalty and love for Garet were put to the test more than once that summer. But you'll forgive the people you love for a lot, I've found.

4

Margaret Parker's Journal

Events of Wednesday, May 23, 1877
Written Monday, October 1, 1877
Heresy Ranch
Timberline, Colorado

When I rode up with Grace riding double, Hattie was not amused.

The trio had changed into their getaway outfits. Hattie had shed her masculine Union army getup for a plain brown dress. The red sash she'd worn around the waist of her coat was wrapped around her head in a turban. The cigar was gone, and her face had relaxed into its normal pleasant expression. The tone of her skin looked different, though I knew that she had done nothing more than change the color of dress she wore. Hattie LaCour was a chameleon and could change her entire demeanor with the slightest rearrangement of her features, going from a brusque, uneducated woman to the plain black woman in front of us to a beautiful seductress, if need be.

The sisters, however, could not. They were farm girls, intelligent in their way, but they would never make a living at poker. They were who they were, and didn't see the need to apologize for it, and, as such, needed more help to hide in plain sight. They'd worn the disguise of innocent sisters easy enough, though Stella had chafed at the lace and frills. It was no surprise to see Stella with her hair slicked back, and wearing pants and a serape she traded for in Cheyenne and a light-gray felt John Bull she stole off a man during our first holdup. Joan's frilly bodice was covered with a tight-fitting short green coat, and she was twisting her little-girl ringlets into one long braid that she liked to wear over her left shoulder.

—What are you doing, Margaret? Hattie asked.

—Margaret? That's your name? Grace said.

Hattie sighed dramatically and walked off toward the cabin.

—Margaret. It suits you.

She was too close for me to focus, so I looked away.

—I prefer Garet.

—Shouldn't have told her your name, Joan said. She shook her head with a maturity belying her seventeen years and tied her braid with a leather thong with wampum beaded on the ends. Stella handed Joan a brown gambler's hat, and the transformation from a child holding a dolly to a young woman was complete.

It's difficult, even now with everything that's happened in the four months since we robbed the Marshall Pass stage, to come to terms with the fact that Joan is a woman. She and Stella came to us when they were twelve and nineteen, respectively. They were wise beyond their years; growing up on the Nebraska plains will do that to you. Joan wasn't so lost to childhood that she didn't enjoy, and take advantage of, all of us treating her like a child. Hattie, Jehu, and I did it out of love, to fill the hole of the children we would never have. Stella did it out of protectiveness, or control, to make sure what had happened to her didn't happen to her sister. Stella succeeded, in a way. Joan was no shrinking violet, and she had more discernment than her sister did, but she was young, inexperienced, and headstrong, no thanks to us petting her. Stella didn't like strangers, as a general rule, and she hated men. She trusted slowly, if at all, and during our hours in the stage together, I'd seen her throw a few smoldering looks Grace's way. Joan had warmed to Grace on the stage, which probably accounted for a fair bit of Stella's animosity toward Grace. I imagine Joan got an earful from Stella about the bluestocking on the ride to the cabin, fueling Joan's newfound guardedness with Grace.

—I won't be any trouble, I promise, Grace said.

—You're already trouble. Look at your horse, Stella said.

I patted Grace's knee and told her to hop off.

She landed on wobbly legs and reached out as if to touch the horse to steady herself. But a strange expression flitted across her face, and she pulled her hand away and stepped back.

My gray's head hung low, and her breath came out in heavy gasps. I'd been careful not to blow her on the ascent to our meeting place, but she was close. I rubbed her sweaty neck and put my mouth close to the mare's ear. "You're my best girl. I'll take care of you, don't you worry." She turned her head to me and nudged me gently with her nose, showing that there were no hard feelings for the extra weight. Old Blue was an ugly horse; her head was too big, her neck too short, and her pale eyes gave her a crazy aspect that didn't match her personality. But she was a devil in the mountains, sure-footed and a smooth ride no matter the terrain—and, if I was honest, probably the smartest member of our gang.

I miss her.

Joan came to take Old Blue's reins to cool her down for me. I pulled Joan into my arms. —You were marvelous today.

—You really think so?

—A natural.

—Not according to Stella.

—She's just afraid you'll be better than her one day.

—Not bloody likely, Stella said.

I winked at Joan, who walked Blue off toward the barn. Stella glared at Grace, her scarred lip curled into a menacing sneer, and followed her sister.

—What is this place? Grace asked, her head swiveling around as she took in our surroundings.

The log cabin sat on the bank of a nameless creek that rushed across gray stones smoothed into perfect ovals from thousands of years of Rocky Mountain runoff. The cabin was small, but tidy and well cared for, and a thin stream of smoke rose from the chimney. Joan and Stella led Blue down a narrow, well-worn path to the small barn and corral. The getaway horses were in the corral getting their reward, while three saddled horses waited patiently, tied to the fence.

I told Grace to help the sisters with the horses and followed Hattie into the cabin.

The inside of the one-room cabin was as tidy as the outside. A brass bed mounded with quilts and thick pillows sat in one corner. An elk-hide rug lay on the floor between two rocking chairs, which faced the small fire crackling in the fireplace. Hattie was at the stove, stirring a pot of stew. I can still smell it, though the thought of eating it right now, months later, makes my stomach lurch unpleasantly.

Hattie handed me a cup of coffee.

—Thank you.

—Would you like to tell me what that woman is doing out there?

Hattie's Creole accent came through her voice clearly when she was emotional.

I sipped the six-shooter coffee, knowing it would be strong enough for Jesus to walk across. I prepared myself for it to be horrible, but still pursed my lips and jerked my head back as the bitter taste hit the back of my tongue.

—Where's Horace?

—Does it matter? Don't change the subject.

The second swallow was always better than the first. I wrapped my chilled fingers around the warm, thick ceramic mug and drank to buy time. I'd asked myself why I'd brought Grace Trumbull along for the last two hours and hadn't come up with a good answer, at least not an answer Hattie would like. I'd left plenty of innocent people in more remote spots, and had never given them or their comfort a second thought. Until Grace Trumbull. Grace, as if sensing my regrets, had been silent for the entire ride, besides a gasp or two as Blue nimbly made her way up the almost nonexistent mountain track. She had clutched my waist so tightly I'd finally had to tell her to loosen her grip, unless she wanted me to die from suffocation.

Hattie waited, arms crossed over her chest. I couldn't tell her the truth. Not yet.

—I don't know. I like listening to her talk.

Hattie slipped back into her ignorant-slave patois.

—Our talk ain't 'telligent 'nuf fo' ya?

—That's not it.

The answer was too quick.

Hattie looked at me from the sides of her eyes and went to the stove to stir the stew.

—She's interesting, Hatt. Lord knows we need a little variety in Timberline.

She rounded on me.

—You're bringing her home? Do you want us to get found out?

—No, of course not.

—We're safe enough now, with her only knowing your name. But when Jehu walks through the door it's all over. You can't put him at risk like that.

—What was that with Jehu?

—Stop changing the damn subject, Garet.

Hattie pointed the wooden spoon at the door. A bit of potato slipped off and onto the floor.

—You take that woman to Gunnison, drop her off outside of town, or we'll all end up twisting from a high branch. That what you want?

—No, of course not.

—You're sure acting like it.

A log in the fireplace settled and fell out onto the packed dirt floor. I used the small shovel leaning against the wall to toss the log back in. When I turned around, Hattie was watching me, the wooden spoon forgotten in her hand.

—You going to tell me what's really going on? You don't do anything without a plan, Margaret.

—That's not entirely true.

Hattie tilted her head to the side, but remained silent, no doubt remembering my trembling, tearful confession about the unexpected direction my first bank job had taken. She was the only person I'd trusted with the knowledge that I'd killed a man, the only person I'd known wouldn't judge me for my lack of remorse.

—Doesn't it just…I squeezed my hands into fists and my voice deepened into a growl. —Infuriate you that we're dismissed? Ignored. Jed Spooner is getting credit for everything we're doing, and why? So men can save face.

—No, so we can keep on doing what we're doing. And I've become somewhat partial to breathing. I'd like to do it for fifty more years.

—Look at Spooner. Angus King. Jesse James. Our jobs are bigger, cleverer. Hell, King can't rob a train without using three times the TNT, injuring innocents. Jesse would just as soon kill someone as rob them. Spooner is a little more cunning, I'll give him that.

—They also have sheriffs and Pinkertons and bounty hunters always after them. Hell, Spooner and his boys have been in Mexico for two years, laying low. You itching to visit Mexico?

—God, no. I hate the heat.

—Me, too. What does all this have to do with that woman?

—Her name is Grace.

—I don't care what her name is.

—You jealous, Hatt?

Hattie scoffed and turned her back to me, giving more attention to the stew than it probably deserved. I went up to her and put my arm around her shoulders.

—Horace leave this for us or you make it?

Hattie shook her head. She refused to cook. Said it reminded her too much of her slave days.

—I want to make sure you get your due. You're the brains of this outfit, Hattie.

—That's true.

Hattie met my gaze, her copper-colored eyes serious, and told me to answer her question.

—I want Grace to be our witness.

—Our witness? For the trial against us when she turns us in?

—She's out here on a grand tour, to write her memoirs.

—Rich white woman memoirs, just what the world needs.

—I want there to be one objective person to know our story. To tell it. No one will believe us. Men will lie about us. Grace won't.

—You sure got a good read on her from knowing her a few hours.

—I know that I can manipulate her into writing what we want. *The Legend of Hattie LaCour.* Has a nice ring to it, doesn't it?

—I don't want to be a legend.

—You will be, though. With a name like Hattie LaCour, how could you not?

—Please. No one will tell a story with a slave as the hero. Especially that rich white woman out there.

—You're not a slave anymore.

—Doesn't matter and you know it. Margaret, you know good and well if people knew for sure that we were pulling these jobs that they wouldn't leave us be. They'd be damn sure to make a spectacle of us so we wouldn't give any other women ideas. There is no way in hell they're going to give a Negro woman her due. They'll be imagining a black uprising before they finish reading a sentence. Have you never thought of what they'll do to me if they catch us? Won't be the same they do to you, I can promise you that.

I looked down and away, ashamed that I hadn't considered it, and sick at the knowledge she was right. She'd never told me about her time in captivity. Not a word. But I'd seen the scars on her back and knew she'd suffered.

She let the silence lengthen, to make sure I felt my shame sufficiently. I embraced her, and after an initial pause, she wrapped her strong arms around me. Hattie was tall and big-boned, with warm light-brown skin. Long eyelashes framed her copper-colored eyes, and once a month one of us takes a straight razor to her head. Not that it matters overmuch, since she wears a tignon all the time. She is quite possibly the most intelligent woman I've ever known, and without a doubt the most beautiful. She enchanted me from the first time I saw her standing defiantly in my barn, wearing my own dress. It was easy enough to see that Jehu was head over heels for her. Loving Hattie, respecting her, was the easiest thing in the world. I can admit now, at the end of my life, that a germ of motivation for most of my exploits was to impress my best friend.

—Henrietta LaCour, I'd die before I let anything happen to you.

She squeezed me close.

—I'd prefer none of us die.

—You're too ornery to die.

—That's true.

We pulled apart and didn't look at each other. We weren't much for hugging or showing emotion, and when we did we tended to pretend it hadn't happened. But it always stayed with me long after, and I knew it did the same for Hattie.

I wish I'd hugged Hattie more.

Hattie ladled some soup into a bowl and held it out to me.

—We're damn lucky we haven't robbed someone who's not too proud to admit it. We will, one day, and soon, probably. Might have today, Hattie said.

—If Jehu wasn't on our side, I'd be worried.

—I was talking about the pissing man.

—I'm not worried about Adamson. But I do want to know what that was with Jehu. And don't tell me I'm changing the subject. You two have a fight before he left?

—Jehu doesn't fight. You know that.

—After what you pulled, I have a feeling he might when he gets home.

Hattie put a spoon on the table next to me and smiled for the first time since we'd left the ranch a week ago.

—Good.

I never did find out why Hattie threatened her lover with a knife.

We ate in silence for a few minutes. I tried not to grimace when the food hit my stomach. I put the spoon down, hoping I'd eaten enough to keep Hatt from being suspicious.

—Grace is only a threat if she can find Timberline. We'll blindfold her, or put a flour sack over her head. We'll take her on a tour of the mountains so that she's so confused by which way is which, she'll never be able to give away our location.

—It's a big risk.

—You remember when we met? I trusted you on a lot shorter acquaintance than I have with Grace Trumbull. Now I'm asking you to trust me.

Hattie inhaled deeply and looked up to the heavens. I knew I had her, but I decided I needed one more bit of assurance.

I reached out for Hattie's hand. My friend looked at me in resignation.

—I won't let my guard down. If I start to suspect she's not on the level, I'll kill her myself.

Grace knocked on the door and opened it without waiting for an answer.

—They rode off without a word.

—That's what dey's 'posed to do, Hattie said.

She'd pushed her bottom lip out, overemphasizing its fullness, and wiped her hands on her apron like a kitchen maid. I half expected her to ladle up some soup for Grace, but apparently Hattie's playacting didn't extend to providing hospitality to a bluestocking such as Grace.

—We haven't been properly introduced. I'm Grace Trumbull.

Grace held out a gloved hand to Hattie, who barely acknowledged it and didn't shake it.

—If it wasn't for you, we'd be leaving, too, Hattie said.

—I don't mean to slow you down.

—Would you like something to eat, Grace?

—Yes, I'm famished. Banditry sure makes you hungry.

Her laughter died at Hattie's stoic silence. Grace couldn't disguise the fear on her face, and decided to hide it through chatter.

—What is this place?

—A cabin, Hattie said.

—Well, yes, of course. But whose is it?

—Eat. I placed a bowl on the table with a spoon and returned to my own.

Grace set her carpetbag by the door. Hatt stood directly in the way of Grace's place at the table. Grace moved to one side, then the other, but Hattie didn't move. Grace laughed nervously, straightened her shoulders, and looked Hattie directly in the eye.

—You don't like me much, do you?

—No.

—Well, I like you very much.

—You don't know me.

—Nor do you know me.

Hattie looked down her nose at the woman, taking Grace Trumbull's measure. The bluestocking wore a copper-colored traveling suit and a feminine John Bull the deep green of late-summer leaves, with a thick silk ribbon that matched her suit. After a long moment in which Grace smiled steadily, Hattie stepped aside. Grace relaxed just enough that I knew the confrontation had taken some courage. With gloved hands she unbuttoned and removed her coat, showing a vest beautifully embroidered with intricately intertwined vines over a bright white shirt. She draped the coat over her chair with great care and sat down to eat. Her hand shook as she picked up her spoon. She blew on the steaming stew before taking a tentative bite. Her eyebrows rose, and she nodded in appreciation.

—Irish stew.

—Squirrel stew, Hattie said.

Grace coughed, spewing her mouthful onto the table. Hattie's mouth twisted into a grin.

—She's teasing you. It's Irish stew.

I caught Hattie's eye and shook my head. She shrugged one shoulder.

With her eyes defiantly on Hattie, Grace took another bite.

—Umm. Whatever it is, it's delicious.

Hattie tossed a towel on the table for Grace to clean her own mess.

—Is this your cabin? Where you live?

—No.

—The owner lets us rest here. Change horses, I explained.

—Where's the owner?

—None of your business, Hattie said.

—I'm merely trying to make conversation.

—You're not making conversation; you're interrogating.

—I hardly call two questions an interrogation.

—You understand every question you ask us puts our lives in danger? Knowing Garet's name puts us in danger? Hattie said.

Grace rested her spoon in her bowl and wiped her mouth with the towel. She cleared her throat.

—What can I do to make you trust me?

—Hmm... Most likely nothing.

—I understand your plight better than you think.

—My plight.

—As a Negro. I come from a long line of suffragists and abolitionists.

—Oh! She's an abolitionist. That makes all the difference.

—My parents and grandparents were. I was too young to do anything. But I eavesdropped on their meetings and have heard them reminisce about the movement and its success.

Hattie's eyes narrowed and her mouth pressed into a very thin line. I wondered, briefly, if Grace was *trying* to antagonize her.

—Well, we sho thankful for dey's help in freein' us.

Grace blushed and looked down at her traveling gloves, but she didn't apologize.

–Where are you from? Hattie asked.

–Chicago.

–What is a woman like you doing on a stage in Colorado?

–Traveling.

Hattie leaned over and looked Grace up and down again, taking in the richness of the woman's dress.

–Your family let you travel like that alone?

–Like what?

–Dressed like you shit gold coins.

Grace stilled and glanced back and forth between me and Hattie, apparently realizing she was a rich woman alone, in a remote cabin with two outlaws. Her gaze settled on me.

–Don't look at her. I'm talking to you.

Grace lifted her chin and turned to Hattie, but she didn't look her full on.

–I think you're trying to scare me.

–Garet said you were smart.

Hattie leaned forward over Grace.

–I'm protecting me and my own.

–I'm no threat.

–You keep saying. Lies are thick on the ground out west. Here we judge people on their actions. Remember that, blue belly. Eat up. We leave in five minutes.

Hattie let the door slam behind her. Grace exhaled and turned to me.

–Why didn't you stand up for me?

–Why would I?

–Because she's . . . I thought we were friends.

–I've known you for a day. I've known Hattie for years, trust her with my life every day. She's the closest thing I've ever had to a sister. She's suspicious of you, and while I don't necessarily agree with her, I respect her opinion.

—You trust me.

—I wouldn't go that far. That'll be the last bit of food you get till morning, probably. Best finish it up.

—Are you going to let her boss us around like that?

—Why shouldn't she?

—Well… I thought you were in charge.

—What gave you that idea?

Grace sniffed, but didn't answer.

—We're equal partners, Hattie and me. The color of her skin makes no difference to me, or Joan or Stella. If it does to you, I'll take you to Gunnison right now. I have no patience for that kind of pettiness, nor do I have time to deal with it. So which'll it be? Gunnison, or Heresy Ranch?

—Heresy Ranch? Is that where you live?

—Yes.

—Where did you…

—Answer the question; we're running behind.

—Heresy Ranch, of course.

I pulled some money out of the saddlebag on the bed and placed it on the small dresser.

—You pay these people to help you?

—Horace hired us to do the job. To get the full worth of his mine back from Connolly.

—You're like Robin Hood. You're stealing to help people.

—I'm doing it for the thrill. Helping people keeps me from feeling guilty that I enjoy it so much.

Grace seemed disappointed, and truth be told, I probably should have let her believe I was all beneficence for a little longer.

—No one does anything out of the goodness of their heart, Grace. Even Mainline philanthropists get satisfaction from their generosity, either self-satisfaction, or, to give them the benefit of the doubt, the pleasure in knowing they have truly helped someone. But everyone wants something in return.

—You want something from me?

—I do. I'll tell you in good time. Are you going to finish your stew?

—No.

She took her bowl to the basin and stared at the water.

—There's…um…remnants.

—Yes.

—What should I do with them?

—Eat them.

—Is this squirrel stew?

—Probably.

She wrinkled her nose and finished her portion in a very unladylike few bites. She turned to the basin and daintily dipped the bowl in the water, trying not to get her gloves wet.

—It would be easier if you took the gloves off.

—This is fine.

She cleaned the bowl and asked me where she could relieve herself.

COLORADO WEEKLY CHIEFTAIN

THURSDAY, MAY 31, 1877

BOLD STAGE ROBBERY AT MARSHALL PASS

The Wells Fargo stage from Cañon City to Montrose was robbed by four masked bandits on May 23. The four outlaws made away with the Connolly Mining Company payroll, making it the third time in a year that one of the late Colonel Connolly's businesses have been targeted. News of the robbery has been sent to Columbia, where his son and heir, Callum Connolly, is working alongside his miners.

A posse left as soon as the stage made it to Gunnison, but the thieves' lead was too long and they successfully used the rocky terrain of the mountains to get away.

It is suspected this is the same Spooner Gang that has been targeting Connolly Industries for the last two years. However, there are conflicting reports about the identities of the bandits. It is rumored that Jed Spooner and his men have been in Mexico since their confirmed robbery of the Cheyenne National Bank back in '75. The Connolly outlaws have given Spooner credit from the beginning, but announcing his name isn't something Spooner has ever done in his confirmed robberies. There are some similarities, though: both gangs hit quickly, are extremely efficient, avoid violence and manage to get away cleanly. Until now. Benjamin Adamson, Connolly's new clerk, was beaten during the Marshall Pass robbery. He is laid up with a concussion, but should survive.

5

Margaret Parker's Journal

Thursday, May 24, 1877
Northwest of Marshall Pass, Colorado

I'm writing this by the glow of a fire under a star-speckled moonless sky. Hattie is asleep next to me, brows furrowed, body tense, head pillowed on the seat of her saddle, her rifle within reach. Grace is across the fire, her face slack, her mouth open in a slight snore, careless of danger, her hands folded together on her chest, her gloves grimy with leather dust from choking the saddle horn for three hours as if her life depended on it. Our horses are picketed just outside the glow of the fire, but I can hear their snuffles, swishing tails, and the occasional stomp of a hoof, and it calms me.

It's hard to believe it hasn't been a day since we held up the stage. This isn't where I'd imagined we would be, or whom I'd imagined we'd be with, when planning the heist. Hattie is beside herself with anger, though her placid demeanor and expression would make a stranger think different. She's never more terrifying than when she's silent. If she'd yell and rail against me, or Grace, it would be a comfort. I can talk anyone, man or woman, out of that kind of mood. Silence, though, always cuts straight through me. Of course, Hatt knows that, which is why she's been spare with her words.

I'm extending my watch a little longer so I can start this journal. I haven't written a diary since the early days of our time in the territory. My journal was the ranch accounts and correspondence. There was too much work and too little time. Writing about my hopes and dreams and wishes and chronicling my life seemed indulgent. Besides, my life was the ranch; there was very little outside of it, until Jehu started bringing strays home, but that's a story for later.

I'm starting with the events from Horace's cabin, because my memory of the robbery is thin. It's always the way. The high I receive from the event seems to wipe my memory clean. There are impressions, but it can take me days to remember the details, what was said, who did what. I want to chew on it for a while and get it down right. I think the last heist of the Parker Gang deserves that much, at least.

Hattie and I were mounted and waiting when Grace finally emerged from the outhouse with an expression of revulsion on her face, complaining about the closeness. I asked if she'd never used an outhouse before and she replied, —I have, only not one so…fetid. Hattie snapped that we didn't have all day and that a posse would catch us for sure if we didn't put some ground between us. When Grace held out her carpetbag and made ready to get on behind me, well, I think Hattie's head would have exploded if it weren't so tightly wrapped.

—What are you doing? Don't you see the horse tied to the fence?

A docile, saddled blaze-faced bay with its back leg cocked turned its head to assess Grace. I'd left a little extra money to pay Horace for the horse and tack, with plans to return it as soon as possible and exchange this horse for Old Blue. I introduced Grace to Rebel, her mount for the next few days. In a faint voice she repeated the name and said she hoped it wasn't indicative of his personality, before cautiously approaching the horse. I assured her Rebel was the gentlest horse imaginable (only a slight lie, but as long as we didn't run across any snakes she would be fine).

Grace hooked her carpetbag on the saddle horn, untied the horse, and started to mount. From the right side of the horse, with the wrong foot in the stirrup. She started to pull herself up, realized she would be facing backward, and stepped back down.

Hattie cursed under her breath and said to me, —You kidnapped her, you help her.

Grace's face was pale and her gloved hands shook. I saw her silence and strong grip around my waist on the ride to the cabin in a new light, and asked her if she knew how to ride. She shook her head and stepped away from the horse. Grace grasped her throat, swallowed thickly, and asked if she could ride with me.

I told her riding double in the mountains was too difficult for the horses, and besides it would slow us down considerably. We needed to put miles between us and the posse that was sure to follow.

Grace acquiesced, but all the color had drained from her face. Even her lips were white.

I led her around the horse and instructed her how to get on, assuring her the whole time that Rebel was a very calm horse. Rebel, as if determined to show me for a liar, threw his head up and down. Grace squeaked.

I placed my hand on her knee and told her horses could feel her fear, to which Grace replied, with a wry humor I hadn't expected, —Wonderful.

Showing humor in the face of fear, well, it made me like her even more. I gave her a few more tips and Hattie'd had enough, saying in a gruff voice that we didn't have time for mollycoddling.

—Then leave, I snapped.

Hattie dismounted and went into the barn.

I adjusted Grace's left hand so that it held the reins correctly and proceeded to explain to her how to ride in the simplest terms possible.

Hattie emerged from the barn holding a rope. She fashioned it into a makeshift halter and put it over Rebel's bridle. Hattie readjusted Grace's reins and mounted her own horse, lead rope in hand.

—Hold on, she said, and clicked at her horse, and they were off.

I watched them ride away with mixture of anger and astonishment. Leave it to Hattie to simplify everything and take action. Her practical streak had saved my life more than once, but it's never stopped chafing me that she sees through all the complications to the simplest answer and course of action.

When I caught up, Hattie handed me the lead rope and loped off.

—Where is she going?

—To scout ahead.

—Am I really slowing you down?

—Yes.

—Tell me what I can do to remedy that.

—Do what you're told, and don't bait Hattie.

—Bait Hattie? She's the one…

Grace saw my expression and finished, —Yes, OK. Don't bait Hattie.

We carried along at an easy trot for a half mile. I watched Grace carefully. For a woman who was afraid of horses, she had a surprisingly solid seat. Her back was erect, from tension and fear, I suppose. She didn't bounce around in the saddle like so many new riders, though Rebel's smooth gait probably helped her. She was comfortable enough to start talking and asking questions.

–That's her name? Hattie?

I'd forgotten Hattie had made a point of not introducing herself.

–Yes.

She started asking questions about Hattie and I stopped her. If Hattie wants to tell Grace her story, as it doesn't relate to us, that's her business. I'm not going to do it, though. Grace was disappointed but said she understood.

Grace waved away a black fly buzzing around her head and almost fell off her horse in the process. When she spoke, her voice was shaky.

–So, Garet, tell me how you got started in the outlaw life.

–We were hungry and didn't have any money.

–But why banditry? Surely there was another option.

–Such as?

–Oh, teaching, perhaps. I hear they're in short supply out here.

–I don't like kids. No one would hire Hattie, and the sisters are illiterate.

–Are? Haven't you tried to teach them to read and write?

–Hattie has. Stella doesn't see the letters in the right order and gave it up pretty quick. Joan doesn't see the need.

–Of course there's a need. Women can't expect to win the right to vote if we aren't educated. By keeping us uneducated, men are able to control us.

–That's not the only way.

–No.

Grace was silent for a bit, then said, –And men aren't the only ones who want to control what's acceptable for women to do, to be. She said it real quiet like, and when I glanced over she was rubbing her fingers against her palms. She stopped when she caught me, smiled, and said, —But we have no chance of slipping off the yoke of oppression if we can't learn, think, and reason for ourselves.

—Is that what you did?

She got all haughty on me.

—I don't know what you mean.

I moved on, but I was sure to keep her actions and words in the back of my mind to ponder later on.

—Oh, then you probably heard it in a women's salon where they talk about women's rights but don't ever seem to make much progress. You're new to the West, Grace, so I'll let you in on a little secret: All this talk of freedom to make something of yourself, the American dream and all that? That's only meant for men. Women alone can't be too successful. Men are threatened by independent women. Especially independent colored women.

Her mouth tightened. Grace really doesn't have a poker face, though I can tell she tries.

—You sound like you know that from experience. Are you speaking of your banditry?

—Not only, no. I haven't always been an outlaw. Have you always been a travel writer?

—No. Do I detect a hint of an accent in your voice? Where are you from?

—England, originally. I've been over here since '63.

—Tell me all about it.

—Later.

—How did Stella get the scar on her lip?

—I don't know.

—How do you not know?

—She hasn't told me, and I haven't asked.

—Aren't you curious?

—Some people don't like to talk about their troubles. Some people do. I listen when they need an ear and stay silent when they want to keep their own counsel.

—It's going to be difficult to write about you all if you won't talk to me about how you ended up here.

—Hattie doesn't want me to.

—And do you do everything she says?

—It's always good advice. I'd be a fool not to.

—Can you tell me how you named your ranch?

—We are heretics, Grace. Didn't you know? Women doing men's work, not knowing our place. Having the audacity to think we should be treated with respect. It's *scandalous*.

—The ranch name is facetious, then?

—It might have started that way, over a few glasses of whisky. Our motto was definitely the result of whisky.

—Motto?

—It's from *The Tempest*. Hattie thought of it. It came later, after our first job in '75. We'd splurged on a good bottle of Kentucky bourbon and got roaring drunk under a full moon. Hattie starts quoting Shakespeare when she gets drunk. She was raised a slave in a New Orleans theater. Knows the Bard's words better than I do, and I'm British. Anyways, we were talking about what the men would do if they found out women had robbed the stage, and that quote just burst from her lips. *Hell is empty, and all the devils are here*. I painted it on the sign a couple of days later, after I recovered from my hangover.

—I like it. All of it.

—You'll probably fit right in.

Hattie rode hell-for-leather around the corner, stopped next to Grace, and told us someone was coming.

Grace was looking at me with a bemused expression and didn't see Hattie pull her gun and swing the polished walnut handle to hit Grace on the back of her head. Grace slumped forward, unconscious. Hattie grabbed Grace by the collar and pulled her off the horse and onto the ground.

—Bloody hell, Hatt. What are you doing?

—Leave her horse and follow me.

—I will not.

—Garet, by God, if you don't listen to me, trust me for a goddamn minute, I'll put a bullet in your head right now.

She would've, too. I dropped the lead line and followed Hattie up into the trees about fifty yards. We dismounted and crept back close to the road. Grace lay there, a lump of fine brown cloth against the road, a sharp gray rock poking into her temple.

—Are you going to tell me what's going on?

—Horace is coming.

An old miner on an ornery old mule of indeterminate color trotted around the curve and pulled up when he saw Grace and Rebel on the road. He dismounted with his canteen and went to Grace's aid. In a few minutes, she had revived and sat up, dazed, her hair flying away, her hat discarded on the road.

—Ma'am, did you fall off your horse?

Grace touched the back of her head, where a large lump had formed, and grimaced. She looked around, her eyes glassy and unfocused. When she saw Rebel standing docilely by, her eyes sharpened slightly. She took in the man and recoiled a little.

—I must have.

—What're you doing out here, riding alone? There's some dangerous bandits on the loose.

—Oh, I... um... rented this horse in...

—Ouray?

—Yes, Ouray, and was just out for a little ride. The livery assured me this was an easy road. I think my horse got spooked by an animal in the woods there. What's this about dangerous bandits?

—Four men robbed a stage this morning. Took a woman captive, they say. A Yankee, like you.

The man looked at her with suspicion, though with his walleye, you'd think he was looking more back down the way he came.

—Heavens. I assure you I haven't seen any bandits or captive women. Besides, I'm not a Yankee. I'm from Chicago.

—Anyways, you shouldn't be riding alone, especially without a gun for protection. I'll take you back to town.

—I don't want to trouble you. I can find my way back, thank you.

I almost laughed at the expression of horror on Grace's face at the idea of riding with this frightening-looking man.

The miner stood and looked around, searching.

—No trouble. Which livery did you use?

Grace touched her temple and looked at the blood on her glove.

—I don't remember. I must have hit my head harder than I thought. You are too kind, but I really don't require assistance. Rebel here is a very capable horse, I've discovered.

The man nodded slowly and agreed.

Hattie came out from behind the tree and walked into the road.

—That was the friendliest interrogation I've ever seen.

—You didn't tell me to scare her.

—Just the sight of you was scare enough, Hattie said.

—That ain't very generous of you, and me doing you a favor.

Grace looked between the man, Horace Whatley, and Hattie, her face darkening. She turned to me.

–This was a test? Were you in on it?

–No, I wasn't. And while I don't agree with the way Hattie did it, I'm glad she did.

Grace looked as if I'd slapped her.

–Don't get your bloomers in a twist. Passed the test as far as I can see, though you ain't much for geography. Ouray's about eighty miles thataway, Horace said.

Grace glared at Hattie. Hattie had a shit-eating smirk on her face. Honestly, I wanted to slap her myself, but I'd take it up with her in private.

–You enjoyed hitting me over the head.

–I did.

–Goddamn you, Hattie.

I stepped between the women.

–What'd I tell you, Grace?

–You told her my name?

–I agreed not to bait Hattie, but I didn't agree to being beaten and thrown onto the road for some sort of initiation, Grace said.

–The initiation is much tougher than this, Hattie said.

–Not helping here, Hatt.

–It's amazing you women get any holdups done at all, the way you fight and bicker, Horace said.

–We got your money back from that crook Connolly easy enough, I said.

–Did you now? How much did you take? His roaming eye wandered around–looking for our horses and stuffed saddlebags, no doubt.

–None of your business, Hattie said. She shoved a few extra dollars in Horace's vest pocket and told him thanks for the help.

—Did you pay for the horse and tack?

—Left extra money, Hattie said.

—I'm coming back for Old Blue. You better treat her right. You better not let that jackass of yours mount her, either.

Horace waved at me as he rode away to his cabin, his mule honking its pleasure at being close to home. Hattie went to get our horses.

I tried to look at the gash on Grace's head, but she moved away. Even when I told her she was bleeding, she refused. A wry sense of humor and grit. I was liking Grace more and more.

She picked up her hat and put it on and was dusting the dirt from her skirt when Hattie returned. Before I could intervene, Grace stepped up to Hattie and raised her hand as if to slap her. She stopped, her hand in midair, and her head snapped back. I moved forward and saw the point of Hattie's knife holding Grace's chin up.

—The last whitey who raised a hand to me got his throat slit. I have no qualms about doing the same to you.

Grace's voice shook when she answered. —Take that knife off of me.

—Or what?

In one deft movement, Grace stepped back and pushed Hattie's hand with the knife away.

—Don't *ever* touch me again, or I won't have any qualms about killing you, either.

Hattie stared at Grace for a long time, and Grace held her gaze. I could see a little muscle working in Grace's jaw. I don't know where Grace's mettle came from. I hadn't expected it, and I'm sure Hattie hadn't, either. One thing Hattie hated was weak-willed women, and Grace showed herself to be anything but by standing toe-to-toe with Hattie and her Bowie knife.

—Fair enough.

Grace looked at Hattie's outstretched hand in shock, but took it. They jerked their hands down once and released. It was a start, at least.

Happy the rest of the journey would be tense only part of the time now, I got us moving.

—Come on, then, or we won't make camp by nightfall.

Grace got Rebel's lead rope and draped it over the horse's neck before she got on. She was still awkward and looked nervous, but had apparently decided to go it on her own. Maybe once she faced down Hattie and her knife, falling off a horse didn't seem so bad. We mounted and loped off. A mile down the road, Hattie reined her horse onto a small animal track that peeled off from the road and wound its way uphill into a colony of aspens. The silvery-green leaves shimmered in the breeze, the saplings swaying on their pliable trunks as we climbed up the side of the mountain.

—Heaven help me, Grace said.

Rebel lunged up the steep mountain, and all of Grace's riding poise on the flat road disappeared. Rebel's neck bobbed up and down with the effort of the climb, and Grace hunched over and grasped the saddle horn, swaying back and forth like a thin spear of grass buffeted by high winds. The incline leveled out slightly, and the horses' gaits smoothed out. We exited the trees and were greeted by a majestic Rocky Mountain sunset. The sky was a mixture of purple, blue, and gold, and shafts of golden sunlight lit up the rocky precipices on the mountain opposite us.

Grace gasped at the sight. The big gash over her left eyebrow from hitting the road had scabbed over.

I asked her if she was glad she came, and she said with an awe-filled voice that she was.

We continued on the trail, which now cut across the open mountaintop. Rocks of all shapes and sizes littered the slope and protected patches of untouched snow on their northern sides. Wildflowers covered the ground like a multicolored carpet. Grace asked for her journal so she could write down what she was seeing. I lied and told her it was with Stella.

Hattie reached a ridge and stopped. Grace pulled up next to her, and I did the same. In the shadow of a massive peak, three gulches met in a riot of undulating rocks and grassland crisscrossed by animal trails. Crooked paths of snow wound down like frozen rivers through the dips and crevices of the uneven ground until finally dissolving into a lake of pale, almost translucent, blue.

—Every scene is more beautiful than the last. How is that possible? Grace said.

I shrugged. I'd long since lost my wonder at the beauty around me, and I mourned the innocent pleasure Grace received on seeing this for the first time.

Across the lake a herd of elk grazed on patches of spring grass. One elk raised his head and looked our way. He surveyed us for a long moment before sauntering off, the rest of the herd following him, oblivious to our presence. The lead elk stopped, lowered his head and grazed, apparently deciding we were no threat.

—Wouldn't he look handsome hanging in our smokehouse? I said. My mouth watered at the thought of a thick elk steak.

—There'll be plenty for you to kill at home, Hattie said.

—You hunt? Grace asked.

—No men around to do it.

—Wouldn't matter if there were. Garet's the best shot in the Hole.

—Hatt only says that so she doesn't have to do the hunting.

Hattie grinned with real pleasure for the first time that day.

We made camp next to the lake. I killed and skinned a rabbit while Hattie showed Grace how to care for the horses. The adventures of the day had exhausted the bluestocking, and she fell asleep almost immediately. Hattie kept her own counsel while the rabbit roasted on the open fire, and we ate. She lay down, giving me first watch, falling into her half sleep while I read Grace's journal. It's not as interesting as I'd expected, her prose is a little too florid for my liking, but it is precisely what she said it was, the journal of a woman traveling alone in the West. I'll let Hattie read it. Maybe it'll put her mind at ease a little more.

I regret my impulsive decision to bring Grace along. I expect we won't be back at the ranch for ten days, taking the circuitous route I promised Hattie. The pain comes and goes, but the doc didn't give me enough laudanum to last two weeks. It'll probably last since I need to keep my wits about me so Hattie doesn't get suspicious.

I long for home, for the comfort of my bed of a night, for the quiet companionship in front of the fire in the evening, for the feel of the cool grass between my toes, the smell of horses and hay in the cozy barn. And a couple of fingers of whisky wouldn't go amiss, either.

GHOST TOWNS OF THE OWLHOOT TRAIL

by Thomas Henery
Published 1935

Chapter Twelve

Timberline, Colorado, 1871–77 or 78

Timberline, Colorado, was marked by tragedy from the beginning. In the spring of 1871, two wagon trains set out for Colorado, one from Independence, Missouri, the other from Austin, Texas. Only one made it. The wagon train through Texas was massacred by a band of Kiowa led by Satanta and Big Tree, leading to a violent shift away from the army's Quaker peace policy. The Comanche and Kiowa would be driven onto the reservation within three years.

Ironically, about the time the Plains Indians were defeated, Timberline was entering its prosperous years. Saying *prosperous* is being generous. Timberline was never much of a going concern, but like all new towns it had visions of grandeur. The characteristics that had drawn the land promoters to stake a claim to the area—a rich river valley surrounded by mountains teeming with wildlife, plenty of wood for construction and minerals to be mined, God willing—were shadowed by the remoteness of the location. Set in a box canyon with a narrow, treacherous pass as the only entrance, the settlers had trouble getting in and out to do business in the closest railroad town, Rock Springs, seventy miles north as the crow flies.

Legend has it Jed Spooner came across the Hole during his flight from his '73 robbery of the Rock Springs Bank, where he and his gang got away with $13,000. He knew immediately it would be a perfect long-term hideout and base of operations for his gang and any others willing to pay him for protection. Imagine his delight when he came across a poor excuse for a town at the southern end of the canyon, on the banks of the Green River. When Spooner and his gang rode into Timberline, the townsmen were considering pulling up stakes and moving somewhere on the rail line, where making a living might be easier. Flush with money, the outlaws spent freely on what little entertainment was to be had. Soon an agreement was made, and Jed Spooner had a hideout on the back range to complement the one he had on the front range.

At its height Timberline boasted a general store, a saloon and whorehouse, a blacksmith, a half-built one-room schoolhouse, and a sheriff's office occupied by Luke Rhodes, a former cattle rustler and friend of Spooner's who decided he'd rather raise the cattle his friends rustled than steal them. When not stealing and killing, Spooner and his gang ran a horse ranch north of the town and trained getaway horses for their outlaw brethren.

The hideout only protected him for so long. In late 1877, Pinkertons hired by Callum Connolly tracked the Spooner Gang down to his ranch, where he died in a firefight with the agents. When Spooner died, the town died with him. But Brown's Hole's role as a hideout for outlaws would continue; it was used by outlaws such as Butch Cassidy and his gang for twenty more years. Timberline, however, remained a ghost town.

The names of the residents are lost to history, and Luke Rhodes disappeared after the 1870 census.

The blacksmith's shop is still standing, but barely, the last remnant of a cursed town. In the western Colorado backcountry, you'll need a good compass, a good topographical map and a sure-footed mule to find it.

CALICO QUEENS OF COLORADO 1859–1899

by Richard Matheson
Published 1930

Chapter Seventeen

The Gem Sisters

As with most whores, no one is real sure where Ruby and Opal Steele came from and we only know where one ended up. Though we don't know the specifics, most prostitutes' origin story is the same: hungry and poor, with no husband, brother or father to protect or take care of them, no education or skills, they use the only possession they own completely to make their way: their body.

Ruby and Opal Steele, the Gem Sisters, as they became known, are historically significant in that they were the preferred whores of numerous outlaw gangs in the mid-to-late 1870s. Little is known about where they came from. Opal, the only sister we know to have survived into the twentieth century, who eventually married a Welsh miner who hit it big in Leadville, told different stories about their origin. In one telling they were black sheep daughters of a Pittsburgh steel baron. In another they were poor farm girls from Missouri, orphaned young and sold off to a pimp by their grandmother. In still another they were nurses in the war who followed the Union army west and became laundresses. What all the stories had in common, I suspect, is they were outright lies. Where the sisters came from isn't necessarily important.

What was important was the role they played on the Outlaw Trail before it became known as such. The 1870s saw the beginning of the outlaw era in the Old West. It would reach its peak a decade later and last until the Wild Bunch disbanded and went into the wind. Ruby and Opal were whores in Timberline, Colorado, a short-lived town in Brown's Hole, in the far northwestern corner of the state. They were brought to Timberline by Hank "Ought-Not" Henry, Jed Spooner's lieutenant, who was half in love with Opal, the younger and the prettier of the two whores, at least according to Opal's account. There is no formal record of Ruby Steele at all, but Ought-Not, the last survivor of the Spooner Gang, told me himself that Ruby Steele was real and was a pretty little thing for a half-breed Chinese. Spooner apparently had a soft spot for her, but he had a soft spot for whores all across the West. Ought-Not said she left the Hole about 1880 and he didn't know what happened to her after that. I asked him if he'd read Opal's autobiography, *Gem in the Rough*, and he said he had no desire to read a bunch of lies and besides his eyes were bad.

According to Opal the two of them joined Spooner's gang sometime in the late seventies—she was never clear on the year. The story she tells beggars belief, and since this is a historically accurate recounting of whores of the Colorado, I'm not going to reprint it here. Ought-Not said it was a bunch of lies, and that's good enough for me. This story goes a long way toward explaining why Opal Steele Driscoll is considered one of the biggest liars from the era.

What's not in doubt is that Opal turned up in Leadville in 1878, married Bowen Driscoll, and became one of the most important society ladies in the area after he hit it big. Occasionally she would be coerced into bringing out her accordion and playing one of the two tunes she knew, as she used to do for her customers. When she played, a wistful expression would settle on her face and her eyes were moistened with tears that never fell.

6

Margaret Parker's Journal

Monday, June 4, 1877
Heresy Ranch
Timberline, Colorado

Grace's exhaustion at camp turned into full-fledged *soroche*—headache, nausea, exhaustion. Her face swelled up and her hands were straining against her gloves, but she never took them off. Staying there and letting her recuperate wasn't an option; we had to get her down out of the mountains to counteract her sickness, and the posse would be in a full-fledged search now. We were already behind on our getaway because I'd brought Grace along. I figured the sisters were at least fifty miles closer to home, and a good thing, too. Someone had to take care of the horses. Business always picked up in the spring and summer, prime rustling season.

We told Grace we needed to take a more circuitous route with her along—three women stood out even more than a black and a white woman traveling alone—but she begged us to get home as soon as possible, said she'd ride as hard as needed to make it happen. And she did. We rode like hell, and she kept up and kept quiet. She didn't become a horsewoman over those five days, but she and Rebel built a bond, which is the first step in understanding horses.

When we got to the ranch, Grace found a bed and fell into it. She's still there. No one begrudges her; we've all had a bout of the sickness and know how miserable it can be.

I spent the first couple of days enjoying being home, getting some sleep. But I can't wait too long for the dispensation or the town gets restless. So today, with a saddlebag full of bundles of money, I rode into Timberline.

I suppose I should explain a little about our town to whoever will bother reading this in the future, if anyone. It's going to be difficult to describe to you, future reader, an environment I take for granted and, frankly, don't think about anymore. I've been too busy surviving and living to think about the colors of the setting sun or the carpet of wildflowers that blankets the valley. But I will venture to add a little bit of description here and there when I think of it.

Despite its bucolic setting, Timberline, Colorado, isn't much to look at. It's a clutch of ramshackle buildings randomly placed along a wide, nameless street and set in a remote box canyon where the borders of Wyoming, Colorado, and Utah meet. Timberline had been on the verge of becoming one of the forgotten towns of the West, a footnote to a far-off massacre that had claimed the lives of half of its settlers, when Jed Spooner and his gang rode into town on blown horses, searching for a safe haven. Spooner, equal parts charming and cunning, saw in the dying town an opportunity. He offered them money for protection and for looking the other way and not asking questions about where the money came from. It was an easy enough deal for the five surviving families to take.

After my husband died, and Colonel Connolly stole my ranch, Jed Spooner brought me and my family here. I'm not naive enough to think there wasn't a strong streak of selfishness in Spooner's action; our ranch on the front range, the Poudre

River Ranch, had been a reliable hideout for him and his boys for years. We traded horses with them and hid them, gave them work in between their bank jobs. Gave them good meals and a warm hearth. Eventually I invited Spooner into my bed. Sooner than he expected, but we'd both known as soon as I buried Thomas that it would happen.

I'd been drawn to the outlaw from the beginning. Jed Spooner was charming and fun loving, gentle with horses and children, and he treated Hattie with a respect you wouldn't have expected from a former Confederate officer, or a man who briefly ran with the James boys. He left the gang, he said, because he didn't see the point in fighting a war they'd lost, and he saw even less point in killing people for money. No, Spooner decided to charm people out of their money at the point of a gun. He said it was more fun, and less messy. He'd seen enough blood to last him a lifetime. Thomas, a veteran of the Crimea, admired him for it, and I wanted him because of it. Of course, you learn a lot about a man by bedding him, and by sharing a pillow after, and it didn't take me long to wonder if Spooner's story had been an elaborate tale to ingratiate himself with Thomas and me. There was a dark streak in Spooner, one he kept a tight rein on, but there were flashes, an edge to Spooner that both repulsed and attracted me.

Bringing us to Timberline did two things for Spooner: It let him feel like a mighty fine man, saving us unprotected women and helping us start a new horse ranch. His boys helped build the Heresy Ranch's cabin, barn, outbuildings, and corrals. In return we agreed to train getaway horses and give them room and board. I offered Spooner my warm bed.

Jed didn't know at the time that Jehu and I had robbed a bank in Denver to keep us from starving. He was impressed when I told him (I left out the part about killing Alfie Gernsbeck;

only Hattie knew that part of the story), but he saw it as a one-time thing. He was there to take care of me now. Jed's idea of taking care of me was bringing me part of his latest haul, eating my food, drinking my whisky, trading some horses, and getting a poke or two before riding off to whatever other woman he was "taking care of."

It really shows Jed's ignorance that he thought I wanted to be taken care of by a man. Thomas was a fine husband, and I loved him dearly, always will, but he didn't take care of me. Oh, he thought he did, of course. Smart women will always let a man think he has the upper hand, but Thomas wasn't endowed with the astuteness required to succeed out west. Being a one-armed man didn't help, either. I was intelligent enough to run the ranch, and crafty enough to let Thomas take the credit.

My arrangement with Jed worked. He wasn't around enough to annoy me or to boss me around. When he was around he was an enthusiastic lover, which is about all I require of a man these days.

It has been two years since Jed rode off through Lodore Canyon, taking his patronage with him. The girls and I have been taking care of the town since. Which is why I rode into Timberline today, to pass out their part of our take.

These ramshackle buildings I mentioned include a livery, a whorehouse/hotel/saloon, a shebang, a half-built schoolhouse, and a sheriff's office that's closed most of the time and has never housed a prisoner. There are four or five vacant buildings waiting to be reclaimed and put to use. They were left abandoned by original settlers who weren't enticed by Jed's offer, and who didn't like the general lawlessness up and down the valley.

I reined my horse up at the livery and dismounted. A scrawny towheaded boy met me.

—Miss Garet, howdido?

—Hello, Newt.

I surveyed the boy. The black eye that had been yellowing when I left had reverted to a deep shade of purple, the white of his eye turned bloody. A few more hits to it would blind him, I suspected. Now that his mother, Lou, was dead and unable to take the brunt of his father's anger, it all fell to this twelve-year-old boy. Newt was still young enough to be saved from his father's violence and his own inevitable violence. I wanted to get him away from Ulysses Valentine, but I didn't know how. I'd done more harm than good when I tried to help Lou, and the fact was Newt was as good as Valentine's property. I would find little support from the townsmen. Timberline was one of the rare towns where women outnumbered men, but men somehow still got their way.

Newt looked past me to the empty street behind.

—Jehu with you?

—No. Should be along in a couple of weeks. Wonder what he's going to bring you this time.

The excitement in Newt's good eye almost broke my heart. He had to hide the little gifts Jehu brought him, usually toys, from his father, who was so drunk most of the time Newt was doing most of the work.

I pulled a paper sack out of my saddlebag. The scent of licorice hung in the air around the bag.

—I brought you this.

Newt's eyes lit up like candles, and he thanked me.

He ripped off a chunk from the rope of licorice and offered it to me wordlessly. I told him I preferred lemon drops and asked after his pa.

Newt's face closed off.

—Around back.

I grabbed Newt's shoulder and squeezed.

—Newt, you know you can always come out to our place. Whenever you want. We've always got a job for a good hand like you.

—Thanks, Miss Garet, but my pa needs me here.

—I know you're a big help. You're becoming a good blacksmith in your own right.

Newt flushed with pleasure. I bent down to be at his eye level.

—We like to go on picnics on Sundays, after we get our chores done. Maybe you could join us one day. Joan will fry us up a chicken and you can try to catch a few fish for our supper.

—I'd like that.

—It's a date. Now, why don't you ride Ole Pete down to the creek, give him a drink. And enjoy your treat with a little privacy.

Newt grinned and gathered up Ole Pete's reins.

—Need a heft?

—Yes, ma'am.

Newt put his booted foot in my cupped hands and I tossed him up the sixteen hands to Ole Pete's back. The sorrel turned his blaze-faced muzzle back to gently nip at Newt's boot, a sure sign of affection.

—Don't let him get away from you.

Ole Pete snorted loudly and nudged me with his nose, as if offended by my suggestion that he'd be anything other than a gentleman with the wisp of a child on his back. I patted the old horse's neck, and he headed off toward the creek.

I walked through the stables, noticing the empty stalls, past the blacksmithing tools and an unfinished ax head on the anvil, and found Newt's father sitting on a camp chair next to the back wall, a jug of whisky at his feet. The blacksmith's rheumy eyes landed on me. Even with him sitting down, I was barely taller than Ulysses Valentine. His arms, strengthened by years of blacksmithing, were as thick as my thighs, his chest as big around as me and Hattie when we hugged. I clenched my jaw as I thought of Newt's black eye and imagined this giant's meaty fist connecting with that soft face.

—I heard you were back.

He held his hand out, palm up. No need for pleasantries. Our mutual dislike was well known, but we managed to get along professionally well enough. I needed horses shod on the regular, and he needed someone to keep him in whisky.

I pulled his take out of my bag and dropped it in his lap. He opened the leather pouch and looked down at the gold and silver coins within. He grunted.

—When's Jehu get back?

—Couple of weeks.

He bit the leather cord and pulled it to close the pouch.

—You know, people are starting to talk about how you're playing both ends here.

—Are they?

—It's not going unnoticed that you get back most of the money you give us when Jehu brings in supplies.

He stood. I pulled my pouch of hashish tobacco and papers from my shirt pocket and took my time filling the blanket. I know very well that Valentine can snap me in two like a twig if he's of a mind to. I wouldn't even have the chance to pull my knife from my boot or my gun from its holster. He relies on the fear of his size to bully and intimidate everyone in town, man and woman alike, except Luke Rhodes.

Sheriff Luke Rhodes, roughly my height but as stout as a bulldog, is the only man in the whole of Brown's Hole whom Ulysses Valentine is afraid of. But I'll be goddamned if I'm going to rely on a man to fight my battles. I've managed to keep my intimidation hidden from Valentine, which makes him hate me all the more. I know when he stops hating me, I'll lose the upper hand. So I stared him in the eye, knowing that Valentine would get what was coming to him, and probably sooner than he realized. God willing, by my hand.

I scratched the match along the livery wall and puffed my cigarette alight. I inhaled deeply, letting the smoke fill my lungs, take the edge off my pain and infuse me with a sense of well-being and invincibility. I looked up at Valentine's heavy face and blew a steady stream of smoke into his flattened nose.

—You're free to travel to Rock Springs to get your whisky yourself. But it takes a helluva lot of effort to get there, and you and I both know you're a lazy bastard.

I kept my gaze level, but heard him growl deep in his throat.

—One day…

—You'll beat me to death like you did your wife?

—That was your fault.

I couldn't let Val see it, but a part of me wondered if he was right. Her final beating came when he found the money I'd been carving out of Val's take and giving directly to her, in hopes she would use it to escape.

—Keep telling yourself that, Val.

Valentine kept his eyes narrowed on mine, but out of the corner of my eye I saw him ball his fists.

—I look forward to cleaning your plow.

—You touch me, or mine, and I will kill you. You'll do well not to anger me, Val.

—Just wait till Spooner returns.

—Unless he's bringing you a mail-order bride, he's not going to be much help.

—I could kill you with my bare hands.

—Yet you never have. Because you need my money.

—When Spooner returns I won't.

—Spooner's been gone for nearly two years. He's probably dead. Until another gang comes along willing to pay for your whisky, you're stuck with me.

I walked through the livery and said over my shoulder, —Jehu probably won't be back for a couple of weeks. Might want to portion out your whisky till then.

—Newt!

I turned and walked back to the giant.

—I sent him to the creek to water my horse. He'll be back directly. And if I see another bruise on his face…

Valentine moved close enough to me I could smell the liquor on his breath over the smell of my smoke.

—You'll what?

—Valentine?

We both turned to see the outline of Sheriff Luke Rhodes in the middle of the wide livery door. Val backed down.

—Sheriff, what can I do for you?

Rhodes walked into the barn and out of the shadow. He wore his sweat-stained hat low on his head, and the sleeves of his shirt were rolled up past his elbows. His forearms are brown and ropy, his hands are scarred with lasso burns from his previous job as a cowhand turned cattle rustler, his fingernails are rimmed with dirt from his current job as a cattle rancher and vegetable gardener.

Rhodes touched his hat.

—Mrs. Parker.

—Sheriff.

—Need you to make me a pickle barrel, Val. Think my cucumbers are going to come in good this year.

Valentine nodded.

—Will do, Sheriff.

—Remember what I said, Val. Good day, Sheriff.

I walked out of the livery and down the wide, nameless main street. The muddy ruts from the spring runoff were hardening in the dry June sun. Soon driving a wagon down the street would be an uncomfortable, bumpy proposition.

I finished the cigarette, enjoying the slight floating sensation it gave me, and put the stub out on the heel of my boot. I entered the shebang to the tinkling of a little brass bell, a small, innocent sound that brought to mind the bustling main street in the village next to my grandfather's Somerset estate. This little general store in the back of beyond was a faint image of the store of my youth.

Rebecca Reynolds looked up from her books, and a smile broke across her face. She came around the counter, hugged me, and told me she was glad I was safe.

—I always come back safe.

—There was the one time.

—Hattie tricked me, told me snuff wasn't any stronger than a cigarette. If you've ever had snuff, you know full well I couldn't help falling off my horse. And it's awfully ungenerous of you to remind me every time I come back.

Rebecca shrugged and smiled.

—Someone's got to keep you modest.

—You've taken it upon yourself, I see.

—Yes. You can't be the best outlaw, the best horsewoman, and the most handsome woman in Brown's Hole to boot. It's not fair.

—I am not handsome.

—You can wear pants all you want, Margaret, but you can't hide that face.

—These are jodhpurs, I'll have you know, and I wear them because it makes riding easier. I bet you'd like pants if you wore them.

Rebecca scoffed.

—But I wouldn't like it.

Harvey Reynolds emerged from the back room with a smile barely visible through his thick beard. Harvey is a good-humored man, despite the fact that his left arm was thrown on a head-high pile of limbs outside the Gettysburg field hospital.

I greeted Harvey and handed Rebecca the pouch containing their take. Harvey intercepted it, hefted it in his hand, and raised his bushy eyebrows.

—A little extra for your little one. I nodded toward Rebecca's swollen belly.

—Thank you.

—Don't tell anyone, especially Valentine.

—Of course not.

There was a flush just visible on Harvey's neck below the edge of his ginger beard. I knew that soon enough his entire face would be aflame, and his shame would be complete. It's why I prefer giving the take to Rebecca. She'll leave it on his desk, and Reynolds can ignore the fact that his business, and his family, are being kept afloat by a gang of women.

—You're too good to us, Margaret, Rebecca said.

—I wish you'd call me Garet.

I looked around the store. The shelves looked significantly emptier than when I left three weeks ago.

—Been busy?

—There's some rustlers camped out where Beaver Creek flows into the Green, rebranding about a hundred fifty head. They've been in a few times.

—Cause any trouble?

—Not a bit. They're friends of the sheriff, so they know better, Rebecca said.

I hid a smile. We all call Luke Rhodes the sheriff, and gave him a dented tin star to wear, but he has very little law to enforce. In Brown's Hole there's only one rule you don't break. Everything else is fair game. Something that Rebecca Reynolds would like to change. If Timberline has any chance of getting civilized, it will be down to Rebecca Reynolds.

—Jehu should be here in a couple of weeks with supplies.

I watched Rebecca and Harvey for any sign of disapproval—an exchanged look, a tightening of their mouths, the aversion of their eyes—and was rewarded with enthusiastic smiles, proof that Valentine is alone in his resentment. Jehu is everyone's favorite, and not just because he brings everyone's supplies and news of the outside world. I figure if anything ever happens to me, the town would mourn the end of their gravy train more than the loss of my company. But Jehu? If anything happens to him, the entire town'll be out for blood. Hell, I can't blame them; I like Jehu more than myself, too.

—Is it true you kidnapped a woman? Rebecca said.

—Stella tell you that?

—Joan. Stella looked pretty put out about it.

—When is Stella not put out? Harvey asked.

—Truthfully, Grace asked me to bring her along.

—I can't believe you obliged her, Rebecca said.

—Nor I. She's back at the ranch, sleeping. Struck with *soroche* on the way back. I'll bring her to town soon enough to meet everyone. Better be moving along. I've got Hattie getting a pale stallion ready for me this afternoon.

—Oh, be careful, Garet.

—I haven't been beaten by a horse yet.

—Except that one time…

As I left, I pointed at Rebecca Reynolds and told her she was an ungenerous woman. Then I walked down toward the Blue Diamond.

Luke Rhodes was leaned against the wall of his office, waiting for me. I smiled, knowing Luke had missed me as much as I'd missed him. I'd never admit it to him, though.

I greeted him, and he opened the door to the sheriff's office and followed me in. I dropped my saddlebags on his desk and his arms were around me, pulling me back against him, his lips on my neck, his luxurious mustache tickling so that I shivered.

—Does this mean you've missed me?

—Would you please wear a dress when you come to town? These pants are a genuine nuisance.

I turned around and wrapped my arms about his neck.

—Will you wear a dress for me as well?

—Not funny.

—Do you want to talk, or do you want to...

Luke and I have been...intimate...for almost a year. Not regularly, and not publicly, but occasionally. When I seek him out. He is too much of a gentleman to do the same, which only makes me seek him out more. I resisted for months after Spooner left, but I have my needs, same as a man, and I couldn't resist the urge to feel if his mustache was as soft as it looked.

It is.

Luke and I have been friends since we rode into town, and it was easy to see that he wanted me. His reticence and respect for me helped heal my poor opinion of men. He reminded me there were plenty of men—honorable, just men—worthy of my respect, and, like a moth to a flame, it drew me in. I'd felt much the same way about Thomas when I fell in love with him. Spooner was an anomaly, a love affair built on desire, not affection, a relationship that required nothing of me so I could focus on my family and my ranch. Luke, though—I think we could have had a good life if Lou Valentine hadn't died the same week I found out I was dying of cancer. When Luke, as sheriff, didn't arrest Valentine for beating his wife to death, I quickly snuffed out the thoughts of the future that had started to worm their way into my brain. Hattie was livid with Rhodes; all the women in town were. But what we thought or wanted didn't matter, because Lou was considered Val's property.

I stayed away from Luke for two weeks to show my displeasure, but eventually went back. I didn't want to die a celibate, and options for companionship are thin on the ground in the Hole.

I've tried my very best to keep my feelings on a… I cannot even find the word for it. We are well beyond platonic, and *disinterested* is laughably incorrect. When we are alone, Luke makes it difficult not to let my mind wander to what it would feel like to wake up with a warm body next to mine.

When we finished, and I was dressing, Luke said he was thinking of getting into a new sideline.

—Already gone sour on the pickle business?

—Now see, *that* was funny.

—Yes, well, the British wit and all. What business? Going back into rustling?

—No. The horse business.

I stared at my lover. His black handlebar mustache is shot through with gray. Today it was unwaxed and looked especially silky hanging down past the corners of his mouth. Right then, though, his mustache barely masked a teasing smirk. I was half-tempted to punch the smugness off his face. Instead I smiled.

—You could, but I wouldn't recommend it.

—Afraid I might be a better hand than you?

—No. I've seen you ride.

—You really know how to charm a man.

—You were pretty well charmed a minute ago.

Luke stood and made himself decent enough we could talk without me being distracted. He knew me and my appetites too well. I was holding on to my irritation at his nerve in challenging me.

—You really are beautiful when you get your dander up.

—I don't take kindly…

He stopped me, pulled me close. My God, I love that mustache.

—Settle down for just a minute and remember not every man on earth is out to get you. Especially not me. I want to work with you, Garet. Not competition.

—You help us every summer.

—You know what I mean.

Now he'd done it, made the subtext text. I wished he hadn't. I was forced to hurt him, to push him away, which I do not want to do.

—What will Ruby think?

He reddened a little. I've made it clear that he is free to find companionship where he wants, as am I. He wasn't aware until today that I know about his occasional visits to the whore.

—Or Spooner?

Luke's bright blue eyes darkened at the outlaw's name.

—Spooner left the field over two years ago.

—Left the field? Is that what I am to you? Some sort of military objective to be achieved, instead of a woman to be won?

—That's not what I meant.

—I'm not the only one who needs to work on their charm.

I went to my saddlebags for Rhodes's take and handed the folded clutch of bills to him.

—I like our relationship just fine as it is.

He stared at me, ignoring the money.

—I want more, Luke said.

—I can't give you more money.

—I want more of you.

—I can't give you any more of that, either.

—Why not?

—I don't have to give you a reason, Luke. You don't own me, and you're perilously close to not having any part of me at all.

He crossed his arms over his bare chest.

—You shouldn't antagonize Valentine.

—Maybe he shouldn't antagonize me.

Luke laughed.

—I think all your success has gone to your head. If you don't watch it, Valentine will teach you a lesson one day when I'm not around.

—Put me in my place, you mean? Show me who's boss? Like he's doing with Newt?

—I warned him to stop.

—Or what, Luke? Are you going to throw him in jail?

—I can, for a couple of days.

—Then he'll get back out and go at him even worse.

—Garet, what do you want me to do? Valentine has every right to discipline his son.

—But he has no right to discipline me, which is what you were implying. If you stand by and let him…

—I would never stand by and let him hurt you. You know that. This would be moot if you'd marry me.

—That's your proposal? *Marry me so Valentine won't kill you*? That's a terrible proposal.

—Well, you've got me all flustered. I had it planned better than this. I love you, and I want to take care of you. And don't get your dander up again. I don't want to control you, not that I could if I tried. You're the finest goddamn woman I've ever met, the way you take care of your family and everyone in town, and my God, you're a hand with a horse. You're pert near perfect, and I'm gonna be selfish for a minute and tell you the real reason I want to marry you. I think you'd make me a better man.

I turned away from him so he wouldn't see my tears. I hated God in that moment, for finally giving me a man almost worthy of taking Thomas's place by my side, only to not give me the health or the time to let it happen. As if to remind me of my mortality, a pain shot through my stomach.

He asked me if I was crying and I told him I was, then I told him why. He tried to talk me out of my decision, saying that the way he saw it, that was more reason than ever to get married, so we could spend time together before the end. I respected Luke too much to tell him outright that I would never take the chance he would claim my ranch after I died. Take it from the girls. I didn't think he would, but there is a germ of mistrust that I just cannot get rid of. Luke is a new addition to my life, and I felt the stirrings of the nascent stage of love, when you want to spend all your waking hours with this new, exciting person, revel in the possibilities. But Luke is lost possibilities; Hattie, Jehu, Stella, and Joan are reality. We are carved into one another's lives and futures like the elaborate designs in a finely tooled saddle.

—I'll forever be grateful for your offer and, if things were different, I might take you up on it. But it's unfair to you, to me, and to my family. I know you and Ruby have a…

—Garet…

—She can offer you a future, Luke. I can't.

I cradled Luke's face and kissed him for the last time.

When I got to the door, Luke called out to me in a gruff voice, telling me to stay away from Valentine and warning me about the one hard-and-fast law in the Hole.

I was glad he did; it reignited my anger and helped diminish my grief at turning him down.

—Everything but killing. I know. Funny how that law didn't apply to Val beating Lou to death. But that was her fault, right?

Justified because she went against her husband by dreaming of being free of his fists. Not the kind of escape she was looking for, death. But Lou knew well enough that there are worse things than death. All women do.

I walked down to the creek to cool off for a bit before seeing Ruby and Opal. I took off my boots and waded into the cold water and smoked another cigarette, wishing I'd cut the tobacco a little more generously with hashish. It helped my physical pain, at least, and the cold water quieted my flush of anger until I was relaxed enough to see the Gem Sisters without showing too much emotion.

The Blue Diamond Saloon is the only whorehouse in Brown's Hole, and Ruby and Opal Steele are the only whores. They say they're sisters, but everyone knows that's a lie. They're both dark haired, of a height and coloring, with one big difference: Ruby is a Celestial, though probably only half, which is why people don't care overmuch. Ruby knows that she's always one mean drunk away from being a scapegoat, so she keeps on the straight and narrow. No one knows where they came from or how they hooked up together. They came into town with a few of Spooner's men and decided to stay on and open the Blue Diamond.

They had the door to the saloon propped open to take advantage of the nice breeze flowing across the cold river and into town, and I could hear Opal playing "Sweet Betsy from Pike" on her accordion. I walked in and let my eyes adjust to the dim light. The Blue Diamond is clean and serviceable, but simple in the extreme. The Gem Sisters, as they call themselves, see no point in fancying up the place. If a randy cowboy doesn't like the surroundings, he's welcome to make the hard journey up the steep, rocky pass to get to Rock Springs to the north or go through the treacherous Lodore Canyon to the south and travel a couple hundred barren miles to get to civilization. Or he could take an easy ride along the Green River through the wide, flat box canyon to Timberline. Most choose the Gem Sisters.

The music stopped.

—Well, well, well. Look who the cat dragged in.

Opal sat at a table holding an accordion on her lap, looking nothing like a whore waiting for her next john to walk through the door. She wore a simple blue cotton dress, and while the neckline was considerably lower than a farmer's wife would countenance, it was nothing to a Denver dove's. Opal was fine figured and saw no need to show off her wares any more than necessary. Men could see what was under her dress easy enough. In fact, she told me once that she'd made more money by leaving it to the john's imagination than by baring all. The battered accordion she was rarely without rested between Opal's spread legs, and her dress was hiked up to show her shins and bare feet. Her dark hair was up in a messy bun, with stray tendrils framing her face.

—Ruby! We got company.

Ruby Steele walked in from the kitchen, wiping flour from her hands with the apron tied around her waist, with no idea I'd just taken Luke to bed and told him he should take her as his wife. I was a little dazed from the encounter with Luke, and Ruby smiling at me, genuinely happy to see me, made me feel unaccountably guilty.

I will dwell on that later. For now, I need to explain about the Gem Sisters.

If people can't see from their faces the sisters aren't related, they sure wonder from their figures. Ruby is thin as a rail, flat chested and taller than any Oriental I've ever met, man or woman. I suppose she got her height, along with her hazel eyes, from the white blood running through her veins. Opal is loud, gregarious, and impulsive. It's difficult not to like her or smile when you're around her. Ruby is all shrewd intelligence, and she shapes her personality to fit whoever she is with at the moment.

When Hattie, Stella, Joan, Jehu, and I rode into Brown's Hole with Jed and his gang, the Gem Sisters met us with expressions fitting their divergent personalities. Opal looked excited and relieved at the increase in female company in their remote corner of Brown's Hole. Ruby glowered at us, seeing us not as potential friends but as competition. The gang had been more than willing to soothe their worries, and spent a week drinking and whoring at the Blue Diamond while my girls and I set to staking a claim on five hundred acres a few miles out of town, to build a horse ranch to replace the one up near Fort Collins. Within a month Spooner and his gang had helped us build a cabin, barn, and corral, and Jehu, Hattie, and I left on a month-long quest to round up as many wild horses as we could before the snow set in. When we drove a hundred horses down Timberline's main street, the residents came out to greet us. Ruby leaned in the door of the Blue Diamond with a markedly different expression. I touched my hat at her, and she nodded, and our mutual respect had been sealed.

Opal played a little celebratory jig, and Ruby rolled her eyes.

—Garet, welcome home.

—Thank you. I hear business has been good.

I pulled the Gem Sisters' take from my saddlebag and handed it to Ruby. She hefted it and dropped it into her apron pocket.

—Better than usual. Want a cup of Arbuckle's?

—Love one.

I dropped my saddlebags on the floor and sat at the table with Opal. Though we are all on friendly terms, Opal and Ruby draw the line at letting customers into their kitchen. It's the only room in the saloon that is theirs alone.

I can be honest with my journal: I've always like Ruby more than Opal. Though more gregarious than Ruby, Opal is shallow, vain, and ignorant. Ruby is highly intelligent and longs for conversation about more than johns, whisky, clothes, and money, or the lack thereof. When we went on our first job, Ruby asked me to bring her back something to read. When I asked her what, she laughed and said anything. She and I always meet later, down by the river, for the exchange, since I never bring anything for Opal, and she wouldn't take kindly to me and Ruby having a friendship outside of her.

Opal put her accordion on the ground. She leaned on the table with her arms and hooked her bare feet around the legs of her chair. Her eyes sparkled with curiosity and mischief. She asked if it was true that I'd kidnapped someone. After I said it was, Opal peppered me with questions about you, Grace.

(I've wondered if I should write this journal as a letter to you, or as a straight journal. I haven't decided, but I think you'll like to know that when I'm writing this, I'm writing it as if it is to you more often than not.)

Back to Opal. She was very interested in you, and I told her what I know. Be prepared for her to bombard you with questions when you meet. Opal is curious and she does have a certain amount of charm. I think you and I are alike, though, and Ruby's quiet confidence and intelligence will be more to your liking.

Ruby asked me why I did it, and to be perfectly honest, I don't have a good answer. I don't want to reveal to them about you telling our story. Not yet. Maybe not ever.

So I sipped Ruby's coffee and let a little groan escape me. Ruby makes a damn fine cup. She swears it's the mountain water, but I wonder if she doesn't have a secret ingredient she slips in.

—Now you have no excuse not to bring me along on the next job, Opal said.

—Opal, Ruby chastised.

—What? She took the child *and* she kidnapped a stranger.

—Joan's seventeen. She did very well. Give her time and she'll probably be better than Stella. Very levelheaded, I said.

—It's too dangerous. What would I do without you? Ruby said. She squeezed Opal's hand. Opal beamed at her sister.

My eyes met Ruby's. Though we'd never discussed it, we both knew the reason I wouldn't take Opal on a job was that she was impulsive, unpredictable, and selfish. Ruby, on the other hand, would make a fine addition to the gang. I couldn't take Ruby without Opal, and she'd never expressed the least interest in outlawing.

—I'm not sure how many more jobs you'll need to do. The Hole is filling up with settlers. Some new miners are prospecting up Cold Spring Mountain. A couple of farmers are breaking ground up on the terraces. And Luke's friends are out by Hog Lake, Ruby said.

—I'd love nothing more than to settle down and sell horses.

—Oh, pshaw. You love outlawing, Opal said.

—The outlaw life is a short one, and I'd rather leave when I want than with a bullet.

—Or a California collar, Ruby said.

—Garet's too good to get caught.

—As soon as they start believing that, they will, Ruby countered.

—Anyways, we need to lay off for a while. Got a little rough with one of the men, and, well, we've hit Connolly one too many times, I'm afraid. Men'll only be insulted for so long.

—You got that revenge out of your system, then? Opal said. She picked up her accordion and started fiddling with it.

—If Dorcas had kept running the company after the colonel died, I wouldn't have hit them. She did business the right way. But Callum Connolly has continued his father's tradition of cheating honest hardworking people to make his fortune. So I take their ill-gotten gains and give it back to those people.

—Like us. And you.

—I hear Callum Connolly's a handsome devil, Opal said.

—Never met him. But I'd be surprised if he is, with half of his face covered in leather.

—I have it on good authority that he is, and the mask just adds to it. He's charming, too. But he can be a rough son of a bitch behind closed doors. Whores talk, you know, Opal said.

—Even more reason to steal from him. Maybe next time we should give some money to the whores he's hurt.

I realized that there wasn't going to be a next time, at least not one I would be a part of.

—You'd be a hero to all the calico queens, Opal said.

—We're thinking of bringing in a couple of new girls. Think your Grace would be interested? Ruby asked.

I laughed. —She's not my Grace, and she's a suffragist. Not sure she cottons to men.

Ruby looked intrigued. —Maybe she is your Grace, then.

—Business is good? I asked.

—Getting better.

—Tell her the real reason, Opal said.

When Ruby remained silent, Opal filled it in.

—She wants to quit whoring. Manage the business.

—Become a madam? I said.

Ruby clasped her hands in her lap but met my gaze.

—Something like that.

—Good for you, I said.

—Ain't nothing wrong with whoring, Opal said. She played a few notes on her accordion.

—No one said there is. But it's a bit like outlawing, there's not a long career in it. Where's Eli?

—Sleeping. Some cowboys came in last night. Ran us ragged.

—Which is why we need more whores. The long stretches of easy living are nice, but we can't take many more weekends like this past one. It's too much, Ruby said.

Opal played the beginning of a jig.

—Think Jehu can pick us up some girls in Rock Springs? Opal asked.

—You can talk to him about it.

He'll say no. Jehu is more likely to save a woman from prostitution than to entice one to the life.

Ruby said something about getting back to work and was retreating to the kitchen when a man walked through the open door. The sun being behind him, he was in shadow, but I knew he was a stranger. I thought he was a cowboy until he stepped inside and I saw him full on. He had a sallow, pockmarked face with a thin, limp mustache that fell past his chin. A band of silver conchos surrounded the crown of his dusty black gambler's hat. He carried a Winchester and two pistols on his hips. The match in the corner of his mouth did nothing to soften the hard line of his lips. I looked to the sisters to see if they recognized him. They didn't.

The stranger asked if they were open.

Opal found herself, smiled, and stood to meet the man.

—Always.

His dusty brown cavalry boots scraped across the wood floors, his eyes scanning the room. They passed Ruby and settled on me.

—You looking for companionship, a drink, or a room? Opal asked.

—All three.

—You're in the right place.

Opal took his free arm as if he were her escort and leaned into him while she directed him to the bar and asked his name. His name is Salter and he looks like trouble.

He lifted his whisky glass, turned to me, and raised it in a toast. I'd decided that was my cue to leave when Luke Rhodes darkened the door. Ruby had inched back to the table and stood beside me. She greeted Luke with his title. The stranger didn't move from his relaxed position against the bar.

Luke greeted us, walked straight up to the stranger, and asked him his business. I'm going to write the exchange down word for word, or as best as I remember it, because it was mesmerizing, seeing these two men challenge each other.

—Drinking, whoring, and sleeping, Salter replied.

—Passing through, then.

—Didn't say that.

Salter pulled a thin cigar out of his shirt pocket and lit it with the match he'd been chewing on.

—Settling down here?

—Didn't say that, either.

—Not saying much.

—My business ain't yours.

—That's where you're wrong.

—Your star's got a dent in it.

—Still works.

—You trying to run me out of town?

—Unless you tell me what you're doing here, I will.

—You can try. I hear Timberline is welcoming to a certain type of man, Salter said.

—We are. There's one rule in the Hole. No killing. You take someone's life, I'll string you up from the nearest tree.

Salter smiled.

—Like I said before, you can try. Can I get another one, honey?

—If you're buying, I'm pouring, Opal said.

—Two, Salter said.

Luke has good instincts, Grace; he's been around enough outlaws, thieves, and troublemakers to spot one, and Salter is one. I have to admit, watching Luke challenge this man was thrilling. Maybe I was still flushed from our encounter. Regardless, I felt the telltale pull toward him.

Opal poured two shots, and we all thought Salter was going to give the other one to Luke, to cement their understanding. Instead he walked over and held it out to me.

—Got a few minutes to spare for a weary stranger?

—She ain't a whore, Luke said, his voice rough.

I admit, Salter raised my suspicions and made me more nervous than I was willing to show, but Luke jumping in to defend me, and insulting the Gem Sisters in the process, doused the desire for him that had bubbled up. I smiled and took the whisky glass.

—I'm visiting my friends Ruby and Opal here, who'll be happy to show you a good time.

—Conversation, then.

—Conversation.

We toasted each other, drank, and sat down at the table. Luke stood in the middle of the room, powerless. I ignored him, lest I lose my resolve and confidence. Eli, the sisters' beefy bartender and protector, had woken up and joined Opal behind the bar.

—Where are you from, Mr. Salter?

—Here and there.

—Me, too. What brings you to Timberline?

He motioned to Opal for more drinks, which she poured and delivered with a frown in my direction.

—I met a woman once who'd been trying to settle here. She went back east. But when I heard Timberline was a welcoming, remote kind of place for a certain kind of man, I had to see for myself. What's your name?

—Garet.

—What brings you to Timberline, Garet? Safe haven from the law?

—How did you know?

—You look like a troublemaker.

—Do I?

—It's in the eyes. I imagine your husband has a time keeping you in line.

—Hasn't been a man yet who could keep me in line, as you so eloquently put it.

—I'd sure like to give it a try.

—Watch your mouth, Luke said.

—Didn't mean to move on your woman, Sheriff.

—I'm no one's woman. Do well to remember that.

It was as much a statement to Luke as to Salter.

I stood and thanked him for the whisky and told him I better be getting on home.

My skin crawled with each of Salter's questions, and it was all I could do to answer nonchalantly under his smirking gaze. I know Ruby and Opal can handle themselves, but I didn't like leaving them with Salter. There's something about his expression, his dead eyes, that makes me think Salter is here for trouble.

I caught Ruby's eye and, from a quick jerk of her head, knew to head down to the river and wait for her. I ran into Newt on the way and took Ole Pete off his hands.

It took thirty minutes for Ruby to arrive.

—Opal just took Salter back.

—And Luke?

—Gone home, I suppose. To brood, it looked like. Did something happen between you two?

—He wants to marry me.

Ruby crossed her arms and nodded.

—I figured as much. Congratulations.

—I told him I'm dying.

—I'm sure he would have taken a simple no for an answer.

—But I am dying. I have cancer. I don't think I have much time left. I haven't told the family yet, so keep it to yourself. Jehu knows. I'm going to tell them all when Jehu gets back.

Ruby sat on the downed tree we always met by and said I might want to work on breaking the news. The blunt version is too shocking. I apologized. I'll be honest, Grace. I didn't expect Ruby to take it so hard.

I handed her the newspapers I'd brought for her.

—I went to Chinatown and picked up a broadsheet. At least I think that's what it is. A newspaper. It might be a menu for all I can tell.

Ruby smiled and thanked me.

—Have you ever heard of this Salter character? I asked.

—No. I know his type, though.

—Is it true, that you want to become a madam?

—No. I want out of the life. Out of the Hole. Opal doesn't. I tell her I want to be a madam because it's easier than arguing with her. I've been doing this longer than her, and I'm tired.

—Is there anything I can do to help?

Ruby stood and hugged me.

—Why do you have to make it difficult for me to hate you?

I pulled away and asked if she was speaking of Luke.

She nodded but said not to worry.

—I'm not heartbroken, and I'm not in love with him. But he would have been safe, Ruby said.

—I told him today he should marry you. Don't give up.

She laughed. —I'm not in love with *him*, but I'm arrogant enough that I want him to be in love with me. At least a little.

We talked a bit about the town, the influx of new people into the Hole, even some families. Rebecca Reynolds has dreams of a school, then a church, the two first steps in civilizing a western town. Ruby was surprised Rebecca didn't ask me for extra money to go toward the schoolhouse. I made a mental note to give a nice donation, if for nothing else than to make sure Newt got an education. Ruby probed about my plans for the future, too polite to ask outright what my funeral plans were. I was vague. I didn't have the heart to tell her that I had no intention of staying home to die.

7

WPA Slave Narrative Collection

Interview with Henrietta Lee

Sunday, September 6, 1936

Those first few days after the job, I made sure to let my displeasure with Garet be known. It wasn't an act, either. Grace Trumbull couldn't ride a damn horse, and she got a bad case of *soroche*. Mountain sickness. Everyone got it when they were new to the mountains. Headache, sick to your stomach, tired. Oh Lord, did it make you tired. That first night in camp, Grace fell asleep like that and slept like the dead. I threw pebbles at her, trying to wake her, and nothing doing. Garet chastised me, but she was smiling a bit, too. I could tell she regretted bringing the woman, but she never admitted it.

"I expected Grace to want to have a lie-in the next morning, but when we woke her at dawn, she made ready to leave without question or complaint. Surprised the hell out of me, but she didn't complain once. In fact, she wasn't much for complaining in general. I figured she was holding back because she knew she was on thin ice with me. I'd done my level best to frighten her when we met, and I think I did. But the more I got to know her, the more I realized she wasn't the complaining kind. She was a lot like Garet, and me, in that way. She saw something that needed to be done and she did it. I liked her more than I ever thought I would, but that was at the end. Right here in this part of the story, I didn't trust her. That was well founded, as it turned out.

"We made it back to the ranch with little trouble. You should have seen that Yankee get off her horse the last time. She could barely walk. I laughed and got a dirty look from Grace for my effort. I knew well enough what she thought of me and my kind by that time.

"Garet had this habit of going off in the mountains by herself after we did a job. She always took a green horse to train 'em in mountain riding and came back with a deer or elk or something across the back of her pack horse to hang in the smokehouse. Usually I didn't mind, but this time it meant I had to babysit Grace Trumbull. Wasn't a problem for the first few days, what with her being rump sore and the mountain sickness still had her, so she spent most of the first week in bed. You shoulda seen her face when she was told Garet was gone and we didn't know when she'd be back. Partly cause I had other fish to fry, I decided to let Stella take charge of her. Mostly I wanted to see how tough Grace Trumbull of Chicago really was.

"I haven't told you about Stella and Joan yet, have I? They were a couple of sisters from Nebraska. Jehu found them begging in Rock Springs, trying to get the money for a train to Frisco. Joan was about twelve, old enough that Jehu guessed some man would try to buy her, or not, which would be worse. Wouldn't no man want to buy Stella. Oh, she wasn't ugly—she was just a plain granger—but you could tell by the set of her mouth and the scar on her top lip that Stella wouldn't be a compliant wife. She got that scar the first time her pa threw a leg over her. Didn't lie down and take it like he expected. Stella was a fighter, and that's a fact. Joan had some fight in her, too, especially at the end.

"That happened then, miners, farmers, businessmen buying wives to do the housework and spread their legs when demanded, squeeze out some children to put to work and make miserable by and by. Pioneering was a hard life for women. They gloss over it in the movies. Make the sodbuster some handsome, good-hearted fella. Make the cowboy honorable. Those types of men were thin on the ground in the West, let me tell you. Jehu? He was different. Everyone loved Jehu. Luke Rhodes was a good man, too. In the end. Ought-Not. Jack and Domino. Guess we had more good men around us than we realized at the time.

"But Jehu. He had the tenderest heart of anyone I've ever known. He couldn't abide the idea of that little girl being sold off to some toothless, dirty miner. Course, he didn't know Stella. Talk about a mama bear. Lawd, she would have slit anyone's throat who suggested Joan for the skin trade.

"Well, thinking on it, she did, but I think she used an ax to the back of his head. She wasn't ever real clear on events, you see, and knowing Stella like I did, there was no telling what she did. She killed her older brother and father when they switched their attention from her to Joan. Not out of jealousy, mind you. I think she'd been harboring murderous feelings since her mom had died and she'd had to fill in for her, in every way. That's how the sisters ended up in Rock Springs, with Jehu, and at Garet and Thomas's ranch, oh, about '71 I guess. I'd been there for a good three, four years by then. Thomas was laid up in bed, and Garet and I ran the ranch. We were a good team, Garet and I.

"We weren't the only vagrants Jehu brought home, but they'd all eventually go their own way until it was only the five of us—Garet, Jehu, Joan, Stella, and me. And then Margaret went and brought Grace Trumbull. Stella didn't like her—Stella didn't like anyone much—and I knew she wouldn't give Grace any quarter.

Grace was a tough old bitch, I'll give her that, and a fast learner. Made Stella right angry, let me tell you. She expected that Yankee to fold in a day. Instead, by the time Garet blazed back into the ranch, Grace was on her way to becoming a good hand. I'd even started working with her on riding.

"I didn't just give Grace over to Stella to torture her, though that was an enticement, but I knew that with Garet gone, Grace would need a shoulder, and I wanted to offer it. I still didn't like her, and trusted her even less, but I wanted her to trust me, to confide in me. I knew I could never earn her trust on my own. She wasn't going to warm to me unless she had no other ally. Stella, God bless her, played Grace right into my hands. I figured if Grace was against us, she'd eventually slip up.

"Why did I think she was against us? Well, I'll tell you. Since we'd started outlawing I'd thought long and hard about what our enemies were doing. I didn't believe for one second they were letting us get away with what we did. Oh, sure, they didn't want the world knowing they were being bested by women. I imagined Connolly had a time of keeping it out of the papers. There's nothing a newspaperman likes more than a sensational story he can make even grander with lies. And sure enough. Years later, when most people who were there were dead and gone, what did I discover but that a big chunk of the Connolly empire is newspapers? That mystery was solved when Dorcas sold to Hearst at the turn of the century. Oh, I'll get to her. She's a big part of the story later on. You better believe Connolly Industries is still around. Bought and sold and changed names, but the colonel's legacy lives on.

"Anyways. I knew that they were after us, and that their plans and strategy would be just as cunning and devious and secret as our plans were. There weren't no bounties on our head, none that were public anyways, so we weren't being chased by those scoundrels. Which left the Pinkertons. But I thought, "What would I do to catch us?" A female gang wouldn't trust a man who tried to get in with them, but they might a woman. And that was the first thing that ran through my mind when I saw Grace riding double with Garet.

"I eventually told Garet my suspicions, but I wanted some time to watch Grace, to win her trust. I knew Grace didn't think of me as her equal, or that I was smarter than her. I might have let her believe it. Might've let her think I was all into voodoo, just to mess with her. Hell, if she was going to write a story about us, might as well make it more interesting than the truth, which was that Garet and I neither had much use for the Lord back then.

"Things were changing in the Hole. More people were coming in, strangers, all up to no good. Apparently word had gotten out about Timberline and how accommodating we were with bandits. There were strangers and threats everywhere. When Garet got back from her walkabout with news that Spooner and his gang were back in town, we were surrounded on all sides by enemies. By the time we realized it, it was too late."

8

Margaret Parker's Journal

Friday, June 15, 1877
Heresy Ranch
Timberline, Colorado

Damn Jed Spooner. Damn Luke Rhodes. Damn all men.

9

Margaret Parker's Journal

Saturday, June 16, 1877
Heresy Ranch
Timberline, Colorado

Thank the Lord, Jehu has returned. I can always find an ally in Jehu. As much as I love Hattie, she's not one to condole with. Her shoulder is hard and bony and she has this irritating habit of telling it to me straight, especially when I don't want to hear it. Her gruff advice is always sound, goddammit.

Jehu rolled in about midday today, his wagon filled to the gills with supplies for the town. Usually we'd all ride into Timberline with him, but since we'd all just made a spectacle of ourselves the night before, we said no. Except Grace. I think she's finding our company a little taxing. Not sure I blame her.

First, though, Jehu went straight to Hattie, got in her face, and cussed her out good for the knife in his crotch at the robbery. She didn't flinch, or show any sort of remorse, which just made Jehu angrier. He's not one to take and hold a grudge, but it's been nearly three weeks since the holdup and I've never seen him so angry. She asked him if he was done with the tongue-lashing, he said he suspected he was, and Hattie took his hand and led him to their bedroom. They were in there for quite a while, making up.

Grace was shocked to see Jehu drive up. We'd never mentioned him in front of her because of Hattie's distrust. I guess Grace and Hattie came to an understanding during my days in the mountains. They aren't quite thick as thieves (ha), but Grace does look to Hattie for answers instead of me. I'm a little put out by it, if you want to know the truth.

I wish Grace could have seen the expression on her own face when Hattie led Jehu into the house and they started with their enthusiastic and noisy making up.

I asked her if it was the sin she minded or the color of their skin.

—It's against the law.

—Yes, we are especially concerned with not breaking the law around here.

Grace turned bright red realizing how ridiculous she sounded, but I could tell her opinion against them being together hadn't changed.

It's uncomfortable when you know what people are doing behind closed doors, so Grace and I went for a ride. She's made amazing progress since she jumped on back of Old Blue. (I need to ride back to Horace's and save Old Blue from that ignorant miner. No telling what he's putting my horse through.) She and Rebel have bonded, and I've caught her giving him sugar cubes and talking sweet to him when she grooms him. You can tell a lot about a person by how they treat animals, and Pinkerton or not (that's Hattie's suspicion), Grace isn't a cruel person. We'd barely gotten out of sight of the ranch when Grace asked if I was serious about Spooner's challenge.

I admit, I wasn't in the right frame of mind last night to head to the saloon and see Spooner for the first time in two years. I was hurting because I'd completely run out of hashish and laudanum, I was trying to keep my pain from everyone, and I was angry at Luke for following me up the mountain and not letting my refusal stand as a final answer. Of course, that was after he'd seduced me to lay with him one more time, goddammit. No reason we can't keep enjoying each other, he said, and I believed him. All he wanted was to try to get my guard down so I would fall into his arms and accept his proposal. I'm not sure what makes me angriest about the whole thing, but I'm pretty sure it's the fact that he thinks I'm weak willed enough to fall for it.

Take a deep breath, Garet. Finish your story. You can stew later. Maybe do some target practice and pretend the cans are Luke's bald head.

Grace and Joan were the only ones of us in a fine fettle to see the boys, not that we had any idea who "the boys" would be by now. Men drop in and out of the gang, some by their own desire, some at Spooner's urging, and some by being propped up in a casket in front of a sheriff's office. Who the hell knew what Jed and his boys had been up to in Mexico for the last two years, or why he'd finally decided to come back, or if he intended to stay and take back up his Lord Bountiful routine? Stella, Hattie, and I knew that if he did, we'd be out of the outlaw line whether we liked it or not. Everyone would expect us to go back to a woman's place.

The thought of it gets my blood up. I want out, but I want out on my terms, not terms set by a man. So when Grace asked me if I was taking the challenge, I said hell yes I am.

Grace was especially anxious to meet a "true outlaw gang." That earned her a glare from Stella and Hattie, but she was too busy adjusting her fancy traveling clothes to make them more festive to notice or care.

I knew everyone in town would be at the Blue Diamond. Being small and remote, Timberline doesn't much truck with the notion of women not being welcome in the saloon. There is little enough social distraction in the Hole, no one sees any point in keeping the women from enjoying Opal's accordion playing. Though I imagine if the Hole ever gets civilized, we'll be shoved back into parlors to play bridge. Eli keeps a bottle of sherry behind the bar for just such occasions, but it was dusty from disuse. We all drank whisky or beer, depending on what our mood was. Last night, I was in a whisky mood.

We got to the Blue Diamond after dusk, and the party was already well on its way to being rambunctious, and Stella tried to take Joan back to the ranch. Joan ignored her sister and sashayed through the door as if she'd walked into a saloon a hundred times. Stella needs to understand that Joan is a woman now and can't be treated like a defenseless little girl. All the same, I kept my eye on her, and I'll continue to. She's green in the ways of men, that'll happen when you're surrounded by women all the time, and these men use, abuse, and toss aside women like her on the regular.

Ruby sat on the arm of Jed's chair. In one hand he held his poker cards, the other was up high on Ruby's thigh. Ruby saw me come in before Jed did, and she look chagrined at draping herself over the man everyone thought was mine. (It's amazing that no one besides Ruby has picked up on what Luke and I have been up to for the last year. Even Hattie and Jehu are ignorant of it, as far as I know.) Ruby took the empty whisky bottle and headed to the bar. Luke Rhodes leaned against the bar, watching the room.

The stranger, Salter, looked up from the cards he held, lifted the corner of his mouth not occupied with a stubby cigar, and nodded at me in acknowledgment. I was glad to recognize some of Spooner's men: Domino Jones, former riverboat dealer turned cardsharp; "Sly" Jack Fox, the best fingersmith in the territories; Scab Williams, powder monkey for the Union navy and a gold-mining company until Spooner offered him the same job in less dangerous circumstances and a bigger return; Hank "Ought-Not" Henry, peterman, whose constant entreaty that "we ought not to do that" kept the gang from being reckless; and I was glad that a couple weren't there. Then "Dead-Eye" Deacon Dobbs walked in from the back, holding his Bible and wearing a priest's collar. Hattie said what I was thinking.

—Shit. When did that bastard hook up with Spooner?

—I don't know.

Deacon Dobbs looked like an outlaw priest with his black suit and white collar, but he wasn't a Catholic. He is a Methodist, or was, I should say. Spooner'd told me Dobbs had been run out of the church when he took too much of a liking to purifying wayward women through a violent ritual that was an amalgam of all the worst teachings and impulses of a variety of religions. Dobbs's reasoning that what he did to the women was nothing he hadn't done to himself to cleanse himself of sin only horrified his congregation more.

Dobbs had come to the Poudre River Ranch with Angus King's gang back in '71 and, though a mite strange, had been quiet enough. He worked hard and said little, but he had a tendency to stare with a dead-eyed expression at Hattie especially. Hattie'd had plenty of experience giving men like Deacon Dobbs a wide berth, but the young woman staying with us, a young whore from Cheyenne, had not. Spooner, whose gang was lying low after a job, had caught Deacon at the beginning of his ritual, thank God, though not soon enough to keep the girl from having scars on her breasts for the rest of her life. We ran Deacon off the ranch, threatened to kill him if he ever came back. Spooner told Angus King he needed to find another hideout. The last couple of jobs that King had pulled had been violent, and Spooner didn't truck with that at all.

Which is why we were shocked to see Deacon with Spooner. I couldn't imagine what a mean old rip like Dobbs was doing riding with him.

Dead-Eye saw us and said, —Hello, Margaret. He ignored Hattie, which I knew was fine with her.

—Deacon Dobbs. It's been a long time. Is your evening self-flagellation over, or is that later?

—Later. Would you like to borrow my whip for your own recrimination?

—I have nothing to repent for, but thank you for the offer.

Spooner looked up about then and spotted Joan. His eyes sparked with a look I knew very well, and I edged over next to the young woman. I didn't care a whit about Spooner not noticing me—Luke Rhodes's eyes were doing enough of that on their own, and Dead-Eye looked at me as though imagining my bare back being riven by the end of his whip—but I wanted Spooner to see that Joan was protected by not only her sister.

Spooner's entire expression lit up with pleasure when he saw me, and my vanity was pleased. I hadn't bothered wearing a dress because I didn't want to bed any of these men and wearing a dress into a saloon you might as well be waving a red flag, so Jed looking at me with appreciation helped smooth the feathers that Luke Rhodes had ruffled a few hours before.

Spooner stepped out from the table, opened his arms wide and said, —Duchess!

I was in a quandary. I didn't want to hug Jed. I looked at him, and he looked well—brown faced and stout, as if he'd been working with his arms for a while—and I could tell that he expected to warm my bed that night. But I felt nothing for him. Not even a little spark. But Rhodes was watching, and I didn't want to give him a hint of hope, so I waltzed right up to Jed Spooner and kissed him like he was my long-lost husband. He still tasted like the mint he likes to chew and the whisky he likes to drink, and I might have felt a little something just then.

The men whooped and catcalled as Jed and I reacquainted ourselves. I heard Hattie say low in my ear, —You're gonna stir up the others and there ain't enough to go around, so I pulled back before I wanted to. Jed, the rascal, winked at Hattie and slapped me on the ass. Jed hollered to Eli he was buying a round, and a cheer went up. He told Domino to deal him out of a round or two and ushered me to the bar, where Eli had our whisky waiting. Out of the spotlight Spooner was always different, gentler and less of a braggart. We'd shared some conversations after lovemaking that I'm sure he'd rather I forget. It was one of the reasons I kept inviting him to my bed. I missed the closeness of a man as much as I missed the touch. Spooner had given me that for years. Of course, Luke wants the job full-time.

But the man leaning against the bar was harder, and there was a different gleam in his eyes.

—Good to see you, Jed.

—And you.

—You're looking well. Mexico agreed with you?

—Stayed in Texas, mostly. Ran into the James boys. They were cooling their heels after a bad Minnesota job. Don't know why he insists on staying back east. Outlawing is much more lucrative out west. As I guess you've learned.

—It is. I definitely understand the appeal of the outlaw life. I guess I learned a few things from listening to your tales over the years. I lifted my whisky. —Thank you.

Jed drank his whisky and gave a tight smile.

—How much have you pulled in?

I shrugged. Something held me back from giving specifics, which turned out to be a good instinct.

—Enough to help out the town, give money back to people Connolly cheated.

—You only went after Connolly?

—Yes.

—You didn't learn that from me. Never become predictable, Duchess.

—They haven't caught us yet.

—No, because you've been giving me credit for your jobs, I hear. I suppose I should thank you. You've burnished my reputation.

—Only for a couple. We've been riding unmasked for the last three. Still, no one wants to give us credit.

—Hell, Margaret, that's a damn blessing, not being in the papers. With that voice, how long until someone puts two and two together? There ain't many Englishwomen in Colorado.

—I lose the accent. Anyways, it doesn't matter now. We're done. Did our last job up by Marshall Pass a few weeks ago.

—Now that I'm back.

—No, that had nothing to do with it. I just, um…want to take it easy for a bit.

Spooner's eyes narrowed, but lost the hard glint.

—You feeling all right? You look a little peaked.

—I'm fine.

He motioned for another whisky, and a muscle pulsed in his cheek.

—How long have you been fucking Rhodes?

—What?

—Why else would he be glowering at me from underneath that stupid hat?

—I hate to break it to you, but Luke has never liked you.

Spooner laughed. —And why do you think that is, Duchess?

Spooner lifted his glass and nodded at someone behind me, which I knew without looking was Luke.

—Why would you care one way or another? We've never had that kind of relationship. Or have you been faithful to me while you were down south?

Spooner motioned for another drink.

—I didn't think so.

Over Jed's shoulder I saw Valentine walk into the saloon. His bloodshot gaze roamed over the room until it settled on me and Jed. He grinned and came our way.

Before Valentine got halfway across the room, Jed lifted his glass to me and said, —To Margaret Parker, the best…

He paused, and there was a brief moment when I thought he was going to toast the gang's accomplishments. I'd given him credit for inspiring us, after all. But the pause was fleeting.

—…the best fuck I've ever had.

He threw back his shot, his eyes never leaving my face, which I'm sure was a mask of astonishment. That turned to anger in a flash. In the silence that followed, Opal stopped playing, and I heard Luke Rhodes's boots scrape the floor as if he was coming to intervene on my behalf. Even Valentine stopped in his tracks, a stunned expression clearly visible on his hirsute face. I lifted my glass higher and said in a strong voice, —To Jed Spooner, the second- or third-best outlaw in three territories.

I slapped the glass upside down on the bar and glared at my former lover. Grace appeared, and damn, Luke Rhodes was right there behind her. I introduced her to both men, told her she could mark meeting an outlaw, a cattle rustler, and a sheriff off her list with one go, then went to the poker table and took Jed's seat. I swept his money off onto the floor and pulled out my own coins. Salter smiled in appreciation, and Domino and Ought-Not stared at me wide-eyed.

—What's wrong, boys? You never seen a woman play poker?

—No one so pretty, Ought-Not said.

—Since when did you become a charmer, Ought-Not?

He blushed.

—I've always been a charmer. You've just been immune to them.

—Much to my detriment.

—He was quite the favorite of the señoritas down south, Domino said.

Ought-Not's face darkened.

—Shut up and deal the cards.

Ought-Not wasn't a handsome man. In fact, he was fairly unmemorable all the way around. Average height, brown hair, brown eyes, thin lips, but a strong jaw. Soft-spoken and polite to a fault, he was the conscience of the group. Spooner got all the credit, but Ought-Not was his right-hand man, watching Spooner's back and looking out for the pitfalls. But there was steel in Ought-Not's jaw, and Spooner respected the Missourian enough to heed his counsel. I suspected Ought-Not was behind the outlaw code that Spooner had followed, which made it so difficult to imagine Dead-Eye's riding with the gang sat well with a man like Ought-Not. Sly Jack came over, plopped a chair down backward next to Domino, sat, and leaned his arms on the back.

—Good to see you, Margaret.

—You, too, Jack. How was the South? I asked.

—Hot.

—Me, Jack, and Ought-Not didn't get south of Fort Worth, Domino said.

—Got on with an outfit west of there. Cowboying. Did a couple of drives to Abilene.

—And Spooner?

—Met up with the James boys and Dobbs in Fort Worth. He and Scab went south in search of a better-paying job.

—Did they find one?

Domino and Ought-Not exchanged a wary glance, and Domino said, —Yep.

They clammed up after that.

I'll finish tomorrow. My hand is cramping up and Cassiopeia has traveled too far across the sky. Sun will be up before I know it.

Sunday, June 17, 1877

It's dawn, and I'm sitting next to Grace on the gallery that circles the house, drinking coffee and watching the sun rise over the mountains behind the barn. I just finished helping Jehu tend the horses, but he's still out there, piddling. I retreat to the mountains when I get back from being away, Jehu retreats to the barn. He's angry at me, but it won't last long. It never does.

A few months ago, on the way home from my doctor's appointment in Cheyenne, Jehu and I had made the decision to stop outlawing, and we were going to tell everyone together after the last job was done. Then Spooner had to go and bait me, to belittle what the girls and I have accomplished as luck or tall tales (he used both reasons, though they contradicted each other) and the next thing I knew we were in each other's faces, throwing down the gauntlet. Our gangs were ranged behind us, some offering more vocal support than others. Ought-Not, Domino, and Jack's support of Spooner was tepid at best. The rest of the town was on the edges of the room—though Valentine was behind Jed as if part of his gang—watching with mixed expressions. Rebecca and Harvey were concerned, Valentine looked at me with murder in his eyes. Luke Rhodes was nowhere to be found.

The challenge was quickly agreed on: One job before the first snow. No killing or violence. Biggest take wins. Winner gets the ranch. My ranch. Loser leaves the area and finds another place to outlaw.

Let me tell you right now: we're going to win this bet, we're going to shut Jed Spooner's mouth, and we're going to finally get the credit for the jobs we've done.

10

WPA Slave Narrative Collection

Interview with Henrietta Lee

Thursday, September 10, 1936

Where'd we leave off the other day? Surrounded by enemies. That's right. The Spooner Gang rode back into town, six of them anyways, the ones who'd been with Spooner the longest, and the ones who didn't have the intelligence to lead their own gang. That's what Jed had done, left the James Gang in Missouri and came west. Used the same Confederate raider practices that old cracker Jesse and his brother Frank used. Guerrilla tactics, he called them. They're the same ones we used.

"Yes, I'm talking about Jesse James. No, I never met him.

"Spooner'd never liked the violence of the James boys, which is another reason he came out west. Managed to be successful, too, without killing or hurting people. When Spooner came back from Mexico he wasn't the same good-time fun-loving outlaw he'd been before. At the time I didn't know what changed him, and it was a shock seeing this good-natured rascal turn into a steely-eyed killer. Turns out he'd met up with the James boys in Texas.

"I heard tell later that what set Spooner off on Garet was Valentine, the town blacksmith who hated Garet something fierce, telling Spooner that Garet'd been going around saying she was a better outlaw than Spooner, that the town didn't need him, that they relied on her now. He believed it easy enough because the town was much better off when he got back than when he left. It was down to us, sure, but like I said, the Hole was filling up, and business was good. Garet's plan to retire wouldn't have bothered people too much, I bet, since they were relying on her less and less. Though you never know; people love to get something for nothing. Course it ain't money they want for nothing from a woman, is it?

"Did I not mention Garet's plan to retire from outlawing? Hmm. Thought I did. That was why she wanted Grace to tell the story, because she wasn't going to be around to do it herself. Me write it? Hell, child. Even if I could get someone to print it, who would believe a Negro? You'll see when I get farther along. It's a hard enough story to believe as it is.

"That was all put on hold when Spooner came back and insulted Garet in front of the town. Didn't give her, or any of us, credit for what we'd done. Hell, we'd improved his reputation by giving him credit for the first two jobs. He didn't care. All he saw was a woman doing a better job than him, and he couldn't let that stand. He challenged Garet to a contest, both gangs pull a job, biggest take gets the Heresy Ranch. Loser leaves Timberline forever. We were all caught up in the moment and egged her on to take the bet. Not that she needed the encouragement. We should've stopped for a moment and considered a little more, but we didn't. Spooner wasn't playing fair, but he'd always been honorable, as far as outlaws go, and we didn't count on his betrayal. We were all, Stella, Joan, and I, excited to be doing another job so soon.

"When Jehu found out about the bet he was fighting mad. If he hadn't been naked in bed with me when I told him, I think he would have gone right then and punched some sense into Garet. It didn't make sense, you see. Jehu'd always been eager for the next job. I distracted him—easy enough to do—and after, he told me why he was so mad. He told me that Garet was sick, dying of a tumor in her gut, and that they'd decided this would be the last job, so she could live out her remaining days at home, at peace. Then it was my turn to be mad. One, that they'd made the decision without me, and two, that Garet hadn't trusted me enough to tell me she was sick.

"I'm a jealous person by nature, and the green-eyed monster got me. Jehu and Garet had a special bond. Nah, they weren't lovers. It wasn't like that, though I think before I came along Jehu was sweet on her. She never thought of him that way, and, well, when I found that out… I think I loved Jehu from almost the moment I met him. I saw in him a gentle soul who would never hurt me. Course, we would have still been just friends, sneaking glances at each other, trying to think of excuses to brush our hands against each other, if I hadn't climbed up in the barn loft late one night. He slept there instead of the house. Said it was comforting. I knew why he slept up there, and I knew he would never approach me, though the air practically hummed with desire when we were around each other. He cried when I dropped my dress, and a woman with less confidence would have probably gone on her way. But I knew Jehu needed me as much as I needed him. You see, human beings can only go so long without feeling a loving touch, and that was something neither Jehu or I had ever felt. Going without deadens you, hardens you. I was tired of being dead inside. It was the most beautiful night of my life. I can't think too much on it. It makes the hole Jehu left ache too much."

Mrs. Lee falls silent, and her eyes pool with tears until they run down her face. I don't say anything; I don't know what to say. She pulls a handkerchief from her pocket, wipes her face and eyes, and continues.

"I got off course there. Jehu does that to me. Back to Garet. Of course, it all made sense knowing Garet was dying: kidnapping Grace, wanting her to "tell our story." Garet saw the end of her life and wanted to make sure it had meaning, wanted to make sure she wasn't forgotten. She sure as hell didn't want men taking credit for our work. None of us did, though I don't think Jehu cared. He'd gotten the idea of settling at the ranch, giving up teamstering, us waking up together every day for the next forty years into his mind, and there wasn't anything that was going to change it.

"I've thought on it a lot over the years, why Garet took that bet. It wasn't just for the glory, or for the thrill of doing the jobs. She didn't want us to be forced back to the life we'd left. Escaped from. She wanted to ensure our independence, if that's what we wanted. In those days the best way to be secure was to marry a man, and most of the women who left our care, protection, whatever you want to call it, eventually got married. There's plenty of good men out there, but child, there are times when it seems like they've gone extinct. None of us, though, wanted to be married. That's why we stayed. That's what Garet wanted to protect. Our choices.

"We all thought if we started planning, Jehu'd go along eventually, but he never did. He wouldn't stand in our way, but he wouldn't take part in it.

"Why? He said it was because he'd made a decision and he was sticking with it. That was part of it, no doubt. He wasn't one to go back once his mind was made up. But when the stage we robbed finally got to Gunnison, the victims were questioned, they told their stories, and they agreed to keep silent on it being women. Except this time at the saloon after, Jehu ran into another teamster who said Jehu had the worst luck of any driver he'd ever known, being held up so much. Jehu worried that one more job and he'd be found out. He understood Garet's reasons for wanting to do it, and mine, which were the same, and he thought not being involved would protect him. It would've, too, if he didn't have a heart the size of the moon. You see, Toddy, the guard, overheard it, but Jehu didn't know that until later."

GUNFIGHTERS & OUTLAWS

by William Gibbons
Published 1922

Chapter Five

The Spooner Gang, 1868–1877

When people think of Old West outlaws, the same gangs come to mind: Jesse James (though he did all of his jobs in the Midwest), Billy the Kid, Butch Cassidy. But there were dozens of gangs and twice that of individual outlaws and gunslingers who worked west of the Mississippi during the late half of the nineteenth century who get nary a mention.

Jed Spooner arrived in Colorado in 1865 claiming to have ridden with the James–Younger Gang in Missouri. No one questioned him; he told detailed stories about their exploits and, as he was a generally pleasant fellow, men tended to take his claims at face value. Now, nearly sixty years on, there's no historical basis for his claim. Neither "Jed Spooner," nor any variation of that name, comes up in research on the notorious James–Younger Gang, nor did any of the gang leave around the time Spooner claimed to have left. Jed Spooner wouldn't have been the first outlaw to lie about his past, and he certainly wasn't the last.

We can confirm a good deal, since Spooner wasn't one to hide his light under a bushel. He came west after the war for the same reason most rebs did, to start a new life and to hit it big in the mines. Spooner never hit it big. Pickax Johnson, a forty-niner who died in 1917 at the ripe old age of ninety-nine, worked with Spooner in the San Juan Mountains around '65, and said the only kind of mining Spooner had any skill for was picking up chunks of gold from the riverbed. Since gold panning was mostly played out by then, Spooner lost interest soon enough and turned to gambling and whoring as his main occupations, though not necessarily in that order. He was a mite better gambler than miner, but not by much. He was a lucky son of a bitch for all that, because he lost his last coin to Hank Henry, a light-fingered safecracker who was looking to change his affiliations. Over the next few months, he and Spooner robbed a bank, a mining office and a general store. They gathered some others on the way, riverboat dealer Domino Jones, pickpocket "Sly" Jack Fox, and powder monkey Maurice "Scab" Williams. Other members came and went, but these five were the core of the Spooner Gang for a decade.

They survived a decade of outlawing without one death and, despite a night or two in jail for drinking and rowdiness, were never caught for their thieving. The debate on whether or not Spooner rode with the James boys rests on this one fact: he was an expert at the guerrilla tactics the James boys learned as Missouri bushwhackers in the war. Though it is largely forgotten now, Spooner's was the first gang to relay horses along their getaway route, a trick Butch Cassidy would use to great effect a decade after the Spooner Gang disappeared. But the best trick the Spooner Gang ever did was to disappear completely for months at a time.

According to Hank Henry, who got his nickname, Ought-Not, while riding with Spooner, they were able to disappear so easily because they had two hideouts to choose from. One was a horse ranch on the front range near Fort Collins. In an interview for the *Rocky Mountain News* in 1910, Henry said,

"It was a nice little ranch, owned by an Englishman and his wife. They'd hire us on and we'd be just like regular cowboys.

There was a cave up in the foothills behind the ranch where we could hide if we felt the pressure was coming down on us. Worked out just fine, but it started getting crowded over there on the front range. People started pouring down the Cheyenne–Denver rail line and, well, some posses started taking trains. Moving faster, you know? Great for targets, but not so great for escaping. We moved west a bit, hit a bank in Rock Springs, and on the run from it found this nice little box canyon out in the middle of nowhere and a booger to get to. That's where we'd go. Till the end. That's where it ended."

The end came sometime in 1877 in a blaze of glory, amid the gun smoke of a posse of Pinkertons hired by Callum Connolly to hunt Spooner down. For reasons that have never been made clear, Spooner took to targeting Connolly's businesses almost exclusively the last two years. According to Opal Steele Driscoll, who claimed to ride with a gang of women calling themselves the Spooner Gang, a Pinkerton named Salter infiltrated Spooner's gang, and that was how their hideout was discovered. Ought-Not Henry called Driscoll an outright liar on more than one occasion, and many other words that aren't fit to print. However, Henry would never clarify what happened. The end result remained the same: Spooner was killed and the gang dispersed.

11

Margaret Parker's Journal

Friday, July 20, 1877
Heresy Ranch
Timberline, Colorado

I have been remiss in my journaling this past month. Much as when I let my writing lapse when Thomas and I started our ranch, I've been too distracted with daily chores, plans, arguments, and agreements to be reflective.

Jehu, Hattie, and Stella left a month ago with a few hired hands to round up mustangs. Grace, Joan, and I have been busy running the ranch. We hired Ought-Not, Domino, and Jack to help out. They rode out to the ranch two days after the bet, said they'd told Spooner they wouldn't work against us, and asked to be taken on. I readily agreed, though part of me wondered if they'd been sent by Spooner to keep an eye on us and discover our plans.

Salter decided to stay in the Hole for a while and came looking for a job, too. Since we needed fence built and I wasn't feeling physically up to helping, I hired him, too. Grace advised against it. When I asked her why, she said she didn't trust him.

—Good rule to follow out here is to not trust anyone.

—Not even you?

—Especially not me. You shouldn't have to interact with Spooner much, but let me know if he does something.

—Like what?

—Starts asking questions.

The four men did their jobs, ate meals with us at the table under the shade of the narrow-leaf cottonwood tree on the north side of the house. Conversation tended to ranch business. They never mentioned Spooner or the bet, but they all went into town Saturday night and didn't return until late Sunday, it being the day off. I never let my guard down, and felt bold enough to start dropping false information, and told Grace to do the same with Salter, who'd taken a shine to her. She did her best to avoid him and rarely spoke more than two words to him at a time.

Jehu and Grace left for Rock Springs today. The plan came together quickly, as if it had been waiting in the back of my mind for four years. It is the perfect period to put on the end of our outlaw careers.

After this, no one will be able to deny us.

Saturday, July 21, 1877

Hattie and I were checking our packs last night before turning in for an early start for Rock Springs when there was a knock on our door. Whoever it was had snuck up the road; no one had heard a horse's hooves. We got our guns, which were always close by these days, and Stella unsheathed her knife. I was about to open the door when I heard something scratch down the front door and fall on the porch. A whimper followed, and I opened the door to find Newt in a haphazard heap.

I checked for Val before putting my gun aside and helping the boy up. When I saw his face, something inside me broke. I took him in, laid him on the table, and went to retrieve my gun.

Hattie caught me halfway across the yard on the way to the barn.

—No, ma'am.

—I'm going to kill him, Hatt.

—Not tonight, you're not.

—Hattie, by God. I *told* Valentine. I told him clearly not to touch that boy.

—You really thought that would matter?

—It'll matter when I blow his head off.

—You do that and Luke Rhodes will arrest you.

—He wouldn't.

—Why? Because you're fucking him? Yeah, I know all about it. Give me the gun.

She put her hand on it, and I tried to pull it away from her.

—Don't be a damn fool, Garet. Valentine probably beat that boy on purpose just to get you to town. Chances are he's waiting with a gun, hoping you'll show up. He might even be sober.

I pushed the gun toward her and walked a little off. I inhaled deeply and raised my gaze to the sky. There was no moon, and the stars were stunning. The only light was the glow of lanterns from the house. I heard Hattie break the barrel. When I turned, she was putting the shells in her front pocket.

—How long have you known?

—Margaret, there's not many women who can hide when they've been loved, and loved well.

—It isn't love.

—Hmm-hmm. That's what I thought, too, until you went back after what happened to Lou. *Only one rule: no killing,* my ass. That only applies to killing men, apparently. I'll never forgive that bastard for not stringing Valentine up. I can't believe that you did.

—That's easy to say for a woman who has someone warming her bed every night.

—I've known you for a decade, Margaret, and you've never disappointed me more than right now.

—You're going to judge a dying woman for finding a little comfort in the arms of the only man around? Sorry I'm not living up to your high moral standards, Henrietta.

—Don't pull that dying card on me. I'm still pissed about that, too.

—Jesus, Hattie! I can't help that I'm dying.

—You didn't fucking tell me, Margaret. Me! Your best friend. How do you think that makes me feel?

I tried to interrupt her, but she was on a roll.

—I know you've known Jehu longer, and you have a special bond. I don't care that you told him, I just wish you wouldn't have kept it from me. You made the decision about our last job without me. You've always said we were partners, equals. But it was all a lie.

—Hattie, shut up for a second. I didn't tell Jehu. He overheard me talking with the doctor. I wouldn't have told anyone if he hadn't overheard. Not until I had to. And you would have been the first person I told.

—Why didn't you?

—Because I love you, and I knew it would devastate you. Or at least I hoped it would.

—Don't joke.

—I'm sorry. I hated watching Thomas die. I didn't want to put you through that. I thought it was the kind thing to do. The loving thing. I didn't mean to make you feel betrayed. When I got back, I went to Luke because dying has this way of clearing your mind. I haven't forgiven Luke for betraying Lou's memory. If things were different, I wouldn't have gone to him. But what can I say? I'm a weak woman, and it's comforting. It lets me forget for a while, makes me feel like a whole woman. I'm not going to apologize for it.

–I'll hate him for both of us.

–*Hate*'s a strong word.

–It fits.

–You know how to hold a grudge.

–I do.

–Let me go to town, see if Luke has him in custody. He might. He warned Val, too.

–Against beating his son? Margaret. Rhodes won't do anything about it because Valentine isn't breaking any laws. If the boy dies…well, that bastard Rhodes still won't do anything. He'd be laughed at by every man in the country if he did. Hell, the world.

–Sometimes I hate men.

–Keep that fire in your belly. We're going to need it to win this bet.

–Do you forgive me? For not telling you straightaway.

–Of course I do.

–We should probably hug. I know you aren't keen on hugging.

Hattie rolled her eyes and pulled me into a strong embrace. We held each other for a long time, until Hattie finally said, –Is that long enough for you?

–I guess if you think that's a long enough hug for a dying woman.

Hattie sighed and said, –Good Lord, but she relaxed into the hug and squeezed me a little tighter. I felt my throat tickle with emotion.

–OK, Hattie. That's enough. Just because Jehu isn't here doesn't mean I want to hug you for hours.

She laughed and playfully pushed me away.

—Next thing you know you're going to want me to cuddle with you at night.

—I guarantee you that won't happen, Hattie said.

—Uh-huh. We'll see.

I put my arm around her shoulder as we walked into the cabin to check on Newt.

Joan had a bowl of water and a washcloth and was cleaning the cuts and bruises on Newt's face. Stella was feeling his arms, checking for breaks. When she squeezed his left forearm, Newt called out in pain.

—I heard it crack when he twisted it, Newt said.

His chin was quivering, and I could tell it was an effort for him not to cry in front of Joanie.

—Someone needs to kill that bastard, Joanie said.

—Spoken like a woman in love, Newt said.

Joan laughed and ruffled the boy's hair. —You must not be too hurt if you're well enough to flirt with me.

—I'll always be well enough to flirt with a beautiful woman.

—I notice you aren't flirting with me, Stella said.

—You've been spending too much time with Sly Jack, haven't you? Joan asked.

—He's given me some pointers.

Newt stopped Stella from touching his torso.

—No need. I can tell a couple are broken.

Stella's face darkened into a dangerous expression. I understood her feelings. It was an abomination that a twelve-year-old boy should know what it felt like to have broken ribs.

I went into my bedroom to get the laudanum. Hattie followed me.

—We can't leave Newt here unprotected. You know Val will figure he's out here soon enough. The men won't stand between him and Newt, you know they won't. Stella and Joan won't be enough, I said.

—I know. That's why we're going to take him with us.

—What? Now we're adding twelve-year-old boys to our gang?

—He's not much of a boy anymore. He'll be thirteen soon, and, well, you see the way he looks at Joan.

—That's puppy love.

—Maybe, but he's going to be a man soon, and the longer he stays around Val, the more likely he'll turn into him. Do you want to inflict another Ulysses Valentine on the world?

—No.

—We're going to take him to Rose and Portia. You know they'll take him in. There's no way anyone from here will find him there, Hattie said.

—We can't ask them to adopt a boy... almost a man.

—Probably better that he is older. You know Rose will put him to work. After the job is over, we pick him up. Bring him back home. If you want to know the truth of it, he's old enough to make his own decision. Go out on his own if he wants. Maybe that's all he wants, a way out of the Hole.

—We'll let him decide. Ask him if he wants to come back to the Hole with us. Once he sees Cheyenne, he probably won't.

—Doubt it. When we get back, with or without Newt, Valentine will die in a freak blacksmithing accident. Maybe a horse will kick him in the head. Or he will be so drunk he'll fall into a horse trough and drown.

—He could do that tonight, too.

Hattie sighed and looked up to the heavens.

—You're trying my patience, Garet. We've got to travel fast and light to beat Grace to Denver. Remember?

She placed her hands on my shoulders. —Let me say it in a way you understand: You can either have your revenge right now and be strung up tomorrow. You'll be forgotten by the few people who know of you, an outlaw lost to history. Or you can pull your last job and let that Yankee immortalize you.

—Sounds like someone's been trying to win you over. Has she done it?

—Nope. Jehu and I still don't want her to put us in her story. Have you told her you're a duchess yet?

—No. She thinks it's a nickname.

—Oh Lord. Wait until she finds out. The myth writes itself.

—It's not a myth. It's the truth.

—Garet. No one cares as long as they're entertained.

—Damn you, Hatt. You could tell me what I want to hear every once in a while. Maybe give me that gift before I die.

Stella walked into the room.

—When it isn't a matter of your life and death, I will. You'll get your revenge on Valentine, I promise. It'll just be delayed a few months.

—I'll do it while you're gone, Stella said.

—No, you won't. There won't be any lynching bee in Timberline, Stella. Once a place gets lynching in their blood, it's tough to get it out. No, we stick with the plan. Garet'll just take a longer stop in Cheyenne on the way to Denver, Hattie said.

Newt was clearly disappointed to be leaving Joanie, but when we explained the danger Joan and Stella would be in if he stayed, he agreed to leave.

Newt assured us Valentine was too drunk to be moving so early in the morning, but to be safe we left well before the sun was up. I suspected Valentine wouldn't chase us, but Newt encouraged us to keep a fast pace in case. We humored him and made good time. Thirty miles in a day through rough country. Newt is set on pulling his weight, even with a broken arm that Hattie could only splint and broken ribs. There's only a small part of his face that isn't bruised or bloody, and he's having trouble breathing from his crooked nose. The first place we will go when we get to Cheyenne is the doctor I nursed for during our brief stay before we moved to Brown's Hole. We'll stop by the general store and kit him up. I can't very well take him to his new home without a change or two of clothes. Besides, he's practically grown out of his own. He's grown like a weed since Lou died, and if Valentine even noticed, he sure isn't the type of man to know how to solve the problem.

Tuesday, July 31, 1877

I met Portia Bright while nursing an old woman who was on her deathbed. Portia was the widow of a minister and had continued the practice of visiting sick people and shut-ins after he died. In the case of the woman I was nursing, she and Portia played bridge together, and Portia visited daily.

Portia was a sweet woman, a little retiring, with a set of mesmerizing blue eyes with pupils rimmed in orange. I told her a little of my story, and she invited me and the girls to her house for dinner. She'd mentioned her roommate, Rosemond, only briefly, so we were all astonished to discover Rosemond was a beautiful, vivacious woman. She owned a sign-painting company and a portrait studio and had recently taught herself photography. There was more money in photography portraiture than painting, though she still painted half a dozen or so portraits a year. She and Portia were both welcoming and understanding. I knew they wouldn't hesitate to take Newt in for a time, and I was correct.

I was worried about Newt's reaction to living in Cheyenne for nothing. As soon as he laid eyes on Rose, all thoughts of Joan flew from Newt's mind. Rose winked at me over Newt's head and led him to the kitchen for a glass of lemonade. Portia rolled her eyes and smiled.

—I've never known a woman who men fall in love with as often as Rosie, Portia said.

—She is welcome to the talent.

—Agreed.

—Thank you for taking Newt in.

—Of course.

—The doc looked him over and did what he could, casting his arm, setting his nose. He's afraid it's never going to be completely straight. Here's some money for his room and board.

—That is not necessary, Margaret.

—I know, but I feel better giving it to you. I did spring this on you last minute.

Portia took the money and put it in her pocket.

—We'll take good care of him. I wouldn't be surprised if Rosie has already put him to work in the shop.

—He'll be a good worker for you.

I said my goodbyes to Newt, who waved me away with barely a glance, and made the train with time enough to buy a bag of roasted peanuts for the trip. Now on to Denver, where I can put my plan in action.

PART TWO

THE DUCHESS

Colorado Woman Suffrage Association

August 1877 Meeting Minutes

Corresponding Secretary and Referendum Committee Chair Alisha Washburn presented a report of the committee's last meeting, and of her correspondence with American Woman Suffrage Association. Plans have been finalized for Susan B. Anthony, Lucy Stone, Henry Blackwell, and Matilda Hindman to join our own Margaret Campbell on a barnstorming trip across Colorado. Aware of our financial struggles, the AWSA will pay the expenses for their leaders, and Margaret Campbell has offered to pay her own expenses, freeing up the CWSA money to be used for the rally in downtown Denver on October 1, the day before the referendum. Though we have met with resistance from local Denver politicians, our esteemed Governor Routt stepped in and secured the approval required for us to march down Colfax Avenue to Broadway, where local and national suffrage leaders will speak on the enfranchisement of women. Grace Trumbull, a lay member of the national organization who recently immigrated to Colorado and a new CWSA member, suggested all women marchers wear the same-color dress to show the solidarity and cohesiveness or our group. The idea was enthusiastically embraced, with a great debate ensuing on what color it should be. Black was deemed too severe; white deemed inappropriate and out of the question for women still mourning the loss of loved ones in the war. Purple was settled on as a compromise, and Miss Trumbull offered to donate purple sashes embroidered with "Votes for Women" for marchers to wear, as well.

THE WESTERN UNION TELEGRAPH COMPANY
21,000 OFFICES IN AMERICA
CABLE SERVICE TO ALL THE WORLD

TO: ALLAN PINKERTON, PINKERTON NATIONAL DETECTIVE AGENCY, CHICAGO, IL
DATE: MONDAY, JUNE 25, 1877

CONTACT MADE WITH GANG. PLANNING BIG JOB BEFORE END OF YEAR. COVER INTACT. LETTER TO FOLLOW.

12

Margaret Parker's Journal

Saturday, August 4, 1877
Denver, Colorado

The plan Hattie and I had put together was to rob the Bank of the Rockies, the same bank I robbed with Jehu in '73. Come full circle and take something from the Connolly family one last time. Grace had a surprising suggestion: use a suffrage march scheduled for the day before the vote as our escape cover. We would be in Denver for a couple of months, establish ourselves as part of the suffrage movement (but strangers to each other, of course), and reconnoiter the bank for a few weeks. Joan and Stella would join us in mid-September so we could finalize everything.

When I told Grace I intended to pay Callum Connolly back the money I stole from his father, the colonel, in '73, with interest, she stared at me in shocked silence for quite some time.

—You can't do that. It's much too dangerous, Grace said.

—At least you didn't call me a prideful, pompous son of a bitch like Hattie did when I told her.

—Why didn't you talk her out of it?

—I tried. But she makes a compelling case, Hattie said.

I explained the reasoning: If Callum Connolly suspected Margaret Parker was the leader of the gang that had been terrorizing his company—and there was no evidence that he did—my arrival on his doorstep with repayment plus interest must surely prove my innocence. After all, what kind of outlaw would put herself at that kind of risk?

The boldest outlaw in the West.

I thought Grace would argue with me some more, but she didn't. She shook her head and said it was a needless risk.

—But it's going to make a great story, I said.

—*Margaret Parker: Prideful, Pompous Son of a Bitch.* There's your title, Grace, Hattie said.

—I won't write it if you do this.

—Do you know something, Grace? Some reason I shouldn't?

—No, of course not. The last thing I want is for you to put yourself in unnecessary danger all for a good story. Hell, Margaret, I can make that part up.

—She has a point, Hattie said.

—No. This is the plan. Hattie and I have planned out what to do if they arrest me. That might even be the better outcome. But it won't happen.

—How do you know? Grace said.

—I don't, and that's the thrill of it.

Monday, August 6, 1877

While I dropped Newt off in Cheyenne, Hattie made it to Denver in time to follow Grace when she got off the train, to confirm or dismiss her suspicion that Grace was a Pinkerton. The first person Grace went to see was Dorcas Connolly. To Hattie it was a done deal; Grace had to die. I asked her to give me the opportunity to show Grace's loyalty. If Grace failed the test, Hattie could kill her. If not, the plan would go on. Hattie thought it was a needless risk, but went along with it.

When I stood in front of the Connolly Building, looking up at its solid brick exterior and down at the blue-and-white CONNOLLY INC. EST 1867 mosaic I stood on, I wondered if I was going to have the wherewithal to go through with the plan. Anger at the colonel's theft of my ranch simmered deep within me still. I felt the dull ache of my tumor and thought of what Hattie said when I told her this plan back at the Heresy Ranch, that this tumor of mine was the physical manifestation of the anger and rage I'd tried to keep tamped down for the last five years. She thinks this last job will heal me, extinguish the fire that's been in my belly, that's fed my sickness. It's one of the most ridiculous things I've ever heard, but I hope she's right.

The Connolly offices were on the top floor. A Negro stood next to a steel cage by the stairs and asked me if I would like to ride the first elevator in Denver, Colorado. I agreed, and after clanging the metal door shut, the operator set us slowly on our way. I grasped the rail as the elevator rose, and the operator smiled and asked me if it was my first time. When I said it was, he told me I had nothing to worry about. It was safe as houses. I wasn't sure about that as I felt the gears grind and lift us to the fourth floor.

I stepped out into a long hallway that stretched out on either side of me. I headed toward the double doors to the left, which had CONNOLLY INCORPORATED stenciled on the frosted glass.

I took a few deep breaths as I stood outside the door, and thought of what I might find on the other side. Whom I might find. What kind of man Callum Connolly might be. How I might best insinuate myself into his life. His business. I also thought of the prospect of the sheriff coming to arrest me, being thrown into jail, the lawyer I would call, the trial that might follow. Hattie and I had talked it through so many times I was prepared for any situation that might arise. When I opened the door and wasn't met with men with guns, I knew Grace was with us. When Dorcas didn't recognize me immediately, I suspected our plan would go off without a hitch.

Dorcas Connolly wore the same high-necked dress and cameo brooch she wore the last time I saw her, standing on my front porch next to her cheating brother. Today she smiled and asked if she could help me in a friendly yet professional manner.

—Dorcas, I said.

She recognized me soon enough.

—Margaret?

—It's been a long time.

—Five years.

—You're looking well.

—As are you.

I'd taken great care with my appearance, needing to show I wasn't destitute, but not to be so flashy as to imply too much wealth. Everything about me was demure, sliding back into the woman I'd been when Thomas and I married all those years ago. I felt constrained, like a completely different person. Which I needed to be to succeed.

—I heard about the colonel's death. My condolences.

—You don't have to pretend to mourn him for me.

—Oh, I didn't mourn him, but I'm sure you did.

—What can I do for you, Margaret?

—I've come to see your nephew. To pay back the loan I took from the colonel's bank back in '73.

—Loan? After a long moment of confusion, Dorcas Connolly's face turned thunderous.

—I should send for the sheriff.

—You could. But then I would tear up the check I brought to pay what I borrowed, with interest.

—Borrowed? You robbed our bank.

—*Our?*

I knew it would rankle Dorcas, and it did. When I knew her, she had lived on the charity of the colonel. Being near neighbors, she and I had had a cordial relationship for years until Thomas died and Colonel Connolly decided he wanted not only my ranch but me as his wife. Friendship had turned to animosity, at first because I might supplant her, and then because I'd rejected her brother's business offer, as well as his personal one. Turned out familial pride and the success of Connolly Enterprises were as important to her as they were to the colonel, despite the fact that she had no ownership in the company, and it would be left to his son in its entirety upon the colonel's death.

Dorcas pressed her lips into a line.

—Come now, Dorcas. You understand what your brother did to me. He left me destitute, with few options. I needed a loan to get back on my feet, to feed my family.

—Your family?

—Family is thicker than blood.

I suggested to her it would be more efficient if I told the story to both her and her nephew. She studied me for a long moment, and the door behind her desk opened. For a terrifying moment, I thought Benjamin Adamson was exiting, but no. It was another of the hundreds of hirsute businessmen "building the West." Jehu had told me that Adamson had died in Montrose a few days after they arrived, of an apparent heart attack. In an opium den.

I forgot all about Adamson when I laid eyes on Callum Connolly for the first time. Callum is a little taller than I, with golden hair oiled back and away from his face and a thick but smartly trimmed beard. He wore gray riding breeches and black boots with soles rimmed in mud. He was coatless and wore a white shirt and a plain black waistcoat spanned by a silver watch chain. But I didn't notice any of that until later; what struck me most was the metal mask that covered the lower half of the right side of his face. Though I'd been expecting it, the sight still stunned me, and I had to click my teeth together to close my gaping mouth. Opal was right, Callum Connolly was handsome.

Callum bid the businessman goodbye with a firm handshake, but didn't take his eyes from me. Gauging my response to his deformity, no doubt.

Dorcas introduced me as the woman who'd robbed the Bank of the Rockies. I amended the introduction to include that I was the widow his father had cheated out of a ranch.

Callum made no secret of his assessment of me, taking in everything from head to foot and back again. I did the same to him, not shying away from looking him in the face. I let my gaze linger on the polished silver mask, the way it cupped his chin, and how a rigid strip of leather attached just below his temple curved around his ear, like the arm of a pair of eyeglasses. But for his deformity, Callum Connolly might have been the best-looking man I'd ever met.

—Have you sent for the sheriff?

—Not as of yet.

—Before you do, and I know Dorcas is champing at the bit, I'd hoped you might give me the opportunity to explain, and to repay you. With interest.

Callum Connolly's office is spare in the extreme, with only a desk, two chairs facing it and a coat rack by the door. A massive map of Colorado with pins bearing little flags with names of mines written on them hangs on the wall behind the desk.

My eyes traveled to the Fort Collins area, where a large plat of land had been colored red by different pencils at different times. I know that map. Had seen it many times in Colonel Connolly's office at his ranch, when the plat in the middle had been white, and all that stood in the way of his fifty-thousand-acre dream.

But the most interesting part of his office was the safe in the corner.

Callum Connolly sat in his desk chair, leaned back, and crossed his boot over his knee.

I sat even though he didn't ask me to and spun him the story I came to tell. It was the truth, for the most part. It had to be, since Dorcas stood sentinel at the door behind me.

—After your father cheated me out of my ranch—

Dorcas grunted in disagreement.

—I was destitute, winter was coming on, and I had a family to feed. I'm sure you understand that making a living on my back wasn't an option. I suppose I could have found a job as a schoolteacher, but the idea of living on the uncertain charity of farmers dependent on how the crops came in wasn't appealing. More than that, I couldn't bear to stay in the territory, not after having my own ranch, knowing that freedom. That happiness. I'll confess, I was angry. More than angry, and the idea of taking something from your father was appealing. I'd been hearing men brag about outlawing for years, and thought, *How difficult could it be?* I would steal from the colonel's bank, get my pound of flesh, and move my family out of the territory. Start a new life. And that's what we did.

Dorcas couldn't believe I'd admitted it.

—I can hardly deny it when I told the teller to send my regards to the colonel.

Callum Connolly raised his eyebrows and glanced at his aunt. He nodded, and she left the room. I swallowed my doubt and continued with my plan.

—This is a check for the amount I stole, plus four years' worth of interest.

—How did you come into so much money?

—I took a page from your father's book; I invested. In the California State Telegraph Company.

—Where have you been these past four years?

—Here and there. When my return was significant enough, I decided it was time to make amends to your father. Imagine my surprise when I found out he'd died.

—Yes. Three years ago.

—May I ask how?

—Peacefully. In his sleep.

I know that for a lie, but it was the story I'd read in the paper as well.

—How odd. He was such a vibrant man.

—Why now?

—Excuse me?

—Why have you decided to make amends?

—Does it matter?

—Yes.

I stood and went to the window that looked out over Colfax Avenue and saw Dorcas Connolly escorting a policeman to arrest me. I turned to my prey with tears moistening my eyes.

—I'm dying, Mr. Connolly. I have an inoperable tumor and have been given a short amount of time to live. Weeks, maybe a few months if I lie in bed. It is what my family wants. That is not in my nature, however.

—Your nature is to take a risk by coming to my office and confessing to stealing thousands of dollars?

—Ten thousand, two hundred forty-seven dollars, to be exact. And this.

I placed the deed to the Poudre River Ranch on his desk.

—I know Dorcas has gone for the sheriff, and I will go without a fight. In fact, I will be happy to stand trial. My affairs are in order, my family taken care of, and there's a good possibility I'll be dead before the trial takes place. But if it did, I would be happy to tell the story on the record about how your father took advantage of a woman alone, how he gave me an ultimatum of marriage or destitution and followed through with the latter. When my terminal illness comes to light, I'm quite sure that the court of public opinion will swing my way. I wouldn't be surprised if other men and women your father wronged and stole from came forward to support me. Is that what you want your business to be known to be built on? Theft of property? The manipulation of a widow? I will be dead and quickly forgotten, but the cloud will hover over your interests for years. I'm offering to settle this quietly, for you and your late father to retain your reputation, and for me to retain mine.

Dorcas entered with a tall, lanky man wearing a tin star.

—There she is, Sheriff. She admitted to robbing the Bank of the Rockies in '73.

—Is this true, Mr. Connolly?

Callum Connolly and I hadn't taken our eyes off each other. He tapped the check on the desk and looked at it.

—She did. But she's also paid what she stole back, with a very generous interest rate.

—Do you want me to arrest her?

—Of course he does.

—No. Sorry to put you out, Sheriff.

The sheriff tipped his hat to Callum and left.

—That will be all, Dorcas.

—You're making a mistake, Callum.

—When I want your advice, I'll ask for it.

Dorcas left the room in a huff.

I asked Callum how my ranch was, and he smiled (though I could only see one half of his lips) and said he'd liked my ranch house much better than his father's and had been living there since he'd come west to take over his father's businesses.

—I suppose you've made it your own on the inside.

—No, actually. It is just as I found it. What my father did to it before I came I don't know.

—I was thinking of riding down, to see it one last time. Could you give me a letter to present to the foreman so I'm allowed?

—I'll do you one better. I'll take you myself.

—Oh. How very kind.

Though hardly part of the plan.

—Are you sure it's no trouble?

—None at all. I planned on going this weekend. I have some business to take care of before I make a circuit of my holdings.

—How long does that take you?

—A month. Depending on what disasters I come across.

—Not many, I hope.

He smiled tightly and stood.

—I will pick you up at ten a.m. on Friday. Where are you staying?

—The American House.

—Pack for the weekend. I'll put you on the return train to Denver on Sunday.

Definitely not part of the plan. I smiled and shook his hand.

—Thank you, Mr. Connolly, for being so understanding. I know you didn't have to be.

—On the contrary. It would be impossible to discover what my father found so appealing about you while you're in jail.

—Yes, I am an acquired taste.

—I look forward to it.

It was too easy. Callum Connolly is up to something.

This is going to be fun.

13

WPA Slave Narrative Collection

Interview with Henrietta Lee

Sunday, September 13, 1936

You hear about that woman who flew her plane across the country? Markham, that's her. Don't that beat all? You know I flew in one of those Jennys once. With Bessie Coleman. Yes, I did. I suppose things are changing a bit. Of course it's tougher to hide women's accomplishments with the radio and movies and telegraph available everywhere. When I was up in that plane, the air in my face, looking down at the earth like that, I sure did wish I was younger. You better believe I would have learned to fly. I think on everything I've seen in my life and I marvel. I was born in 1844, did you know that? Louisiana. Nah, haven't been back there since the end of the war. No good memories for me there.

"Travel back in 1877 was slow, especially when you're twisting and turning through the mountains. Take us ten days to get to Rock Springs from the Hole in a wagon. It was probably a hundred miles as the crow flies, but the only place in the West you could travel as the crow flew was the plains. Doubt there's an automobile road to the Hole today. Sure as hell too remote for telegraph, then or now. Made it a great place to hide. You could go faster on a horse, of course. I like to imagine what the view would look like flying over the mountains, along the Green River valley that made up Brown's Hole. I bet it's a pretty sight. It was pretty on the ground, and that's a fact.

"Right, right. We got to get going. Meeting the president by the fireside tonight. That radio, Lawd, what an invention that is. My mind spins with all the stuff we have now, it really does. I wish Margaret had lived to see it.

"Margaret made the bet, so we had to come up with a plan. We didn't have time for Jehu to scout us a target, and anyways he wasn't interested. He made himself scarce during our planning sessions. I wasn't sure how smart it was to have Grace Trumbull in on everything, but she argued that this last big job would be a great centerpiece for the book. I let it go. I had plans for Grace Trumbull. And I knew I could kill her anytime I wanted.

"Garet wanted to hit the first bank she robbed, the Bank of the Rockies. Connolly's bank. She said it would be a fitting end to go back to where she started. I thought there were easier, more remote targets to hit, but since we had to best Spooner, she convinced me we needed to hit a big target, and a Denver bank sure was that.

"We couldn't rely on Garet's knowledge from '73 since Denver had changed a lot in four years. We planned to go to Denver at the end of the summer, after rounding up a new batch of mustangs and spending a few weeks breaking them. We were a working horse ranch, after all, and we couldn't put it all on hold to go outlawing. We had given ourselves enough time to get to Denver, watch the bank for a week or two, pull the job, and get back to the Heresy before winter set in. We targeted being in Denver by the first of August, pulling the job no later than October first and riding hell-for-leather back to the Hole.

"Grace had been pretty silent, taking notes—which I didn't like one bit—but when Garet said October first, she startled. She asked what street the bank was on, and when Garet told her, she smiled. She was a suffragist, you see, and had been to a meeting in Denver before leaving on her travels. Colorado was set to vote on women's suffrage on October second, and the association that was advocating for it was going to have a rally, a march, traveling right down the street in front of the bank. You can use it as escape cover, she said. Garet was impressed, I could tell. I was suspicious and determined to get a look at that book Grace was always scribbling in.

"Jehu and the girls were going to stay at the ranch and keep it running. Hire some cowboys to help, and that was just fine with him. If he didn't need to be out on the trail, searching for jobs for us, then he'd just as soon be at the ranch taking care of the livestock. The ranch would be ours when Garet passed, and though he'd never said a word against Garet's running of it, I knew he was eager to be the one in charge. I wasn't eager to leave him, though. I didn't like being apart from him, and this job was going to keep us separate for at least two months. It had taken me a long damn time to find a man who loved me like Jehu did, who took care of me in the little ways. Rubbing my shoulders after a long day. Waking me up every morning with a cup of coffee and a light kiss on my forehead. Try as I might, I could never get out of bed in the morning before Jehu to return the favor. I finally gave up trying. I liked the attention too much. He'd bring me little gifts from his trips, a soap with rose petals in it, a lotion he used to rub on the scars on my back. Said it was supposed to help them fade, but it never did. They'd been healed for too long, I suppose. That didn't mean Jehu would stop rubbing it on my back, though. Course, you know what a good long back rub would lead to. To this day I can't smell camphor without longing for Jehu's touch. Never been a sweeter, kinder, or gentler man than Jehu Lee.

"I've gotten off track. That'll happen when I start thinking about Jehu. There'll be days when I'll sit here on the porch and think about him, and Garet and the girls, the times we had, for hours. Five years is all it was, but we lived a lot in those five years, and we were happy."

We take a break here. I help Mrs. Lee into the house and to the bathroom. She uses a cane, but isn't slump-shouldered like so many elderly women. She has a regal bearing, and I'm struck by the brightness in her copper-colored eyes. She pats my arm before going into the bathroom and says, "I like our chats." I tell her I enjoy them, too. I get us some iced tea and we settle back onto the front porch.

"I went with Jehu and Stella and some cowboys to round up mustangs, which gave Jehu and me time to talk without Garet around. I told him I suspected Grace was a Pinkerton, and he said I was probably right. That was all I needed to hear. Jehu wasn't suspicious by nature, and if he had reservations about Grace, then that was as good a confirmation as any that she was against us. We went to Garet with it when we got back, and goddamn if she didn't smile and say, 'She may be, but I want to give her a chance to do the right thing.'

"Garet had somehow lost sight of how the right thing to most people would be turning in a gang of outlaws. But she was stubborn about Grace, said that she was damaged, like we all were, and that made the difference. 'She's looking for acceptance,' Garet said. 'We give her that, and she won't turn on us.'

"Jehu and I both thought it was a damn fool idea to be trusting our lives on a white woman's better nature, but Garet said giving her a chance wasn't the same as trusting her, and my job while in Denver was to shadow Grace, find out if she was a Pinkerton. We could feed her false information about our plans, because wouldn't it be better to have the Pinkertons looking one way while we were pulling our job the other?

"Damn that Garet, she was a clever woman. I was angry I didn't see her play from the beginning. While we'd been gone rounding up mustangs, she'd been softening up Grace, getting to know her, getting Grace to trust her. Grace had a crush on Garet, and Garet was fostering it, and she told me it was time to put my animosity on the shelf and to gain her trust. I told her she did trust me, as long as Garet wasn't around, but that Grace was always going to go to Garet before a colored woman.

"Grace suggested she go to Rock Springs and catch the train to Denver alone, that the three of us traveling together might stand out. We agreed, and Jehu took her in the wagon so he could do another supply run. As I said, the wagon took a while and Jehu might have driven slower than usual, so Garet and I easily outpaced them to Rock Springs by following animal trails instead of the road. I went on to Denver, to pick up Grace when she got off the train. Garet detoured to Cheyenne, took this boy Newt who'd been beaten half to death by his pa, to the doctor, then left him with some friends of ours. She needed to pick up some hemp. Reefer, I think they call it these days. She liked smoking hemp to keep the pain at bay more than laudanum. That opium-laced shit will kill you.

"I knew Grace never suspected I was shadowing her, because if she had, she would have never led me straight to her meeting with Dorcas Connolly. Garet took the news better than I expected. She apologized for doubting me, for not trusting my instincts, but said we'd know if Grace had betrayed us to Dorcas as soon as she walked into Connolly's office. If she did, I should kill Grace and skedaddle.

"We didn't have to worry about that, though. She went into the lion's den and came out with an invitation to stay the weekend at her old ranch. It wasn't the plan, it was better. It would give her the chance to snoop in Connolly's office, see which businesses we should hit. The Bank of Denver was a decoy for Grace. The real plan was bigger. Bolder. And a great way to go out."

14

Margaret Parker's Journal

Letter to Grace Trumbull
Written between August 6-10, 1877

Dear Grace,

You don't know what I have in mind for you yet, the role you will play in my legacy. You may turn down my offer. You may be a Pinkerton plant and readying a trap to catch me. Regardless, this journal will be read by someone, and they will most assuredly want to know how I, Margaret Elizabeth Standridge Parker, came to be a Colorado outlaw in 1877.

I was born in Somerset, England, in 1843 to the third son of an earl who reluctantly went into the Church, but never took to the job, or the teachings. He was a libertine and a gambler and by the time I was five he'd lost his curacy and was disowned by his family. He died not long after and is buried in an out-of-the-way portion of the family plot, with only a small, flat stone marking his existence. Thankfully, the Earl of Standridge was a fair man and allowed me and my mother to stay under his guardianship, and let us live in a little gamekeeper's cabin on his estate. My mother's family lived in genteel poverty in Derbyshire; my grandmother married my mother off to the Standridges because they couldn't afford to take care of the six daughters they had. Returning to them was never considered.

My mother tutored me in all the ladylike accomplishments that would be required for me to make a good match, freeing both of us from the earl's charity. I excelled in my studies, but what I loved more than anything was being outdoors, especially riding and spending time at the stables. I learned everything I know about horses—evaluating, training, riding—by shadowing my grandfather and his head trainer, Ransom. The earl was a famous horseman and breeder and had seven grand champions in his lifetime. The earl and Ransom doted on me, enchanted with my enthusiasm, my intelligence, and my ability to listen and learn, and to stay out of the way when I needed to. My first lesson in relationships with men had nothing with to do with my mother's daily tutoring in accepted female accomplishments. Make men feel important and smart, take an interest in what they love, and their loyalty knows no bounds. My grandfather bought me a pony when I was seven, Tulip, a lovely little sorrel, and as I grew and became more skilled, my horses became feistier until I was riding a beautiful blood bay hunter as large as my grandfather's. When I came out, I was known far and wide to have almost as good an eye for horseflesh as my grandfather, and a better seat than any other debutante in England.

That made me attractive to a certain kind of man, namely Captain Thomas Parker, Crimean War hero, veteran of the Charge of the Light Brigade, and second son to the Duke of Parkerton. Thomas lost his left arm in the battle, but he was charming and handsome and almost as knowledgeable about horses as I (though of course I let him think his expertise exceeded mine). We fell in love almost instantly. The earl approved; the Parkers were an old family who were more respectable than wealthy, and my grandfather gave me a generous dowry. If he had known it would eventually lead to me living thousands of miles away and that I would never see him again after I embarked on my honeymoon journey, I'm not sure he would have been so generous.

Since the colonies were embroiled in a civil war, Thomas and I made our way to the American West via Canada for our honeymoon. Thomas was eager to try his hand at mining, to refill his family's coffers with the spoils of the American Rockies and to prove that he was a whole man, that his missing arm didn't matter. Of course, many more people went bust than hit the motherlode (the newspapers and land promoters always elided over that fact), but it was hard not to dream when you saw the West. Thomas dreamed of riches; I dreamed of horses. When I saw my first herd of mustangs, all that horseflesh free for the taking, my entire body thrummed with energy as a vision of our future, in Colorado Territory, bloomed in my mind. With our knowledge of horses and the growth of the West that I saw with the construction of the Transcontinental Railroad, we could fill the Parker family coffers with money from ranching. Thomas had to be led away from mining and toward ranching in such a way that he believed the idea had originated within himself, but I was persuasive, and subtle. Soon Thomas was as enthusiastic about mustangs as he had been about gold.

With my dowry, we staked a claim on five hundred acres by the Cache la Poudre River and built the required cabin, or had it built, I should say, along with stables and a corral. Thomas hired some men, and they went off in the mountains to round up our first herd of mustangs, and I went about trying to learn how to cook and clean and run a house without servants. Colonel Connolly and his sister, Dorcas, were our nearest neighbors and welcomed us to the area with open arms. Dorcas lent me her cook so I could learn the kitchen basics I would need, and the colonel and Thomas spent many nights in the colonel's library, talking about their army exploits.

The first few years were exhausting, not only because of the backbreaking work of running a household in a remote area, but also because it became apparent pretty early on that Thomas was ill prepared to run a working horse ranch. He had no eye for business, and, though he knew a lot about horses, he wasn't as skilled at breaking and training them as he believed. Two very fortunate events happened within a few months of each other, saving us from total ruin: Jehu and Jed Spooner.

It was a Saturday, and Thomas and I were in Fort Collins procuring supplies for the next week. Thomas had gone off to the blacksmith to discuss a wagon repair, and I was shopping at the general store for flour, salt, ribbon, and fabric. A loaded wagon came down the street, and the driver tipped his hat at me. I smiled and dipped my chin in acknowledgment. I didn't know the man's name, but it seemed that I saw him in town every Saturday, without fail. I call him a man, but he was so slight he looked like little more than a boy.

I took my time shopping, knowing full well that Thomas's business would be concluded quickly and he would head to the back room of the hotel and play faro for a few hours. I purchased a sandwich and a bottle of ginger beer and took myself to the river for a picnic and a few hours of glorious solitude. I'd finished my repast and was having a lie-down in the cool grass to let the sun warm my face and listen to the gentle sound of the flowing river when a shadow was cast over my eyes. I had a moment of pure terror; I was alone and quite away from the town. A man could have easily overpowered me in my vulnerable state. I sat up quickly and moved away before my eyes had the opportunity to focus on who stood near me. When they did,

I saw the young teamster holding his hat close to his chest, an expression of mortification on his face.

—I'm sorry, ma'am. I didn't mean to startle you.

My answer was curt and more than a little rude. I can still feel the heavy beating of my heart. The man apologized again and turned to go. I stopped him and asked him his name.

—Jehu.

—Like in the Bible?

—Yes, ma'am. I'm a fair hand at teamstering, especially for one my age.

Jehu's face was soft, but nothing else about him was. He was wiry, a little taller than me, perhaps. He looked as if a stiff wind would blow him over, but his strong hands and corded forearms gave the impression of greater strength than evident at first glance.

—You're a teamster?

—Yes, ma'am.

—I see you every weekend.

—Yes, ma'am. I drive the Denver Road every week from Cheyenne to Denver. When you see me on a Saturday, I'm on my return trip to Cheyenne.

—By yourself?

—No, ma'am. I have a guard that rides with me.

—Stop calling me ma'am.

—I would, but I don't know your name, ma'am.

—Right. Margaret Parker.

—Mrs. Parker.

—Call me Garet.

—Yes, ma'am.

During this exchange, Jehu's eyes never met mine, and he fiddled his hat around and around in a circle.

—Was there something I could help you with, Jehu?

—Yes, ma'am. Garet. I wondered if there might be a job for me out at your ranch?

—Tired of teamstering?

—Yes, ma'am.

—What do you know about horses?

—I know the best way to get them to do what you want is to be gentle with them.

I raised my eyebrows at this, since most of the men Thomas had hired to break our mustangs thought force and abuse the best way to train a horse. I disagreed, of course.

—You can drive a horse, but can you ride?

—Yes, ma'am.

—Do you know what we do at the ranch?

—You round up wild mustangs and break them for sale to the army or mines or whoever needs them.

—How do you know that?

—Everyone knows about the Englishman's ranch.

—Do you also know that we are probably going to go bankrupt if we don't do a better job of breaking our stock?

—Heard rumors. I can help. I want to help.

—Why?

Jehu gathered the courage to meet my eyes for a brief moment, and his face reddened quicker than I'd ever seen another person blush.

—Ever broken a mustang, Jehu?

—No, ma'am. But I've ridden plenty of green horses in my time.

—How old are you, Jehu?

—About twenty, I expect.

—Family?

—Been an orphan since before the war.

—I'll pay you a dollar for every horse you break to start. Plus room and board. Does that sound fair?

Jehu agreed, met my eyes, and smiled. He had a set of surprisingly straight teeth, more than I can say for myself.

After Thomas's initial shock at the skinny man sitting next to me in the wagon, and my declaration that Jehu was our new cowboy, Thomas quickly warmed up to him. It was difficult not to. Jehu was quiet, respectful, attentive, intelligent, and a quick learner. I saw a lot of myself in Jehu's ability to endear himself to Thomas, and me. Soon he became like family, though he steadfastly refused the idea Thomas had of building a room onto the cabin for him. Instead Jehu slept in the barn loft, said he liked the comforting smell of horses and hay. I didn't understand until later what the true reason for his shyness was. I assumed it was because he wanted to keep his distance from me, a married woman he was sweet on. You could say it was my vanity talking, but I wasn't entirely wrong, merely right for the wrong reason.

I helped break horses under the guise of teaching Jehu, and by the time Jed Spooner and his gang rode up to our ranch looking for fresh mounts to trade, we had plenty on offer. We didn't look too close at the money, or ask aloud where a gang of six rough-looking characters might have gotten the cash to buy six horses in addition to the six they traded for. It was the first major sale we made, kept us from going bankrupt, and we were thrilled to get six seasoned horses in the bargain. It wasn't until Jed and his boys rode away that Jehu told us who they were, and that we might have gotten ourselves into a relationship it would be tough to get out of.

We never wanted to get out of it, least of all me. With the sale there was a subtle shift in the responsibilities at the ranch. Thomas couldn't deny how good a team Jehu and I were, and he understood that the more horses we trained, the more money we would make. He focused on rounding up the horses, general ranch maintenance, and the other livestock. I still had the housework, as well as the books to keep. I slept like the dead for five hours a night and got up the next day to do it all again. I didn't care. I felt more alive and significant than I ever had in my life.

There was another reason I didn't want to jeopardize our relationship with the outlaw. I was drawn to Spooner from the moment I set eyes on him. Spooner is handsome, as you know, Grace, and there's a rough edge to him that Thomas never had. I was never disloyal to Thomas while he was alive, and Jed never approached me. Thomas was, and is, the love of my life. He is the reason I never remarried. He saw our marriage as a partnership and knew how integral I was to the success of the ranch. I know I will never find that with another man, least of all Colonel Connolly or Jed Spooner. Not that Spooner has ever hinted at matrimony.

Thomas was drawn to Spooner, as well, though for different reasons, of course. He saw in Spooner a man he could never be again. Someone daring and whole. You would think that would make Thomas resentful, but it was the opposite. He respected Spooner, despite the fact he was an outlaw and a rebel. Spooner got his start with the James Gang in Missouri, but came west when their brand of outlawing got out of hand. The war was over, and he felt like the James boys were still fighting it, would be until the day they died. Spooner wanted to make enough money to help his friends when they needed it, to work as little as possible, and to gamble, drink, and whore the rest of the time. He knew himself for the libertine he was, and didn't think other men should have to die so he could partake in his vices. I suspect it was similar to the life Thomas had prior to the Crimea, when he was a young, dashing officer, though his reputation was as no more than a high-spirited man in the regular way. By all accounts, the Crimea changed Thomas. There wasn't a hint of vice about him when we met, nor was there a bad word to be said of his reputation. He was gregarious, friendly, and charming when we met, and he remained so until the day he passed. But he would fall into a brooding mood from time to time. Was he remembering scenes from battle, or mourning the life he lost when he lost his arm? He never said, and I stopped asking. He lived vicariously through Spooner and his gang. Spooner invited Thomas to go with them on a job, but Thomas refused. He said he would never be so desperate as to steal from another, but I wonder if he wasn't afraid his deformity would hinder his ability to help. It was of little consequence, as Spooner was a raconteur and would regale us with stories of his exploits so detailed we almost felt as if we were there.

Soon we had a deal with the gang. They would use our ranch as a hideout, cowboy for us, round up mustangs, and we would always have a ready supply of horses for them to use in their jobs. We went on like that for a few years, made a good living. Other gangs started using us as a way station, too. We sold horses to the army and anyone who would give us a fair price. We bought a thoroughbred stud, and the quality of our stock rose.

Jehu would leave to haul freight occasionally. He loved us, and having a home, but he also liked his freedom. At least that was what I thought until I realized his hauling coincided with the arrival of Jed and his gang. We'd built a little bunkhouse out back behind the barn for the seasonal cowboys we'd take on, but Jehu never lived in it. Insisted on living in the barn. Still, when the ranch would fill up with strangers, Jehu would get itchy feet, and decide it was time to make a little extra money. He always brought home something pretty for me, a new dress, a hat, soft leather gloves that I had no occasion to wear but loved anyways because they were such an extravagant and lovely gift. He would bring gifts home for Thomas as well. Tobacco, a finely tooled belt, a new dove-gray gambler's hat, one time a brightly colored vest. Thomas always thanked Jehu, but would tease me in private that Jehu's gifts to Thomas were only to make his puppy love of me less obvious. I think he was a little in love with me, but that all changed when Hattie arrived.

You haven't spent much time with Jehu, which is the more pity for you. You would know he is the gentlest man you'll ever meet. He couldn't abide seeing young girls degrade themselves to eat and would give them as much money as he could and still have some for us. After one trip he came home with a woman and son, her face bruised and swollen (much as Newt's was). Thomas and I welcomed her into our home, gave her a job cooking and cleaning, and let her heal. Eventually she and her son moved on, took a job in Golden, I think. After that the ranch became known as a safe haven for women, a place they could come, earn some money, and be on their way. Our first priority was helping these women, but their arrival had the added benefit of freeing me up to work outside with the stock. Some women stayed longer than others. Jehu found Stella and Joan in Rock Springs, trying to get money for a train to Frisco, and he found Hattie hiding in our barn.

I will leave you there, desperate to know what happens next. Maybe I should be writing my story instead of taxing you with the job. But no. I need to be more succinct and remember that after I'm gone, you will have Hattie, Jehu, Stella, and Joan to fill in the blanks. Hattie would probably tell her story better than I would, anyways. Don't forget to talk to my enemies to get the full picture of my personality. After all, how do you know I'm being completely honest with you?

August 6, 1877

Pinkerton,

The Spooner Gang is holed up in a town in Brown's Hole called Timberline, Colorado. They arrived in June, and for the last two months I've been ingratiating myself with them, working on their ranch, to get information about their next job so we can catch them in the act.

Spooner and his gang have been working the area for years and deserve to be arrested. But our theory that Spooner and his gang were responsible for two of the five jobs against Connolly and behind the other three was wrong. The women who have been doing those jobs are led by Margaret Parker and a Negro named Hattie. They dressed as men and wore cloth hoods as masks for the first two, and for the last three, which they pulled as women, they were sure to let the men they robbed know that they were there on Spooner's behalf. When Spooner got word he was being blamed for the big jobs that were happening a thousand miles away but not receiving any of the compensation, he decided to head back up to Colorado and teach Parker a lesson. He's challenged her to a competition—one heist each, biggest take wins the ranch (which Spooner and his men helped build; he was formerly Parker's lover), loser has to leave the area and take their trade elsewhere. Parker took the bet and she and Hattie left a few days ago for Denver. Spooner and his gang immediately moved into her ranch.

As I said above, I'm in with the gang, and it didn't take long to discover that Spooner has no intention of doing a heist, and he has no intention of giving up the ranch when Parker returns. It was a ploy to get her out of the Hole and set her up to be captured when she tries to pull the job. I'm not sure how he intends to discover what she is targeting to set her up, but he seems confident that information will be readily available when he needs it.

He isn't getting much help from the town besides from a blacksmith named Valentine. Spooner and the sheriff, Luke Rhodes, hate each other, and I'm guessing it's over Margaret Parker. Rhodes wants her, Spooner had her.

Parker and her girls give a portion of the money they steal to the town, to keep it afloat, and Parker and her girls are well liked. The women are protective of her, and even though their husbands hate taking money from a woman, they don't want Parker and her family to leave the area.

I recommend biding our time with Spooner, discovering what Parker's plans are, and both hitting Spooner in the Hole and catching Parker red-handed when she tries to pull the job. You should ready agents at Rock Springs, the closest railroad town to the Hole, and Denver, apparently where Parker plans to work.

Salter

15

Margaret Parker's Journal

Friday, August 10, 1877
Cache la Poudre River Ranch
Fort Collins, Colorado

Callum and I took the train to Greeley and rode from there. The rail line between Fort Collins and Denver should be finished by September. Connolly's company has an interest in it, of course. Unfortunately, I'll be retired or dead and not able to rob it. Maybe Hattie and the girls will. I suspect they will continue with their outlaw ways when I'm gone.

Connolly had a man at the Greeley station with two horses for us to ride. I was surprised and pleased when I saw the mount he had brought for me: a strapping gray stallion with plenty of life. Connolly had sent me a note the day before we left and told me we would ride part of the way, so I'd dressed appropriately, and smartly. I've always filled out a riding habit well, and Callum Connolly looked on me with appreciation and a little astonishment.

—Have you never seen a woman wear britches before, Mr. Connolly?

—Not one so beautiful as you.

—It is awfully early in the morning to be so charming, Mr. Connolly.

—Please, call me Callum.

—Callum. It is quite shocking, isn't it? I suppose when you know almost the day of your death, what other people think about what you are wearing matters little. I've always thought riding was easier in pants, and since I don't ride sidesaddle, it's pointless to pretend to be coy.

We rode through Greeley, and I was shocked to discover it had changed so much in the time I'd been gone—more buildings, though no saloons. I'd never liked Greeley much; it is full of pious teetotalers. You couldn't fault them for hard work and good business sense, though. But the railroad worked its magic wherever it went, which is why so many small connecting lines were being built to towns off the main line. I wondered how long until the entire country would be accessible by train, and realized I wouldn't be around to see it.

These past weeks, I've felt my life picking up speed to its destination. I don't feel appreciably worse, though the doctor told me that in the end the pain will be unbearable. The certain knowledge of the misery that awaits me doesn't worry me, it frees me to take chances I might not otherwise take. I've had to rein myself in more than once; I still want to win this bet, I *need* to win this bet, to set up Hattie, Jehu, and the girls, to give them a comfortable nest egg and a ranch free and clear, so they can live out their days. It is the thought of and Hattie, elderly and sitting on our porch watching the sun rise over Cold Spring Mountain, that keeps me from recklessness.

But today, nothing could keep me from giving my horse its head and enjoying the wind whipping my hair out of its twist, of leaning low over the horse's neck to encourage it to go faster, faster, faster. I thought of my mother and grandfather, long dead, and how proud my grandfather would be of me despite the fact that I was an outlaw.

I outpaced Callum and his horse by at least three lengths. I stopped when I reached the Cache la Poudre River. My horse danced beneath me, excited after the long run. My heart beat rapidly in my chest, but I couldn't keep the smile off my face. I've always felt most at home astride, and always loved more than anything the smell of horse sweat and leather, the feel of the powerful animal beneath me combining its energy with my own, feeling more alive than I've ever felt at any other time in my life. The closest I've ever come to that transcendental feeling was after I'd robbed my first bank. Callum Connolly must've seen something of my thoughts on my face when he caught up to me because he smiled and said, —Dorcas said you were a good horsewoman, but I didn't believe her.

—Dorcas complimented me? I can't believe it.

—If it makes you feel better, she said it as an insult.

—Much better. Thank you, Callum, for putting me in my place.

—I don't know what I'm going to do now Dorcas isn't accompanying me to my other businesses.

I asked Callum why Dorcas wasn't coming with him as planned.

—She was attacked last night. Robbed.

—Was she injured?

—She has a splitting headache and a lump at the base of her skull. The doctor diagnosed her with a concussion and told her not to get out of bed, let alone travel.

—It seems working for you is a dangerous occupation.

—It does seem that way.

—Do you not have another clerk?

—No. I had a potential secretary die an untimely death in Gunnison a few months ago.

—Oh dear. What happened?

—He was a weak man in a rough town. Come, let's cross upriver a bit.

It was a companionable ride. We made small talk about the weather and the beauty of the area, but mostly we were silent. The river was languid, meandering along the valley floor, and we could have easily crossed at any point. I was getting nervous, wondering if this hadn't all been a ruse to get me away from town. I was alone with a man I didn't know, but who was rumored to be violent with whores behind closed doors, without my gun. He could do whatever he wanted with me and I had no recourse save Hattie's Bowie knife secreted at the small of my back beneath my vest. It wouldn't be easy to get to if he did attack me. I should have put it in my boot.

Callum rode with his masked profile toward me and his black Stetson pulled low over his eyes. A cloud drifted across the sun, throwing us in shadow. A chill went down my spine. I was opening my mouth to say I was crossing the river when Callum said,—We're here.

Ahead of us, around a slight bend in the river, was a copse of trees. Beneath the largest tree, a cottonwood of course, were a table and two chairs. The white tablecloth fluttered in the gentle breeze. A wagon with two mules in the traces was parked a little ways off. A Chinaman stood off to the side of the table, hands folded in front of him, waiting.

—I thought we'd have a picnic, Callum said.

—How lovely. Thank you.

We dismounted, and Callum took the horses upriver to drink. The Chinaman bowed as I approached the table. I smiled, greeted him, and asked his name.

—Bohai, madam.

—Pleasure to meet you.

He bowed again and went to the river. Bohai pulled on a rope that led into the river, and a bottle of white wine bobbed on the surface. The table was laid with china, silver, and crystal, with a bowl of floating flowers as the centerpiece. There were a silver platter with a large ham, a plate of rolls that looked soft as air, deviled eggs, a bowl of grapes, a wedge of red-rind cheddar cheese, and a smaller glass next to the wineglass, which foretold a bottle of port or sherry miraculously appearing.

Bohai poured a glass of wine and handed it to me, bowing yet again.

—Thank you.

The wine was crisp, dry, and fruity. Bohai showed the label; it was from France.

Callum returned, clapped his hand together, and said, —This looks wonderful, Bohai.

—Thank you, sir.

—This is more feast than picnic, I said.

—Dorcas told me you were royalty. I couldn't very well have you sitting on the ground eating hardtack, could I?

—Ah, is that what Dorcas said? She said it derisively, didn't she?

—Of course.

He held out a chair and I sat. Bohai carved the ham.

—I'm not royalty, you know.

—I didn't imagine you were, but Dorcas was ranting and raving, so I didn't ask her to elaborate. It's usually best to let her vent, then ignore her. Why did she think you were royalty?

—My husband was the second son of a duke. The Duke of Parkerton. In England, the first son is the heir, the second son goes into the military, the third son goes into the church.

—What about the fourth son?

—Law most likely, possibly a doctor. But they're all libertines. They marry plain heiresses who silently suffer their peccadillos and watch their fortunes evaporate in the London gambling halls. My husband, as a second son, went into the army. Was a hero of the Crimea.

—The Charge of the Light Brigade?

—Yes.

—My father told me in one of his letters. He liked your husband very much.

—Hmm. Well, turned out my father-in-law and his heir, Edward, were the gamblers. By the time we married, there was very little Parker fortune left, and Thomas's brother had risen to the dukedom. Thomas was determined to strike it rich in the West, to help refill his family coffers.

—He didn't, though?

—No. His brother died without issue, and the title went to Thomas. By the time we got the letter, Thomas had died as well, and with him the line. So yes. Technically for three months I was the Duchess of Parkerton. But not according to any official records. Thomas hadn't returned to claim it, you see?

—If he had, would you have inherited the title?

—No idea, though it's highly doubtful. I made the mistake of telling a friend of the title, and Duchess has become somewhat of a mocking nickname.

—May I call you that?

—I'd rather you not. Garet is fine.

—I will stop peppering you with questions. Eat. Please.

I did, and it was delicious. For his part, Callum ate the rolls and the deviled eggs, avoiding the ham, though it was succulent and tender, and drinking half of the bottle of wine before I'd finished a glass. I ignored Callum, though I felt his eyes on me, and focused on my meal, the sound of birdsong, the rustling of leaves in the breeze, the gentle bubbling of the river, the stomp of a horse's hoof. My senses have been highly attuned to the world around me, as if longing to take everything in so the memory of it will stay with me, manifest itself in the afterlife. As if I deserve to be surrounded by things I love. As if I deserve heaven.

Forgive me, Grace. I'm becoming maudlin. It happens more often than not, though I have done a magnificent job of keeping those thoughts out of this journal.

When I finished, I sat back in my chair while Bohai poured the sherry. I sniffed it, toasted Callum, and drank it in one shot.

—Is this my last meal, Callum?

—I'm sorry?

—You obviously hold Dorcas and her opinions in little regard since you've ordered an elaborate picnic of silver and china for the woman who confessed to stealing from your father.

—You see, there is the key point: you stole from my father. I couldn't care less. By the time I came to Colorado, that loss had been absorbed. The check you gave me was, to my mind, pure profit. You confessed, you seemed to have a legitimate complaint against him. For me, it's ancient history.

—And for Dorcas?

—Oh, she holds a grudge. She doesn't understand why you would turn my father's marriage proposal down. I, on the other hand, admire you for it.

—Why?

He leaned forward. —I like strong women.

I laughed. —Do you?

—Indeed, I do.

—You like the idea of strong women. When confronted with a woman who speaks her mind, who challenges you, who won't do as you bid, your opinion will change quickly, I venture.

—Are you willing to challenge me, Garet?

—Are you propositioning me?

He leaned back in his chair and hooked his arm over the back in an insouciant manner. —Isn't that why you're here? Why you came with me?

—To be your lover? No. I came to see my ranch.

—That is disappointing.

—Why would you think that?

—It's widely known you took Jed Spooner into your bed almost as soon as your husband was buried. Knowing your husband was missing an arm, I thought that you had a soft spot for deformed men.

—Jed wasn't deformed.

—But he was an outlaw. That is its own kind of deformity.

—You think so?

—Deformity of the soul.

—If Jed suffers from that, then so does every businessman I've ever encountered, especially your father. Businessmen are as much outlaws as gangs like Spooner's, or even the James Gang.

—Murderers?

—You aren't so ignorant as to think your business decisions don't affect people's livelihoods and in turn their health and well-being. You may not pull the trigger, but you are responsible for their deaths.

—Interesting argument, but full of holes. You forget we live in the land of opportunity. If a man works hard he can, and will, succeed.

—And a woman? I worked hard. My family worked hard. We succeeded, but in the end, our livelihood was stolen from us.

Callum shrugged. —I don't make the rules, Duchess. I just play by them.

—Don't call me that.

Callum stood and stretched.

—This conversation took a turn I didn't expect, though I suppose I should have. Dorcas told me you were opinionated.

—I prefer *intelligent*.

—I'll get the horses.

We swam our horses across the river and continued on at a sedate pace, though I was stewing in anger at Callum's proposition and our infuriating conversation. Too many businessmen were crooks and liars, but society rewarded them for their transgressions. Whereas women…

I'm sorry, Grace. No more talk of that. I've thought of it too much these past five years, the injustice, and I just do not have the energy to put it all down on paper. I'm sure you understand my thoughts. You are an intelligent woman trying to make it on your own. If you don't understand yet, you will one day.

The sun was high overhead, and it didn't take long for our clothes to dry. The land around became familiar, and I started recognizing landmarks from my past. We were getting closer to my ranch, and the only way to keep my anger at bay was to keep talking.

—What have you done with your father's business since he died? It's quite the empire, I understand.

—Empire? My father would be pleased to hear you call it that, but it is much too grandiose a name for a group of businesses, most of which barely break even, and the others are so expensive to run they're almost not worth it. This weekend, I look to remedy that.

—How?

—By stealing from and murdering people, of course.

—Touché.

—I didn't mean to anger you earlier, Margaret. You are correct that bad behavior in men is seen as strength and rewarded, but in women as weakness and punished. I am correct in that I didn't make the rules, and I would be a fool to not play by the same set as other, more ruthless men.

—Justify it however you want. I, for one, don't want to talk of it anymore. You and I won't change anything this weekend.

Am I to understand Dorcas ran your business while you were in South America?

—For someone out of the territory for years, you know a lot about my family.

—I read the papers, and I'm always on the lookout for news about Connolly Enterprises. To torture myself, you know.

—Yes, Dorcas ran the company. Made a few solid moves, but most of her acquisitions are the failing ones.

I made a noncommittal noise and suspected he was lying.

—I confess I was surprised to hear that you had come out west to run your father's business. You and your father had…a strained relationship, from what I remember.

—He spoke of me to you?

—Not frequently, which is why I assumed your relationship was strained.

—He wanted me to come west with him, take advantage of the distraction of the war. I decided to stay, and then I fought for the wrong side.

—You were a rebel?

—I was, and I do not apologize for it.

We rode in silence for a mile or more. Soon we came to the fence line that delineated my old ranch. Colonel Connolly had not been pleased when Thomas and I decided to fence off our land. But it made sense since our stock was our livelihood, and we couldn't very well have it running off into the foothills to return to its herd of wild mustangs. I was surprised to see the fence still there and in good repair. I'd expected the colonel to tear it down as soon as the girls and I rode away.

Mares and foals grazed in the distance. Ducks swam in the tank that provided water for the herd. The mountains behind hadn't changed, nor had I expected them to. Memories of sitting on our back porch together, Thomas and I, drinking coffee in the morning, whisky at night, watching the sun rise behind us and set in front of us, conversations about running the business, about the horses to keep, the ones to sell, and the ones to breed. In the distance some seemed familiar, though none of those horses could be from my stock, stolen by the army.

Colonel Connolly had planted trees along the fence line near the entrance to our ranch, but they were young enough I could see my house before we arrived. A sharp pain shot through my abdomen, and I grasped my stomach and leaned over.

—Duchess, are you ill?

I glared at Callum for the use of that infernal nickname, said that the pain comes and goes and that I had a tincture I could take once we dismounted. He nodded and looked me up and down. I think that until that moment, Callum had doubted my illness. I smiled. It was one of the few things I hadn't lied to him about.

When we turned onto the lane leading up to my house, I kicked my horse into a lope, eager to arrive, to see if Callum had been truthful himself when he said my home hadn't changed much in the preceding five years. I pushed my horse faster and faster until his hooves thundered on the hard ground, kicking up dust, alerting the cowboys in the corral that we had arrived. I reined in my horse, and he slid on his back legs to a stop. He reared when I gave him his head, and I knew I had to have this horse.

—How much for him?

—Too much for a woman with only months to live.

—I can't imagine anything I'd rather do than ride this fine animal every day until then. It helps me forget my pain. What is his name?

—Whatever you like.

—Me?

—He is yours.

–Oh, I couldn't let you give him to me.

–Of course you could. He's from your stock, anyways.

I paused.

–The army took my stock. There was nothing left.

–They gave most of it back to my father.

-What are you saying? That the army did not requisition my horses? That not only did your father steal my ranch, but he stole my horses as well?

–That's about the sum of it, yes.

–And you think giving me a horse will make up for all your family has taken for me?

–I did not take anything from you, just as you have not stolen anything from me. Right?

–Yet here you are living in my house, riding my horses. I was left destitute, Callum. My family and I were starving, and all because of your father's greed. When I speak of the consequences of greed, it isn't hypothetical. I lived it. Barely survived it. And you seem to have no remorse whatsoever about what was done to me.

-This is why women should not be in business. They're too emotional and take everything that is done to them personally, just as you did.

–Yes, I consider starvation personal. Though I imagine you have never wanted for anything in your life.

–You know nothing about me, *Duchess*. There're plenty of times during the war where me and my men went without food. We boiled leather to soften it up to have something to eat.

–You expect me to feel sorry for an army that fought to enslave others? You will not get my sympathy, Mr. Connolly.

–And you will not get your ranch back.

A cowhand arrived and Connolly gave him the reins of his horse, and I did the same. Thrumming with rage, I followed

Connolly up the steps of my house and walked to the front door for the first time in four years. Connolly was right, nothing had changed. And that makes it all the worse.

The main room was the original cabin Thomas and I had built when we arrived in 1864. Over the years, as we accumulated family members such as Jehu and Hattie and Joan and Stella, along with countless other women who used our ranch as a way station to get their lives back together before moving on, we added rooms as they were needed until we had four bedrooms, a kitchen, and the main room with an office in the corner where I would do our books every night. The rag rug Stella and Joan had made when they first arrived still lay in front of the fireplace. Thomas's desk, which in truth was *my* desk, hadn't moved, though it didn't look as well lived-in as it had when it was mine. The leather chair behind the desk showed more wear, and a rack of moose antlers hung on the wall behind the desk.

—Those are new.

—Those were here when I arrived. I suppose it was my father's trophy.

A Chinese woman came in from the kitchen wiping her hands on a towel and stopped at the sight of me. My anger dissipated at the sight of my old friend.

—Hello, Zhu Li.

—Miss Margaret.

—I suppose Julie came with the ranch, too, Callum said.

—Something like that. How are you, Zhu Li?

—Good. Was lunch to your satisfaction?

—It was delicious, thank you, Callum said.

—Yes, it was. I should have known you were behind those rolls.

—It is Hattie's recipe.

—I realize that now.

—Would you like to see the barns? Callum said.

—Yes.

I grasped Zhu Li's hand as I passed and told her we would talk later.

The barns and corrals had been expanded to accommodate the larger horse operation. A bunkhouse had been built behind the barn near the creek. I counted ten cowboys within my sight and knew that to run a ranch as large as what Colonel Connolly had obtained through cheating and theft, there had to be at least as many more out working the land.

I stood on the corral fence and inspected the herd. Fully half of the herd came from our best stud, a gray thoroughbred that had somehow been bought, sold, and traded from Kentucky to Colorado, losing an eye and most of his value along the way. He didn't need two eyes to mount our mustangs, and that he excelled at. Jehu pampered and petted Crockett, and Thomas remarked more than once that there wasn't a man alive who didn't envy a stud's life of rutting every female in his sight and having his every whim indulged.

—No wonder I liked my mount. He's from Crockett.

Callum leaned on the fence.

—The one-eyed horse? Yes. Most of the mares here are. The foals aren't. Crockett broke his leg last year. Had to be put down.

It was a blow, but time waits for no man.

Callum regaled me with the statistics of the ranch, how many acres it was, how many horses they had, cows, sheep, goats. He didn't sound as if he was bragging, so what else could he be doing, telling me these things? He had to know it would infuriate me, especially after our conversation from earlier. But I would not rise to his bait. I would get back at him later by hitting as many of his businesses as possible before I died. So I congratulated him on his great fortune, on his ability to turn my ranch into the success I always knew it would be. I even said something about how since I wouldn't be around much longer I was happy that my horses—his horses—would be so well taken care of, and that I had always worried about the life my stock had as army beasts. Apparently he liked the sentiments because he offered me a warm smile. His gaze slid down to my lips and back as he pulled a silver case of prerolled cigarettes from his inner pocket.

—Would you like one?

—May I smoke my own?

I hoped to shock him, but he merely said, —By all means, and lit my cigarette when I produced it. I blew a long trail of smoke.

—Why have you never married?

—Isn't it obvious?

—Not to me, no.

—Hmm. I was engaged before the war to a South Carolinian girl. She is why I went into the Confederate army. Her father wouldn't let us marry unless I did. I didn't care one way or the other about slavery or states' rights, but I loved Constance. We wanted to get married before the fighting started, but her father refused. I think he was afraid I would desert to the Union, as if having me on their side would turn the tide of the war. I never wanted to be a soldier, but if I was going to enlist I wanted it to be as an officer. I was commissioned as a lieutenant in the Army of Northern Virginia. The first couple of years weren't terrible. We won more than we lost, at least. When we finally started to lose, their belief in the South, and states' rights, and the inferiority of the black man hardened. They never lost faith, but they were no longer fighting for a noble idea. Fear drove them.

—Of?

—What the world would be like with Negroes walking down the street next to them. Losing all that free labor.

—And your injury? Is it from the war?

—Yes. It happened in a skirmish after the surrender at Appomattox. My fiancée preferred the whole, handsome version of my face. In the years since, the only women who will look at my face I pay handsomely. Besides you, Garet.

—I know that there is more to a man than what you can see. I also know I'm not the only woman who can see past your…

—Deformity.

—Injury.

—Possibly. But how would I know they aren't merely interested in my empire, as you called it?

—I suppose it would be difficult to know. Which is why you're lucky you have Dorcas, who is family and has only the family's best interest at heart.

Callum laughed.

—Dorcas's interest lies with herself. She knows that I'm the only thing keeping her from destitution, so she does whatever I ask, no matter how demeaning.

—That is unbelievably cruel, to treat a woman, your own flesh and blood, like that merely because society allows you to.

—Do you think Dorcas, if the situation were reversed, would treat me any differently?

—Yes, I do.

—You're wrong. She would see in me what I see in her: a threat. She loved running the company and would like nothing more than for me to be met with a freak accident so that she would have control of the company once again.

—If you two worked together, you would be a formidable pair.

—You sound like you admire her.

—We were friends before I turned down your father. Why she hates me now I can't even begin to imagine.

I flicked the end of my cigarette onto the dirt and ground it out under my boot.

—I'm going to rest before dinner, if you don't mind.

—Of course. Though I do have one question.

—Yes?

—Why didn't you go back to England to see your family? To be with them in your last days?

—They are all dead.

—What about friends?

—They moved on.

—You're alone in the world?

—No. Since I've been in Denver, I've made friends in the suffragist movement.

—You're a suffragist?

—Of course. I've been thinking it would be a good way to spend my final days, helping future generations of women, especially since I leave no children of my own.

—Why do you want to vote? It's only more to worry about, to think about. The issues are complex and women do not have the education, or the turn of mind, to understand them well enough to make informed decisions.

—I think we understand the complexities more than men. We are less concerned with what men think of us and with our own importance, and want to do what is fair and just, and to get things done.

—Yes, of course. You think we are all thieves and murderers.

—Men want to do what will serve them, and their pocketbooks, best. I suppose there are some men who care about the good of others before themselves, but they are rare indeed.

—Like that Blackwell man.

—You're familiar with the cause? Is Dorcas part of it?

—I'm not sure if she attends meetings, but I know she sympathizes with them. It's all over the papers how the easterners are coming out here to give talks on the amendment. It is a tactical error by Governor Routt. People don't take kindly to outsiders telling them what to do.

—Unfortunately, being an Englishwoman, no one will want to hear my take on women's suffrage.

—If England had given women the vote, they might.

—There goes my idea of riding my horse through the mountains, saying goodbye to its glorious beauty, and stumping for suffrage along the way.

—You are welcome to come with me on my tour.

—Another proposition?

—This one is purely professional. You can act as my secretary, as Dorcas would have. Are you well enough to come? It will be two weeks, at least.

—I am fully supplied with hashish and laudanum.

—I thought your tobacco smelled funny.

—Why would you want me along?

—I like arguing with you.

I laughed. —Well, I imagine we would do plenty of that.

—There is one condition.

—Yes?

—No stumping.

—Agreed.

Saturday, August 11, 1877
Poudre River Ranch, Colorado

I feel a little taken in. Callum told me this morning over breakfast that guests would be arriving today and he would be having a dinner party tonight. When I said I didn't have anything to wear, he smiled and said he'd taken the liberty of bringing a dress for me and that it would be in my room when I finished breakfast.

It is a shocking red dress with a fitted bodice and a straight skirt with a small bustle in the back. Black lace trims the three-quarter sleeves and frames the small opal buttons that run down the center of the bodice. I suppose I should be thankful the neckline is modest, but everything else about the dress is horrid, like nothing I would ever wear. Zhu Li came into the room, sewing kit in hand, and told me she would alter it however I wanted. There wasn't much hope that I would like the dress no matter what she did, but I had her remove all the lace, making it nominally less offensive. The dress fit me perfectly, a fact I didn't examine too closely.

Callum left to help round up cattle while I was working with Zhu Li, which suited me perfectly. It gave us a chance to catch up without fear of being interrupted. It has been three years since I saw Zhu Li, and she hadn't changed a bit. She still wore a beige linen tunic and pants and her hair in a long ponytail down her back. She still covered her mouth when she giggled, to hide her crooked teeth. Her eyes still crinkled when she laughed, and she talked to herself under her breath in Mandarin as she worked.

Jehu had brought her home from Denver about six months after Thomas died, and she had immediately taken over our kitchen. It never ran so well before or since, even though Joanie learned a lot about organization and timing a dinner at Zhu Li's elbow. In an effort to beat me by attrition, Colonel Connolly had enticed Zhu Li to work for him for double what she made with me, which was still well below what she was worth. The women who stayed with us worked for room and board and a little Saturday spending money, so it hadn't taken much for the colonel to lure her away. We didn't blame her in the slightest; a woman alone had to look out for herself and her own financial well-being.

When she finished pinning my dress I asked after the man she had been seeing three years ago, and with a beaming expression she told me they were married and that he was Bohai. No children, and she said they would most likely not come, that she was too old to have children. It shocked me. I'd never known how old she was, but her smooth face and dark hair made it difficult to believe she was past the childbearing age. She didn't ask after my family, knowing that my answer would have been much the same as it had been the last time I saw her.

I told her that I would be writing letters at Callum's desk. She told me to come to her if I needed anything at all and went into the kitchen, where Bohai and another man were sweating over a worktable and stove, getting ready for the dinner.

I closed the door without latching it and went to the desk. This had been the objective: Callum's office. In the absence of being able to break into his Denver office, I hoped to be able to parse enough information about his businesses from correspondence here to know which were the best to hit. I'd never dreamed he would ask me to go on his business tour with him. I suppose I should thank whatever poor, starving man mugged Dorcas two nights ago for this great stroke of luck. But it didn't hurt to do a little snooping when I had the chance.

I found a piece of paper and pen and started a letter to give a sheen of truth to my lie in case I was caught. I looked out the window and saw the cowboys busy in the corral, went to the door and listened and heard only the faint sounds of the cooks.

A stack of letters revealed negotiations for investment in a smelter near Oro City, a letter from a marble miner trying to gin up interest for a mine in the Crystal River Valley, an update on mining operations in the Sweetwater area of Wyoming, a raunchy love letter from a woman named Daisy accompanied by a racy photo. She was rather pretty, but she surely must be a whore. A respectable woman, even a mistress, wouldn't have such a photo taken. I flipped it over and saw a familiar mark denoting the photographer, though no name. I shook my head. Looked like Rosemond had expanded her portraiture business. I hoped she kept Newt out of it.

These letters, while interesting, did nothing to further my purpose. The bottom desk drawer was closed and locked but was easy enough to open with the letter opener. I grinned and pulled out a ledger. I flipped through it and discovered it was merely the accounts for the ranch. I ran my finger down the details of their horse operation. The army was a big client, which was no surprise. I swore under my breath when I saw the profit line. The Connollys were reaping the benefits of the ranch I'd started, the herd I'd nurtured and bred into the horses they were selling the army, and others, at a pretty penny. Goddammit.

I stared out the office window, not seeing what was in front of me, seething with the injustice of it all. I had never understood why the colonel had been so hell-bent on destroying me. We weren't in direct competition, so why couldn't we have coexisted, helped each other out? It could only be pride and greed that had driven the colonel. Two of the seven deadly sins, three if you count what he did to me as wrath, and I do. I take some comfort in knowing that the colonel is burning in hell, but not much.

I need to get out of this house.

Saturday, August 11, 1877 cont

I am dressed in this red monstrosity and have a half hour before dinner to put down the events of the remainder of the day. I hope the dinner will be dull and end early so I can go to bed. Pain ramps up in the evening.

This afternoon I changed into my habit and went to the barn. I retrieved my horse (whom I have decided to name Storm after his dark-gray coat) from his stall and tied him to a ring fastened to the wall outside the tack room.

—Can I help you?

I jumped and turned. A cowboy stood in the door, bright light framing his silhouette and casting his face into darkness. Fear pulsed through me.

—I'm sorry, I was looking for brushes.

—Miss Margaret? Is it really you?

The cowboy removed his hat and moved closer. I could see that he was young, no more than twenty, I guessed. He wore khaki pants and a denim work shirt with a red bandanna knotted around his neck. His fair hair was flattened against his head, and he had deep brown eyes framed with dark eyelashes. The memory of a small, shy boy clinging to his mother's leg came into my mind.

—Ezekiel?

His face flushed red with pleasure and he stammered out, —You remember me?

—Of course I do.

He and his mother, Lana Barnes, had been the first people Jehu had brought home with him. I told her she was welcome to stay as long as she needed if she pulled her weight. She and Zeke had stayed for six months, enough time for her to heal from her outer wounds, as well as her inner ones. She'd answered an ad in the paper for a housekeeper at a boardinghouse in Golden and had gotten the job. When she and Zeke left, Lana asked if she could tell others about the ranch. I said of course, there would always be room for those in need. In addition to the women Jehu rescued, our ranch became something of an underground railroad for women who wanted to escape abusive, drunken husbands, controlling pimps or madams, or, sometimes, overbearing families.

—It's so good to see you, Zeke. How is your mother?

—Good. She and her husband live in Black Hawk. They own a boardinghouse.

—Does she? That's wonderful.

—It's all thanks to you.

—Oh, Zeke. No. Your mother was a wonderful woman. Smart and strong. I had no doubt when you left that she would do well. Look at you, all grown up, and a cowboy, just like you wanted.

—Yes, ma'am. I came back here in '75, looking for you and Mr. Thomas and Jehu.

—You came here for us?

—Yes, ma'am. I wanted to thank you, maybe see if you would take me on.

—I sure would have.

—I was right angry when I learned what happened to you. I didn't know the details when I took the job, I want you to know that.

—That's very sweet to say, Zeke.

—It's the truth. If the old man hadn't died right before I got here, I would have killed him myself.

—Oh, Zeke, no.

The boy's expression had an intensity, and his voice took on an urgency, that caught me off guard, but made my heart swell with emotion.

—Miss Margaret, you don't understand. I don't think my ma ever told you the whole story about us.

She hadn't told me anything, and I hadn't asked. It wasn't my place to pry into people's business, into what had brought them to us. Lana Barnes's cuts, bruises, and skittishness told a story well enough.

—Y'all saved us. We'd have been dead for years now if it wasn't for Jehu buying me an ice cream. And then you and Mr. Thomas treating us so nice. My ma does the same now, you know. Helps people in need like you did. She married a good man who's plumb happy to let her boss him around.

Emotion clogged my throat, but I laughed. Lana *had* been a little bossy, once she got used to us.

—That's so wonderful to hear, Zeke. Tell her I am happy for her.

—You should go see her. She would love it.

I smiled, swallowed the lump in my throat.

—I might just do that. But right now, I want to go for a ride.

—I've got something for you.

He went to the back corner of the tack room and pulled a cloth off a saddle horse. There, bright and shiny as new, was my husband Thomas's English saddle.

I gasped. —Zeke.

After the colonel stole the ranch from me, and we went through what little money we had, the first things we sold were our horses and tack. We had the idea to make a go of it in a town, thinking there would be more opportunities available for us. There were, of course, but nothing that any of us wanted to do for a living. When Spooner took us to Timberline, we kitted up with western saddles and mountain ponies. No one wanted a horse broken with an English saddle, and there wasn't enough time to ride for pleasure.

—I found this ole pancake back here in the corner all dusty and cobwebby when I was cleaning out the tack room. I knew it must have been yours. It took me a while to get the leather supple again, lots of soap, a little bit of linseed oil, and it's good as new. Want me to saddle your horse with it?

—Yes. You think he'll take it?

—Sure thing. Broke him myself. He can be ridden without a saddle or bridle.

—Jehu would be proud of you.

—How is Jehu? Is he with you?

I told him Jehu was doing fine and tried to tell him as much as possible about our life without revealing too much. When he finished I thanked him and asked him for a favor.

—Anything.

—Don't let anyone know you know me, especially Callum. And keep what I've told you to yourself.

Zeke nodded.

—Whatever you say, Miss Margaret. Don't forget to go visit my ma. Anything you need, anything at all, she can help.

I put my foot into his cupped hands and he boosted me on Storm's back. The horse danced a little, as eager to let loose as I was.

—He's a fiesty one, but he's got a sensitive mouth, so…Zeke stopped and blushed, realizing whom he was giving advice to. I thanked him anyway and with a nod, I trotted Storm out of the back of the barn toward a stagecoach trail up beyond the first row of foothills. Storm summited the hill easily. We turned right, and I gave the horse his head, toward Colonel Connolly's ranch.

Though I don't need another reason to want this beautiful horse, when I'm riding I forget the pain in my stomach, which is growing more insistent with each passing day. I'm weaker, as well, and it is taking all of my mental acuity to hide the depth of my sickness from everyone: Callum, Hattie, Grace. I'm thankful I have planning the heists to occupy my mind, otherwise I would be curled into a ball in bed. When I'm busy, I'm distracted, and if I don't think about the pain, it recedes. The challenge then becomes fatigue. I can either have less pain and be tired, or rest and be in pain. I'll take the former, thank you very much.

I wonder if I will survive the trip with Callum. I imagine that if there's an issue with a business, he'll extend his trip. Do I want to die in a strange hotel, away from those I love, with a man I'm ambivalent about as the only witness to my last moments on earth?

I don't want to die in bed, that I know for certain. I watched Thomas waste away, fully aware that he was wasting away. It was a humiliating and shameful way for a man, once so strong and full of vigor, to leave the world. When I think of Thomas, I think of him as a living cadaver in our bed, the sheets folded across his chest, his arms thin and spindly outside the blanket and next to his body. I want to be remembered as healthy, vibrant, clever, resilient, and most importantly, selfless. Asking my family to watch me die would be cruel, and I hope I've never been that.

If it wouldn't be a betrayal to my family, to the bond I have with Hattie, Jehu, and the sisters, I would ride off on my own, south to the Grand Canyon, find a ledge to sit on, watch the sun rise and set, see firsthand the brilliant colors I've heard so much about, and fade away. With a large bottle of laudanum and whisky, of course. I don't want to die in pain if I can help it. But surrounded by beauty? That's the way to go.

Maybe I should have a gun on the ledge with me, too.

I reined up, dismounted Storm, and tied him to a scrubby tree. I clambered up a small rocky rise, sat down heavily on the outcropping, and looked down upon the colonel's ranch in the distance. I let my mind wander to Zeke and his mother and the dozens of other women and children and the few men who came through our ranch. A few had kept in touch, written us letters letting us know where they ended up, what they were doing. Others left and we never heard from them again. I wish I could say that helping people became a mission of mine, a calling (though by now, Grace, you know I don't believe in God), but it was simply the right thing to do. Thomas and I didn't have much, though I could see how someone might think we did, looking at our tidy little horse ranch on the Poudre River. But turning away people who asked for help was never considered. Thomas and I never discussed it, though he would joke about Jehu bringing home strays.

Zeke's compliments and effusive thanks embarrassed me, if you want to know the truth of it. I hardly deserve credit for changing their lives when I offered them room and board in return for an honest day's work. I'm glad to hear about Lana's happiness and success, and Zeke has turned into a dab hand at breaking horses if Storm is any indication.

I unbuttoned my vest, lay back on the rock, covered my face with my hat, and listened—to the insects buzzing nearby, the *pit-er-wick* and *hoodle-hoodle* calls of birds in the trees high above, the wind rustling the leaves, the shush of brush disturbed by an animal. Peace and quiet. Only the sound of a bubbling brook would make the moment more perfect.

I felt the lump in my abdomen and wondered if I hadn't made a mistake in not going east and having an operation. Or at least going to Denver and having another doctor examine me. But there hadn't been any pain at that point, and part of me hadn't believed there would be any pain in the end. I felt great, after all. Life went on, we did another job, had horses to break, a ranch to run, winter to survive. By the time it started hurting I figured it was too late. I didn't want to take the chance I wouldn't return from Chicago. So I've been going about the process of tidying up the last few months, making sure that Jehu, Hattie,

Joan, and Stella know everything they need to know, that they are prepared for a time when I won't be around. They are. In fact, I've started to feel a little superfluous and wonder what I contribute to the ranch at all. I see my last days spread out in front of me, sitting by the fire, a Navajo blanket on my lap, being waited on by everyone, the dog at my feet looking up at me with sad brown eyes. The stagecoach job was a welcome distraction, one last hurrah before Margaret Parker faded into history. Then you had to tempt me with immortality, and the idea of fading away, already anathema to me, became unbearable.

I suppose I should thank Jed Spooner, the bastard, for throwing down this bet and giving me a reason to live. I haven't told Hattie yet, but I don't intend to return to Timberline. I haven't quite figured out how I'm going to slip away from her, or you, Grace, but I am. I said my goodbyes before I left the Hole.

If our mark is big enough, the take will set them up for years, and I can die knowing they are taken care of. That's why I have to go with Callum on this tour, to find the best target, the most lucrative one, the one where we are least likely to get caught. Maybe there's one. Maybe there's five. Maybe it's as simple as robbing the safe in his Denver office. In three weeks I'll know.

I dozed for a while, and when I woke up the sun was just above the foothills. I had no idea what time dinner was, or when the guests would be arriving. Luckily, I had a fast horse who was well rested. I could be at my ranch in thirty minutes or less.

I grimaced against the pain as I rose and took a few deep breaths. Sweat beaded on my upper lip and was dried by the wind almost immediately. Down below, to the north of the colonel's house, cowboys were driving a large herd of fat cattle toward the ranch, bringing them in from summer grazing to be sold to the army, or shipped off to the meatpacking plants in the East. A thin stream of smoke rose from the house, and near the barns cowboys readied the corrals for the herd. I noticed for the first time that Connolly had fenced in the pasture near the house. I suspected it was Callum's doing, since the last time I'd been at this spot, observing the house, the fence hadn't been there.

No, this wasn't my first time back, Grace. I'm not sure if I trust you with that story yet.

Three men walked out of the back of the house. It was too far away to make out their faces, but the glint from Callum's metal mask flashed in my eyes. I'd been around long enough to recognize the stance of one of the men as that of a cowboy or rustler. The other was rotund and most likely a businessman. I imagine I will meet them at dinner. Hours of talking to businessmen, or listening to them talk about business. It won't occur to them to ask for my opinion. Little do they know I will give it to them anyways.

Sunday, August 12, 1877 (midnight)

I feel like a Christmas goose right now, stuffed past the point of propriety. Zhu Li helped me out of my dress and took it away (I wonder if to keep it handy for the next woman Callum brings to his house), and I'm sitting at the small writing table, in my loose shift, writing this. The wind has picked up outside, and the house is creaking in response. There is a full moon as well. Perfect conditions for a midnight job. I've got the fever to do a job. I'm not sure I can wait until October first.

As much as I didn't want to participate, as much as Callum sprang the dinner on me last minute, it was possibly one of the most enjoyable dinner parties I've ever been to. Granted, I haven't been to many since I left England, and even then I was young and not expected, or able, to participate in "real" conversation. So, thinking on it, saying this was the best dinner party of my life is rather faint praise. It does make me wonder what I've missed. How many dinners like these would I have attended if I'd married the colonel. Probably countless, but I doubt the colonel would have let me speak as freely as his son did tonight, or enjoyed the spectacle of conflicting opinions as much as Callum did.

First the actors. Governor John Routt and his wife, Eliza; Nathaniel P. Hill, a gold smelter; Lewis and Dorothy Wilson, dry goods proprietors with stores in Cheyenne, Denver, and Golden, and a contract with the military for sutler stores; Callum's lawyer, Alexander Bisson, and his companion, Evangeline White. Bisson was an unwelcome surprise; he had been the colonel's lawyer as well, and had done his bidding, namely going to every bank within fifty miles and threatening them with retribution if they lent me money to keep my Poudre River ranch going.

Callum must have warned Bisson I would be in attendance, at least. Bisson greeted me as an old friend. I told him he'd gotten fat. His companion, pleasantly plump and pretty and obviously being paid for her time, covered her smile by looking away. Bisson's face froze in a ridiculous grin before sliding into a frown.

—I hear you're dying.

—We're all dying, Alex. I just have a better notion of the date.

Callum intervened and ushered me away. I chastised him for not warning me about Bisson.

—I didn't make the connection you two would know each other.

—Liar. He knows I'm sick, you must have discussed me.

Callum's eyes narrowed slightly, and he dipped his head in a semblance of contrition, saying he hadn't realized we had an antagonistic relationship.

I laughed, then dropped my voice so the others wouldn't overhear.

—We are having dinner in what was *my* house, the house my husband and I built together, and you didn't think I would have an antagonistic relationship with the lawyer who helped steal it from me? I am not stupid, Callum. I don't know what game you're playing, but know this: I'm not easily manipulated.

—Neither am I.

Callum pulled out the chair at the end of the table, where the hostess would sit.

—Do me the honor, he said in a low voice.

I looked down the table and realized all of the places were assigned, and the men were waiting for me to be seated. I had little choice, so I sat down, and his hands lingered on my shoulders. He put his masked face close to mine and whispered that he had known red would be my color. I shivered, not in pleasure.

Bisson glared at me, and I pointedly looked at his stomach, which touched the edge of the table. Evangeline White raised her eyebrows and glanced between Callum and me with a knowing expression, and I realized she thought I was Callum's lover. He sat at the other end of the table and smiled around at his guests, looking relaxed and in charge. He leaned forward to listen to something Eliza Routt said and laughed, his blue eyes almost sparkling. He was in high spirits, and I wondered why.

It didn't take long to realize he was in his element. He was charming and engaging, and he put all his guests at ease by talking on a variety of subjects, subjects the women could discuss as well as the men. We were barely into the soup course when the subject of suffrage was brought up. Apparently the governor is a supporter, his wife is heavily involved in the cause, and he had arranged for the East Coast suffragists to tour Colorado promoting it.

—You have school suffrage, which is perfectly adequate. Child rearing is the purview of women, so of course they should have their voices heard on education, Lewis Wilson said.

—You approve of women running for the school boards, then? Eliza Routt said.

—Heavens, no. Leadership is the purview of men.

I asked why he thought men were better leaders than women.

—It is the natural order of things, of course. Men have the mental capacity for complicated issues and make decisions based on facts and not emotions.

—That's ridiculous, Eliza Routt said.

—We have a perfect example of the failure of women's leadership and business acumen sitting at this table, Bisson said, looking directly at me.

—Women need capital to run a business, same as men. It is difficult to do when banks are strong-armed into not lending to you, I said.

—That's why I own a bank, Callum said, and he turned the conversation to Nathaniel Hill's smelter.

Hill enthusiastically took over the conversation and talked of his plans to expand to other towns, wandering into a tangent about how he'd gone to Wales to work with the miners and perfect their process for Colorado gold. We were well into the main course by the time he finished explaining, in painstaking detail, how it worked. He was a scientist who had at least had the business acumen to open his own smelter instead of working for someone else, though I imagined the pitch of an investment opportunity would come Callum's way when the men had retired to drink whisky and smoke cigars.

The governor didn't seem to want anything from Callum, but instead was eager to do for Callum, one of the largest investors in the state.

—I can assure you, reining in the crime in this state is my administration's top priority. There are difficulties, of course, with policing the central areas, let alone the remote ones.

—As my client is well aware, Bisson said.

—Yes, I heard you were robbed again, Connolly. I've upped security at my smelter as a precaution. How much did they get? Hill asked.

—Eight thousand.

There were gasps around the table. I did my best to look shocked as well.

—Callum, I had no idea, I said.

—I would imagine not, just returning to town as you did.

—I thought you'd hired Pinkerton to take care of it, Hill said.

Yes, and I am in the process of turning her outlaw. I hid my smile of pleasure behind my wineglass.

—I did, and he protected the wrong shipment. The gang is a clever bunch.

My ears perked up at that. *He*? Who is Grace working for if not Callum?

—How many times have you been robbed? Evangeline asked.

—And by the same group? Eliza Routt said.

—Four times. I'm not sure it's the same gang. The descriptions of the bandits change every time. They do appear to be targeting my businesses exclusively.

—You are one of the biggest investors in Colorado, and I suppose the risk goes with the territory, I said.

—You could be right.

—What is Pinkerton doing now? Hill asked.

—He has sent his best agent to infiltrate the gang.

—Sounds a good idea, Governor Routt said.

—I've heard rumors they're a female gang. Is that right? Evangeline said.

The men scoffed, all talking about how ridiculous an idea it was. Except Callum. He was watching me while the others talked over each other about how women were more moral, lacked the intelligence, the mental capacity, the courage, and John and Eliza Routt defended women's intelligence, but didn't approve of criminal activity no matter the sex.

—Margaret, you're quiet.

—As are you.

—What do you think of the idea that the gang is female, pretending to be men?

—What does it matter if it's women or men? You are still being robbed.

—True. I just thought you might have an insight into the possibility since, of the people surrounding this table, you are the only one who has befriended an outlaw.

I glanced at Evangeline, who had taken a keen interest in cutting her steak. I wouldn't be surprised if she's serviced an outlaw or two in her time, maybe even Spooner. She was his type: voluptuous, blonde, and willing.

—Are you asking me if I think women have the intelligence and cunning to be outlaws?

—Yes.

—Of course they do.

—They would never get away with it, with the way women like to talk so, Hill said.

I found that a highly ironic statement coming from the man who'd spent almost two courses talking without pause. By her chuckle, Evangeline did, too.

—That's unfair. I know plenty of women who keep their own counsel. I doubt it because of the immorality of it, Dorothy Wilson said.

—Stealing is stealing. Why should it be more amoral, more shocking, for one sex to do it than the other? I asked.

—It's not in women's nature, Hill said.

—Precisely, Dorothy Wilson said.

—I assure you, human nature is the same for women and men. Men can love with the same depth women do, and women can hate with the same intensity as men.

—But women would never do such a thing. It wouldn't cross their minds, Dorothy Wilson said.

—You don't know of one woman who would *admit* to it. Think of the women who steal to feed their families. Is there a difference between a woman and a man who steal bread, or fruit, or money, if the purpose—taking care of their family—is the same?

—There is not, Eliza Routt said.

—So why should there be a difference if a female outlaw gang steals from a larger…target than a bakery or fruit stand? If their goal is the same as men's, then the morality behind it is equal.

—I don't even understand what you're saying, Dorothy Wilson said.

—You think women should be held to the same moral standard as men, not a higher one, Callum said.

—Why are women held to higher standards, except to let men have their vices without guilt? I asked.

—You don't give our sex much credit for goodness, do you?

—To those who deserve credit for goodness I will.

I thought of Luke here, wondered what he was doing, and almost lost the thread of the conversation.

—Equality for men and women is what you want?

Wilson and Bisson laughed long and hard, as did Dorothy Wilson. Evangeline and Eliza watched with expectation, the governor with consternation, as if it suddenly occurred to him that the cause wouldn't end with suffrage, that women would continue to agitate for more rights. Callum watched me with level eyes, waiting for my answer. I understood his implication well enough; equality in credit meant equality in punishment. It was a trap and I refused to be caught.

—I fear we will have to wait decades for that to come to fruition. And I was talking in generalities about women. We aren't given enough credit for our intelligence, and too much credit for our morals. Evangeline, what do you think?

—Oh, I…uh…

—Jed Spooner is taking credit for the robberies. Tell me, Mrs. Parker, you knew Jed Spooner once, does that sound like something he would do? Callum asked.

—Rob you? Yes.

Everyone around the table laughed.

—It's almost as if he has a vendetta against me.

—I wouldn't know anything about that.

—How did you know Jed Spooner? the governor asked.

—My husband hired him on at our ranch, and they became friends, after a fashion. Jed would come and go, and he always had fantastical stories to tell on his return. We didn't believe half of what he said. To answer your question without being glib, Callum, do I think Jed would go back to a well over and over that had been so fruitful? Yes.

—I can't believe you harbored an outlaw, Eliza Routt said.

—We didn't know he was an outlaw at first. Jed bought our horses, and brought us business, and had become our friend by the time we discovered it. So we looked the other way. As far as I know, he has always eschewed violence. I assure you, if that were not the case, we wouldn't have offered him sanctuary.

—What is Spooner's goal? To feed his family? Callum asked. Our eyes were locked, and I knew he was playing with me.

—Because he wasn't good at anything else. He rode with Jesse James, did you know that?

—I did not.

—He left because James can't seem to let go of the war, and he is violent. Spooner avoids violence wherever he can. He outlaws because it's fun, and he's good at it. Sometimes there's a purpose; he robbed a bank once to get the money to pay a lawyer to get one of his men out of jail.

—Why not just break him out?

—Maybe he's a coward? Maybe he was afraid to get caught? Maybe it was in Montana Territory, where he made an agreement to never set foot again on threat of hanging. I don't remember. It was all a long time ago.

—Maybe Mrs. Parker can help you find him, Callum, Hill said.

I laughed and told them I'd been out of the territory for years and hadn't spoken with Jed Spooner since I left.

—I imagine Spooner was disappointed to see you leave, Bisson said.

—Why is that, Alex?

—He stayed on at your ranch after your husband died.

—And he left a good year before your boss stole it. So what are you implying, exactly?

—Maybe if he'd stayed on you wouldn't have lost your ranch.

I laughed long and hard.

—Jed is a terrible businessman. Why do you think he's an outlaw? Are you sure that's what you were implying? That I would miss Jed's...business skills? Or were you implying he was my lover, Mr. Bisson?

—Mrs. Parker, I think you've dominated the conversation long enough, Lewis Wilson said.

—Yes, what's for dessert? his wife asked.

I was angry now, and I wasn't going to let this man insult me with insinuations. I wanted to shock the group, and why not? The hit my reputation would take would be short-lived.

God, Grace, dying is so freeing.

More to the point, I was ready for this dinner to end.

—You aren't going to answer, Alex?

—You're embarrassing yourself.

—Very likely. But you see, I don't care. That's the freedom of knowing you have little time to live.

—What? Evangeline said.

—I have cancer, Evangeline. Please don't pity me. I'm not afraid of dying, and I'm obviously not afraid of not being "respectable" by calling Alex out for the... subtext in his conversation. Since I'll never see any of you again, I'll answer: yes, Spooner was my lover. It was one of the reasons I turned down the colonel's marriage proposal. I couldn't very well have a lover on the side, and I wasn't quite ready to give Spooner up. By the time Spooner left, I'd insulted the colonel too much to go back on my rejection. I didn't want to marry him anyways. After Spooner... Well, I'll leave it to your imagination.

—You are a harlot, Lewis Wilson said.

—Mr. Wilson, your opinion matters not at all to me.

—What about your reputation? Eliza asked.

—I'll be beyond caring soon enough. Now, if you don't mind. I tire easily these days and must beg to be excused.

Callum nodded his head and said of course I could be excused.

—Thank you. It was a delicious dinner, and I hope I was adequate entertainment, which I believe it was my role to play. Good night.

So here I am. In my room, unable to sleep. The pain comes in waves, and since we are leaving tomorrow I don't want to take too much laudanum. I am going for a smoke and will have to get dressed in case the men are still awake talking, drinking whisky, and smoking.

August 12, 1877 cont (2:00 a.m.)

My heart is racing and my hand is shaking after the encounter I had with Callum. I'm almost certain he suspects me. I need to get the events down in case…

I'd planned to smoke the cigarette outside on the back porch, maybe nick a sugar cube from the kitchen to take to Storm, and if the house was quiet when I was done, do a little more snooping in the office.

I found Callum sitting in front of the fire. He turned his head slightly when he heard my footsteps and said he hoped he hadn't woken me. I demurred, said I've been having trouble sleeping for weeks. He was solicitous about my pain, said he had something I could take if I liked.

I showed him my cigarette, lit it with a punk from the fireplace and leaned against the mantel. His mask was balanced on his knee. His face was in shadow.

—I was going to smoke this on the porch. Would you like to join me?

—Would you like a whisky?

—I never turn down good whisky.

—I didn't say it was good.

—I never turn down bad whisky, either.

—Go on out. I'll bring you one. Grab my coat off the hook there. The temperature has dropped thirty degrees.

In the short moments before he came outside, I allowed myself to inhale the cold night air, to help it reinvigorate me. I looked at the night sky full of stars and marveled at how beautiful it was, and how small and insignificant I was. My problems. My goals. My death.

Callum handed me the whisky, keeping the injured side of his face turned away from me, but I noticed he didn't wear his mask. I thanked him and we drank in somewhat companionable silence for a few minutes. He spoke first.

—Did you enjoy dinner?

—It was delicious.

—That isn't what I meant, and you know it.

—Did I embarrass you?

—No. I've never enjoyed anything more than Bisson being put in his place. He's a terrible hypocrite, a gluttonous man with appetites that exceed his reach.

—Why do you keep him around?

—He has no scruples, and he's loyal as a dog.

Zhu Li brought a coat for Callum and helped him get into it. Callum said thank you in Chinese, and she bowed and left, but not without a quick questioning glance in my direction.

—You know Mandarin?

—That's the only phrase I know, Callum said.

—Zhu Li taught me a few phrases when she lived with us.

—Why didn't she leave with you?

—Your father hired her at his ranch a few months before my husband died.

—I have been trying to figure out why you turned down my father's offer of marriage.

—Because most women would jump at the opportunity to be taken care of by a wealthy husband?

—Yes.

I smoked for a bit before answering.

—My husband was a wonderful man, but the success of our operation was down to me and Hattie and Jehu. Of course our neighbors believed he was the brains behind the outfit, and it was easier for me to go along with the ruse. Why encourage people to be suspicious of me, of the type of woman I was…?

—Intelligent?

—Men don't particularly like intelligent women. Neither do women, for that matter. Or at least they don't like it when you show it. It's our great secret, you know? That we are smarter than you.

—I didn't know that.

—Your father did. He knew I was in charge. If he would have come to me with a proposal of a partnership instead of a marriage, I would have agreed. I might have even eventually agreed to marry him. I liked your father very much. Admired him, even. I didn't love him, and I never would have. But in the years since, I've imagined a scenario where we were partners in business, family, marriage. We might have been unstoppable. Your father didn't want a partner, he wanted a wife. Funny thing was, I realized after my husband died that I'd never particularly liked that role. It is very restrictive. Duplicitous.

—Because you pretended you were less than you were?

—Yes.

—What about Spooner? Did he respect you for your mind?

I heard the sneer in his voice.

—Heavens no. That was purely physical.

—You are an astonishing woman.

—You say that as if it's not a compliment.

—It isn't. Do you know where Spooner is?

—I told you…

—Yes, I know. I thought he might have told you places he liked to hide, when he was telling you and your husband stories.

—Most of the time he would merely go into an adjoining state since the sheriffs didn't have jurisdiction. He didn't hide so much as blend in. They would use different names, get jobs on ranches, like ours, until the money ran out. Honestly, the outlaws were the best workers.

—Did you harbor more than Spooner's gang?

—We didn't ask questions.

Callum chuckled.

—No wonder my father wanted to marry you.

—Are you propositioning me again?

—No.

—I would be the best kind of wife to have. You'd be rid of me in record time.

He hummed a response and looked at me full on. The moonlight lit up the scarred side of his face and I saw it for the first time. His entire cheek and part of his lips were scarred from burns. The scars were a silvery white and stretched across his face, pulling the side of his mouth into a constant smirk. I didn't look away, though.

—If I asked you into my bed, would you come?

—Is that why you asked me to travel with you?

—Yes. I want to have what my father couldn't.

—I do like your honesty. I wondered if you would try to seduce me again.

—I'm not seducing you.

—Yes, I know. It seems very transactional on your part. A power play. Much like your father's marriage proposal. If you'd taken a different approach, we might be in your bedroom by now.

—I don't need your permission.

—I suppose not. You are stronger than I. But know this: I will kill you if you do.

We stared daggers at each other for what felt like an eternity. Finally he smiled and chuckled.

—I suppose I'll try a softer touch next time.

He shifted away from me and sipped his whisky.

—Why did you come, Duchess? And do not lie to me and say it was to see my ranch. You could have ridden here and seen what you wanted without ever talking to the foreman, without them even knowing you were here.

—Curiosity. I wanted to see what had been done, if there was even a trace of my hard work left. Imagine my surprise when I saw my herd expanded and healthy.

—You didn't need my permission for that.

—I was curious about you, also. Your reaction, first to my confession, then to my request. I wondered if you were a better man than your father.

He turned back to me.

—And what have you decided?

I looked up at him for a long moment, not shying away from his deformity, and lied.

—A much better man.

—Dorcas thinks you are the head of the gang that's been stealing from me these last two years.

—I have to say I'm flattered.

—To be suspected of being an outlaw?

—From what everyone says, this gang is brilliant. But there is no proof they are women. Only rumors, which everyone dismisses as ridiculous.

—Yes, ridiculous. But you made a very convincing case that women are capable of being as immoral as men.

—Of course they are. That doesn't mean I am.

—You did just threaten to kill me.

—Because you threatened to rape me. I believe I would be justified. Though I also know I would swing if I killed you. Of course, if you raped me, I would be blamed for that as well. I wouldn't be killed, just shunted off to the county hospital with all of the other inconvenient women.

He gently touched my cheek, and for a brief moment I thought he might kiss me. I hoped my revulsion didn't show in my expression.

—I don't make the rules, Duchess.

—But you benefit from them nonetheless.

He leaned toward me.

—And I will do everything I can to protect and enforce them. He kissed me on the cheek and whispered, —Sleep well. We leave for Cheyenne after breakfast.

Before I could catch my breath, he was gone.

There is no doubt in my mind that he suspects I'm behind the heists. I cannot sleep tonight; I suspect he might make good on his threat. Regardless, there will be Pinkertons waiting for me somewhere along the line. Cheyenne, most like, since our biggest job against him was in Wyoming. No question about jurisdiction there.

Now, Grace, I must—

16

Margaret Parker's Journal

Thursday, August 23, 1877
Black Hawk, Colorado

Garet,

I am writing this in your journal because Hattie is reading mine. Technically she's reading case notes. Or they are supposed to be. They turned personal soon after I met you, as soon as Jehu delivered my trunk to me at the ranch. The number of sighs and harrumphs from Hattie has decreased as she's read further along. I hope that means my storytelling is riveting. I need it to be to tell your story.

You are sleeping upstairs, Hattie is reading, and there is a very real chance she will kill me when she finishes. So I decided to take this time to update your journal since so much of what has happened did so while you were absent, delirious, or unconscious. I suppose you won't mind, since you want a clear telling of your story.

Where to start? Do I start when you and Hattie arrived in Denver, and the argument between us all about your plan to approach Callum Connolly? You seem to have elided that event. (Yes, I've read your journal to this point, and was interested to see a very different perspective of our acquaintance from mine.) Should I go back further in the story and retell my version of events? Or do I honor your desire to tell your own story and leave the recollection as it is, such as it is? Or do I start from when you left on your trip with Callum Connolly, catch your journal up as you surely would have done after we met and discussed everything?

Though I doubt highly I would have been a part of the conversation, since neither you nor Hattie trusts me completely.

I can't say that your instincts are wrong, only that mine have been.

I will start with the here and now and go where the muse takes me from there.

A man knocked on the door of Hattie's room two days ago, introducing himself as Frank Chambers. He told us you were at his boardinghouse, beat to hell, broken collarbone, and sick and in pain, going in and out of consciousness. Hattie, ever suspicious, asked how we were to know he was telling the truth.

"She told me to say, 'The Legend of Hattie LaCour.'"

Hattie grasped the back of a chair and nodded.

"She said that'd mean something to you."

"It's a private joke."

Since Hattie was shaken, I quizzed Chambers pretty thoroughly, and though he didn't know exactly how you made it to Black Hawk, his wife, Lana, knew you from years back. The doctor staying at their boardinghouse—part of the suffrage group traveling around—was set to operate on you. In one of your rare moments of lucidness, you asked for Frank Chambers to find and bring Hattie back. I said we'd go, of course we'd go.

Chambers would fetch us in the morning and take us to Black Hawk. Since time was short, he promised to rent us two horses and tack so we could travel the thirty-five miles more quickly than in a wagon.

Hattie was quiet when Chambers left. I asked her if she knew this Lana woman and she said she didn't, but that she was probably one of the women you'd helped before Hattie found the ranch. I asked her if there was anything I could do for her, anything she needed. She shook her head no and thanked me. I made her promise to wait to leave until the morning. She smiled sadly and asked, "How'd you know?"

"Because it's precisely what I want to do."

"It's too dark, and we don't know the road. I'll stay."

Neither of us got much sleep.

The next morning, we received a letter from Rebecca Reynolds. If Hattie doesn't kill me, I'll copy it into your journal. Loose documents so often get lost over time. The gist is that Spooner has taken over the ranch, most likely deflowered Joan, and has no intention of leaving the Hole to make good on the bet. I theorize that his plan all along was to get you out of the Hole and set you up to be caught. It would be an easy thing to do since Salter, the man you hired on at the ranch, is a Pinkerton agent, though Spooner didn't know that when he made the bet.

I know, I know. I should have told you all weeks ago. By not warning you, I've put you in danger. I am to blame for you being in this bed. I take full responsibility. But I truly thought I could protect you. I didn't count on Spooner's duplicity.

I guess I'm not as good a detective as I think I am.

PART THREE

THE PINKERTON

Monday, April 30, 1877
Chicago, IL

Dear Mr. Pinkerton,

I am tendering my resignation from the Pinkerton National Detective Agency, effective immediately.

I will forever be in your debt for trusting me with your female detectives after Kate Warne's sudden death, may she rest in peace. On the whole, I have enjoyed my time as part of your organization and have always cherished the respect you have given me and my girls, treating us as, if not quite equals, at least women worthy of being listened to and taken seriously.

As per our last conversation, there seems very little room for a woman of my skills in an agency that is increasingly becoming known for strong-arm tactics and bullying instead of honest investigations. Not all poor people are criminals, and all rich people are not saints.

Yours sincerely,
Claire Hamilton

17

Claire Hamilton's Case Notes

Tuesday, May 8, 1877
Chicago, Illinois

Tomorrow I leave for Colorado, my next great adventure and the most challenging one I've set for myself. It is strange, embarking on this investigation on my own. Though I've always worked alone, the safety of having an organization behind me, supporting me, was more comforting than I ever realized. The financial support was nice, as well. I estimate I have the funds to survive for three months. It is critical I convince Callum Connolly to hire me if I am to have any chance of starting an agency in my own right.

Thursday, May 10, 1877
Cheyenne, Wyoming

Twenty-four hours on a train is a miserable experience. No one tells you that when they tout the speed and ease of traveling across the country. From what I gather, the trip across the plains is the easy part. My train now leaves for San Francisco and will have to travel through, over, and around the mountains to get there. The description of the Dale Creek bridge west of Cheyenne is enough to make me never want to go one step farther west.

Only a few more hours until I arrive in Denver. I pray there is a soft bed waiting for me somewhere.

Tomorrow I go to Connolly Enterprises' Denver office to state my case to Callum Connolly.

Friday, May 11, 1877
Platte River Boarding House
Denver, Colorado

After a wonderful night's sleep and a hearty breakfast, I made my way down Colfax Avenue to Connolly Enterprises. A woman in half mourning, with salt-and-pepper hair pulled back into a tight bun, sat behind the desk in the main office. Her name is Dorcas Connolly and she is the sister of the late Colonel Connolly and the aunt to Callum Connolly. She was cordial, but stiff and professional, as if she thought, apparently without irony, it was quite out of the ordinary for a woman to be conducting business. I asked her what her role in the family business was, and she had the grace to blush, if ever so slightly. She informed me that Callum was out of town, in Columbia checking on their mine, most likely working it, if Dorcas knew her nephew. She offered to make me an appointment for when he returned, though she wasn't sure when that would be. Callum tends to be single-minded when he is doing something he loves, and he loves mining, she said.

I asked about the possibility of me traveling to Columbia and received her full attention. She looked me up and down as if a new idea of my objective had been revealed. What is so pressing you want to travel by stage through rough country to talk to my nephew? I laughed and assured her my interest was purely in business, which seemed to offend her as well. There didn't seem to be any winning with the woman. So I decided to take her into my confidence.

On my request to talk privately, she ushered me into Callum's office and shut the door. I sat down without being asked, hoping to prompt her to sit behind the desk, which she did. She rubbed her hands on the desk with an expression of longing before remembering herself and shuttering her face with a bland, businesslike mien.

My plan had been to make the same case to Callum Connolly I'd made to Allan Pinkerton: a female operative was much more likely to infiltrate a female gang than a male, and I'd been trained by Kate Warne, the best undercover detective Pinkerton had ever hired, male or female. It was a straightforward and logical argument, which typically worked on men.

Pinkerton had laughed, saying that infiltrating wasn't the goal. It took months, maybe years, to infiltrate a gang, to gain their trust. The client wanted the job done quickly, and Pinkerton had his best agent in Cheyenne available. I knew who Pinkerton's "best" was, a reprehensible, violent man named Salter whom Pinkerton had bailed out of scrapes, usually involving dead women, many times. But Salter got results for our clients, which I'd come to realize was all Pinkerton cared about. Salter was the last detective to send after a group of women, and I pleaded with Pinkerton to reconsider and to send, if not me, at least a different male detective. He refused, and I resigned.

When I saw Dorcas Connolly's expression, I knew straightforwardness and logic would need to be paired with a little manipulation.

I told her I was a detective, there to infiltrate the female gang terrorizing Connolly Enterprises and bring them to justice. "Mr. Pinkerton changed his mind, then? Or has he sent two detectives for the job?"

"No, he did not. I am here of my own accord."

"If my nephew has already hired someone from your company, why would he hire you?"

"Because I am a woman."

She laughed. "You don't know my nephew."

"I beg to differ." I pulled a file out of my case, opened it, and read its contents to Dorcas: her nephew's birth date, where he was born, when his mother died, his engagement to a southern belle, his estrangement from his father and his injury in the war, the severing of the engagement, years spent mining in South America, learning of his father's death and returning to run the business.

"All very well and good, Miss Hamilton, but you do not know Callum's temperament, and he would never hire a woman to do a man's job."

"Yet you sit in his front office."

"I'm family."

"Oh, you have an equal say in the running of his empire? No surprise, since the company flourished under your short tenure leading it after the colonel died. Congratulations, and I apologize."

Dorcas's nostrils flared and she told me Callum ran the business and she assisted him when asked.

I returned my file to my case and rose, but not to leave. I walked around to the map of Colorado on the wall. I asked if the pins were the locations of his businesses, and Dorcas said they were. I recited the holdups I'd copied from the agency file before I left.

"Late spring 1875, a stage carrying the payroll for the Sweetwater mine in Wyoming was held up by masked bandits between Rock Springs and South Pass City. October 1875, a Connolly bank was robbed in Golden in the middle of the night. No one saw the bandits, so everyone assumed it was men. May 1876, Connolly Enterprises' mining office in Silverton was robbed by two white women. Fall 1876, the Breckenridge branch of Bank of the Rockies was robbed by two white women and a black woman. In each instance, they claimed they were part of the Spooner Gang."

"You've done your homework."

"Of course. Are there any more?"

"No."

"The dates are consistent, which means..."

"They're going to strike again, most likely this month," Dorcas said.

"Has anyone been injured?"

"No."

"Is there anything connecting the two masked robberies with the ones with the women?"

"The dates. The lack of violence. The efficiency."

"Efficiency? Interesting word choice."

"You live in the West long enough, you hear and read about robberies and outlaws weekly, at the very least. They're nearly always caught; do you know why?"

"Why?"

"They can't resist bragging. This gang does a job and disappears for months. Not a word. Does that sound like men to you?" Dorcas asked.

I had to grin. "No, it does not."

"If you don't work for Pinkerton, why are you here, Miss Hamilton?"

"Are men ever asked why they do the jobs they do? No, but for women there always has to be a reason. Here is my reason, Miss Connolly: I'm good at my job, and I love it. These women are criminals, and I want to catch them. I want to start my own agency and need an independent investigation, a successful one, to do so."

"Pinkerton won't give you a recommendation?"

"My work was unassailable, but our personalities weren't always compatible. I think he kept me around mainly because Kate Warne was my best friend, my mentor, and he didn't want to lose that connection. He wanted to have someone to talk to about her. To reminisce. She was a calming force on him, a moral compass if you will. I never had that amount of sway." *Because I wasn't sleeping with him*, I thought.

"You're hired."

"Excuse me?"

"I'm hiring you. Callum has his man for the job, I have my woman. I can pay you out of my own pocket."

"I accept, of course, but now I must ask you why, Miss Connolly."

"Imagine the headlines, Miss Hamilton, if a female detective catches a female gang, and on the eve of the vote for suffrage in Colorado. I think it would help the cause, don't you? Showing female competence in a man's profession?"

She'd hired me, so I agreed with her, but thought it more likely that the sight of a woman with four other women in chains might do more to defeat the amendment than help it.

There were two possible targets for the outlaws to hit: an eastbound train carrying a safe full of gold, the other a stage from Cañon City carrying the first payroll of the season to the Columbia miners. Callum was counting on the train to be the more enticing target, as it was what he would rob—why take a risk if the reward wasn't large enough?—and had the train loaded with guns for hire. Dorcas disagreed, but her entreaties had been dismissed until Callum finally agreed to have his new clerk travel with the stage for extra protection. I told her I would bring my gun, as well, and asked her to tell me everything she knew of the gang's previous heists. We spent the next hour discussing my plan.

As the payroll isn't scheduled to leave for a week, I have time to settle in to Denver, look around the town, and get my bearings. Tomorrow I will go to the newspaper offices and read their dispatches on the robberies.

COLORADO WEEKLY CHIEFTAIN

FRIDAY, MAY 14, 1875

MASKED OUTLAWS ROB STAGE BETWEEN ROCK SPRINGS AND SOUTH PASS CITY

Four masked bandits robbed the stage carrying the payroll for Connolly Enterprises' Sweetwater mine on Thursday last. The whole event took five minutes, including looting the safe box and unhitching the team from the stage. The driver balked at doing it, but the bandits threatened to kill the horses, even though the outlaw said he was trying to help them out, as finding a new team would be a damn sight easier than removing four dead draft horses from the road. The driver saw the logic, and he and the guard did as told.

The outlaws were polite and efficient and said very little. They were all slight of build, which led the victims to believe they were young men, possibly not past their twentieth year. They took $7,000 from the strongbox but did not loot the passengers' possessions, or ask them to empty their pockets. Harvey Quartermaine, who has had the unfortunate luck to be present at four robberies, (two trains and now two stages), said it was the most pleasant experience of the bunch.

The bandits rode off in four directions and used the rough terrain around the area to escape. A supply wagon happened along about twenty minutes later and took those it had room for on to South Pass City. By the time the robbery was reported to the mining office, the bandits had a four-hour head start. Darkness and a heavy thunderstorm meant the posse couldn't chase until the next day. By the time the sun rose, the posse had been called off, owning to lack of will as well as the sure knowledge any sign of the retreating bandits would have been washed away in the storm.

GOLDEN WEEKLY GLOBE

TUESDAY, NOVEMBER 2, 1875

MIDNIGHT ROBBERY

BANK OF THE ROCKIES

$10,000 IN CASH AND BONDS TAKEN

NO CLUES OR SUSPECTS

Sometime after midnight on Thursday, October 28, outlaws entered the Golden branch of the Bank of the Rockies through the back door, cracked the safe and walked out with $10,000 in cash and bonds. No one saw them enter or leave, and they left the bank in pristine condition, so the robbery wasn't discovered until the bank manager, Edwin Kiester, opened the bank at ten o'clock Monday morning.

With no clues, witnesses or suspects, speculation is running high as to which outlaw gang might be responsible. Because of the skill and lack of force in opening the safe, it's considered a good bet that Hank "Ought-Not" Henry was the culprit. Henry rides with Jed Spooner and his gang and is thought by many to be Spooner's second in command. The heist has the typical Spooner Gang hallmarks: no violence, efficiency and a large take.

Pug McDougall, who used to ride with Angus King, says Spooner's gang beat it down to Mexico last June after coming close to being caught by Sheriff Cooper and the Cheyenne posse, who were on the chase after the robbery of the Union Pacific office.

Callum Connolly, son of the late Colonel Louis Connolly, was in Golden when the robbery took place. This reporter happened to be standing in the lobby of the bank, waiting to speak with Mr. Kiester, and through a closed door heard Mr. Connolly dress down his bank manager. The younger Connolly slammed the door when he left the office, shattering the glass and leaving poor Edwin Kiester, a good, honest Christian man, shaking from head to toe.

Mr. Connolly didn't respond to questions about a reward for the capture of the bandits. When one is issued, you can be sure to find it in this broadsheet.

LA PLATA MINER

WEDNESDAY, MAY 24, 1876

OUTLAWS TARGET CONNOLLY BUSINESS IN SILVERTON

THIRD ROBBERY IN LAST 18 MONTHS

Two men robbed the Connolly Mine office in Silverton on Friday, May 19, the third Connolly business theft in 18 months.

The men walked in and politely asked for their pay. The manager, Edgar Agnew, didn't recognize the miners and asked them for their names to check against the register. The men pulled out their guns and said that was all the name they needed. It was lunchtime, and Agnew was in the office by himself, and his gun was out of reach. No matter, as the younger man confiscated his gun before Agnew could take a breath. There was nothing for it but to acquiesce to the villains' demands. The leader tied Agnew up and closed him up in the storage room, looted the cash box and left.

Agnew's assistant returned and released him, and they went directly to the sheriff to report it. The town was filling up with miners coming down from the hills for the weekend, and a large supply train had just rolled in from Ouray. The chaos of the influx of people allowed the two bandits to vanish without a trace.

ROCKY MOUNTAIN NEWS

THURSDAY, NOVEMBER 2, 1876

"THE SPOONER GANG SENDS THEIR REGARDS"

CONNOLLY BUSINESS HIT AGAIN!

FOURTH ROBBERY IN TWO YEARS

PINKERTONS BEING CALLED IN

The Breckenridge branch of the Bank of the Rockies was robbed by three men in masks last Friday night, October 27, The men came in at the end of the business day when only the bank manager, Wesley Loren, and his clerk, Josiah Smith, were closing up. Two bandits easily subdued the men, tied them to chairs and shoved kerchiefs in their mouths while the third cracked the safe with a stethoscope. They got away with $13,000 in cash, gold coins and bonds.

The gang used the festive air in the town due to the opening of two new saloons and the competing shows of beautiful dance hall girls as cover for their flight out of town.

As they left the bank, the leader told the bound men to tell Callum Connolly "the Spooner Gang sends their regards."

This is the fourth time in less than two years that outlaws have robbed a Connolly business, but the first time that the Spooner Gang has specifically taken credit for it. Each job has been pulled off with little fanfare and no violence, hallmarks of Spooner's gang. Though Spooner is an efficient crook, he tends to go for more showy displays of his banditry skill, such as the train robbery near the Dale Creek bridge in Wyoming. Rumors have swirled that Spooner is south in Mexico and that this gang is a new group using Spooner's name to hide their identities. Another possibility that has been floated by former outlaws is that this gang consists of members who didn't want to go south and are trying a different type of banditry. Whatever the case, these bandits have been successful enough and have angered Callum Connolly enough that he is hiring Pinkertons to run them to ground.

18

Claire Hamilton's Case Notes

Saturday, May 19, 1877
Platte River Boarding House, Denver, Colorado

There are days on this job when you walk for miles, talking to dozens of people, and seem to make no progress, and feel less informed, and more confused, than you were when you started, until you realize the lack of information is the biggest clue of all. Today was one of those days.

It turns out, this female gang is a figment of my overwrought female imagination. I went to the three major daily newspapers and the smaller weekly ones and found no mention of them in their pages. Dorcas was correct in that there are numerous stories of robberies, some large, most small, but the only crimes women seem to be guilty of are hysteria, prostitution, drunkenness, and stealing food for their children. One woman stabbed her husband and was sent to the county hospital for her trouble. There are lots of articles on both sides of the suffrage amendment, with "against" getting the loudest voice and the best placement. There is talk of a coming silver boom in the area near Oro City in California Gulch.

To a man, the editors from large and small newspapers looked at me as if I were mentally unsound when I asked about the female gang terrorizing Connolly Enterprises. Outrageous.

Preposterous. Women don't have the mettle to be outlaws. Or the intelligence. Too emotional. Besides, what man would let his woman go and do such a thing? Besides, women don't think that way. The fairer sex is too upstanding and moral. The ones who aren't are sent to mental hospitals, where they belong.

At first I was perplexed, then I was angry, but by the end of the day *I'd* started to believe I was mentally unsound.

That's when I knew the gang was real.

Regardless of what transpires, of how this case turns out, I've decided to settle in Denver. An impulsive decision? Possibly. But the air is invigorating, the skies are a beautiful blue, the weather is outstanding, and the snowcapped mountains in the distance are awe-inspiring. Denver is a large town and growing more and more every day. I feel at home here in a way I never did in Chicago. Tonight I'm attending a meeting of the Colorado Woman Suffrage Association. Tomorrow I leave for Colorado Springs and on to Pueblo, where I will catch a stage to Cañon City. It is a good thing I enjoy traveling, because I will not see Denver again for at least two weeks.

I have purchased a traveling outfit with Dorcas's advance on expenses. They are easily the nicest togs I've ever owned. If I'm going to pull off the ruse of a rich travel writer, I need to look the part.

Sunday, May 20, 1877
Colorado Springs, Colorado

A man was shot and killed not five feet from me today. I'm ashamed to say I fainted dead away. I came to in a bed with a tired-looking woman wearing a linen shift that left nothing to the imagination pouring whisky down my throat. When I sat up and looked around, I discovered I was surrounded by similarly clad women staring at me with a range of expressions, the most dominant one being impatience. I realized I was in a whorehouse and that I was interrupting the only time of the day they had to relax and sleep. I tried to stand, but stumbled. The woman who had given me whisky told me I'd hit my head and that I should sit down.

"Fell face-first, you did. Never seen a woman faint like that."

I touched my forehead and felt the bump square in the center and discovered a headache behind my eyes.

"Don't worry, we sent for the doc."

I told her I didn't want to trouble her, and one of the younger girls said, "Too late for that." The woman shooed everyone out of the room, telling them to get some sleep, as it was a Sunday. When we were alone, I asked if Sunday was a busy night.

"Every night is busy. What's your name?"

I decided taking an alias would be wise, so if I crossed paths with Salter, Pinkerton's agent, he wouldn't recognize my name. "Grace Trumbull."

"What're you doing out here alone?"

"How do you know I'm alone?"

"Haven't asked for me to fetch anyone, have you?"

I attribute my mistake to my light-headedness. "What is your name, and where am I?"

"My name is Sally Dove, and you're in the Dove's Nest."

"And you are a house of assignation?"

"We're a whorehouse, if that's what you mean."

"Yes, indeed. Did you know the man who was killed?"

Sally Dove shrugged. "We see lots of men. Very few are memorable."

"I suppose you hear lots of news. Gossip."

"Most of it's lies."

"I read about a new silver seam being found somewhere in the mountains?"

"That's real. Probably head out there soon, change of scenery. Men are free with the coin when they think it'll never play out. Always does, though. That's why you get there early and get out."

My head was starting to throb, and I wanted to lie down in my hotel bed instead of this one, so I decided I couldn't be subtle in my information gathering. "I'm out here traveling. To write a book about what I see and whom I meet. May I mention our interaction?"

"No skin off my nose."

"I wondered if you might be able to help me, since you hear so much in your line of work. I overheard a man on the train talking to his companion about a gang of outlaws."

"Colorado is lousy with outlaws. Pay good after a job, though."

"But this gang is unique. They're women. Have you heard of them?"

"Why didn't you ask the man?"

"I did, and he clammed up."

Sally Dove's shift slipped off her shoulder, exposing a breast with a large pink nipple. I looked away, felt my face flush and my heartbeat throb in my temple.

"Not surprised. They only talk of them when they're drunk."

"They are real?"

"Yep. Said to be part of the Spooner Gang, but I don't believe it. I've bedded Jed Spooner, and he's more respectful than most, but he's a man, and I ain't never met one who would stand for a woman showing him up for two years."

"He doesn't know?"

"Last anyone heard of Jed, he was heading south, away from the law in Utah. That was two years ago. My guess is news hasn't traveled to Mexico yet, but when it does, he'll scamper back."

I glanced at Sally Dove, hoping she'd made herself decent. She hadn't, and when I lifted my eyes to her face, it wasn't tiredness that I saw. She moved close to me. Touched the bump on my head with gentle fingers. She offered to make me feel better.

"Do you have any idea who they are?"

"No."

"Where they go between jobs?"

"No."

"How many of them there are?"

"You aren't writing a book, are you?"

"No."

"I tell you what. I'll ask around for you. You come back through and visit me again, and I'll tell you what I know."

Monday, May 21, 1877
Pueblo, Colorado

Spent a sleepless night with a pounding headache, and decided to use the time to write a different journal, one that will show me to be what I claim, a travel writer. Will hide this one in the false bottom of my trunk.

Tuesday, May 22, 1877
Cañon City, Colorado

I have visited the papers in Colorado Springs, Pueblo, and Cañon City, receiving the same answers as in Denver. Never heard of a female gang. Not in women's nature. It's little wonder these women have been so successful, as no one believes they exist.

I admit to being fascinated by them. What drove them to steal? Are they hard, uneducated women? Or are they respectable women doing these things on a lark? What do they do with the money? Where do they hide? In plain sight? A schoolteacher? A widow? A group of whores? They cannot be married. I can't imagine a husband who would willingly let his wife put herself in danger and provide for the family. Unless, of course, he had been severely wounded in a mining accident and otherwise they would starve.

There I am, letting my imagination run away with me. But it is a game I have played since I was a child, imagining strangers' lives. It was a quiet game I could play while looking out the window of our house. Quietness was critical to the peace of our house, critical to making sure I wasn't on the receiving end of my mother's ire, as were obedience and hard work. Curiosity about others is what led me to detective work. Some might call it being too nosy for my own good. Regardless, it has made me successful at my profession.

The idea of being a travel writer was an in-the-moment inspiration, but the more I think on it, the more I like the idea. Why not tell the story of my time in Colorado, much as Isabella Bird did in 1871? I suspect this journal will become a little more florid as a result. It is a case report in name only.

The stage ride from Pueblo was rather miserable. Six people jammed into a small space, three of whom hadn't bathed in what smelled like quite a while. One man, named Benjamin Adamson, I soon discovered is the clerk Connolly sent to add extra protection to the payroll. I was taken aback that Connolly would think this nervous little man would offer any sort of security to so important a load. A little subtle prodding and questioning and I soon learned Adamson and Connolly had never met, that Adamson was traveling to his new post almost directly from Iowa. I didn't doubt it; he had the look of a harried traveler too long on the road. Poor man looked ready to burst into tears at any moment.

The stage for Gunnison, then on to Ouray, Silverton, and finally Columbia leaves at eight a.m. I do hope it isn't as crowded as today's. I hear that it is difficult going from here on out. I hope Adamson can hold himself together.

Saturday, June 16, 1877
Heresy Ranch
Timberline, Colorado

I've never been so happy to see a traveling trunk in my life as I was when mine was hauled into the ranch house. I didn't have time to properly think of what it meant to have all my clothes and new gloves and this secreted journal back because I was so stunned to see Jehu, the stage driver, walk through the door. In all our weeks together, Garet and Hattie hadn't mentioned him or his name once. A piece of the puzzle fell into place as to how these women who lived so remotely were able to target specific lucrative jobs. Jehu was their scout. Being a teamster, he traveled all over the state, hearing all sorts of gossip. Driving a stage, he would know better than anyone when valuable cargo would be on board. He's a sweet man. I wonder if he realizes the danger he has put himself in.

Since my last entry there is so much to relate, to put down, I hardly know where to start. I don't feel entirely safe writing in this journal. Garet stole my fake journal and took it upon herself to read it. It was meant to be read; this one is not. My entries will have to be short, and I will go in chronological order, though it's all I can do not to detail the events of last night at the Blue Diamond Saloon first.

There are four members of the gang, five if you count Jehu. Margaret Parker is the leader, a British lady, of all things, though she rarely lets her British accent slip. She is of average height and beauty, with a rather long face and dark hair, but she has a certain charisma that draws people to her. She drew me in rather quickly—on the stage, in fact—and I have to watch myself to make sure I don't fall further under her spell. I keep reminding myself she is a criminal, and apprehending her is the key to my future, my independence.

Hattie LaCour, former slave and Buffalo Soldier, is the second in command (though they both claim they are equals, and Garet does show more deference to the Negress than I've ever seen from a white woman). She is quite beautiful, with smooth bronze skin that seems to darken and lighten depending on what she's wearing. Dark freckles are scattered across her nose like tiny stars in the sky, and she has full lips. I've never thought of lips as beautiful before, but Hattie LaCour's lips are beautiful, and quite mesmerizing as a result.

Hattie takes on different personas depending on the situation; she robbed the stage as a cigar-smoking, ignorant former slave wearing men's clothes, but her true self is a well-spoken, possibly educated, and cunning woman. She wears brightly colored turbans and moves with an enviable grace. Hattie doesn't trust me one bit, and I don't trust her, either, but I have to respect her love of her family, the protective streak that is what I believe fuels her distrust of me. Of course her skepticism is warranted, which means she has the gift of discernment. I'll have to be careful around her.

Two sisters, Stella and Joan Elbee, round out the group. Stella and Joan are uneducated and ignorant, though Joan is uncommonly pretty. Stella is a mean son of a bitch who wears a poncho and a sombrero and hates everyone but her makeshift family. All three older women have a tendency to pamper Joan, to treat the young woman as if she's a child. She uses that against them, and, surprisingly, they don't appear to realize, or if they do, to care. Joan is sly and used to getting what she wants.

I met Margaret (who goes by Garet), Stella, and Joan as we waited for the stagecoach to leave Cañon City. They gave fake names, which means four of the five people in the stage were pretending to be someone else. Garet was a consumptive widow, Joan and Stella were sisters going to meet their father at a mining town, and I had kept my story of being a travel writer. They gave nothing away about who they were or what their purpose was. Even now, thinking back on our conversation in the stage, I can't point to one thing they did or said that raised my suspicions. I assumed the outlaws would ride up somewhere along the route, not have planted three people inside the stage to increase their odds. If Hattie had been in the stage, I might have figured it out earlier. They are incredibly disciplined, and it was illustrated perfectly when they held the stage up.

Garet feigned a coughing fit, and I was eager to help her. She had told me previously she had medicine in her trunk, but she'd hoped she wouldn't have to use it. I had the driver stop and get her trunk down. She insisted on finding it herself, and I thought nothing of it. She played me brilliantly. She had befriended me on the journey, taking my side in an argument with Adamson about suffrage, sitting by the river with me at our extended stop for lunch, drawing me out without revealing anything of herself. If she weren't an outlaw, she would make an excellent detective.

When she pulled the gun on me I realized that this was the best possible outcome for me, having met and made a connection with Garet before the robbery, so I eagerly did everything she asked. There had always been a large hole in my plan, namely how to infiltrate the gang, or how at the very least to follow them and discover where they holed up. Especially since I had run into roadblocks everywhere I asked for information (except from Sally Dove, but I couldn't rely on a man being killed in front of me to get me into the door of every whorehouse in the mountains). Garet befriended me to manipulate me, but she gave me the in to her gang I would have never had otherwise. When she started to ride off, I asked her to take me with her, so that I could write about them in my book. "No one believes you're real; I can change that."

It turns out Garet is more like male outlaws than she wants to admit. She wants to brag about her exploits, too. It's just that no one wants to listen.

Sunday, June 17, 1877 (sometime after midnight)
Heresy Ranch
Timberline, Colorado

Jehu and Hattie are a couple. It's highly unlikely they are married since she's a Negress and he's white, but that doesn't stop them from loudly enjoying marital relations. There was yelling earlier, but I don't think it was related to...well, you know. They seem a passionate couple.

My bed is a pallet in the main room by the fire. It is the most uncomfortable thing I've ever slept on. Garet offered to share her bed, but I demurred. I wanted the opportunity to write late into the night and try to catch up with everything that's happened. I won't get a bit of sleep.

When I asked Garet to take me with her from the stage, she took me with little hesitation. We rode up the mountains to a small cabin, where Stella, Joan, and Hattie were waiting for Garet with a change of horses. They were all surprised to see me. Hattie was livid. I've learned since that Stella doesn't like anyone. It was easy to tell that of the other women, it was Hattie I had to win over, and I did it in a very unexpected way: by standing up to her.

It took us a week to ride to their ranch at Timberline, and I was sick as a dog during the entire ride. It's called mountain sickness, and I thought I was going to die. But I couldn't show weakness, or slow them down any more than I already was. The threat of a posse being on our tail was ever present. Garet was accommodating, if not necessarily nurturing. I think she regretted bringing me along, which broke my heart a little. I admire her more than I should, since she is my adversary and my goal is to bring her to justice. As her story and Hattie, Stella, and Joan's stories come out in dribs and drabs, I find myself marveling at their resilience, their determination to survive. I expected to find greed and arrogance at the root of their outlawing, but have found the opposite. They give away much of their money to the struggling residents of Timberline, and in return the town is their safe haven from the law. Garet's desire for the world to know what they've done has less to do with arrogance than with the injustice that women are always overlooked, shoved into the margins of history, or erased altogether.

I was so ill I slept most of the first few days back at the ranch. When I awoke I discovered Garet had gone to the mountains. It was her way, to disappear for a couple of weeks after a job, have time alone. Which meant I was left with Hattie, which would give me the perfect opportunity to befriend her, to glean as much information as possible. Hattie wasn't having any of it; she put me to work and had Stella in charge of me.

I have always been terrified of horses, a fear I had to quickly overcome on our seven-day ride to the ranch. I'd hoped to be done with riding when we arrived, so imagine my surprise when I discovered these women own a horse ranch in an area they call Brown's Hole. They round up wild mustangs and train them. They trade and sell them to rustlers, cowboys (one and the same most times, it turns out), outlaws, miners and anyone else who happens to accidentally stumble into Brown's Hole. Which means I'm surrounded by the beasts and can't do anything but pretend to like them and try to get better at riding. I think they would forgive me anything but disliking horses.

That is wishful thinking, of course. Hattie said she would kill me if I'm lying to them, which I'll admit gave me pause. In the course of my investigations, it's the first time I've been directly threatened. I have no doubt that Hattie means it or that she has killed before. It's in her nature. There is something cold and unforgiving in her eyes, at least when they're turned in my direction. She does smile and laugh, and when she does the sound is beautiful. Then she will notice me laughing with her and the humor will leave her face. I considered running away, but I am trapped here. I can't ride out, and I don't have the money to pay anyone to take me out. Not that anyone would. The gang is this town's bread and butter.

While Garet was gone, the only one who was forthcoming with information was Joan, and she swore me to secrecy. I told her that if I wanted to provide a full accounting of the gang I would have to include their background in the book. She agreed, but said the printed word didn't matter since Stella couldn't read. I couldn't let on to anyone, especially Stella, that she'd told me how they came to be there. I agreed, and she told me a story so brutal that I almost didn't believe her.

She and Stella are from Nebraska, the daughters of a cruel sodbuster and a sickly, overworked mother. There were six children, but only an older brother and the two girls made it out of the cradle. Their mother died ten years ago, of overwork Joan said, when Stella was thirteen and Joan seven. Being the oldest, Stella took over their dead mom's responsibilities. Joan helped where she could, but even at that age, Stella was protective of her sister.

"I was too young to understand what my father was doing to my sister every night. On the days my father would leave the farm, my brother would do the same. The first baby lived for three weeks. The second for four. I didn't realize what was happening until I saw Stella holding the third upside down in a barrel of water."

I clutched my throat, trying to massage the rising bile down so I could hear the rest of the story.

"Stella went to the local midwife, and I don't know what she gave her, but she didn't get pregnant again. Papa didn't like that. He needed children to help on the farm. Judah, our brother, had become a man and was itching to leave. Papa couldn't run the farm on his own. Stella and I tried to keep my bleeding from them, and we did for a time. But we couldn't hide my buds. Stella tried to keep me in her sight at all times, but she couldn't. I couldn't disobey my father, and when he told me to help him in the barn, we both knew what was going to happen. I followed, and Stella said, 'Don't worry.'

"He'd unbuttoned his pants and was pulling out his thing when I saw Stella behind him. She raised the ax at her side and killed him with one stroke. He fell forward onto me, the ax sticking up out of his head. Blood was everywhere, and he was twitching like a dead snake. Stella dragged Papa off me by the ax handle, told me to look out for Judah, and dragged him to the back of the barn out of sight. I heard five or six more thumps before she returned, blood splattered all over her and dripping from the blade. She told me to change and go get Judah, to tell him there'd been a terrible accident. To run into the barn and get out of the way, quick. I was shaking from head to toe, knowing what she'd done and was she was going to do. She slapped some sense into me and said unless I wanted Judah to kill her, and to do to me what Papa had done to her, I needed to do exactly what she said. So I did."

Joan told me all of this in a calm voice while kneading a loaf of bread. I was...speechless. How do you respond to a story like that? I was horrified, though I know that I'm no better. I understand what it is like to be pushed past your limit.

The sisters ran, of course. Stella had been putting back money for a while, knowing it would eventually come to this. They only had enough money to make it to Rock Springs, which is where Jehu found them begging for money to make it to San Francisco. He took them to Garet and Hattie at the Poudre River Ranch, their first ranch on the front range near Fort Collins, and they took them in.

I asked if Garet's husband was alive when they arrived, and she said yes, though he was a lunger and died that winter. Joan wasn't clear on the year or specific date Thomas died, only that he spent most of his time in bed and Garet and Hattie spent most of their time nursing him.

"They did that, taking people in, especially women. Somehow word got out that the Poudre River Ranch was a safe place for women and outlaws." Joan's eyes lit up at that. "Jed Spooner and his gang, a few others I never knew the name of. They'd come and trade horses, sometimes hole up in the cave in the foothills at the edge of the ranch; other times they'd stay out in the open as cowboys. They didn't talk about their exploits, at least not in front of me and Stella, so we could say with truthfulness that we only knew this one and that one as cowhands.

They overpaid for the horses, so as to pay for the food that we'd feed them while they were there."

"You know a lot about the workings for a young girl."

She looked sly. "I was small and could hide easy to listen without being noticed." She leaned close to me, though we were the only ones in the kitchen. "Garet and Jed took up together the very night they planted Thomas in the ground. Out behind the barn. Against the wall. Didn't even..."

"Stop. I don't want to hear it."

Hattie walked in, so I didn't have time to ponder the knowing look Joan gave me.

When Garet returned to the ranch from her hunt she was in a high dudgeon, ranting and raving and damning men to hell. When she settled down, she told us that Jed Spooner was back in Timberline. I couldn't believe my luck. My success would be assured if I could bring Jed Spooner *and* Margaret Parker in. While I was planning for my big moment, Hattie was quizzing Garet about how she knew, since she went in the opposite way of town when she left. She blushed and said Luke Rhodes told her. Then she started cursing again, this time about manipulative men, and I knew that she and Rhodes were romantically involved.

I met Rhodes briefly when Stella and I went to the blacksmith to have her knife sharpened. He's a short, bowlegged cowboy with a magnificent mustache and a craggy brown face. I suppose he's handsome, if you like your men rough-hewn. He was polite, and his eyes were good-humored. He was a rustler in former days, until he broke his leg in a stampede and decided he'd never much liked cows anyways. He was elected sheriff because no one else was qualified and there wasn't much sheriffing to do in a town as remote as Timberline. He mostly farms, but Hattie says he helps on the ranch when they drive a new herd of mustangs home every summer.

There's one law in Timberline: no killing. He doesn't mind if outlaws use it for a safe haven, but if they're running from a killing, Rhodes will mete out the justice himself. He's only had to do it once, so the story goes. Garet's gang doesn't go in for violence, Stella pistol-whipping Benjamin Adamson notwithstanding. Adamson was staring at Joan in an inappropriate way. I was glad he got a little punishment for it.

My hand is hurting, but there's so much more to tell and so much I have left out. But I cannot go on. Tomorrow night I will tell the story of the events at the Blue Diamond.

Sunday, June 17, 1877 cont

My head had barely hit the pillows before the rooster crowed and Jehu was up making coffee. He greeted me and apologized for waking me and for me having to sleep on the floor, saying one of the sisters would give up her bed that night. I demurred, though my back popped and creaked when I stood and stretched. Luckily Jehu didn't hear it. Garet came into the room braiding her long hair and wearing jodhpurs and riding boots, looking and sounding every bit the Englishwoman, telling Jehu she'd offered half of her bed to me.

"I didn't want to impose."

"Are you a rough sleeper, Grace?"

"No, I..." I felt myself blushing and was thankful the light in the room was dim. "I do have a tendency to kick. Or I used to. I haven't shared a bed in..." I cleared my throat. Why was I stammering like a fool? "This is fine." I folded the blankets and put them on top of my trunk, a hopeful extra layer of protection from prying eyes. I had faith in the false bottom, but didn't want to take a chance. After I placed the blanket on the trunk I realized my hands were bare. I shifted to shield my scarred hands from the other two and quickly retrieved a new pair of gloves from the trunk. My brown traveling gloves, sturdier than the cotton ones I put on, were coming apart. I would need to sew them tonight, alone, when I could do so with bare fingers.

When I turned around, Garet stood near me, holding out a mug of coffee. Her eyes stayed on mine, but my clean white gloves glowed in the semidarkness. I held her gaze and tried not to look guilty or mortified. My scars and my past were my own, and none of their business.

"I have a sturdier pair of gloves, for everyday work, if you would like to borrow them."

I swallowed the lump that had traitorously formed in my throat and croaked out a thank-you. Garet smiled and turned to Jehu. She offered to help him with the horses, and when I offered to help as well, they told me it would be faster if they did it themselves.

Through the kitchen window I watched them enter the barn, and I followed, leaving my coffee cup on the arm of one of the rocking chairs in the gallery.

I went around the side of the barn not visible from the house and stood next to one of the open windows. The horse in the stall nickered, and I shifted out of sight when I saw Garet throwing hay to it.

"I have to do it, Jehu."

"No, you don't. You want to do it."

"So what if I do? Bloody Jed Spooner."

"Garet."

"Don't Garet me. I'm dying, or have you forgotten?"

"No, I haven't forgotten. That's why this is foolishness."

"You weren't there. You didn't hear him humiliate me. Treat me like nothing more than a whore. That's all he's ever thought of me."

"I don't think that's true."

"Why are you defending him? You hate him."

"He lost face as a man, that's all."

"Oh, and I suppose you'd know all about that."

"Garet."

She paused. "I'm sorry."

"You're not yourself, Garet. First you kidnap that woman."

"She asked to come."

"You didn't have to bring her! You don't know anything about her!"

"She's going to tell our story."

"Yeah, Hattie told me. If I'm getting this straight, you'll be dead, and whatever that woman writes will lead the law to us. To Timberline. That sounds like a great idea."

Garet laughed. "There is no way she can find her way here. I've never met a more helpless woman when it comes to directions or riding or any sort of hard living. Anyways, I trust her for some reason."

"Hattie doesn't."

"Hatt doesn't trust anyone."

"I told her last night. About your cancer."

"I figured that's what all the yelling was about."

"You should have told her."

"Bloody hell, Jehu, you only know because you're an eavesdropper."

"How are you feeling?"

"Fine if I have my laudanum and hashish. Thank you for bringing me some."

"Welcome. Is it getting worse?"

"It's nothing I can't handle."

"Why do you want to go off and do a job instead of staying here, enjoying your days with us, with your horses? It doesn't make sense, Garet."

"No, I suppose it doesn't. The truth is, I feel most alive when we're pulling a job. I love it, even more than breaking horses. If I stay here, I feel like I'd be giving up on life, saying it's time to die. I'm not scared of dying, Jehu. I've got a lot of people waiting for me. I'm just not ready to do it yet."

They worked in silence for so long I wondered if they'd left the barn. I peeked through the window and saw slivers of them through the stall slats. Jehu finally answered. "OK."

"You'll do it with us?"

"No. I got it in my mind that was the last one, and it is for me. I'll stay here and watch the place. Hire a few cowboys to help me run it while you and Hattie go plan the job. I'm not leaving the Hole ever again for anything other than a supply trip to Rock Springs."

"Fair enough. Let's water these horses and go drink some coffee."

I scurried back to the house and settled into the rocking chair, taking up my mug and sipping it as if I'd been sitting there the whole time. I barely had time to register what I'd learned, that Garet was dying, when she walked across the yard and said, "I think I'll join you."

She returned with her mug and the pot of coffee. She freshened mine up, put the pot between our rockers, and sat down. "You hear all that?"

"I'm sorry?"

"I know you were eavesdropping."

"I didn't..."

"Look straight ahead."

I did, and from the rockers I could see Jehu clearly in the barn.

I dropped my chin to my chest and cursed myself. An amateur mistake.

"Why were you?"

"I'm nosy."

"That all?"

"If you want me to write your story, to tell the full story, you have to be more forthcoming with me and not be so suspicious when I ask questions. I'm not trying to pry. I want to get it right. Now more than ever."

Garet narrowed her eyes and chewed on the corner of her lip. "Don't pity me, Grace Trumbull."

"I would never."

"Are you going to help?"

"With what?"

"Our heist."

"You... you want me to help?"

"What better way for you to write about us than to be one of us?"

There is no way to describe what I felt at that moment, the conflicting emotions that pulled against each other. To admit my conflict, to put it down on paper, will give it power I can't afford. My answer, though, was never in doubt. Being brought into the fold completely was a good thing.

"I suppose that means I'm going to have to get better at riding."

"It does."

"I hate horses."

"I know." Garet patted the back of my gloved hand gently and stood. "But I can fix that."

Now, as promised, the events of the Blue Diamond on the night of June 15, 1877.

I'll confess I was anxious to meet Jed Spooner. What kind of man would Garet have relations with before her husband was cold in the ground? It seemed so out of character for her, though what I'm basing my opinion on I'm not sure. I imagine it's more a case of me not wanting her to be that kind of woman.

Even if Jed Spooner hadn't been an enticement, the novelty of going to town, drinking a pint of beer, and finally getting to listen to Opal play the accordion would have been exciting enough. Stella donned her serape and sombrero, checked her gun was loaded, and drove it into her holster. Hattie pulled out the outfit she wore when they robbed the stage—a hodgepodge of army clothes minus the army insignia, but instead of the kepi she wore her bright-red turban, but tied to the side in a more jaunty, celebratory style. There was an argument between Stella and Joan about Joan's dress, which looked demure enough to me. Hattie leaned in and told me in a low voice that it was always a good idea to wear pants to the Diamond, so as not to draw unwanted attention. "There's only two whores, you know."

I changed. Garet didn't, and neither did Joan. But they all wore guns. Garet buckled an extra holster around my waist and, with a warning that it was loaded, gave me my Peacemaker.

Hattie joked that it was a lot of gun for a blue belly. She was right, and I blushed.

"I'm not a very good shot. Would you teach me?"

Hattie chewed on the cigar she had in the corner of her mouth and studied me, her chin lifted. "Well, you took to riding good enough. Maybe you'll take to shooting."

"Want me to teach you to throw a knife?" Stella asked. "Ought to know more than one way to kill a man."

"I suppose, though I—"

"I'll teach you how to kill one with your cooking," Joan said. "Poisonous mushrooms, or berries, are usually the best.

Jehu won't bring us arsenic for some reason, so I have to make do."

The three women all looked at me with completely serious expressions. My mouth gaped, and I said, "Um, well, I really appreciate the..."

"They're teasing you," Garet said.

"Oh."

The three women started laughing.

"We had you going, though, didn't we?" Stella said.

"Yes, yes you did."

Stella came up to me and patted me on the shoulder. "I'll still teach you to throw a knife. And to use it up close. Might need to protect your virtue one day."

"Let's hope not."

Hattie, Stella, and Joan went out to get the horses ready. I was following them when Garet stopped me.

"They like you."

"Do they?"

"Can't you tell?"

"They still threaten to kill me on a daily basis."

"They won't do it now that I'm here." She threw her arm over my shoulder. "Now it's me you have to worry about."

"Funny."

We mounted our horses, who were prancing a bit more than made me comfortable. I placed my hand on Rebel's neck to calm him. Garet's horse high-stepped around, feeling the excitement that was clear in his expression and in his bright eyes.

"Come on. Let's go show those men what a real gang of outlaws looks like."

She kicked her horse and he reared slightly before lurching off. The other three whooped, spurred their horses and followed. I watched them race down the lane, my chest filling with a sense of freedom I've never felt before. I didn't have time to enjoy it; Rebel was too difficult to hold back, so I gave him his head, hung on for dear life, and prayed to God that I wouldn't kill myself trying to catch up.

It was amazing how different the Blue Diamond looked when full of people and music. It all died down when we walked in. I didn't need to be told that it was the arm of Spooner's chair that Ruby sat on. There was an air of power about him and he was handsome, quite possibly the handsomest man I've set eyes on to this point, and I maybe understood, a little, how easy it would be for a woman to fall under his spell.

Spooner stood and opened his arms to Garet, greeting her as Duchess. She went to him reluctantly (or did I want it to be?) and kissed him, leaning away from him as much as she could, as if she wanted it to be perfunctory. Spooner didn't, and soon the feeling was mutual. I glanced away, embarrassed at the public show of passion. Luke Rhodes leaned against the bar, his hat pulled low but his eyes clearly riveted to the spectacle. A tall, cruel-looking man was at the end of the bar, his boot resting on the brass foot rail. He was more interested in his whisky than in Garet and Spooner, who were moving to the bar.

Ruby came over, and we were making small talk about the Hole, how I was finding life at the ranch, a shockingly normal, guileless conversation. I asked her to fill me in on the members of the gang.

Ought-Not Henry is the gang's conscience and is in love with Opal. Domino, a black man with a long white birthmark on one cheek, and "Sly" Jack Fox are joined at the hip, and have a tendency to finish each other's sentences. Scab Williams is mostly deaf, so he rarely speaks, and whenever he does, it's a shout. The preacher's name is Deacon Dobbs, and he has this way of looking at women that makes my skin crawl. Ruby chuckled when I told her and said that's why they call him Dead-Eye. I have to hand it to Spooner's gang, they have some original nicknames.

No one was expecting the toast Spooner gave, least of all Garet. I've never heard a man be so crude about a woman, and to her face, in my life. I wondered that Rhodes didn't move, only stood there. Garet gave her toast to Spooner—"To the second-best outlaw in Colorado"—and Rhodes's mouth quirked into almost a smile. He knew Garet could handle herself and would be insulted if he tried to save her. I decided then and there that Luke Rhodes would not be an ally to bring Garet in, but that he would willingly take Spooner.

I moved next to Rhodes, who acknowledged me with a nod. He lifted a finger, and the bartender poured me a shot of whisky. It would have been rude to refuse, so I drank it and only partially choked. Garet and Spooner were in each other's faces, hashing out the bet. Hattie was in the background shaking her head, Stella was watching Joan watch Spooner with a dewy-eyed expression that didn't bode well at all. Stella was right to be worried, though, knowing her story, Spooner might need to be worried, too.

Bet laid down, Spooner went back to his poker game, but not before going on about how little Joanie had grown into a fine woman. The bartender slid Ruby a bottle and glass. She went to the man at the end of the bar. "Need another, Mr. Salter?"

"Right as rain, thank you."

My head snapped to the man, and he noticed. I blushed and felt as if cold water ran through my veins at the same time. So Salter has found Garet, and Spooner, just as Pinkerton said he would. Salter wasn't known for going by the book, including writing updates and reports in a timely manner. Which also meant he most likely didn't know about me, or my idea to infiltrate the gang. I was safe as long as Salter didn't report in. There isn't a telegraph in the Hole, and the mail comes sporadically.

Hattie and Garet had pulled Ruby into a low conversation, but I was too involved in my own calculations to care, which is why I didn't notice Salter move next to me until he was there, pouring me a shot of whisky and introducing himself. I told him it was nice to meet him and drank the whisky. He smiled and asked me my name directly. I silently thanked God for my foresight and told him Grace Trumbull.

"The woman they kidnapped."

"I asked to come."

"Turning outlaw?"

"No. Writing their story."

He laughed. "No one will buy it, but good luck all the same."

"Are you part of Spooner's gang, Mr. Salter?"

"Just Salter. No. I like to work alone."

"You're an outlaw, then?"

"Sometimes. Where are you from, Miss Trumbull?"

"Chicago."

"Nice town. Haven't seen it in a while."

"I imagine it's difficult to leave the West. I find myself wanting to stay."

"It's fruitful."

"For men, I'm sure it is."

"It can be fruitful for a woman, too. There are plenty of men on the lookout for wives."

"I am not on the lookout for a husband."

"Is that so? What'll you do if you stay? Teach? Whore?"

"Are those the extent of my choices, Mr. Salter? A wife, teacher, or whore?"

"You could be a dressmaker. Or a milliner. Those are acceptable."

"I don't sew."

"I know a woman in Cheyenne who's a photographer. She started out as a whore, though. Knew a female doc once," Salter said.

"I know one as well. A female physician. In Denver."

"There seem to be a lot of women trying to do a man's job these days." Salter looked me up and down. "Maybe you don't need to be anything. By the looks of your clothes, you're living just fine."

"I'm a writer, Mr. Salter. Here to tell Margaret and Hattie and the girls' stories."

"Are you, now? Are you going to include me in your tale?"

"I imagine you would add a certain amount of…menace…to it."

"Menace? Hmm. And here I thought we were having a nice conversation." Salter leaned close to me. "Now, why do I get the feeling that you know of me?"

Hattie stepped up to us so closely that Salter had to lean back from me. "Don't think we've met. Hattie LaCour." She held out her hand to Salter. He looked at it, met Hattie's eyes, and walked away.

Hattie shook her head and turned her back on him, motioning to Eli for another drink. "What was that about?"

"Just a friendly chat."

She drank her shot, tossed a coin on the bar, and turned to me. "Then why do you look like you want to vomit?"

"I'm not used to drinking whisky."

"Mmm-uh. If you're going to stay in the West you need to fix that, because that look right there? Signals you as weak. Are you weak, Grace Trumbull?"

"I've never thought so."

"You're a woman living in a man's world. You're weak by default. That's why you have to be hard, with men, with women, with everyone. Otherwise they'll take advantage of you."

"I know that."

"Just friendly advice. Let's go, get Garet out of here before she makes another damn fool bet that's gonna get us killed."

I didn't realize until later how silent the ride back had been. I was too wrapped up in my own problems to think about the family drama brewing with every step we took toward the Heresy Ranch.

Salter is here, in Timberline. He is as dangerous and menacing as I've always heard. I have three choices. I could go to Salter, tell him who I am, and coordinate our cases. Hope he doesn't betray me to Hattie and Garet. Of course, he would. He's survived in the West for over a decade, done some truly horrible things, and yet walks free precisely because he is ruthless. It was evident from a five-minute conversation the amount of respect he would give me if we worked together.

Second option: remain silent and rely on the remoteness of Timberline to protect me. This is my best choice, though there is no way for me to keep tabs on Salter. He could ride out of town tonight and be back with a posse of Pinkertons in two weeks.

Third option: tell Rhodes that Salter is a Pinkerton, here to capture Garet. That's ridiculous; I would have to say how I know who Salter is, and I have no good explanation.

When we arrived at the ranch house, Stella lit into Joan, telling her in no uncertain terms that she wasn't to leave the ranch and that she wasn't to go near Jed Spooner.

"I'm a grown woman. You can't tell me what to do."

"I can, and I will."

"How exactly do you expect to keep me here, huh?"

Stella put her hand on her knife and stepped forward. Garet moved between the sisters.

"Everyone calm down. Joan, Stella is right. You need to stay away from Spooner. You're too young and inexperienced."

"You're just jealous because he..."

"You might want to be careful what you say there, Joan," Hattie said. "Tough to take back cruel words once they're said."

"The only reason that bastard is sniffing around you is because you ain't never been with a man," Stella said. "He'll take that from you and throw you away, mark my words. Or he may use you to death. He ain't gonna marry you, that's for goddamn sure."

"If I want Spooner and he wants me, there's nothing you can do to stop me. Any of you."

Stella stared at her sister long and hard. Finally she nodded. "You're right, and you're sneaky enough to do it. That's our fault. We've petted you for too long, you being the baby." She stepped forward and put her finger in Joan's face. I could tell it took something for the girl to stand toe-to-toe with Stella. "When it all goes south, and it will, don't come running to me to save you. Again."

She slammed the door on her way out to the barn. Joan stood in the middle of the room, looking from Hattie to Garet to me as if wanting us to console her, be on her side. None of us did. She stomped off into her and Stella's room. Garet turned and went to her room and closed the door with a solid thud. Hattie chuckled, said, "Isn't family grand?," and bid me good night.

Sunday, July 1, 1877

Ten days ago, Jehu, Hattie, Stella, and five hired cowboys left to rustle mustangs for not more than a fortnight. It's a short roundup, to meet the timeline Hattie and Garet have set for the heist. Garet hired Ought-Not, Domino, Sly Jack, and Salter to help us out on the ranch and do the more physical labor. She,

Joan, and I work from sunup to sundown. Any downtime we have, Garet spends teaching me to ride and to be comfortable with horses. I am sore in places I didn't know I could be sore in, and by the time we we're finished at night, I can barely keep my eyes open, let alone organize my thoughts well enough to interview Garet on how she ended up an outlaw. I've given up trying to think my way out of the Salter situation. I was alarmed when Garet hired him but decided it was the best option in a bundle of bad ones. I can keep an eye on him and feed him misinformation while not being tricked into revealing anything about myself. Seeing his swarthy, smirking face every day has motivated me more than anything to bring them in, and Spooner, too, just to prove to him a woman can perform more than three roles in life.

There is one solution that solves every problem: killing him. I just don't have it in me.

Today is a Sunday, which means we did only the bare minimum of chores, and we took the afternoon off and went to picnic by the river.

We rode, of course, but Garet took the day off from correcting me about my riding. The optimistic part of me hopes it is because I am improving. I don't have the courage to ask her.

While Garet and I tended the livestock this morning, Joan made our lunch: fried chicken and whole roasted potatoes, with fried blackberry pies for dessert. She is an excellent little cook, and she enjoys it. She doesn't like working outside, and everyone else hates inside work, especially Stella and Hattie.

Newt met us at the river with a fishing pole and a promise of catching dinner. We washed our lunch down with a bottle of beer each. Joan brought Newt a jar of lemonade, and he was so grateful and calf-eyed I was embarrassed for him. The beer spread a pleasant warmth through my aching muscles. Joan, smaller, younger, and less used to alcohol, fell asleep almost immediately after. Robbed of the chance to impress Joan, Newt took his pole, a spade to dig worms, and a pail and went down the river to fish.

Garet and I lounged on the blanket and stared up at the clouds. My heart swelled with appreciation for the beauty around me, and I forgot about my Salter worries for a while.

"I never realized how beautiful nature could be."

"They didn't have clouds in Chicago?"

"There were beautiful days, of course, and there were times when the skies over the lake could take your breath away. But there was also smoke and dirt and masses of people. No, I much prefer Colorado."

"Even this remoteness?"

"I might require a little more civilization."

"I'm offended."

I could tell from her voice she was teasing me.

"How did you come to be in Colorado, Garet?"

"I came to America on my honeymoon, and we decided to stay."

I propped myself on my arm and looked down on her. "I can't decide if you're being intentionally vague because you don't trust me, or you want me have the room to embellish your story with my imagination."

"Do you have a good imagination, Grace?"

"I like to think so."

"I'm keeping a journal now. You inspired me."

"Did I?"

"Yes. I kept one in my youth, of course. It was full of horse talk and observations about training and riding, breeding."

"Why am I not surprised?"

"The most interesting entry was the one after I saw a stud mount a mare for the first time. What a shock for a twelve-year-old. It was horrifying, mesmerizing, and"—she looked out of the corners of her eyes at me—"erotic, though I didn't understand that at the time. I knew that tingling meant something, but not what. All of my entries tended that way for quite a few weeks. It was breeding season, after all. Honestly, I can't believe my grandfather let me watch. I don't think he saw me as a girl, or at least not one turning into a woman. My mother found the journal, and I'm sure I don't need to tell you it was quite a scene."

I hated that I was blushing, so I lifted my face to the sun and closed my eyes, as if this were any other story, and any other day.

Garet touched my arm. "Don't worry, there are no such entries in this journal. In it I intend to tell you all about my past. In detail. But today is too beautiful to waste on talk. I have a better idea."

"What?"

She stood and toed off her boots. "A swim."

"In the river?"

"Yes, goose. In the river."

"But the current?"

"It deepens here and slows the current down. Besides, I won't let you get washed down the river." She undressed and I looked around in a panic. "Newt is serious about his fishing. We will be out before he gets back," Garet said. She shed her pants and her shirt, and her undergarments, and I looked away. "You can keep your clothes on, if you like. But there's nothing more invigorating than jumping naked into a cold river." She ran to the bank and, with a shout, leaped in. When she emerged she shouted again. "Oh my God that's cold!"

"I don't like bathing in cold water."

"You'll get used to it. I already am."

"Your teeth are chattering."

"I thought you were a risk taker, Grace."

"Whatever gave you that idea?"

She mimicked my voice. "'Take me with you!'"

"I do not sound like that."

"Now you're avoiding the question. Are you going to get in, or will I have to get out and throw you in?"

"You wouldn't. You couldn't."

Garet spit an arc of water in my direction. "I will and I can. Come, Grace. I'll let you feel my tumor."

"Hardly an enticement." I turned my back and started to disrobe. I heard Garet splashing around behind me, laughing. "It doesn't sound like you need me."

"Find fun where and while you can, Grace."

I looked down at my naked body and cringed at my prominent hipbones, my small breasts, the dark thatch of hair where my legs met, my gloved hands. It seemed ridiculous to leave that part of me obscured when nothing else was, but wearing the gloves had become a habit. At first I wore them because I didn't want to be reminded of what happened, of why it happened. Later the idea of showing my scars to others, seeing the pity in their eyes, the questions, filled me with terror. There was no one alive who knew of my scars, who had seen them, who knew the story behind them. The gloves had become my armor, protecting me from others, from being hurt.

With shaking hands I removed them. When I turned, Garet was floating faceup in the water, her eyes closed. At that distance I could see the abnormal bump in her abdomen. My stomach clenched with grief. How long did she really have? How did she live with the pain? I rarely saw it flit across her expression, and she never seemed to show the effects of laudanum, either. Margaret Parker was an enigma, one that I wanted to solve.

I approached the river cautiously and dipped my foot into it. "You can't be serious. That isn't cold, it's frigid."

"Jump in. Makes it easier."

"I don't know."

"Oh my God."

Garet stood up and waded through the river. I tried to concentrate on her face instead of the water streaming down her body, and almost succeeded. I tucked my hands under my arms, covering my scars and my breasts. Garet noticed the movement and held out her hand. "There's no need to be shy with me, Grace." Droplets of water ran down her face, one hanging on the tip of her nose. I found myself removing one hand and putting it in hers. She looked down at it for a long moment before tracing the iron-shaped scar gently with a finger. Her eyes met mine. "Both?"

I nodded and gave her my other hand, showing the less defined scars. "I knew what was coming with this hand, you see."

"Who did it?"

"My mother. She's dead."

"I hope by your hand."

I looked away to tell the lie more easily. "No, God's. She died in the fire of '71. Burned to death. So you see, God does have a sense of justice."

"So does man. Although it is unevenly meted out."

"How so?"

"Outlaws when they're caught go to prison. If they're caught. Other men protect them more often than not. If a man kills, he will hang most of the time. But everybody out here is stealing something from someone. Some of it's legal, some of it isn't. Seems the legal side is weighted to the rich men and their business. People who are struggling, trying to get by, are treated more harshly. Didn't you find that in Chicago, too?"

"Yes."

"What do you think would happen if we were caught? Four women, getting the best of men?"

"You'd go to jail."

"Assuredly, but not before they thoroughly humiliated us. Made a spectacle of us to discourage other women from following suit. The loudest and angriest voices against us would be women's, because we threaten their idea of their selves, their lives. There is no telling what they would do to Hattie, but it would be many degrees worse than what they do to me."

When I'd thought of the spectacle, I'd been focused on the glory I would receive as the woman who brought them to justice. Whatever consequences they suffered they deserved. But "consequences" had always been a vague idea. Humiliation in the papers, jail time since they've never hurt anyone. My imagination amounted to slaps on the wrists, which is, I see now, completely ridiculous. They would be made examples. Dorcas would probably make sure of that. I'd never considered that Hattie's consequences might be different, harsher. Outside the law.

"Is that justice?"

I shook my head, my throat clogged with shame and fear. Fear that I'd put in motion something I wasn't sure I could stop.

"I don't know much about you, Grace. Only impressions, a gut feeling. I suspect you feel the injustice of your place in the world, the limitations placed on you, as keenly as I do." Her gaze bored into me, seeing me in a way few others have. My breath caught. "Am I right?"

I could barely find my voice. Her words, the low tenor she spoke them in, opened up the tender areas in my soul I thought I'd long hardened against this grief, this longing not to feel imperfect and wanting in the world. "Yes."

"My hope is this job, this telling of our story, will set us both free from what limits us. Me from ignominy. You from whatever it is that haunts you."

"Haunts me? Nothing..."

She put her fingers to my lips. "That will be my parting gift to you."

"Please don't talk of dying."

"Everyone dies, and I will die on my own terms. Will you live on your own terms?"

"I...um..."

"Promise me, Grace."

She didn't realize what she was asking. To live on my own terms, I needed to betray her, to bring her to justice as I originally intended. But the idea that had been niggling in the back of my mind since I'd heard she was dying came forth fully formed: What was the point of turning her in? Was I the type of woman who would sentence someone else to living their last days as a focus of ridicule and derision?

No, I wasn't.

"I promise."

Garet hugged me and, before I knew what was happening, launched us sideways into the frigid river. We plunged into the water, falling down to the bottom. I opened my eyes and saw Garet grinning at me. I pushed up and broke through the surface, wet hair covering my eyes, goose bumps popping up all over my body. Garet shot up next to me, laughing.

"Oh, you vile, tricky woman," I said.

Her joy and mischievousness were infectious, and I started laughing, too. She flicked water into my face, and I returned the favor before turning and diving into the deep center of the river.

Garet had been right; we were packing up when Newt returned with a string of brown trout for dinner. We rode home, took care of the livestock, and ate Newt's catch, which Joan sautéed in fresh butter. I'm not sure I've ever had a more wonderful meal.

Newt rode home, and the three of us spent a pleasant night around the fire. Garet read, I darned my traveling gloves, and Joan played on the floor with Buster, her retriever. It was the perfect ending to the most companionable day I've had since my days with Kate Warne at the agency. On the ride home, I'd asked myself what Kate would do, and hadn't liked the answer.

Now it's midnight, and I am in Jehu and Hattie's room. The bed is soft, and there is a comforting lethargy to my limbs and a quietude in my mind that comes only from the assurance of my place in the world and the path I must take.

Thursday, July 19, 1877

Tomorrow Jehu takes me to Rock Springs to catch the train to Cheyenne, then on to Denver. Garet and Hattie will follow a couple of days later so there is no chance we will be seen together. Over the last month I've grown attached to the ranch, the town, and the people. I'm loath to leave it, but it is time to put Garet's plan into action.

Wednesday, August 1, 1877
Train to Cheyenne

I'm worried Garet isn't going to make it to the day we have targeted for the heist, Monday, October first, the day of the large suffrage march through Denver, rallying for the amendment that will be voted on the next day. We will use the march as a distraction and cover for our escape. I've been watching her, probably too closely, and I can see the strain around her eyes.

She told me that the doctor she saw in Cheyenne told her that he thought the tumor was too far along to operate on, but if she wanted to have it done, she would have to go to Chicago or St. Louis to find a doctor with skills enough to do it. Garet is a homebody and didn't want to take the chance the trip might be one way. So she stayed and has tried to manage the pain with laudanum and hemp for the last three months.

Garet could tell I was worried she mightn't make it to Denver, and she gently chided me when we were saying goodbye. "You're not done with me yet. I will frustrate and irritate you many more times before I'm gone."

I shook my head and looked down at my bare hands. No one had mentioned the scars. The shift in Hattie and Stella's attitudes toward me had been slight, but I'd noticed. I suspected we were all of us scarred in one way or another, and it bonded us together as nothing else would.

Hattie had put a small jar of salve on the arm of my chair one night as I read by the fire. There was no comment or eye contact. I looked up and saw Garet watching with amusement. She lifted one shoulder and returned to her work. The salve smelled like camphor, and I could only assume it was for my scars. I applied a little on the back of each hand and smiled at the comforting coolness.

Jehu, of course, became even gentler with me. He stands out from the others because he is the most respectful of the bunch. With every question there is a please, with every action there is a thank-you. He answers my questions with "Yes, ma'am" and "No, ma'am," and covers his mouth when he laughs. His voice fluctuates between deep and not, as if he's still going through puberty, which is probably why he talks so gently, and his tanned face has a softness Luke Rhodes's hasn't had since childhood, I'd wager. You couldn't help but like Jehu, and within a very short time, he's won me over completely. Without me ever learning a thing about him. I was excited to have a few hours alone with him while we traveled to Rock Springs.

He held the wagon laces softly in his hands, but had complete control of the pair of draft horses in front of us. We were silent, but it was companionable. I wanted to know more of him, and he wouldn't offer it up freely.

"How long have you and Hattie been a couple?"

"Oh, I don't know. A while."

"You were terribly angry with her at the stage."

"Well, I wasn't expecting what she did."

"You made up quickly, though."

"Sure. I'm her man, and she's my woman. We don't stay mad for long."

"Where are you from?"

"Missouri."

"Which part?"

"Moved around a lot."

"How'd you make it out here?"

"Got on as a teamster for a wagon train in '63 and decided to stay. It was real pretty. The mountains."

"They are beautiful. I'm thinking of staying, too. For the very same reason."

"You seem like a real nice lady."

"Thank you."

"Hattie don't like you much."

"Oh, I'd hoped I was winning her over."

"She's a tough nut to crack."

"Do you have any tips for me?"

"Standing up to her was a good start."

"She told you about that?"

"She did. Should have seen the grin on her face when she did. Between us, I think she likes you more than she lets on, but she has a reputation to uphold."

"I will by no means deprive her of her tough reputation."

"She's slow to trust, but when she does, she'll never let you down. My advice is this: don't lie to her. If you do..." Jehu shrugged. "She won't let it pass without meting out consequences."

"I wouldn't imagine." I grabbed the seat as the wagon lurched over the uneven ground. "Tell me, Jehu: What was your role in the robberies Garet and Hattie did?"

He looked at me sideways. "Why do you want to know?"

"I'm writing a book about you all, remember?"

"Guess I forgot, since you haven't been asking many questions since we've been back from the roundup."

"We've been very busy, haven't we?"

"That we have. You've turned into a right good horsewoman."

I blushed with pleasure. I had. Garet had been correct when she said she would fix my fear of horses. I would never love them as she did, but we'd come to an agreement: I wouldn't be afraid of the beasts if they wouldn't throw me. "Thank you. I've worked very hard."

"My role was to tell them about easy targets." He shrugged. "I only helped Garet with the first bank robbery. Didn't like it much."

"The first? I thought your first job was a stage?"

"That was in '75. In '73 she robbed a bank. The Bank of the Rockies. Same one you're robbing October first. Coming full circle, Garet says. She did most of the work, I came at the end, tied the clerk up."

"She did it herself?"

"During the day, too. She was tying up the clerk when I walked in. Stole about ten grand from Connolly that time."

"He owned the bank?"

"That's why we hit it. Has she told you about losing her first ranch?"

"No. What happened?"

"She can tell it better than I can."

"She says she's writing a journal for me."

"I'll let her tell it. But I can tell you the after. We were desperate, and Garet was angry. There was a certain amount of revenge in it, which is why I went along with it. I thought she'd get it out of her system, get her pound of flesh, get us a stake to start over, and that would be it. Never thought we'd do it again. Then we did. She was good at it. Loved it."

"I see."

"Don't judge her too harshly."

"I'm not judging her in the least."

Jehu pulled up the horses, stopping the wagon on the narrow part of the pass. To my right the mountain fell off into a deep ravine. I gripped the side of the wagon. "What are you doing?"

"Hattie thinks you're a Pinkerton."

"What?"

Jehu didn't answer. He knew I'd heard his statement.

"That's preposterous."

He waited. The wind whipped through the mountain pass, and the aspen trees below swayed and shimmered.

"No, I don't work for Allan Pinkerton."

"Who do you work for?"

"No one. Myself. I'm writing a travelogue of the West. Now I'm going to write your story."

"No, you're not."

"What?"

"We don't want you to."

"Who? Garet?"

"No, Garet wants it, and you let her think you're doing it. She'll be... Well, she won't know the difference soon enough. But if you write it, they'll find us. How many white teamsters are married to black women? Not many. Probably none but us. I told Garet I'm not leaving the Hole for the rest of my days, and that's a promise I intend to keep. I won't be able to do it if you go blabbing about us, who we are, where we live."

"Jehu, I would never put you in harm's way. Please believe me."

"Let me put this another way. If you write one word about us, I'll find you and kill you."

I couldn't help myself, I laughed at the idea this soft-spoken man could ever do such a thing. "You?"

"You don't want to test me to see what I'll do to protect me and my own."

The smile faded from my face, and I glanced over the side of the mountain. It would be so easy for him to push me over, and no one would be the wiser. He would tell Garet he'd dropped me at the train station, and if I never arrived in Denver everyone would assume I'd gotten cold feet and moved on. I'd never felt so vulnerable in my life.

My voice was faint when I replied. "What can I do to convince you I won't betray you, that I won't write about you?"

He pulled out a knife, and I flinched. He sliced his right palm open, and I grimaced. He handed the knife to me and held out his hand as if to shake. I swallowed the bile that rose in my throat, closed my eyes, and slit my palm. I gasped in pain, but Jehu grabbed my hand and squeezed our blood together. "Say it."

"I promise I won't betray you, or your family."

"Say you won't write about us."

"I won't write about you."

"Blood oath. To break it is to curse yourself."

"To what?"

Jehu pulled out a handkerchief and handed it to me. He grinned. "Hattie's vengeance."

The train is pulling into Cheyenne. I'm going to stay the night at the Rollins House hotel to gather my thoughts. I will need to check in with Dorcas Connolly, and I need to have a solid lie ready for her, one that will satisfy my assignment and earn me some money but won't betray five people who are doing more good than bad, and who have threatened to kill me more than once.

The first thing I need to do is find a doctor to look at my hand and bandage it better than this bloody, soiled handkerchief.

It would be easier if I kept going east, back to Chicago. I could write the book, publish it as Grace Trumbull, and disappear. Grace Trumbull doesn't exist, after all. I confess, I miss Claire Hamilton.

Thursday, August 2, 1877
Platte River Boarding House
Denver, Colorado

I arrived in Denver this afternoon. Garet and Hattie will arrive in a couple of days. Tonight I go to the women's suffrage meeting and set our plan in motion. Tomorrow I visit Dorcas Connolly.

Friday, August 3, 1877

We met in a café across the street from the Bank of the Rockies, the very bank we plan to rob on October first. Dorcas didn't want to take the chance of me running into Callum Connolly at the office. I was relieved; it meant Dorcas hadn't told her nephew about me, who I was, what I was doing.

Dorcas was glad to see me. She'd started to fear for my safety when she didn't hear from me in so many weeks, or that I'd discovered the task was too difficult and had moved on. Her nephew arrived in Denver a week ago, and after a little coercion Dorcas was able to discover that yes, there had been a woman on the stage, and she had gone off with the bandits.

"Was it Margaret Parker?"

My heart leaped into my throat. "Who?"

"She may have called herself Garet?"

"No. The leader is a woman named Sally Steele. She and her gang are former prostitutes who decided they'd rather rob rich men than lie with them."

Dorcas's disappointment was apparent. "But the black woman..."

"A prostitute, as well."

"I was so sure."

"Who is Margaret Parker?"

"Someone I used to know, who might have held a grudge against us." She stared into her china cup of coffee before snapping her attention back to me. "Where have you been for the past two months?"

"In a remote cabin in the mountains. That's where they hide until interest in them dies down."

"Then where do they go?"

"I don't know. They took me to Pueblo, and I caught a train from there."

"So they're somewhere south?"

"That is where they hide, yes. In an old mining cabin."

"What else can you tell me about them?"

"That was their last job."

"Was it? Why?"

"They have enough money, and they feel like they won't be ignored forever. They were a little afraid pistol-whipping Mr. Adamson would change the tenor of the search. How is Mr. Adamson, by the way? Has he settled into his new job?"

"He's dead."

"What? Not from being hit in the head, I hope."

"No. He died in Gunnison."

"I didn't particularly like him, but to die so senselessly."

"It happens more often than not here."

"Yes, I know. A man was killed in front of me in Colorado Springs."

"Adamson is no great loss, according to my nephew. A sniveling coward, I believe is what Callum called him. Enough about the dead man. What now, Miss Hamilton?"

"I'm sorry?"

"How do you plan on apprehending this Sally Steele and her gang of whores? You went to the sheriff in Pueblo and told them all you know?"

"I had an unpleasant experience with the Pueblo sheriff when I went through there in May. He didn't take kindly to a woman questioning him, and he firmly denied women were robbing around his area. I am following them to San Francisco."

"San Francisco?"

"Yes, that's where they're headed to open a general store. I'll leave in a couple of weeks, give them time to establish themselves. They will be easier to locate. There can't be too many women opening general stores in the city, can there?"

"What makes you think they weren't lying to you?

"Because they don't know I know. Being a master eavesdropper comes in handy in my line of work." I remembered Garet catching me easily and hoped I didn't blush too much.

"Why did they let you go?"

"They believed I was a travel writer. I told them my time with the Steele Gang would be the best chapter in the book. I would do them justice, but I had a steamer ticket in New York City waiting for me."

I watched Dorcas sip her coffee as she took this barrel of lies in. "Has your nephew heard from the Pinkerton?"

Dorcas studied me. Finally she smiled, though no humor was in it, and said, "Not that I know of, but Callum likes to keep his secrets. When are you leaving for San Francisco?"

"August fifteenth, I think."

"That won't work. I am traveling with Callum through the middle of September."

"I'm sorry, I don't understand."

"I'm coming to San Francisco with you."

"What?"

"Oh yes. I want to be there when we catch these women."

"It may take me a while to locate them."

"If I'm there to help, we will cut the time in half."

"Do you not trust me to do the job?"

"You haven't done it yet. Callum's trips are always open-ended, so you'll need to be flexible."

"Of course."

She left a ten-cent piece to pay for our coffee and stood.

"Miss Connolly, I will need payment for my time."

"I gave you an advance."

"Which went to expenses, travel, clothes, food, board."

"How much?"

"Fifty dollars should suffice."

"I'll send it around to your lodgings."

"Thank you."

Sunday, August 5, 1877

Garet and Hattie arrived yesterday and told me today about Garet's big plan to visit Connolly. It is an enormous risk, a danger I'm uniquely positioned to tell her about, but I cannot. To do so would be to admit I'm a Pinkerton, to admit to the ruse I've been playing. Hattie would surely kill me, as she has threatened to do. Who knows, Garet might kill me. Either way, it would be the end of friendships I've grown to cherish, and I cannot risk that. I need more time to gain their trust, to help them in their heist. To misdirect Dorcas.

Tomorrow she is going to Callum Connolly's office to repay the money she stole in the first bank robbery, in '73, when they were starving and needed to eat. She claims arriving, a dying woman wanting to make amends for past mistakes, will divert suspicion from her being involved in any of the other heists. It was the only one they could definitely identify her from, since she'd had the audacity to tell the clerk, "Tell Colonel Connolly Margaret Parker sends her regards."

I admit, it has a certain flash, but it was a colossally stupid thing to say.

What's interesting, though, is that Dorcas never mentioned the '73 bank robbery to me, either at our original meeting or yesterday. I guess she is basing her Parker Gang theory on two members being white women and one a black woman, and her belief Margaret would have a significant enough chip on her shoulder to harbor enmity toward Connolly's empire for all these years. Did the clerk not give Connolly the message? Or did Dorcas hold back the information from me? I can't imagine why she would, especially based on our first meeting. She had given the robberies enough thought and consideration that she had spotted a pattern and had directed me to take the stage, which had turned out to be correct.

I argued with Garet that admitting to one robbery would only bring suspicion on her for the others. Margaret argued for the opposite, that a dying woman making restitution would be seen in a sympathetic light, and she would say she was going to England to live with family, or some convincing lie. She hasn't settled on it, she says. She waved away my arguments, said her decision was final and I was wasting my breath.

I asked Hattie what she thought, to back me up. She studied me for a long time, and I remembered Jehu's confession: "Hattie thinks you're a Pinkerton."

If there was a moment to confess, that was it, but I didn't, and now...I'm not sure if Garet would change her plan even if I told her about working for Dorcas, Dorcas's suspicions, and the chance that Salter has revealed her identity. Garet suffers from an outsize case of hubris, and I suffer from a case of chronic longing. Longing to be independent, to be accepted, and to be loved.

Tuesday, August 7, 1877

Garet's ploy appears to have worked better than she expected, and I can only surmise that Salter hasn't been in touch with Callum Connolly since Connolly refused to have the sheriff arrest her and instead invited her to see her old ranch. I don't understand why she wants to visit a place that will only bring back bad memories, and said as much.

"Even a Connolly is human enough to give a dying woman her last wish. We leave on Friday."

"We?" Hattie asked.

"He's taking me."

"That was not the plan."

"No, but it is now. If I want access to his office, I have to go with him."

"It's too dangerous," Hattie said.

"I can handle Callum Connolly."

"It's a damn fool thing to do, go alone."

"Do you have a better plan?"

Hattie left in a huff. I soon followed, citing a suffrage meeting that didn't start for three hours.

Since divulging her terminal diagnosis, Garet has been free to talk about her imminent death, to joke about it, to almost embrace it, never considering that every remark she thinks of as so witty cuts to the bone those who care about her. I can't afford to let her, or, God forbid, Hattie, know the depth of my feelings, lest I invite ridicule.

I've never felt the sharpness of mortality before. Kate died quickly of an unexpected illness. My grief for the loss of my friend was inexplicably intertwined with the shock of seeing a woman who was healthy on Monday fall ill on Wednesday and die on Friday. Garet talks about death but hides her deterioration so well there are long stretches when I forget, when everything feels normal. But there is nothing normal about this situation, helping these women plan a heist while watching a woman I admire smile and laugh and live while she slowly dies.

The suffrage meeting was precisely what I needed to break myself out of the doldrums, at least for a couple of hours. There is nothing quite like the energy of a hundred women united in a common idea, who believe in the righteousness of their cause and that our side will win in the end. As I looked around the room, I wondered how many of these women would stand up for Garet and Hattie if they were caught, if their belief in women's rights extended so far as to support women who clearly broke the law, though with the best of intentions. I decided to see, and introduced the rumor of a female gang into a group of seven women I was talking to.

"Women outlaws? Why, I've never heard of such a thing." That was Patricia Perkins, a bubbly, vacuous woman whose husband owned a general store downtown.

"Most likely because they're so much better at it than the men," said the president of the group, Dr. Alida Avery. Everyone laughed and nodded. "Women should have equal rights in everything, including the ability to do wrong."

"And be punished equally for it?" I asked.

"Oh no," Patricia Perkins said. "I'm sure if this hypothetical gang exists, they have a pure motivation for it."

"For breaking the law?" said Kaye Hunter, the wife of a state legislator whose support of suffrage extended only to letting his wife attend meetings. "If we want equality, we have to be treated equally under the law."

"So, what? Are you advocating for hanging women who kill drunken, abusive husbands?"

"Of course not. But these are women who are stealing from hardworking men."

"They haven't injured anyone," I said.

The women looked at me. "Are you implying this gang is real?" Alida asked.

"That would be disastrous to our cause," Kaye Hunter said.

"Why?"

"Because it would give our opponents another arrow in their quiver of arguments against us."

"We are trying to convince them we would be a morally upright, balancing effect on voting. If there are a bunch of women running around the country acting like men, it would give them the opportunity to say that we bring nothing to the voting booth."

"That's ridiculous," I said. "It makes no sense."

"Which is precisely why it will work brilliantly against us," Alida said.

The secretary came up and told Alida they needed to start the meeting, and the small group dispersed. Alida touched my arm to signal me to stay. "Are these women real?"

I nodded.

Alida inhaled. "Tell them to keep quiet until after the election. They very well may be the difference between us winning or losing."

Wednesday, August 8, 1877

Dorcas came to see me today. Thank God Hattie and Garet weren't here. She was in a rage and accused me of protecting Garet. I asked her what she was talking about, and she relayed Garet's meeting with Callum Connolly the day before.

"She came in and confessed! To a crime we didn't realize she committed!"

I asked her to explain, and she said that the clerk who had been pistol-whipped didn't remember the event. He remembered locking the door to the bank, but everything after that was a blur. I cursed inwardly. Goddamn Garet and her arrogance. If she would have just listened to me.

"Did she confess to the other robberies?"

"No. But I know it was her. Are you working with them?"

I was taken aback at how clever Dorcas was, how she had not only pegged Garet as the culprit with little to no evidence, but had also surmised I could fall under her spell. My shocked expression served me well as I lied in my own defense and put the blame back on Dorcas.

"If Margaret Parker is the leader of the gang, I do not know it. The name the woman gave me was Sally Steele. If you had bothered to tell me of your suspicion of this Margaret Parker I would have approached my time with them differently. Asked different questions, probed in different ways. If they fooled me, you have only yourself to blame."

Dorcas's nostrils flared, a mannerism I realized happened when she was challenged or angry. "I will prove it myself, then."

"How?"

"Callum invited Margaret to visit her ranch this weekend. Of course I am going as well. We leave for the business survey from there. By the time we leave, I will have outed Margaret Parker for the thief and murderer she is."

"Murderer?"

"There was a man, a newspaperman, killed nearby in the moments before the bank robbery. It was suspected that the thieves did it as a distraction."

"Oh, I..." I clamped my mouth shut, lest I say I didn't believe Garet would do that. "The women I was with weren't violent in the least. It was one of their firm tenets to not hurt anyone."

"She played you very well. But that's no surprise. She is a manipulative, selfish woman. You can salvage your case."

"How?"

"Come to the train station tomorrow. I will point her out and we will know once and for all if Margaret Parker is the fiend who has been terrorizing our company."

"Of course," I said. "I would be happy to."

Dorcas left, and I collapsed into this chair. Garet a killer? I didn't believe it. Hattie I would believe it of. And Stella, of course. But would Garet take another person's life, and as a distraction? No. Impossible.

Dorcas is the biggest threat to Garet's being able to live out the rest of her days in peace. She's a threat to Hattie and Jehu and Stella and Joan's freedom, and I am the only one who realizes.

Thursday, August 9, 1877

I'm shaking as I write this, which explains my crooked, jittery writing. I ball my hands into fists to stop the trembling, with little success. I have done something I never imagined I would do, but I had no choice. I had to protect them, even when it means I—

Friday, August 10, 1877

Garet left today, and I immediately started worrying. Dorcas was out of the way, but there was no way to know if she'd worked on her nephew, told him of her suspicions, laid out her very clear and accurate case. Save the murder. I will not believe that. I have done what I can, but I fear my choice of silence will come back to haunt me.

I went to see Dorcas, as well. Not knowing how delirious she might be from the blow to her head, I knew that if she was of sound mind, she would expect me to come, she would wonder where I was. The nurse wouldn't allow me to see her, so I wrote a note, telling Dorcas I was at the train station and that the woman with her nephew was not Sally Steele.

I am relieved, but I fear . . . there is something that I'm missing.

Sunday, August 12, 1877
Centennial Women's Boarding House
Denver, Colorado

This morning I changed boardinghouses in case Dorcas recovers and comes looking for me.

Hattie received a note from Garet that she was going to travel with Callum Connolly as his secretary, to visit his holdings. She expects to be gone three weeks, until September second. How am I going to survive with Hattie for three weeks? She is suspicious of me, and I suspect she's following me wherever I go.

Wednesday, August 15, 1877
Colorado Springs Hotel
Colorado Springs, Colorado

I need to establish myself as a member of the suffrage community to keep abreast of the plans for the march the day before the election. On a personal level separate from this case, it is a cause that is close to my heart. I want it to succeed, and I want to do what I can to help.

"Negro women going to get the vote, too?" Hattie asked.

"Of course. Negro men received it with the Fourteenth Amendment. Negro women shall be enfranchised, as well."

"Humph. I won't believe it until I drop a ballot in a box."

We had this conversation on the train to Colorado Springs. I'd felt jittery in Denver, afraid that Dorcas wouldn't believe my lie and would come searching for me. I had switched boardinghouses as a precaution, telling Hattie the cost was better (it was worse; my funds were dwindling), but I knew enough of Dorcas's intelligence and her determination to know I wasn't safe. When I heard of a suffrage talk in Colorado Springs, I told Hattie we should go, establish her as a member of the movement. I explained to her that I'd given a fake name when I attended, so that there would be no connection with Grace Trumbull, the woman kidnapped by outlaws, and I suggested she use a different name, as well.

"What name did you use?"

"Claire Hamilton."

"Claire. It suits you."

I blushed at the compliment and the pleasure of hearing my name at long last.

"Thank you. What name will you use?"

"Henrietta."

"It's beautiful, and close enough to your name it won't be too confusing."

"It *is* my name. But of course you think I'm not smart enough to use an alias."

"No, I didn't mean it that way."

"Sure sounded like it."

"You're determined to think the worst of me, aren't you?"

"Haven't done anything to ease my mind yet."

I huffed and looked out the train window at the flat landscape sliding by. If she only knew what I'd done to protect them. We were silent for the remainder of the ride.

When we arrived and checked into the hotel, Hattie requested her own room. I was relieved; I was still smarting from her insult. This would give me a chance to pay a visit to Sally Dove without needing to evade Hattie.

19

WPA Slave Narrative Collection

Interview with Henrietta Lee

Thursday, September 10, 1936 cont

You should have seen the relief on Grace's face when Garet came back from Callum Connolly's office, and the fear when she heard of Garet's plan to visit the Poudre River Ranch with him and Dorcas. She and I both tried to talk Garet out of it, for different reasons. Finally Grace gave up and left. I asked Garet if I could kill her now and she laughed and said no. 'Keep doing what you're doing. You'll know when you should kill her.'

"I was plumb tired of Grace Trumbull, and that's a fact. I was either with her or following her. I knew that woman almost as well as Jehu by the time it was all over. I found myself wishing she would make a wrong move so I could kill her and put myself out of my misery. But after that first meeting with Dorcas, she never met her again.

"I'd received a letter from Jehu, which was a surprise. He wasn't much of a letter writer. It wasn't a love letter. It was full of news of the weather, the progress on breaking the fresh mustangs, talk of the cowboys we'd hired to help him, news of Stella and Joan. He mentioned that Joan was becoming a woman, with womanly thoughts, and wished I was there to be a settling presence on Stella, who looked about ready to murder any man who tipped his hat at Joan.

"Joan, that girl. I think she was doing it on purpose to irritate her sister. She'd always gone along with Stella's overprotectiveness, but she'd had her fill. Stella hated all men, which made Joan love them. It was a disaster waiting to happen with Spooner sniffing around. It's easy to say that now, with decades of hindsight. I figured Spooner would have her and leave her and she'd grow up a little. Learn a lesson. Wish I would have taken Jehu's concerns more seriously.

"But reading Jehu's letter made me miss him something fierce. I hated sleeping alone, and more and more I was coming around to the idea of hanging up our outlaw hats and settling down. I was feeling my age, and I was just past thirty at the time. Hard to believe I've lived more life in the sixty years since. Back then, I thought my life was almost over.

"I missed Jehu, and I was worried about Garet. A day or two after she'd left she dropped a short note telling us she was going on Connolly's annual tour of his businesses as his temporary secretary since Dorcas had fallen ill. But goddamn was Garet lucky. She'd gone to case the ranch and ended up being handed the opportunity to case every one of Connolly's businesses. We could hit more than one, go out with not a bang, but an explosion. I kept telling Garet we needed to move on from the Connollys, but she would not listen. Lots of heartache and lives would have been saved if she'd listened to me. But this was her last hurrah, and all I could do was to make sure me and mine didn't die, and that I could kill Grace if she betrayed us.

"I kept expecting the sheriff or Pinkertons to bust through the door for me, to get a cable that Garet had been taken into custody, but it never happened. None of it. Grace and I disguised ourselves and watched the bank, made false plans about how we were going to rob it, sewed suffragist sashes for the march we were never going to attend. Grace seemed to give her all to our cause. We were rarely apart, but when we were, I followed her.

"Even though I knew her for a traitor, damn if Grace wasn't growing on me, and I think I was growing on her. It was a gut feeling. You ever have one of those? I do, and usually I'm right. I had one about you. I knew you would treat my story with respect, not dismiss me. I know you are, child. It feels good to get this all out, you see. It's been bottled up way too long. You know, I can see now why Garet wanted Grace to tell our story.

"Grace was distracted and fidgety. Couldn't sit still. I think she felt the walls closing in on her. Or maybe her conscience was getting to her. When she said she was going to Colorado Springs for a suffrage meeting, I said I was going along. She didn't like that one bit, but she could hardly stop me. My money spent as well as hers, and Colorado didn't have the Jim Crow laws. Jehu and I couldn't marry; that was illegal. But otherwise Negroes were supposed to be afforded the same rights. So I went with her. We were almost to Colorado Springs when she told me that she'd used a different name for the suffragists. Claire Hamilton. She suggested I do the same, so there wouldn't be any tie between us and the gang, if word finally got out about what we'd done.

"When we got to the hotel, I got my own room. Grace was surprised, and a little suspicious, since I was always going on about money and our lack of it. Told her I didn't like to share a bed with anyone but Jehu. Our rooms were next door, and we said we were going to rest a bit, then go to dinner. The meeting wasn't until the morning. I had no intention of resting, and neither did Grace. I changed clothes, and when she left about a quarter hour later, I followed.

"She'd changed clothes, too, into a plain dress and drab gloves. She walked aimlessly, peeking into store windows, taking her time, and I started to think she was just out for a stroll. Then she made a turn into the tenderloin district. She went down an alley and knocked on the back door of one of the houses. A whore opened the door, and with a casual, knowing smile, and a very friendly caress, let her in.

"I found the nearest saloon and went in for a drink. Was dressed like a man, but kept to myself in the corner just in case. Grace's attachment to Garet took on a whole new tenor, let me tell you. I remembered Garet saying Grace had a crush on her. I hadn't seen any harm in Garet fostering it and had liked watching Grace go all moony over Garet, had laughed at her, truth be told. I never laughed with Garet, though. I wondered then if Garet hadn't been working on making Grace fall in love with her. It made me angry. No one deserved to be led along the garden path like that, and I found myself feeling protective about a woman who I'd never trusted, and still didn't one hundred percent.

"Grace never said a thing about her meeting, though I knew she wouldn't. I never mentioned it, either, even later on when we were on the same side. I didn't want people messing with my private life, I sure wasn't about to mess with hers.

"That was a silent ride back to Denver, let me tell you. Grace had something on her mind and kept rubbing her hands together. She wore gloves all the time, have I mentioned that? Covering up scars on the back of her hands. She rubbed on her hand like she wanted to clear them away, to be free of them. I understood the feeling well enough. I was lucky that it took an effort on my part to see my physical scars. Oh, I feel them all the time, even now. There's a tightness to the skin that has never gone away, but I'm used to it now. It's part of me, just like those scars were part of Grace Trumbull. Maybe seeing them all the time, being reminded of the why, haunted Grace. No, I don't know how or why she got them. I never asked, and I'm not going to speculate out loud. Like I said before, some things are best kept private, and it's not my place to go gossiping about it.

"When we got back to Denver, we were met by a man who said Garet sent him. Don't remember his name, but I remember what he said. Garet was in Black Hawk on her deathbed, and a doctor was about to operate on her to try to save her. If we wanted to say our goodbyes, we best be ready to leave first thing in the morning."

20

Claire Hamilton's Case Notes

Tuesday, August 21, 1877
Centennial Women's Boarding House
Denver, Colorado

A man named Frank Chambers just arrived, saying he was here on Garet's behalf. She is at his boardinghouse in Black Hawk, beaten to hell and in excruciating pain. A doctor was to operate on her after Chambers left to remove the tumor, which the doctor expected was giving her so much pain. Chambers said he would take us to Black Hawk first thing in the morning.

There are so many questions! How did Garet get to Black Hawk? Who beat her up? When did she leave Callum? Was a posse after her? I was eager to talk everything over with Hattie, to hash out what could have possibly happened, but Hattie didn't seem eager to talk. She went to her room, and I went to mine.

Maybe tomorrow, though there may be no point. Garet could be dead by now.

Wednesday, August 22, 1877
Denver, Colorado

A quick note before we leave for Black Hawk. Hattie was given a letter from Rebecca Reynolds when she left the Black Hawk forwarding address at the front desk. Things are not good in Timberline. Spooner has taken over the ranch, and he apparently had no intention of following through with the bet. He just wanted to get Garet out of town.

Thursday, August 23, 1877
Chambers Lodge
Black Hawk, Colorado

I was stunned to discover Alida Avery was the doctor taking care of Garet. She had been traveling with Susan B. Anthony and they were boarding at Frank Chambers's lodge when Garet arrived, delirious and near death. Being in residence, Alida took charge of Garet's care. We had just missed Miss Anthony; there was a schedule to keep and she was due to be in Golden that afternoon. Alida stayed behind to take care of her patient.

By the time we arrived in Black Hawk yesterday, Dr. Avery'd removed a five-pound tumor and Garet's left ovary and had dressed her cuts and scrapes and wrapped her broken ribs. Alida told us the cancer has spread to Garet's other organs, which explains the heightened pain she's been having. Lana said the doctor doesn't expect Garet to ever leave the bed, or wake up.

Hattie tried to stay strong, but I could tell she was devastated. She'd convinced herself on the ride to Black Hawk that the operation would save her best friend.

Hattie and I sat next to Garet's bed all that night. I worked on sewing the sashes I'd agreed to provide the suffragist march, and Hattie read Garet's journal. When she got to the end she stared at Garet's bruised and scratched face for a long time. Finally I couldn't wait.

"What does it say, Hattie?"

She rose from the chair slowly and handed me the journal. Her face looked as if it had aged ten years in a few hours. "It cuts off midsentence, right after she writes about how she was sure Callum Connolly suspected her."

I opened the journal to the end, and my shoulders slumped. "This was written almost two weeks ago."

Hattie was next to the bed, stroking Garet's hair gently. "What did he do to you?" she whispered. Garet's breaths were coming in shallow bursts, and her face was pale with a sheen of perspiration on it.

"I need to get back to Jehu at the ranch, but I can't leave Garet to die here alone, among strangers."

I didn't argue with her that I wasn't a stranger, because I understood what she meant. She wants Garet to die with her family around.

"Why do you need to go back? Jehu is a man, he can handle Spooner."

A strange look crossed her face. "It's not just him, it's Stella and Joan, too. I don't trust Jed Spooner an inch. I need to get Spooner out of there."

"What if I tell you we can get him out of there without you leaving Garet's side?"

"How? Are you going to do it?"

"With a telegram to my old boss, Allan Pinkerton."

21

WPA Slave Narrative Collection

Interview with Henrietta Lee

Thursday, September 10, 1936 cont

We got to Garet at Black Hawk and it was worse than I thought. She was beat to hell, pale, breathing shallow. She looked dead, or near to it. I had to face it, Garet's dying. Made myself think of the what after, the hole she would leave in our family. We might have been equal in the outlawing, but the ranch was almost all Garet. We worked it, did our jobs, but she was the spirit of it.

"I didn't know then that Garet would be my last white friend, but she was. She sure was. Course Jehu was my friend, but lovers, husbands, are different. Summer of '77 there was still hope in some quarters that Negroes could keep our rights, the few we were granted before Lincoln was killed. I'm skeptical as a rule, even more so now that I've lived sixty more years, so I never had much hope about it. But a part of me did, and I think being friends with Garet, being treated as her equal, did it. When she died, that seed of hope died, too.

"Standing there, staring at my friend, wondering what she'd been through to end up here, looking like that. I figured Connolly not being around meant that it had been his fists that had done that to her. I was ready to leave right then and go kill that son of a bitch.

"Grace stopped me by finally coming clean that she had been working for Dorcas Connolly all along. I'd known it, but hearing it made me angry, angry that we'd left a pattern so easy to follow that they were able to pinpoint the Gunnison stage as our target. But I was kinda proud of the fact it had been two women to figure it out, instead of the men. Proved my point about the best person to catch a woman was a woman.

"I did want to kill her. Mostly because I wanted to take my anger at losing Garet out on someone, and I had a legitimate reason with Grace, and she was handy. I pulled my gun out and realized it wasn't loaded. She stole my damn bullets." *Laughs.* "She didn't trust me, either.

"Hell yeah I woulda killed her by Garet's sickbed. Garet woulda understood. Not proud of it, but I wanted Garet to live and recover enough I could say I told you so. But as long as Garet breathed, Grace living or dying wasn't up to me.

"Guess our voices were raised higher than a sickbed whisper, because Garet spoke up, in an almost unrecognizable voice. It was faint, and she sounded more like the Englishwoman she was than I'd ever heard before. 'Stop arguing.'

"Grace started fussing over Garet, giving her a drink of water, asking her how she felt, trying to fluff her pillow. I was embarrassed for her, with what I suspected about Grace's feelings. Garet waved her fussing away with a thin, weak hand. She was diminished, and it occurred to me Garet wasn't going to leave this room alive, that she might not live until the morning. What good would it do to confirm to her that Grace was a Pinkerton? It would've made me feel good, to be able to say I told you so, but it would have burdened Garet, and that was the last thing she needed. So I watched Grace, or Claire, stand across the bed from me, her hands clutched in front of her, her shoulders thrown back, waiting for my verdict.

"Thank God Almighty I was saved by the nurse showing up. She shooed us out of the room, and Garet didn't have the strength to argue. When we were alone, Claire thanked me for not telling Garet, and I got in her face and threatened her a few more times. It'd become something of a habit, a stress reliever. She stood there and took it. When I was done, she rustled through her carpetbag and pulled out a journal. She put it on the table and placed my bullets on the top.

"'Read this. If you still want to kill me after, you're welcome to try.' She pulled a Peacemaker out of her bag, clunked it on the table, and sat right down, arms crossed." *Laughs.*

"Every goddamn time I thought I hated that woman more than anything on God's green earth, she'd do something like that and by God if she didn't redeem herself. I can tell you now, sixty years on, what I woulda never admitted at the time: Gr—Claire Hamilton was a fine woman, and woulda made a damn good outlaw.

"I finished Claire's journal and it didn't make me want to kill her, but I sure as hell wasn't going to let her know that. I needed her on edge to keep her in line. I thought she was on our side, but the fact was she'd spent months lying to us. She could have told us the danger Garet was in going off alone with Callum Connolly, but she didn't. I still suspected her priority was saving her own skin, so I made sure she knew she was one bad decision away from me blowing her fucking brains out. You better believe I told her that. Got right up in her face. Her Peacemaker didn't scare me none.

"She had a plan and I had a plan. I don't remember either one. It's been sixty years, and we never used them anyways, because Ruby Steele showed up. The Celestial whore. She was the last person we expected to see coming out of the pouring-down rain. She told us Jehu had been thrown in jail in

Cheyenne. I wanted to leave right then, middle of the night in a bone-rattling thunderstorm. Didn't matter. Jehu needed me. I couldn't do anything about Garet, but I could save Jehu, and he needed saving. Jail was the last place he needed to be. I would have left, too, but Callum Connolly showed up and we pulled off... Well, this is the part I don't think you're going to believe. Hell, I lived through it and I have trouble believing it myself.

"You know what a con is? Cons weren't our specialty, though I think we missed our calling after Black Hawk. We might could've gone all over the country and pulled cons, the four of us. Ruby, too. We didn't meet up with the sisters until we sprung Jehu out of jail in Cheyenne. It was an eventful week, and that's the truth."

PART FOUR

THE KILLER

22

Claire Hamilton's Case Notes

Thursday, August 23, 1877
Black Hawk, Colorado

I told Hattie everything, drawing out the story longer than necessary, my voice trembling by the end, my body shaking, sure when I finished that she was going to kill me. She prolonged the agony by silently staring at me with dead eyes for what felt like hours. Though my body was quivering, I didn't speak, didn't cry, didn't beg her for my life. I clasped my hands, kept my chin up, and waited for her to declare my fate.

"I've suspected from the first, and have known since I followed you to your meeting with Dorcas at the tea shop."

"You were following me, then?"

"Yep."

"You didn't kill me."

"Garet wouldn't let me do it until you betrayed us." She pulled out her gun. "Looks like it's time."

"No, please. I haven't betrayed you. Dorcas has no idea it's you. She only suspects." I told her the lie about Sally Steele and the gang of whores.

"Where's your real journal?"

"I... Why?"

"I wanna read it."

"No." My case notes had become more personal than professional, and I knew Hattie was clever enough to read between the lines. I'd rather have her kill me than have to face her after she read my innermost secrets.

"What are you hiding?"

"Nothing to do with the investigation, I assure you. I swear to you."

"You swear to me? That fixes everything. You've been lying to us for nearly three months, but now I'm supposed to believe what you say? You've put me and my family in danger."

"I never meant—"

"You never meant what? Look at her face! She lost a battle with someone."

"I don't think so, Hattie. Look—"

"You're gonna argue with me?"

"No, I'm not arguing. Something went wrong, terribly wrong. Why else would she stumble into this town half-dead? And maybe Callum did this; we won't know until she wakes up. But I'm a detective; I'm showing you what I see. Her face is covered in scratches, especially the side that's bruised, the same side with the broken ribs. I bet if we looked, that side of her body would be bruised, too."

"What are you saying?"

"I think she fell off her horse."

Hattie side-eyed me, but she didn't yell at me. I was making progress.

"She's the best—"

"Horsewoman you've ever seen. I know. But even the best fall off a horse sometimes. The point is, let's not fly off the handle, do something impulsive we might regret. We need to wait for Garet to wake up, talk to her, hear what happened."

"And if she doesn't?"

"We go to Timberline and get your ranch back."

"You? How could a rich blue belly like you help? Unless you want to give us some money."

"I'm not rich. Far from it. I dressed that way because I was undercover. I came from nothing, just like you."

"Don't you go comparing your life with mine. As bad as you had it, it wasn't nothing to mine."

"You're right. Of course. I apologize. I want to help. I already helped. When I thought Dorcas was a threat to Garet, I got her out of the way."

"You? You attacked Dorcas?"

"Yes. I dressed as a man. Unfortunately, I was too late. She probably told Callum her suspicions before they left."

"If she'd been there, she might have been able to keep Callum from doing whatever he did. Dorcas isn't a cruel woman, she's just a rule follower. Garet would have gone to jail, to trial. Instead she's on her deathbed."

I covered my mouth and started crying, because I knew the truth of her words. I'd brought all of this on Garet. I should have disappeared when I returned to Denver, never gone to Dorcas, never tried to help.

I retrieved my journal from my bag and held it to my chest.

"I know that I'm partially responsible for Garet laying here, for whatever she went through. But you have to give me the chance to make it right."

"How are you gonna do that?"

"Well, I'm not sure yet. We will decide together. I'll do whatever you want." I gave her my journal. "If you don't trust me after reading this, then kill me."

She holstered her gun.

"If I don't trust you after reading this, I'll let Garet have the honor of killing you."

Thursday, August 23, 1877 cont

Alida is in with Garet right now, so I am going to take this time to write down what's happened since my last entry, little clues, since we aren't sure if Garet will be able to let us know what happened to her and how much danger Hattie, Jehu, and the sisters are in. I suppose I should include myself in that number, since it seems I'm part of the group now.

Hattie finished my journal and asked, "What next?"

I wasn't dying today, at least.

Hattie and I had just about agreed that our plans were overly complicated, with too many points where things could go terribly wrong. We'd danced around the simplest answer: if Garet died, half of our problems went away. I felt horrible thinking it at all. I didn't want Garet to die, but we had to assume that Callum Connolly knew she was the leader of the gang that had been terrorizing him, and that the towns within a hundred miles would be on alert. So we would have to make a run for Timberline through the mountains, which Garet could hardly do after having her guts pulled out, cut apart, and shoved back into her stomach. Not to mention the broken ribs.

"We have to assume Salter is part of this," I said. When she got to that entry, she'd berated me well and good about keeping quiet on the Pinkerton. "He may be leading a group of agents in search of her. How far is Black Hawk from your old ranch?"

We were in the kitchen drinking coffee. Sunrise was a gray affair. Storm clouds were gathering over the mountains; it was going to come a gully washer soon. Lana had told us her relation to Garet, and we saw in her someone we could trust. She went in and out of the kitchen during her daily chores, catching snippets of our conversation and occasionally offering her own two cents.

"Here to where?" Lana said.

"North of Fort Collins."

"'Bout a hundred miles, going up through Estes Park. Takes my boy Zeke a good week to get home. Though he don't get much time off. Always horses to be broken. Why?"

"That's where Garet was, last we knew."

"At her ranch?"

"Yes."

"You can add about twenty more miles on to that. Easy riding, those twenty miles. The other hundred'll be tough." Lana furrowed her brows. "What was she doing there?"

"Garet went with Callum Connolly to visit it. The last letter we received was postmarked from there. Said she was heading into the mountains with Callum to visit his other businesses," Hattie said.

"I wonder if she saw Zeke? My son works for Connolly at Garet's old ranch. He went back a few years ago hoping to get on with Garet and Jehu. When they were gone, the new foreman took him on. Zeke woulda been plumb pleased to see her. They took a shine to Zeke, Miss Margaret and Jehu. It was fine by me at the time. I was too worried about Homer finding us to be much of a mother. Was Jehu with her?"

"No. Jehu's at our new ranch," Hattie said.

"Were you one of Miss Margaret's girls?"

Hattie looked at Lana for a moment and I could tell she wanted to snap at her that they were partners, but instead she said, "Yeah. I found my way there."

"Then you know. I'd do anything for Miss Margaret or Jehu. Zeke would, too. You don't think he done this to her? The younger Connolly?"

"We don't know," I said. "We won't know anything until she wakes up and can talk."

"Well, it's a good thing she just did. That's what I was coming in here to tell you. Doc's in with her now."

23

Margaret Parker's Journal

Events of August 12–19, 1877
Dictated by Margaret Parker, transcribed by Claire Hamilton
Chambers Lodge
Black Hawk, Colorado

Hattie told Margaret we had read her journal and that she should start where it left off.

"Zeke. He knocked on my window. Told me there were a bunch of Pinkertons in the bunkhouse and they were going to take me in the morning. After midnight; we didn't have much time. He told me to get together only what I needed and to wait for his signal. He was gone before I could ask what it would be.

"An hour later, I heard a scratch on my door. Zhu Li was outside. She stepped into my room and gave me a flour sack of food. She told me Callum was asleep by the fire and Zeke was waiting for me up on the stage road. I climbed out the window and made my way around the house. The fastest way to the road was by the bunkhouse.

"Drunk cowboys in the bunkhouse, one alone next to the barn, passed out. I'd shoved my hair in my hat and wore Callum's coat. Stole the drunk's whisky, tossed some on me, drank a swig, and decided to brazen it out. Walked like a man past the bunk just as two men walked out. Salter. Spoke to me, I kept going. Saw my face, yelled to raise the alarm. Pulled out my gun..." *Garbled.* "...Took off running.

"Lucky they were drunk, but thought I was done for. Horses would catch me before I made it halfway across the field. Heard yelling and running, but no horses. Scrabbled up the hill and found Zeke. Had Storm and another horse. Told him I think I shot Salter, begged him to go opposite direction as me so he wouldn't be blamed. Said the bridles he stole would only buy us so much time, and we needed to go. Ten miles on we tossed the bridles hanging over our saddle horns into the brush."

"That's my boy," Lana said.

"Rode up the Poudre River toward the park. Thought we were home free. Couldn't go to the Hole, might lead them there.... though Salter knows.... needed Hattie. Suggested I hide in Black Hawk, send for you. Four days out, they find us south of the park. Don't know how. Thought we covered our tracks.

"We were by Grand Lake. Stopped there to rest. Had ridden hard five days, horses almost done for. Zeke said might could trade at the Fraser post office, or somewhere along the way. Didn't want to part with Storm, so I..." *Garbled.*

"We were on a ridge when Storm was shot out from under me. Threw me down the mountain, he followed. He broke his neck. I was knocked out."

"He? He who?" Lana asked.

"Storm. My horse. Don't think I was out too long, but I'm not sure. Zeke nowhere to be found. I couldn't call out to him or they'd find me.

"I'm sorry, Lana."

"Don't you worry. Zeke'll come through. He's some smart, that kid."

"I hope they think I'm dead. Doc thinks I'll soon be dead anyways."

"You didn't walk here from Grand Lake, did you?"

"Made it to Fraser, caught a ride back to Idaho Springs with a teamster delivering mail and supplies. I don't remember the man who brought me here.

"I'm so tired. Tomorrow I die. It's the only way…"

24

WPA Slave Narrative Collection

Interview with Henrietta Lee

Thursday, September 17, 1936

Now, Grace Williams, don't be angry with me for making you wait a few days for the story. I'm old and needed time to think on it. Wrote me some notes, too. See? You can have them if you want, but I doubt you can read them.

"There we were in Black Hawk—the date? Hell, I don't remember. August or thereabouts. Garet was in bed upstairs, unconscious, high on laudanum. Claire and I were downstairs in the kitchen, trying to figure out what to do. Storm came that night. Bad one. All the typical dramatics—thunder, lightning, rain hitting the roof so hard you thought it might burrow through, wind making the house creak so much you thought it might just give up the fight and fall down. No sensible person would've been out in it. But in walked the whore Ruby Steele, soaking wet and shivering.

"House went into an uproar. It ain't every day that an Oriental walks into your house with gallons of water streaming off her clothes. Goes without saying she brought a lot of questions in with the rain.

"While Laurie, that was the boardinghouse owner, was taking Ruby to change into dry clothes, Frank, her husband (I remembered his name) made a new pot of coffee.

"Let me just stop right here and tell you something real quick. I mentioned how Jehu brought women to the ranch, to help them out? Laurie and her son were the very first ones. Long before my time. Saved from a cruel husband, I think. Anyways, whatever it was, Laurie was as loyal to Garet as I was.

"Back to the story. Waiting on Ruby to get dry, Claire asked me if I thought Garet was giving up.

"We'd seen Garet, she'd woken up to talk to us. Told us how she got to Black Hawk. Not many details, but she hadn't been beaten, we knew that for sure. Fell off her horse trying to escape from Connolly. So he wasn't blameless.

"I stayed after everyone left her room. I'd been shocked when Garet said she was ready to die. I sat on the edge of her bed and held her hand, stroked it. Garet had strong hands, all that work with the horses and on the farm. That blood vessel on the back of her hand stood out—weren't no fat to mask it—and it always looked like a river branching off in all directions. Crazy the things the mind remembers. Can't hardly remember what I ate yesterday, but I can remember tracing that blood vessel with my finger and trying to find words to get past the rocklike lump in my throat.

"'Worried I've thrown up the sponge?' she asked me with something close to a shit-eating grin. As close as a woman on her deathbed could come to one, I suppose.

"Told her the thought had crossed my mind. 'You know me better than that,' she said. And she told me her plan.

"So when Claire asked me if she was giving up, I said hell no. That woman always had a plan. I laughed and told Claire that Garet didn't have any give up in her. And neither did I.

"Connolly thought she was dead, so we might as well finish the job. Obituary, funeral, plot, the whole works. That would give us a lot of leeway in what we did next, if robbing Connolly was still on her mind, and I guessed that it was.

"Not a bad plan, a hell of a sight better than what we'd come up with before. Then Ruby showed up and by God, everything went to hell.

"You know, Claire and I had spent a couple of weeks bored to tears of each other, of purple sashes, of nothing happening. But when things started moving, it happened all at once.

"Ruby told us her story: Spooner got tired of the lack of variety in Timberline and left the Hole to do some carousing up and down the line. A few days after Spooner left, Jehu decided to make his supply run to Rock Springs. Ruby went with him to pick up some new girls. The Hole was getting busy, and it was too much for two women. Luke Rhodes went, too. She never said what for. They all split up in Rock Springs to do their own business. They were staying overnight, so she didn't see Jehu, or expect to see him, until the morning. When breakfast came around, no Jehu. Went to the stables where the wagon was, no Jehu. Luke found him easy enough. He'd been arrested the night before. Spooner saw him at the saloon and turned him in as part of our gang. A man was there who had been the gun for a couple of Jehu's trips and he confirmed it, said he'd started to suspect him after the Gunnison stage. Didn't matter to the Rock Springs sheriff that Spooner was an outlaw, and that the jobs took place in Colorado and not Wyoming. Angered Luke something fierce, Ruby said. Luke went to fetch Stella and Joan and sent Ruby to Denver to find us. We were all to meet up in Cheyenne.

"That was it. I was leaving, storm or no. Claire managed to hold me back, to ask me if I would ever go into a job half-cocked and upset like this. Course I wouldn't, and it stopped me. I couldn't have made it to Rock Springs. I wasn't familiar with the territory around Black Hawk and would have most likely fallen down the side of a mountain. But we needed to get to Jehu, quick. The doc told me in no uncertain terms that Garet couldn't leave that bed for a week, at least, or risk infection, the wound opening and her bleeding out. Doc would've got a lot bloodier in her descriptions 'cause she saw the determination in me, but we were interrupted by the bastard himself, Callum Connolly."

Mrs. Lee pauses here for a good amount of time, but I don't pressure her. I let her sit with her memories awhile.

"Those Pinkertons barged into that boardinghouse like they were breaking a strike instead of walking into a house full of women and one man. There might have been four guns between us, and there were three Pinkertons, including Salter. Yeah, that bastard was a Pinkerton. We were lousy with Pinkertons. He had a bandage on his left ear that was wet with rain and blood, and he looked none too happy. They held their rifles across their chests like an honor guard, and Callum Connolly walked into the room.

"Never met the son, but of course I recognized him with that mask covering half of his face. Injury in the war, I think. We were in trouble, and I knew it, so of course I got smart with them. Never a good thing for a black woman to sass an angry white man. But the longer I distracted them, the longer I had to figure out how to get us out of the mess. I'd managed to drop my gun belt and slide it under a worktable, and I had my knife at the small of my back, up under my vest. I'd heard those kinds of footsteps before and knew they forebode nothing good. Best for them not to know I'm armed.

"'You must be Callum Connolly.' I looked that man up and down like I was inspecting a prize hog. 'Nice mask. Leather, isn't it? Bet that's gonna shrink up in this rain.' Salter punched me in the face, but I was expecting it. I wiped the blood from my mouth easy as you please, even though my ears were ringing. Loosened my turban, too. I wouldn't've lasted long beneath his fists. Connolly stared at me over his mask with these blue eyes that almost glowed when the lightning flashed. 'You look more like a precious metals man than leather. Or is this your traveling mask?'

"'Where is she?' he asked.

"Told him he was going to have to be more specific and got another blow to the head for my trouble. Claire stepped between me and Callum. Told him to stop it. Callum looked right through her to me. "You must be…the slave. Prettier than I expected. So few of them are pretty,' he said to the men. 'You have to close your eyes when you fuck them.' Grace leaned back against me, or maybe I pressed forward, but she stood her ground. 'You seem to have survived your captivity unscathed.'

"I wanted to pull my knife out and gut him. Never wanted anything more in my life. What did he know of what I had and hadn't been through? What did he know of the scars that criss-crossed my back? Course they never touched my face, I was worth more when I was pretty. Anything else, though. That was fair game, and let me tell you, they played. You're goddamn right they played. For years. I knew then, and know now, that there are men who play, who torture us, abuse us, treat our bodies like they're nothing but chattel, still. Nothing's changed. All these years. Still black people are being punished.

"Connolly pushed Claire aside and she fell onto the floor. He got right up next to me, looked at me with an expression I'd seen many times before from a white man. It's this queer mixture of lust and hatred. You know the look. 'Tell me where she is and I won't let my men touch you. You have my word.'

"It was a lie and everyone in that room knew it. Those men's cocks were getting hard just thinking of it. I couldn't gut him because I wasn't sure his men would empty lead into me. Most like they'd injure me, beat me maybe, but keep me whole enough they could have their way. That was not going to happen. I'd been raped by my last white man back in '68. I would've slit my own throat before I let another white man touch me. I couldn't kill Connolly, though goddamn, a lot of trouble would have been saved if I had. No, I had to think of Jehu. I tried to tamp down my anger and stay focused on Jehu and what he was going through.

"So I told Connolly he was too late, that the cancer had finally got Margaret Parker. She wouldn't leave the bed.

"He said he wanted to see her and Grace jumped up and said no. He looked at her then, and she quailed under those glowing eyes but caught herself. 'This is my case, and these are my prisoners. I've been working for Dorcas for months, I infiltrated the gang, gained their trust.'

"'Yet you've never turned them in,' he said. I'll never forget Claire's laugh. She sounded plumb crazy, then what came out of her mouth sounded even crazier. 'Of course not. What would have happened if I turned them in? Would it have made the papers? Probably not. You've done a stellar job of keeping their exploits out of the public eye. No, they would have been quietly dealt with.' She gave Salter a disdainful look. 'I know enough about Mr. Salter over there to not wish that on any woman, even if they are hardened criminals. I need Margaret Parker's arrest to be a splash, you see. A spectacle, so I can open my own agency.'

"The Pinkerton men laughed at that and said some pretty offensive stuff. Claire, though, she stood toe-to-toe with

Connolly. She knew the only thing that made those men dangerous was their guns.

"Claire went on about how she had planned on turning us in until she learned how extensive Margaret's plan was. Garet wanted to humiliate Spooner, not just win. So Claire got rid of Dorcas so Callum would take Margaret to all his businesses. She knew enough about Margaret Parker's cunning mind to rest easy that she would do it. 'She's an arrogant, greedy woman,' Claire said. 'Hubris is what would have brought her down, if the cancer hadn't.' She laughed that laugh again. 'Guess my own ambition has worked against me. Margaret is almost dead, and no one will believe a nigger and two ignorant girls have the intelligence to pull off the jobs they have.'

"I believed her. I thought she was turning on us, confirming every goddamn suspicion I'd had of her from the beginning. She was that good. Then she said, 'They're no threat to you. They couldn't pull off Margaret's ideas if they wanted to, and honestly? They don't. Margaret is manipulative and had three easy targets with her gang. They would do what she said because they admired her. I've lived with them for three months, I know them. All they want to do is to raise horses and live in peace.'

"I could tell Connolly wasn't buying it, but Claire's nonsense was giving me a chance to plot, to watch the men with him, to gauge their weaknesses. Connolly asked who the Chink was. I'd forgotten Ruby was there. I knew that whore well enough to know she was reading the room, figuring out where best to land. That woman, Ruby Steele, she was a stone-cold survivor.

"Claire told him Ruby was with her, she'd enlisted her help to spy on Spooner in the Hole. 'She's had no part in the jobs at all. Come on, I'll take you to see Margaret. You can see for yourself that the threat against your business is over, from this gang at least.'

"Ruby went back with them, and I stood there, watching the Pinkertons, reading on their faces easy enough that there was no way in hell they would let me get back to the Hole alive. By the time Grace came back to the kitchen they'd taken my knife, found my gun belt, and put me in irons, but not without a fight. Busted one man's lip pretty good, but got knocked out for my trouble. I'd just come to and stood up, leaning against the wall to hold myself up, when all the shooting started."

25

Margaret Parker's Journal

Events of August 23-24, 1877
Written September 30, 1877
Heresy Ranch
Timberline, Colorado

Filling in the gaps of my story as best I can with the little time I have left.

I don't remember much about being at Lana Chambers's boardinghouse, but what I do remember is crystal clear: Alida Avery gently telling me I would most likely never leave the bed, Hattie stroking my hand, Grace and Callum looking down on me, talking about me as if I were already dead.

He sat in a chair next to the window and pulled out a cigarette.

—What are you doing? Grace asked.

—Watching the storm. Smoking. Waiting for her to die.

Dr. Avery had watched the scene silently. —You may be waiting a long time.

—How long?

—Days? Weeks? Maybe hours. There's no way to tell.

—We aren't leaving until the storm passes, and this is as good a spot to watch the storm as any. Claire? That is your real name, right?

—Yes.

—Get me some coffee and a sandwich.

Grace, or Claire I suppose, shocked me by readily agreeing. Dr. Avery left the room, too, saying she would bring some broth back for me.

Lightning flashed across Callum's face as he stared out the window and smoked. When I spoke it startled him.

—So you've come to watch me die. That's rather vindictive. I would expect it of Dorcas, but not of you.

—You're stolen more from me than you did from my father.

—So all that talk of understanding and ancient history was a lie.

—Not at all. I couldn't care less about the '73 robbery. But your gang will pay for the other five.

—You want your pound of flesh. Kill me. Now.

—Unsatisfying. You're dying anyways.

—Do whatever you want to me, then kill me.

Clouds of smoke drifted up, obscuring his expression, but he remained silent. A dull pain started in my stomach. My limbs were growing heavy; it was the latest dose of laudanum taking effect. My tongue was thick and dry when I tried to talk.

—Punish *me*. Make me pay. But please, let my family be.

Callum stood. He stubbed his cigarette out on the windowsill, lifted the chair he'd been sitting on, and wedged it beneath the doorknob. His footsteps echoed in the room between booms of thunder, like the beat of a military drum leading the guilty to the firing squad. He stared down at me in my sickbed—wasted, perspiring, malodorous—and shook his head.

—Punishment is only effective if it has long-term effects. You'll be dead before the night is over. You will be spared, Duchess, but examples have to be made. I'm especially going to enjoy the slave. She is a beautiful woman.

I wanted to rise, I tried, but my limbs were too heavy, as if someone were holding me down. He saw my struggle and smirked.

—I'm going to kill you, just like I killed yo—

A volley of gunshots rang through the house. Callum ran out of the room, gun drawn. I tried to get up, to help, to make sure Hattie was OK, but Alida and Ruby appeared, and held me down.

—Let me go. He's going to hurt—

—Drink this, quick, Alida said.

Another gunshot rang out.

—What's happening? Who's shooting? Where's Hattie?

—We don't know, Ruby said. A gunfight wasn't part of our plan. Drink this, Garet. We have to make Connolly think you're dead. Can you play dead?

—Not going to be much of an act.

—I can't believe I'm doing this, Alida said, pouring the potion down my throat.

—It's just hawthorn, Ruby said. You're not breaking any oaths.

—If it kills her I am.

—Garet, listen. This will slow down your heartbeat enough so that we can fool Connolly.

—This a stupid plan. I can't believe I agreed to it, Dr. Avery said.

—When Dr. Avery puts a mirror up to your nose to prove to Connolly you're dead, hold your breath.

I nodded and grabbed Ruby's arm.

—Make sure nothing happens to Hattie. Don't leave her side.

I don't remember anything until I woke up in a coffin. That was an interesting experience. A sliver of light streamed into my eyes, and when I raised my hand to block it, I hit the rough wood of the coffin top. A man's voice asked about the noise. Hattie replied, —Didn't hear nothing. Hard to hear anything with the river on one side and this godforsaken road knocking us around like tenpins. Might be able to keep from knocking if you'd bind my hands in front of me.

The man laughed.

We drove on, my mind cleared, and I took stock. I'd played dead pretty well, it would seem. Hattie was in chains, which meant she would be no help. But she was near, and alive. There was a gun by my side, hidden beneath my skirt. I picked it up slowly and felt it. Sawed-off double-barreled shotgun. I remember thinking, *This is going to be messy.*

Grace's voice sounded rather close by.

—This is an uncomfortable ride, Salter. Why don't you let Ruby and me take your place? You know how to drive a wagon, don't you, Ruby?

—I do.

—There you go.

—I'm not about to put you in charge of driving the wagon.

—You don't trust me?

—No, I don't, Claire Hamilton. Pinkerton told me about you, how softhearted you are.

—I know all about you, too. And I know the chances of us making it to Denver are slim. Especially since you're heading north, not east.

—You probably would make a good detective.

—I *am* a good detective.

—Not as good as I am, and not for much longer, you aren't.

I took a deep, steadying breath, and the stitches in my stomach pulled tight. I gritted my teeth to keep from crying out.

Grace and Hattie had painted the scene for me as best they could. Two men on the driver's bench, three women in the wagon bed with my coffin. A lid that was open just enough I could hear easily, and I could see the dark-blue fabric of a woman's dress to my left. I lifted my head to see toward my feet. Lighter-colored fabric next to the blue. The side of the wagon visible through the right edge. I thought the head of the coffin was closest to the end of the wagon, but I wasn't sure. I pushed against the lid and, after the smallest resistance, it released, widening the crack a quarter inch. I breathed deeply and wished I had a bit of the hawthorn to slow my racing heart down. It was nothing like the adrenaline rush I got from outlawing. Taking a man's life is a sobering proposition, even if it is in the service of saving someone else's.

It's been a few weeks. I'm over it now.

I lifted the lid a bit more and saw Ruby's face. I pointed toward my feet and mouthed, –Two men? She nodded. I held up three fingers and counted down. When I hit one, I curled my hand into a fist and pushed against the lid. I sat up and pumped the rifle at the same time. Hattie, directly in front of me, ducked. I put a hole the size of a melon in one man's back, pumped the rifle again, and blew half of Salter's head off. In the split second before Salter realized he was dead, I saw his shock that he had been bested by a bunch of women.

The gunshots echoed off the canyon wall, and the wagon horses bolted. Hattie got up unsteadily, realized her hands were cuffed behind her back.

–Grace, she shouted.

Grace climbed over the coffin and around Hattie and got the reins.

–Pull back, pull back, Hattie yelled.

–I am, goddamn it. They're strong.

–Well, you better hurry the hell up because see that curve up there? The horses are gonna make it, but this wagon sure ain't.

I pushed myself to my feet for the first time in I didn't know how long. The world went sideways, and I nearly fell over the side. Ruby caught me and told me to sit down.

—Give me one, Ruby said, and together she and Grace were able to slow the horses down enough that the wagon didn't go careening over the side of the cliff and into the river. It took them about a hundred more yards, but they were finally able to stop the team.

The last thing I saw before I passed out was Ruby and Grace hugging, and Hattie telling them to stop celebrating and find the damn key.

BLACK HAWK BULLETIN

TUESDAY, AUGUST 28, 1877

CHARNEL HOUSE ON GREGORY STREET

FRANK & LANA CHAMBERS AMONG FOUR DEAD

Frank and Lana Chambers, owners of the Gregory Street boardinghouse bearing their name, met a bloody fate on August 23, when an argument turned deadly. Mrs. Chambers, whom residents of Black Hawk know as feisty, pulled a gun on a Pinkerton who was there looking for her son, Zeke. Frank Chambers defended his wife, as any husband would, and the result was a pulpy mess of dead bodies on the kitchen floor. Two other Pinkertons survived the onslaught to give testimony of an event no one else witnessed.

The fourth fatality was a woman who succumbed to cancer after a lengthy illness. Dr. Alida Avery, a doctor who accompanied Susan B. Anthony to her speech at the Methodist church, attended the sick woman, as well as those who met with violence, though nothing could be done to help.

Lana and Frank Chambers will be buried in the Masonic Cemetery on Saturday at two o'clock, with a short service performed graveside.

The boardinghouse, located in a prime part of Gregory Street, will be auctioned off by the town on Tuesday next. There have already been rumblings from some that the auction is for show only, and that Nathaniel Hill has already reached an agreement with the mayor for the vacant house, for use as a dormitory for the smelters he is bringing in from Wales. The auction is expected to be eventful, so get there early, and bring a picnic lunch.

ROCKY MOUNTAIN NEWS

SUNDAY, AUGUST 26, 1877

OBITUARY

DUCHESS OF PARKERTON, MARGARET ELIZABETH STANDRIDGE PARKER

Born in 1843 in Somerset, England, died August 23, 1877, Black Hawk, Colorado. Preceded in death by her husband, Lieutenant Thomas Parker, veteran of the Charge of the Light Brigade. Mrs. Parker and her husband toured the West on their honeymoon in 1863 and decided to settle in the territory. Lieutenant Parker claimed 160 acres for himself and 160 for his wife in the Cache la Poudre valley and started a horse ranch, which was stolen from her by Colonel Louis Connolly after Mr. Parker, then the Duke of Parkerton, died from a long illness. Since she cannot be buried next to her husband on their ranch, she will be buried in Riverside Cemetery.

26

Margaret Parker's Journal

Sunday, August 26, 1877
Denver, Colorado

I woke in a lumpy bed in a seedy room, with Alida Avery listening to my heartbeat with a stethoscope. She smiled when she saw I was awake, shook her head, and said I might live forever.

—Don't say such a thing. What day is it?

—Sunday, August twenty-sixth.

—The vote is almost upon us. What do you think of your chances?

—I'm not sure bringing in Miss Anthony and her comrades has been to our advantage.

—I'm sorry to hear that. I would like nothing more than to see the amendment pass before I die.

—So would I.

—Where is everyone?

—They have gone to rescue someone named Jehu.

She told me not to sit up, but I ignored her and regretted it. She helped me lie back down, gave me a sip of water, and wiped the perspiration from my forehead.

—Rescue him from what?

—He's in jail in Cheyenne, I believe. That was where they left for yesterday, at least.

—Yesterday? How long have I been here? When did I ki— When did they bring me to Denver?

—Two days ago. The ruse worked, against all odds.

I steeled myself against the pain and sat up again. She asked me where I thought I was going.

—To help my friends.

—Hattie told me you would do this.

—You're goddamn right I'm doing it.

—Really, your language is unnecessary.

—I apologize.

She handed me a letter, which I've already lost, of course. In it Hattie told me to sit still and recover for a day or two. If things went as expected, Joan and Stella would be in Cheyenne and they would easily be able to spring Jehu with five people, maybe six if they could talk Rhodes into helping. When they got back with Jehu, the real planning would begin. The job was still on, as far as she was concerned. The only thing that could muck it up was if I got it in my mind to come save the day. She had it under control.

What was unsaid, but in between every line, was that it was about time they went out on their own. I wasn't going to be around much longer, and they had to learn how to rely on themselves.

—They left you a loaded shotgun. And a box of shells, which is a bit much for a bedridden woman, don't you think?

A gunshot rang out in the distance, and Alida jumped.

—I suppose not, she said.

I started laughing and grabbed my side in pain.

She repositioned me in bed and gave me a draught of laudanum, a small one at my request.

—What happened to your escorts?

I shook my head and didn't answer. A pained expression crossed her face.

—I am afraid I'm mixed up in something that will haunt me, she said.

—No. I promise. When they return I will leave Denver and never return. I will be dead soon, and none of the gang will give you up. I swear it.

She took a deep breath as if steeling herself to believe me.

—I feel I should tell you something, though Hattie asked me not to.

—What is it?

—The shooting, at the boardinghouse. The Chamberses were killed.

Though she hadn't witnessed it, she was able to fill me in on the details she'd heard secondhand from Claire, which led to one inescapable conclusion: Lana, Zeke, and Frank were all dead because they'd helped me, and Callum Connolly was responsible.

—Was he arrested?

—Who? Connolly? No. He didn't kill anyone, as far as I know. He left soon after, remember?

—Yes, of course. Was anyone arrested?

—No.

—Dr. Avery? What are you not telling me?

She cleared her throat. —It was blamed on the Chamberses. Hattie, Grace, and that pretty little Chinawoman tried to tell the sheriff what happened, but he wasn't interested. The newspaper article wasn't terrible, at least. I'm sorry to be the bearer of bad news.

—Thank you for telling me.

—From your expression, I'm afraid I shouldn't have.

—No, Doctor, this is my *I probably should have a stronger dose of laudanum* expression.

—I knew it.

She turned away to mix the drug with whisky, and I snatched her stethoscope from her bag and put it under my blankets. She placed the drink on the small table next to my bed.

—When you are better, will you go home, Margaret?

—You mean there's the possibility I will get out of this bed?

Dr. Avery looked sheepish. —A small one, yes.

—Well, if I am so lucky, I'm not sure what I'll do. In truth, I'm not sure there's a home to go to.

—Where else would you go?

—I hear there's a canyon in Arizona Territory worth seeing before you die.

Dr. Avery's mouth tightened, as if my death, and her inability to stop it, were somehow her fault.

—I've thought a lot about it, my death. That's a benefit of knowing it's coming sooner rather than later. Of course, we are all terminal, but I've been given a gift, don't you think? I can determine how and when I die.

—You wouldn't...?

—Take my own life? Hmm. No, not personally. There's more than one way to die.

—Oh, Margaret. I wish I could do more for you.

I didn't know what to say to her, how to make her feel better, if it was even my responsibility. Dr. Avery had removed the tumor, and I was generally more comfortable for it. How could I not be with a five-pound solid mass no longer poking out of my abdomen? But her news that the cancer had spread to other organs, while expected, was still devastating.

Dr. Avery was quiet for a moment.

—Can I ask you something?

—Of course.

—Are you an outlaw?

—Did Grace give you that idea?

—Who's Grace?

—Right, Claire Hamilton. Former Pinkerton agent.

—Is she truly? I had no idea. But it makes sense. At a meeting last month, she asked a group of us about a gang of female outlaws and if we'd heard of them. She was talking about you, wasn't she?

—Do I look like an outlaw?

—No.

—Have you ever met an outlaw?

—No, but with everything that happened in Black Hawk…

—Of course.

I drank the opiate-laced whisky and felt the familiar rush of numbness almost immediately. I hated myself for the weakness, for choosing this little bit of oblivion for the night instead of facing what I've wrought, but I'm just so damn tired. I'm alone, and don't have to be strong for anyone. Not for a few hours. The reckoning will come soon enough.

—Promise me something, will you, Dr. Avery?

—Yes.

—Don't believe everything you hear about me.

—What if I hear good things?

—Especially not the good things.

—I have only known you for a brief time, and much of that time you've been unconscious, but there is something about you that is fascinating.

—Claire said the same thing the first day we met. Once she got to know me, I think the fascination wore off.

Dr. Avery laughed.

—Hardly. I'll come check on you tomorrow afternoon. If you need anything at all, this is how to find me. She placed a small card on the desk next to the box of shells, which sat on top of a familiar-looking notebook.

—I can't believe that made it back with me.

—Is it your journal?

—My memoirs, in fact. I need to work on them with all this free time I have.

—I hope I get to read them someday.

—So do I.

Sunday, August 26, 1877, cont

I'll confess I'm disappointed there wasn't a funeral for me. Rather difficult to have one when the two men returning you to Denver are dead and had been rolled down the side of a canyon, I suppose. The obituary ran, so I am officially a dead woman.

It is rather freeing.

Indulge me while I imagine what my funeral would have been like if I hadn't shot Salter and the other Pinkerton full of lead. It would have been held on a Saturday afternoon, in a small church near the Riverside Cemetery. You know the one, all out there by itself three miles down the Platte toward Nebraska. The wind would have been blowing across the plains, whipping the mourning dresses worn by Claire, Dorcas, and Alida Avery. Her presence would have been necessary to put the final nail in my coffin, so to speak. To complete the ruse. I would hope that they would let Hattie out of jail for the service, but most like not. If she could go, she'd wear the bright red tignon, in one of her more fanciful styles, tied on the side like I like. Ruby would be there, too, I suppose. I still haven't gotten a clear story on how she came to be in Black Hawk. There's going to be lots of explaining to do when they return with Jehu.

But since there was no funeral, Dr. Avery doesn't have her reputation staked on my death. None of us will rat her out; the only man who knows she confirmed the death is Callum Connolly, and, well, I have plans for him. He doesn't expect any of us to come back from Black Hawk alive, and he won't miss Salter or his henchman for a while. Which buys me some time.

It's Sunday afternoon and the business district is quiet. I stared into a shop window at the building behind me. Dark and quiet at the front, as expected. I walked down the street, stopping at every window, a man out for a morning stroll. The truth was the laudanum had worn off and I needed to stop frequently because of the pain in my stomach. It felt as if someone had taken a whisk to my insides, and the stitches holding everything in were tight and painful. In an hour or less I could drink the laudanum in my pocket. It would be my reward for a successful job.

Pain or no, I knew when I saw that safe in Connolly's office a month ago that I had to crack it.

Years ago, when Spooner and his gang first started using the Poudre River Ranch as their hideout, Ought-Not taught me how to crack a safe. He needed to practice for the job they were planning, and our safe was the same brand, only significantly smaller, as the one they were robbing. I stood over him to make sure he kept his eyes averted from the dial. When I asked to have a go at it, he handed me the stethoscope, and I cracked it on the third try. Ought-Not was impressed, said I had a career in crime. When Jehu and I robbed Connolly's bank back in '73, I didn't try to crack the safe. I was too nervous and not confident enough in my skills. It was easier, and more of a sure thing, to use the clerk.

I went down the alley at the back of the building and found the service entrance. I knocked and waited, listening for footsteps. When none came, I pulled out the twelve-inch crowbar I'd borrowed from a blacksmith near the tenderloin district (one of my first rest breaks), wedged it between the door and jamb, and pried open the door, leaving more damage than I'd wanted.

I walked through the building as if I were supposed to be there. It's easier to pull off a lie if you're confident about it. I saw no one, thought, *This is too easy,* and smelled cigar smoke at the same time I saw the light on in Connolly's office. I shoved the crowbar beneath my belt and pulled my sawed-off shotgun out from under my coat.

Grace, or Claire, you may be wondering right now what's gotten into me. When did I turn into a cold-blooded killer? November 19, 1873. The day I robbed my first bank.

What follows isn't a justification of my actions, and it isn't an apology. I did it, and I don't regret it. At least not anymore. I stopped regretting killing men when I poisoned the colonel in '74.

Alfie Gernsbeck caught me on a bad day, one of the lowest of my life. Instead of trying to help a woman who was clearly starving and without a coat at the start of winter, he decided taking me to a back alley and *fucking* me was what I needed. I needed his coat, and a distraction, so I blew his brains out, much like I did with Salter. It was an impulse born of months and months of being taken advantage of, of being dismissed, betrayed, talked down to, being insulted by almost every man I came in contact with. I didn't think of men as individuals, but as a toxic hole whose only goal was to protect their power by keeping women down, subservient. By taking me into that alley, Alfie Gernsbeck showed himself to be just another man, like all the others who had put me in the position of needing to rob a bank to survive.

After the job, I wasn't sure if my elation was from robbing the bank or killing Gernsbeck. I didn't analyze it too much. We had money, Spooner took us to the Hole that next spring, and we started over. I should have been happy to move on, content, but I kept thinking of the adrenaline of that day, how alive I felt. I knew I was going to do another job, I just wasn't sure when. As I replayed that day over and over in my mind, reveling in getting away with something so brazen, of making a fool of Connolly, I started seeing the colonel's face when I lifted the gun and pulled the trigger. It was the colonel's skull I saw splattered on that wall. You imagine something like that enough, and it gets in your brain. I knew that I'd killed the wrong man, that it should have been the colonel, and that my mind wouldn't be at rest until it was.

Of course, I couldn't blow his head off. He was too big a man for that, big in importance, that is. I figured that the law would do everything they could to find his killer, and suspicion just might fall on the widow whose ranch he'd bought for pennies on the dollar a year or so before. No, poison was best, and I knew just how to give it so that no one else would get hurt.

Like most men who come from nothing, the colonel liked to impress people with expensive things. He took great pride in bringing out a fine bottle of Kentucky bourbon when he wanted to show he was so rich that cost didn't matter. But the colonel was a poor man at heart. He came from nothing, but you would've never known it from his appearance, his accent, or his deportment. He had transformed himself into a man of means first in South Carolina, then in Colorado. But blood will out, and when he was alone, he pulled out a bottle of moonshine from the bottom left corner of his credenza. I know because he trusted me enough to tell me, though he wouldn't insult me by offering it to me. He gave me bourbon. This was before I turned his offer of marriage down, of course.

I had the how, now I needed the when. The colonel would go out with his cowboys to round up his cattle from the summer grazing grounds in September, and I targeted that as the right time. I had the perfect cover for Jehu and Hattie; I'd been going into the mountains for a while to be alone and to hunt. No one but me knew that the hunting wasn't merely to stock our smokehouse for the winter. Killing animals sated the bloodlust in me that had been awakened with Gernsbeck. For a year that need tortured me. What kind of woman gets a thrill from killing? You almost expect it from men, especially here in the West, but a woman? I convinced myself that poisoning the colonel would eradicate it from me, that I could move on, so by the time I left for my hunt, killing the colonel had become life or death for me.

I watched his ranch from the foothills for three days. The first day they were preparing for the drive, shoeing their horses, stocking the chuck wagon with food, cleaning and oiling tack, taking care of their guns. They left at dawn on day two. I lay on a flat-topped boulder and watched the ranch through my husband's spyglass, the same one that had ridden with him during the Charge of the Light Brigade. A couple of green cowboys were left behind, and Zhu Li was going in and out of the kitchen.

The morning of the third day I went farther back into the foothills and killed and dressed a deer. I was back at my post by ten a.m., cooking deer steaks to sear in the blood. I watched and waited through the third day, to be safe, but nothing wavered. At midnight I made sure my horse was hobbled, took my saddlebag full of cooked meat and my sawed-off shotgun, snuck down the hill, and crept across the pasture. Clouds snuffed out the stars, and it was a moonless night. I made it almost to the barn before the dogs started barking. I dropped down onto the ground and waited for the green cowboys to come and investigate. They were into their whisky, as I suspected, and were more annoyed with the dogs breaking their peace than concerned there might be a legitimate reason for the barking. One of them kicked a dog, who slunk off whimpering, and the others went with him.

—Bastard.

I waited until I was sure the threat was gone and made my way to the barn. The dogs growled at me but didn't bark. I pulled out chunks of deer meat and tossed it to them. I waited while they ate it eagerly, and they came over for more. I let them smell me, scratched them behind the ears, and murmured a few sweet words. When they started licking me, I knew they wouldn't trouble me again. I dumped the rest of the deer meat from the saddlebag and made my way to the house.

In the middle of nowhere, there's hardly a need for locks on the windows, which made getting into his office easy enough. I was putting the poisoned moonshine back in its place when Zhu Li walked into the office, a gun on her shoulder. She said something in Chinese, and I held my hands up. She moved forward and lowered her gun when she finally saw me.

—Miss Margaret?

—Hi, Zhu Li.

—What...

Her eyes went to the opened cabinet, and I closed it slowly.

—How is he treating you? Good?

—OK, for a white man.

—You can come with me, you know. I have a place, I think you'd like it.

—You aren't mad at me?

—Why? For taking a job? No. Never.

Her shoulders relaxed and she lowered the gun.

—You're a better boss.

—That goes without saying.

—How is everyone? Jehu? Hattie?

—They're...

I stopped and smiled at my old friend.

—I haven't seen them since we left.

She knew I was lying, and why. I picked up my gun and stepped out the open window. I tossed my waiting saddlebag on my shoulder and asked her one more time if she wanted to come.

—No. I have a man, working on the rail to Santa Fe. He won't know where to find me.

—Good for you.

—He's a nice man.

—Then you need to keep hold of him.

—You take care, she said.

—You, too.

I never considered killing her, though leaving her alive was a risk. The poison was slow acting; it would take weeks for him to die, and by the time they needed to plant him, the ground would be frozen solid. I like to imagine his dead body in the ice house, covered with horse blankets, during the long, dark winter.

I pushed open Callum's slightly ajar office door with the barrel of my gun. He looked up from his ledger and stared at me almost as if he'd been waiting for me. He sighed, dropped his pen into the crease of the ledger, and leaned back.

—You're like a damn cat, you know.

—Or a bad penny. That's probably a better analogy for you. What are you wearing today? Nickel? Tin?

He narrowed his eyes but didn't take the bait. I watched him put his arms on the sides of his desk chair.

—Salter and Wilson?

—Both dead.

He nodded.

—You really are a killer. I didn't believe Dorcas.

—You'll be dead before you pull that gun from under your desktop.

—Maybe I'm going to shoot you through—

His chest exploded in a spray of blood. His head dropped forward and he patted ineffectively at his gaping wound. Blood bubbled from his mouth and he tried to speak.

—Or maybe not.

I set the gun on the desk and swiveled Callum's chair to face me. I put my hands on the arms and leaned down. He was still alive, but just barely.

—You should have never threatened Hattie and killed my friends, you son of a bitch. You tell your father when you see him in hell that a woman has fucking beat you all, at every turn.

I pushed the chair away and went to the safe. It took me six tries to crack it, but considering I'd been cut open barely a week ago, had sweat running into my eyes, and had a dying man groaning behind me, I'd say I did all right.

The safe was full of cash, papers, and a gold-plated version of Connolly's mask, one I hadn't seen before. I stuffed the cash and papers in my bag and lifted the mask. It was heavier than I'd thought it would be, too heavy to wear. I turned it over and saw the stamp of Nathaniel Hill's Black Hawk smelter. I used a letter opener to scratch a deep groove in it. Solid gold. I put it in my bag with the cash.

I flipped through the blood-splattered ledger. Callum was correct: some of his businesses were bleeding money, others were leveraged to the hilt. Only a few were healthy (the ones Dorcas acquired, I imagine), and he was using those profits to invest heavily in a lead smelter in Oro City. Still, there was loot here to be taken.

I rifled through the papers on Connolly's desk, jotted notes down on a scrap of paper, closed the ledger, and rolled the dead man back to the desk, facing the wall. Dorcas is in for a shock tomorrow morning.

I made it back to my bolt-hole drenched with sweat and bleeding slightly from my bandages. No one asked any questions or offered to help me up the stairs, that is the kind of place this is, they just watched me with calculating eyes, gauging how vulnerable a mark I am. I felt the bag, heavy with the mask, knock against my thigh. I pulled my jacket back, exposing the shotgun hanging on a leather strap from my shoulder to an especially seedy-looking woman, and made myself take the stairs with a strong tread. It took every ounce of my strength to move the dresser in front of the door, and I collapsed onto the flea-ridden mattress.

I woke to a gunshot in the distance, the sound of music floating from the saloon and brothel across the street. The dresser was firmly across the door, and my bag lay where I'd dropped it, the mask bright against the wood floor. I rose shakily to my feet, put the mask on the dresser, and saw the blood spot on my shirt. I found my spiked whisky and took a large swig. The alcohol burned my throat and I coughed, spitting a portion onto the dresser mirror and mask. A few deep breaths later and my arms relaxed with the comforting buzz of eighty-proof alcohol and laudanum.

Bandaging myself took considerably longer, and by the time I was finished, I was sweating and breathing heavily. I lit a cigarette generously seeded with hashish and sat down to write today's events.

It's nearing dawn now, and my cigarette butt is cold, but it snuffed out the jitteriness left over from the job, and the pain is dulled, which was the goal.

Five thousand dollars lie on my bed, as well as four government bonds that Hattie and Jehu can hold on to for the future.

This, plus the value of the mask, is enough. I know it is. Well managed, they won't ever have to worry about money again. I should go back to the Hole, run Spooner off, and—

The thought of returning to the ranch to die fills me with an unexpected terror. Sitting in a rocking chair on the gallery, people waiting on me, dissecting my every move, wondering when the inevitable slide to mortality will happen, wasting away… Does that actually appeal to people? It doesn't appeal to me. I watched Thomas die, and it isn't an experience I wish on anyone else.

The bed is too inviting. I have to rest.

I dreamed of outlawing. Seven of us: me and Grace, Hattie, Stella, Joan, Ruby, and Jehu, raiding up and down the range. Split up and hitting targets at the same time, confusing the inept businessmen. We are never disguised and take full credit for our success. Women and girls line the street cheering for us when we ride into town, tossing gold coins shaped like lemon drops to everyone we see. The men want to chase us, but they have no bridles, and when they realize they aren't wearing britches, they run away, screaming with embarrassment. The women of the town throw a party for us, and there is dancing and singing and the whisky bubbles out of the ground like a spring. Opal plays the accordion, and we all dance until we are dizzy. Luke watches from the end of the bar with a smile hidden beneath his luxurious mustache. Ought-Not, Domino, and Sly Jack play poker in the corner, a small volume of Walt Whitman's poems in the middle of the pot. Jehu and Hattie slow dance, and Grace and Ruby sit in the corner, heads together, plotting our next move.

I woke up with a start when someone knocked on the door. Dr. Avery. She comes and leaves. Remembering her concerns from before, I donate handsomely to the cause to buy her silence and hopefully assuage her concerns. I won't live to see suffrage, but I hope Hattie and the girls do.

She was impressed with my bandaging skills, told me to change my bandages regularly, and gave me a bottle of diluted carbolic acid to put on my bandages to decrease the risk of infection. I wondered aloud if I should bother with it, all things considered. Part of me was hoping she was going to change her diagnosis. She closed her medical bag and remained silent.

I'm alone again, and all I can do is wait for you all to return. Two more days is all I'm waiting. I don't want to die alone, but I'm not going to die here.

27

Claire Hamilton's Case Notes

Friday, August 24, 1877
Denver, Colorado

I am in over my head.

In the last forty-eight hours, I've seen five people shot and had a few stray buckshot pellets picked out of my arm. Tomorrow I'm leaving with Hattie and Ruby to hopefully meet up with Stella, Joan, and Luke Rhodes to try to break Jehu out of jail.

How did I get here? More importantly, how do I survive?

I hardly know where to start. I'll skip over Margaret's account of how she ended up in Black Hawk, incomplete as the story was. If things go as planned, the journal I transcribed her story into will be in my possession. 'If things go as planned.' What plan?

This is not the time to be despondent.

At Lana's boardinghouse, Hattie was in the kitchen, being held under a gun by two Pinkerton thugs and Salter. Ruby and I had taken Callum to see Margaret on her deathbed. He settled down to wait for her passing and sent me downstairs to make him a sandwich. I readily agreed, and Ruby went with me. When the door was closed behind us, I said we had to find Alida. Ruby crossed her arms and refused to move.

"What was that in the kitchen?"

"Me, buying us some time."

"Are you a Pinkerton?"

"I was, but I'm not anymore. I mean, I'm a detective, but not right now."

"You're either the law or you aren't."

I could tell from her stance that she had no good opinion of the law. "I was, and I hope to be again. But right now, I'm trying to save our lives. I know Salter, and he would make sure our end was miserable."

She uncrossed her arms. "I know. What's your plan?"

I grabbed her hand and pulled her toward Alida's room. "It's so crazy, I'll talk myself out of it if I tell it twice."

Alida agreed with me. "You want me to give hawthorn to my patient, who is recovering from a major surgery? I'm dreaming, aren't I? Because that's an insane idea." She clasped her robe together at her breast. We'd woken her from a deep sleep.

"I know it's used for rapid heartbeats, yes?"

"Yes. To slow them down to normal, not to mimic death. Who would even think of that?"

I placed my hands in front of my lips in a prayer pose. "You've been asleep, so you are unaware that there are three Pinkertons in the kitchen with guns trained on Hattie, and Callum Connolly is in Garet's room, waiting for her to die."

"Callum Connolly!"

"Do you know him?"

"I've been called to treat some women who have been on the receiving end of his…"

"We get the picture," Ruby said.

"We need him to believe she is dead. The hawthorn is in case he wants to listen to her heartbeat. Hopefully a mirror test will do. What we really need is for you to put your name on the death certificate."

She reared back at the idea. "Claire, you're asking too much."

"I promise, if you have to sign one, the death certificate will never make it into the official record," Ruby said. "We need you to convince Connolly she's dead. That's all."

"And give her hawthorn."

"Can we put it in broth?"

"Yes, or tea or whisky. It's a tincture."

"Put it in laudanum, then," I said.

"Do you want to kill her? Yes, right. You do." She pulled two bottles from her doctor's bag, a pint of whisky and a smaller brown bottle. She mixed them together in a glass and handed it to Ruby. "I can't believe I'm doing this."

"I've got to go make that bastard a sandwich."

The scene in the kitchen was much as I'd left it, except Salter was sitting at the table, carving up a block of cheese and eating it off his knife. Hattie was bound and had been beaten. She leaned against the wall, keeping a wary eye on the two other Pinkertons. She glared at me when I walked in, and I had a moment of doubt about my plan. But she was playing her part, just as I was.

"There's the detective," she sneered.

I asked where Lana and Frank were.

"Haven't seen them," Salter said.

"Callum wants a sandwich."

"Make him one," Salter said.

"See there, Grace. Or should I call you Claire? No matter what you do, they won't treat you like an equal," Hattie said.

"Shut up, Hattie."

"Truth hurts, don't it?"

I saw the guards look at each other and snicker.

"I'm going to find Lana."

"Here I am," she said, and by God she walked into the kitchen holding a Peacemaker in front of her with both hands. Salter didn't move, but the two henchmen swung their guns around.

"Put it down, lady," one of the men said.

"Where's my son? Where's Zeke?"

"Was that his name?" Salter said. He put another hunk of cheese in his mouth.

"What did you do to him?"

"I didn't do anything. George back there is the one who shot him. I've never been good at distance shooting. I'm more of a ten-paces-and-turn kind of man, or hiding behind a corner and shooting from safety. You live longer that way."

"My boy is dead?"

The pleading in her voice broke my heart. Hattie nudged my arm. I moved close to her. "Get ready to duck," she said in a low voice.

"I imagine he is by now. We left him a canteen of water, but the way his leg wound was seeping, he probably didn't last for long."

"What kind of man leaves a boy to die alone?" Frank Chambers asked. He stood a little behind his wife.

"He wasn't a boy, and he made his choices. Now, you have a choice, too, Mrs. Chambers. Put the gun down."

Lana's arms were shaking with the effort to hold the gun aloft. They dipped, and everyone relaxed enough that she had a split-second advantage. But it wasn't enough. She'd barely got the hammer back before a Pinkerton shot her. Frank produced a sawed-off shotgun from somewhere and got a shot off at the same time as the other Pinkerton shot him. Within a space of a few seconds, three people dropped to the floor, dead or dying. My ears were ringing, and I felt like the house was tilting. The thick scent of blood made me gag, and I covered my mouth. Hattie said my name, although I couldn't hear her. Why couldn't I hear her? Behind her, Lana's hand twitched, and a thick pool of blood ran along the wooden floor and drained down through the cracks. I couldn't hold it back any longer, and I lunged for the sink.

I stared at my sick and swallowed, trying to keep the rest down. With shaking arms I worked the handle of the water pump and rinsed my mouth out. When I'd regained my composure, I surveyed the room. Hattie was back where she'd been before everything happened, Callum stood in the door with a thunderstruck expression on his face and a gun down to his side, and Salter sat at the table still, eating cheese.

"What in the hell happened?"

Salter pointed at Lana with his knife. "That's the cowboy's mom."

"We knew that."

"She didn't know her son was dead."

"You told her? Are you a goddamn idiot?" Callum said.

Salter stabbed the table with the knife. He leaned his chair back on two legs and said, "No, but I've killed a few in my life."

Connolly laughed. "If you want us to take each other's measure later, fine by me. But finish this job, the job you were paid handsomely to do. Start by cleaning this up."

His eyes settled on me. "You. Where's my sandwich?"

Alida and Ruby came into the kitchen. Alida covered her mouth and said, "Oh, good heavens," but moved forward to check the victims.

Ruby came to me. "Are you hurt?"

"No."

"I'm fine, too," Hattie said.

"They're past your help," Callum said to Alida. "You're needed upstairs."

He left the kitchen. Alida finished checking the victims for signs of life and rose slowly, her face a mask of grief. Salter told her to go on, and she went upstairs reluctantly, tiptoeing her way over the blood-splattered floor.

"Go fetch the sheriff, Detective," Salter said.

"You do it. This is your mess, not mine. I'm taking my prisoner upstairs so she can sit by her friend's deathbed. Do you have a problem with that?"

"Nope."

We went up the stairs, and George the Pinkerton followed. Last I saw, Salter sat at the table still, his blade flashing in the lightning.

I'm exhausted and don't have much time if I want to get any sleep before we leave for Cheyenne in the morning.

Salter paid the sheriff to write the deaths off as self-defense, caused by Lana shooting first. Alida pronounced Garet dead at four in the morning. Callum and Salter had a private conversation on the front porch, and Callum rode off at dawn. We never had time for me, Ruby, and Hattie to be alone to talk through our plan, it was mostly made through silent gestures, occasional whispers, significant looks, and the fact that George was distracted from not eating a real meal in two days. Salter sent me down the street for some bacon and biscuits and allowed Ruby and Hattie to put Garet's body in the coffin. When I returned, Hattie and George were putting the coffin in a wagon.

"We're leaving now?"

"Yep," Salter said.

"Other way," said Hattie.

"It don't matter."

"I want her facing east, like she's supposed to."

"That's just for burying."

"No. All the time. You didn't know that dead bodies are laid out in state facing east? In case the Lord comes back before they're planted in the ground. It's the least I could do for Garet, her being so religious."

"Just fucking put the coffin in," Salter said.

Hattie got her way and didn't even resist when George slapped irons on her wrists.

It became clear that Salter had no intention of bringing us to Denver alive. I'd just about decided we should all start taking stock of our lives when I heard a knock from the coffin. She was alive. I should have never doubted it, nor should I have doubted that she would know exactly what to do when the time came. What I never expected, though, was the expression on her face when she shot those two men in the back. It's not something I'll soon forget.

28

WPA Slave Narrative Collection

Interview with Henrietta Lee

Thursday, September 17, 1936 cont

All I could think about was Jehu, what he was going through. How alone he must have felt in that jail cell. As far as he knew, we were in Denver, an easy train ride to Rock Springs or Cheyenne. It had been a week or more since he'd been jailed, and we hadn't come. I had to hope that Luke Rhodes had made better time back to the ranch, and I sure as hell knew that Stella and Joan would ride hell-for-leather to Jehu. But he would be expecting me, wanting me, waiting for me, and I was failing him. I'd never failed him before.

"We made Connolly believe Garet was dead, and we escaped from Salter and the other Pinkerton on the way to Denver. How? Garet rose from her coffin and shot those boys' heads off before they even turned around. For sure, we hid a gun in there for her. She fainted away after, right back into her coffin. She had been half-dead, after all.

"Took Garet to a boardinghouse near the tenderloin district. Where the whorehouses were. May still be there. The district. Haven't been back to Denver in sixty years. There's probably still a warrant out for me." *Laughs.* "They aren't ever going to catch me. I'm the last one alive. Maybe you should write this up yourself, call it *The Legend of Hattie LaCour.* Won't sell a copy, but it'd be a great story.

"Where was I? Oh yeah. Tenderloin district. We pulled up and I told Claire to go get us a room. She was on edge from seeing five people killed and no sleep, and I was on edge because of Jehu and no sleep. She snapped at me that she was tired of being bossed around like a slave. And I told her I was tired of having to spell everything out to her. The only one of us who was still levelheaded was Ruby, and she stepped in. 'She's a nigger and I'm a Chink. They won't rent a room to us.'

"Claire apologized and went inside. 'You didn't have to call me a nigger,' I said. Ruby asked if I wanted to fight with a half-breed about who's talked to the worst. Weren't no need to be fighting each other. It was hard enough dealing with the crackers all the time.

"We settled Garet in and sent for the doc. As soon as she got there and I had her word she would check on Garet, I was off. Claire tried to stop me, to guilt me into not leaving Garet, and I just had enough. I told her what we all knew but didn't want to say, what the doc had been trying to tell us for days—Garet was on borrowed time. Jehu was alive, and it was my responsibility to save him. She could either stay in that dump and watch Garet die, or she could come with me and save a good man from humiliation.

"'Humiliation? He's in jail. Isn't that practically a rite of passage for men in the West?' I told her he was different and I didn't have time to explain it to her. Ruby and I left, and sure enough Claire came after us. All that arguing was for nothing. We missed the last train. Left the next morning.

"Where'd we get the money? Stole it from the Pinkertons. Salter'd been flush. We might have enough to bribe the

Cheyenne sheriff, but I suspected we were past that point, and we were. Too many people knew about Jehu, how he'd been helping some mysterious gang rob the Connollys. Course, there were holes all in the story. Spooner turned him in, but Spooner was the one who'd been blamed for all the robberies. Whatever, the story they cooked up was ridiculous. It was true, you say? I guess if you looked at it a certain way, it was true. But that didn't matter. We needed to get him out.

"Why? That's what Grace asked when we all finally got together—the three of us, Stella, Joan, and Luke Rhodes. We were all talking to each other, around her and Rhodes, to be fair. We knew Jehu's secret hadn't been revealed, or it would've surely been all over the territory. Back then, you might not hear about important news for weeks, but something personal like that would spread like wildfire.

"'Tell me what the hell is going on! What are you talking about?' Grace yelled. She was one of us by then, and she deserved to know. Ruby told her; Jehu was a woman pretending to be a man.

"I'd known since I met him. I'd pretended to be a man for the better part of a year, and I grew up as a slave to an actress. Worked in a theater until I was about twelve. I knew all about disguises and playacting. Jehu fooled everyone but me and, well, you can't live with someone for years without figuring it out. Sure, everyone else knew. You're blushing, Grace Williams. Is there something specific you want to ask me? I didn't think so.

"Let me just tell you something. You're young and haven't lived a whole lot, God willing you will. It's not easy for colored people now, I know it's not. I've lived in this skin for ninety-two years and it's never been easy. The only time I've ever found peace is with Jehu Lee. Man, woman, whatever idea you have about him, don't matter a hill of beans. It wasn't never about the sex, but let me tell you, we enjoyed it, yes we did. Love. Trust. Respect. Passion. Oh yeah, passion's important, too. When you touch souls with someone, well, it's a spiritual experience. I hope you have that one day. You'll know what I mean. You'll think of that crazy old slave you visited for a time, and remember."

29

Claire Hamilton's Case Notes

Sunday, August 26, 1877
Cheyenne, Wyoming

Just when I thought there was nothing in the world that would shock me about this bunch, they reveal that Jehu's a woman.

When Ruby told me, she was so matter-of-fact, as if it were the most natural thing in the world. "She pretends to be a man."

"He's not a woman," Hattie said.

"What?"

"It ain't hard to comprehend," Stella said. "Jehu's got our parts, but he's a man inside. What does it matter?"

"It doesn't. I've just never… My friend Kate, she would go undercover as a man when needed, and I'll confess I've been intrigued by the idea myself. But to live as a man all the time…?"

"He's been pretending as long as we've all known him," Hattie said. "I don't know when he started. He doesn't talk about life before Garet and Thomas."

"Makes life a helluva lot easier," Stella said. "I've done it a few times when I've gone to town. Got lots more freedom."

"I made fun of him when I found out," Joan said. "Hattie tore my hide, but Jehu sat me down later and explained it to me. He feels more comfortable in men's clothes and being considered a man. As long as he gave me piggyback rides and brought licorice home it didn't matter to me. Women's parts or not, he was still Jehu."

"But if he's a woman, and he's your man…What do…" My thoughts trailed off, and I blushed. I looked away from Hattie, and Ruby gave me an encouraging smile.

Luke Rhodes had been leaning against the door, silent. I asked him if he'd known.

"Suspected."

"Bullshit," Stella said.

"Question is, does Spooner know?" Rhodes said.

"He does," Joan said.

"How do you know?" Stella said.

"We talked about it."

Stella and Hattie talked over each other, but their thunderous expressions were identical.

"When did you talk about it?" Stella said.

"You told him?"

"No, of course not. He acted like he knew all along. That Garet had told him."

"That's a lie," Hattie said. "You tell Garet a secret and she takes it to her…" Hattie cleared her throat and looked away. The weight of inevitability pressed against us all. Hattie continued before we became too maudlin. "But it doesn't matter if Spooner knows. We need to focus on the job. Jehu's out there, alone, probably scared like we are, and Spooner is going to use it against him in the trial, I'm sure of it. No way he survives the penitentiary."

"We need a plan," Joan said.

"Guns blazing sounds like a good idea to me," Stella said.

"Maybe later," Luke said.

"What we need is a distraction," Hattie said.

"Two," Joan said.

"We need extra horses on relay in four directions," Hattie said. "That's fourteen horses. I've got the money for maybe half."

"Which means we'll also need money for the run," Ruby said.

"Distraction number one, robbing a bank," Stella said.

"I don't want to ruin you girls' fun, but we could do this the easy way," Luke said.

"You're right, there ain't no fun in that," Stella said.

"But you'll live," Luke said.

"I like that idea," Joan said.

"How?" Hattie said.

"Walk in and walk out with him."

Everyone laughed. "You going to do it? Because there's no way a bunch of women are walking into a sheriff's office and walking out with a prisoner. Unless you want us to bribe the sheriff, which I'm not opposed to," Hattie said.

"Maybe later. Thing is, we don't have time to buy horses and take them to relay stations."

"We?" Hattie asked.

"I'm helping."

"Because you hate Spooner, or because you like Jehu?"

"Or because of Garet?" Ruby asked.

"Let's just say it's a little bit of all of that. And I'm a little jealous that you girls have all the fun."

"Women," I said. "We're women, not girls. And Hattie's in charge. What she says goes."

Everyone looked to Hattie. With a wry smile, she asked Rhodes if he was OK with that.

"I'm outnumbered, so yeah."

"That's a ringing endorsement," Ruby said.

"Keep talking, Rhodes," Hattie said.

"I was talking to a deputy, and he told me Salter, who is a Pinkerton, by the way..."

"We know," Hattie, Ruby, and I said.

"He's coming today to take the prisoner to Denver for trial, which starts in two days."

"Salter's not coming, I can guarantee you that," Hattie said.

Rhodes narrowed his eyes at Hattie, who held his gaze without flinching. "We aren't in the Hole, Luke, and you don't have jurisdiction over any of us. Remember that."

He nodded, and Hattie went on. "One more thing, and this goes for all of you: if you're not willing to do what needs doing, I don't want you along. Doubt, hesitation, will kill someone. Probably yourself. I won't think less of anyone who wants to stay behind. But tell me now. If we get in it and you put the group in danger, I won't hesitate. Understand?"

We all nodded, but Hattie said, "I want to hear you say it."

A chorus of *I understands* rippled around the room.

"First choice is to have a plan where no one gets hurt," Hattie said. "We've done it five times now, we can do it one more."

Rhodes said, "If Salter doesn't show up this afternoon, the sheriff is going to have to send his men to transport Jehu, which will mean overtime that has to come out of his office until he's paid back by he's not even sure who."

"We need a Pinkerton," Ruby said, "and they know you."

"Who better to play one than a former Pinkerton?" He looked at me.

"How did you know that?"

"Spooner. Don't ask me how he knew."

"I was afraid Salter saw through me at the Blue Diamond."

"Will you do it?" Joan said.

I stared at the four women arrayed in front of me and thought of Garet—all of them tough, arrogant, vulnerable, intelligent, loyal—and finally, for the first time in my life, knew what family felt like. My voice cracked with emotion, gratitude at being trusted, at being included, at finally being one of them.

"Hell yes, I will. But I need a bodyguard. So I can convince them the two of us are enough to transport the prisoner by train."

I caught Hattie's eye, and she smiled real slow.

"Hattie, can you pretend to be a man?"

"Give me an hour, and you won't recognize me walking down the street."

"That's what I'm counting on."

Monday, August 27, 1877
Somewhere between Cheyenne and Denver

Hattie was as good as her word; she was unrecognizable beneath her bowler hat and glued-on mustache. I was shocked to see her hair was close cut against her head and almost entirely gray. In all the months I'd been with her, I'd never seen her without a turban. I hadn't paid her hair much attention at the holdup, which seems like a lifetime ago. A plug of tobacco in one side of her mouth helped camouflage her high cheekbones. The wad made her mumble, and with her voice lowered, she sounded manlier than even Rhodes. She wore gloves to mask her long, thin fingers, and had padded her midsection to mask her figure. We knew it was a good disguise when Ruby came in the room and didn't recognize her.

Forging a letter from Pinkerton wasn't difficult. I didn't bother disguising my feminine hand, and explained it away by noting at the bottom that the letter had been transcribed by Chloe Anderson, secretary. I had Rhodes scribble a signature, knowing the sheriff wouldn't know if it was authentic or not. I considered having the letter come from the Connollys, but figured the chances the sheriff would want to telegram Denver and wait for the response was greater than the chances of his doing the same for Chicago. Luckily, the trial was supposed to start in two days; there wasn't time to lose.

Hattie and I arrived at the sheriff's office at eight a.m. Rhodes, Joan, Stella, and Ruby were hidden along the path we would walk with Jehu to the train to make sure we weren't followed. We had purchased tickets for everyone the night before, separately, for the 8:25 a.m. train, including a first-class cabin to transport the "prisoner." Twenty-five minutes didn't leave us much time to pull off our ruse, but the sooner we got out of Cheyenne, the better.

The sheriff sat at his desk drinking coffee and flipping through a stack of wanted posters. He glanced up when the door opened and did a double take when Hattie walked in after me.

"What can I do for ya?"

"I'm here to escort the prisoner, Jehu Lee, to Denver for trial." I held the letter out to the sheriff. He looked at the letter, at the gun on my waist, at Hattie, who held a rifle down to her side and was looking around the place. The sheriff looked up, turned his head to the side without taking his eyes off me, and shot a stream of tobacco juice into the nearby spittoon.

"You're not Salter."

"Salter has been relieved of his responsibilities in this case. I am the agent in charge now. This letter from Allan Pinkerton explains everything."

The sheriff took the letter, opened it, and read it with deliberate slowness. "Who's the nigger?"

"My guard."

"He a Pinkerton, too?"

"Yes."

"He's not mentioned in the letter."

"I met him this morning. It seems agents have been dispersed to other cases, and this is the best Mr. Pinkerton could come up with on short notice. Show him your papers, Henry."

Hattie held out the forged Pinkerton credentials, and I handed him mine as well. Mr. Pinkerton hadn't asked me to relinquish them when I resigned, and I'd kept them for just such an eventuality.

"Women and nigger detectives, huh? If that don't beat all."

"Women and Negroes break the law, too, Sheriff…?"

"Cooper."

"Sheriff Cooper. We have reserved a cabin on the eight twenty-five train to Denver. It was alluded to me that the reason I have been taken off my own case to do this errand is that you do not have the manpower or the funds to pay your men the overtime it would require to deliver Mr. Lee to Denver. Mr. Pinkerton and Mr. Connolly have gone to the trouble of getting me and Henry here to do your job. I'm sure they won't be pleased to learn you made me miss a train, which we've already paid for, because you didn't trust a woman and a Negro with legitimate credentials to do their jobs."

The sheriff laughed and stood. "Lady, you must be new at this, because disappointing rich men isn't a threat that's going to get me to do what you want." He stood between us and the door leading to the jail cells, one hand resting on his gun. He spit another stream of tobacco juice and adjusted the wad in his mouth.

I snapped my fingers and held out my hand to Hattie. She placed an envelope in it. I held it out to the sheriff, but pulled it back before he could take it.

"Is everyone in the West corrupt?"

"Just about," he said.

"I'll take our credentials back first, if you don't mind."

"I'll keep the letter, if it's all the same to you."

"Of course. Henry, see to the prisoner while I sign him out."

My hand shook as I wrote my name in the log. When I lay the pen down, a sense of inevitability came over me. By signing my name, I'd passed the Rubicon, thrown my Christian name, Claire Hamilton, in with a group of outlaws. I was helping a prisoner escape, and if caught would go to prison myself. The full import of that hadn't hit me until I dotted the *i* and crossed the *t* in my last name. Had I been swept along in the energy and the excitement of the events? Or had I been manipulated? Or had I gone into this with my eyes open, knowing deep down where the end was and not caring? I could have left many times. But I never had. What a dull, boring life I'd led to this point.

The jingle of chains announced Jehu and Hattie's arrival. For a moment I didn't recognize either of them, Hattie's disguise was that good. When it snapped into place, I gaped at Jehu. He was a shell of the man who had threatened to throw me over a cliff a little more than a month earlier. The yellowing bruises on his face were almost as shocking as his sunken cheeks, dark-circled eyes, and stooped-over shuffle.

Hattie was managing to keep it together, somehow, but I saw the fire in her eyes.

I tried to keep my voice neutral despite the pounding of my heart in my ears. "What happened to him?"

"He didn't want to come in quietly."

"He looks ill. Has a doctor seen him?"

"Yep. But ain't our fault he won't eat or drink."

"Very well. Thank you, Sheriff Cooper. Good day."

The sheriff got his gun from the cabinet behind his desk and said, "I'll walk you to the train. Just to be on the safe side."

"I hardly think he's in any state to attempt an escape."

"No, he's nice and compliant now. But he has friends, or so they say. Only person that's visited him besides the preacher's widow is a little boy. Works at the blacksmith shop."

"I certainly understand the need for the escort, then."

It was Sunday morning, so the main thoroughfare was mostly deserted. The gang was well hidden; I never saw them.

Sheriff Cooper checked the compartment before we entered and waited until the train was pulling out before leaving. We pulled the window shades down and Hattie hugged Jehu. He grimaced at the pressure on his arm. "Sorry, sorry," she said. "Go get him some food, Grace."

"What is she doing here? She's a Pinkerton."

"Not anymore," Hattie said. "Go, Grace."

I left the compartment under Jehu's glare and ran straight into Rhodes and Newt Valentine.

"What are you doing here?"

"Found him staking out the sheriff's office."

"I've been waiting on y'all to bust Jehu out for a week. Where've y'all been? He was dying in there."

"We've been busy."

"I was about to ask Portia and Rosie to help me bust him out. I bet they would have, too. They're two fine women."

"Don't let Joan hear you say that."

"Go on, Newt. Joan and Stella are in second class. Whatever you do, don't talk to them, especially about Jehu or breaking him out," Luke said.

"Can I have a dollar for some food? I left before I et."

Luke gave him a quarter and gently pushed him down the hall.

"Why is Newt in Cheyenne?" I asked.

"Garet and Hattie rescued him from Valentine, took him to some friends to stay. The bastard didn't even care. Joined up with Spooner when he realized Newt was gone. Talked big about Garet stealing his boy and taking his revenge, though."

"You won't let that happen, will you?"

"No."

"I need to get Jehu some food. He looks half-starved." Rhodes started to enter the compartment to give Hattie the bag he carried, but I stopped him. "Give them a few minutes. Come with me to get him something to eat. I gave the sheriff all of my money."

We bought a sandwich from the steward, and when we returned to the compartment Jehu had settled down, but he still didn't look happy with me. He was still in irons.

"Did the others make the train?" Hattie asked Rhodes.

"As far as I know. Newt did, too."

"That's all we need is a boy getting in the way," Hattie said.

"Don't you worry about Newt. He'll do what he's told," Jehu said.

"Stand there and guard the door, Grace."

Luke removed the irons and Jehu rubbed his wrists. I held the sandwich out to him. He took it, sat down, and tore into it.

"You didn't tell us they beat him, Luke," Hattie said.

"I knew you'd go off half-cocked if I did."

"Don't you act like you know me."

"It's what I would have done if I'd been in your shoes. Let's argue later. Did you tell Jehu the plan?"

"A bit, not enough to make me rest easy. I'm not going back to jail. Haven't been able to take a shit in a week," he said.

"Don't you worry, baby. You'll be able to take a shit whenever you want for the rest of your life."

"You sure know how to charm a fella."

"It comes natural. You two skedaddle. We have to get changed."

Rhodes told me Ruby was in second class, and he was going to the back. "I'll meet up with you in Denver. Good luck."

Somehow Ruby was sitting on a bench alone, and I asked if I could sit next to her as if we were strangers. She smiled at me and raised her eyebrows in question. I nodded and winked at her. Ruby's expression changed ever so slightly. I blushed and buried my head in this journal. It means nothing. Nothing at all.

I cannot believe we pulled it off. My heart is still racing, though I've been on the train for over an hour. I'm not sure when I will come down from this high. I understand the appeal now.

THE WESTERN UNION TELEGRAPH COMPANY
21,000 OFFICES IN AMERICA
CABLE SERVICE TO ALL THE WORLD

TO: CALLUM CONNOLLY, DENVER, CO
FROM: SHERIFF CLAY COOPER, CHEYENNE, WY
DATE: AUG. 27, 1877

PINKERTON CLAIRE HAMILTON AND A NEGRO GUARD TRANSPORTING JEHU LEE TO DENVER. ARRIVE ON 5:20 TRAIN.

REPLY
TO: SHERIFF CLAY COOPER, CHEYENNE, WY
FROM: DORCAS CONNOLLY, DENVER, CO
DATE: AUG. 27 1877

C CONNOLLY MURDERED YESTERDAY, 8/26. DIRECT ALL CORRESP TO ME. C HAMILTON NOT A PINKERTON, PART OF OUTLAW GANG. SEND SALTER TO DEN WHEN ARRIVES.

THE WESTERN UNION TELEGRAPH COMPANY
21,000 OFFICES IN AMERICA
CABLE SERVICE TO ALL THE WORLD

TO: ALLAN PINKERTON
PINKERTON NATIONAL DETECTIVE AGENCY, CHICAGO, IL
FROM: DORCAS CONNOLLY
CONNOLLY ENTERPRISES, DENVER, CO
DATE: AUG. 27, 1877

CALLUM MURDERED 8/26. JEHU LEE RELEASED TO C HAMILTON TODAY, UNDER YOUR NAME. BOTH EVENTS DOWN TO M PARKER. SALTER MIA. SEND 5 MEN TO CE OFFICES IN DEN + I WILL DO WHAT YOUR BEST MAN COULDN'T: CATCH THE PARKER GANG.

30

WPA Slave Narrative Collection

Interview with Henrietta Lee

Thursday, September 17, 1936 cont

Taking Jehu out of that Cheyenne jail was the easiest job we ever did. You expect me to tell you about some sort of doom and gloom right now, how everything went to hell. It didn't. Everything went right to plan." *Laughs.* "Shocked the hell out of me, if you want to know the truth of it. Stealing a little gold is a lot different proposition than walking a prisoner out of jail and into freedom. But the plan worked because it was so simple. Claire Hamilton and I walked into that sheriff's office, I was dressed as a man, of course, and she gave him a forged document from Pinkerton and a bit of cash, and we walked right out. Let that be a lesson for you, Grace Williams. Simple plans and simple lies are always the best options.

"There was one unknown with the plan, who would be waiting for us in Denver. We figured a cable would be sent telling of his transfer. We had to look out for both Callum and Dorcas to be staking out the station. Claire needed a good disguise. No doubt Dorcas had an eagle eye out for the detective who betrayed her. A dark dress and a thick mourning veil did the trick just fine. But it'd been years since we'd seen Dorcas, and neither I or Jehu had spoken more than a dozen words to her in our life.

"Still, to be safe, I asked Jehu to wear a dress. He stared at me long and hard and I thought he was going to refuse. I'd brought some facial hair to glue on him just in case, but I didn't want to go that route unless he threw a fit. All I cared about was getting us all out of Denver safely, and that meant Jehu needed to wear a goddamn dress for a few hours. When he finally spoke, he asked about his hair. That's when I showed him the plain Quaker dress and poke bonnet. He bent his head and shook it a few times. Told me he hadn't worn a dress since he was twelve years old. I thought he might tell me a little about that, about his early life, but he didn't. He never did, and I respected that. I never told him all of my past, neither. As I said, it didn't matter. Our lives began when we met, and everything before was what we had to go through to find each other. I'd go through it again if it meant I got to spend fifty years with Jehu."

Mrs. Lee choked up here and asked if we could continue another day. I agreed, of course, and we scheduled for me to come two days later. The time of each session was dwindling markedly, so that now I am lucky to get an hour's worth of conversation out of her. I fear she is nearing the end of her story and is wanting to drag it out for dramatic purposes.

ROCKY MOUNTAIN NEWS

MONDAY, AUGUST 27, 1877

PROMINENT BUSINESSMAN FOUND MURDERED

VICTIM OF ROBBERY

MURDERER LEFT NO CLUES

NO SUSPECTS

Callum Llewellyn Connolly, aged 34, was found brutally murdered in his office Sunday night. His aunt, Dorcas Connolly, found the body after she became worried when he didn't return home from his errand to the office. The safe had been robbed of $20,000 worth of cash, bonds and gold.

Sheriff Brandon Smith says it was one of the worst scenes he has witnessed, but refused to give details so as not to "shock your female readers." Sheriff Smith said there are no suspects at this time, but the detectives would be interviewing numerous people in the course of the investigation. They would also work with the Pinkerton National Detective Agency, which had been hired by Mr. Connolly to find the gang that has been targeting his businesses for the last two years. If anyone has information that might help, they should contact the police.

Mr. Connolly was the son of the late Colonel Louis Connolly, a cattle rancher turned investor turned philanthropist, who died three years ago. In his two years managing the business, Callum Connolly has expanded the company's mining interests, lately investing heavily in the strike in Oro City. He was also in talks to invest in the expansion of Nathanial P. Hill's smelting company.

Mr. Connolly leaves no heirs and, according to Dorcas Connolly, she will inherit Connolly Enterprises.

PART FIVE

FAMILY IS THICKER THAN BLOOD

31

Claire Hamilton's Case Notes

Monday, August 27, 1877
Denver, Colorado

When we got off the train, a newspaper boy was hawking the afternoon paper with the headline "Break in Callum Connolly Murder Case!" It is a good thing my face was covered with an opaque veil or everyone on the platform would have seen the color drain out of it. Ruby, dressed in a light-blue, loose-fitting tunic and trousers, walked a few paces ahead of me. I kept my eyes on her shoulders for want of anywhere else to look. I knew Dorcas Connolly was on the platform, waiting for me. I remembered Hattie's advice: Don't walk too fast or too slow. Walk like you know where you're going. Believe you're a widow, kill someone from your past if you want. Believe in the disguise, and you'll be that person.

Kill someone from the past? Such as my mother? Not too hard to imagine, since that was essentially what happened. Oh, it was an accident, I was defending myself, after all. But I saw the fire engulfing house after house on our street, and I left her unconscious body to fate. I'd never mourned her, and no one else did, either. Very few people were at the funeral, and there wasn't much to bury anyways. I'd never bought a marker, so Judith Hamilton was one of hundreds of anonymous graves in Oakwood Cemetery.

I found myself suddenly out of the station and on the street, confused because I wasn't in Chicago on Van Buren Street. I glanced around and saw Dorcas deep in conversation with a man with a sheriff's star on his breast. She wasn't looking in my direction, so I stepped off the curb and walked the opposite way. I didn't exhale until I'd rounded a corner and was out of sight. I found an alley and leaned against the wall.

How in the world did they do this all the time? I would have long since died of heart failure. The excitement from going undercover for Pinkerton (and that was the most thrilling part of the job) pales in comparison to being on the wrong side of the law.

Hattie's plan was simple: Disguise ourselves, leave separately, and meet up at Garet's room. Take your time. Make sure you're not followed. If you are, walk into a crowd, lose a piece of your disguise, walk out a different person. Hattie was the only one of us who knew everyone's disguises. To keep us from looking out for the others, she said.

I have to give Hattie her due: she is brilliant. The plan was all hers, with each of us suggesting little fixes. I had the impression they were all things she'd thought of, but that she let us take the credit for morale, for everyone to be invested in the plan. No matter, it worked. We all did what she said, and we all arrived back at Garet's without a problem. I was the last to arrive, and the expressions of relief on their faces did not go unnoticed.

I smiled to see Garet up and about. "Worried I wouldn't make it back? Or were you worried I was going to betray you?"

"A little of both, if I'm honest," Garet said. She hugged me.

"Don't take the 'I'm dying, so I can be brutally honest' tack for the next few…months. You want us to have good memories of you, don't you?"

"If I'm too perfect, I won't make a good heroine. All the best heroines have a fatal flaw, you know."

"Yours is talking too much," Stella said.

A knock on the door, and Joan put her hand on the knob, pulled her gun, and asked who it was.

"Rhodes."

Garet's face fell, and I laughed. I'd forgotten all about our token man. "What's he doing here?" she whispered.

"He helped us," Hattie said.

"You worked with Luke Rhodes?"

"I was in charge, and I haven't forgiven him. You want me to tell him to go away, I will. With pleasure."

When Garet didn't answer right away, Hattie moved to the door.

"Wait."

"That's what I thought," Hattie said.

Joan let in Rhodes and Newt, who ran to Garet and threw his arms around her waist. She was shocked and grimaced with pain, but soon returned the boy's embrace.

"Thank God you're here, Newt. I have a hankering for some brown trout."

"When we get near a river, I'll get you some. How are you feeling? Are you healed?"

"Almost. Seeing you is the best medicine I could have."

When Garet looked over in Rhodes's direction, she straightened. No amount of bravado could disguise her illness. I thought I saw her chin quiver, but when she spoke, her voice had a teasing tone to it.

"Well, well, as I live and breathe. Look who's turned outlaw," she said.

"Righting a wrong, is all."

"I appreciate it," Jehu said. He stepped forward and shook Luke's hand. "Thanks, Sheriff."

"Don't mention it. You ladies did a fine job. Can't even really say I'm surprised. But it was a sight seeing you in action."

"Don't be thinking you can join our gang," Stella said. "Women only. And Newt."

"Where's Spooner, Luke?" Garet asked.

"Why?"

"I need to know where to take the money we're going to steal."

A chorus of voices filled the air: some whoops, a few *What the hells* and a *You just don't quit, do you.* I have no idea who said what. For my part, I said, "What the hell."

"There's no way the company will be ready for a heist, not with everything that's gone on. The company is probably in disarray with Callum's death."

"Did you kill him?" Luke asked.

The room fell silent, and everyone turned to Garet. She smiled and said, "There's only one rule: no killing."

"You didn't answer the question."

"I'm offended you even asked it. What kind of woman do you think I am?"

Luke broke out laughing. "The killing kind." He took off his hat, wiped his brow, and cleared his throat. "Someone killed the men who were bringing your dead body to Denver. No way Grace or Ruby have it in them—"

"Don't bet on it," Ruby said.

"—and Hattie was in irons. That leaves you."

Garet pursed her lips as if considering and held Luke's gaze. She looked at Newt and hesitated, but when she started speaking, there was no remorse in her strong voice.

"In Black Hawk, when I was recovering, Callum showed up." She walked forward as she talked. "He'd killed a young cowboy who helped me escape his ranch. Zeke was his name. We were hiding at Zeke's mom's house. That's how he found me. When I was visiting my ranch and we were alone one night, he threatened to violate me. He could have overpowered me easily. I was in the middle of a pain flare and was weaker than I was letting on. He wanted to, I could tell, and if he hadn't had a houseful of guests he probably would have. So he didn't come all the way to Black Hawk to hold my hand and wish me well into the great beyond. He came to watch me die and to make sure I knew he would make my family pay." Garet turned to Hattie. "You were right. About everything." Hattie nodded slowly.

Garet's voice was quiet, so we all had to strain to hear her. "It was Sunday, I was bored, and I couldn't get the big safe in Callum's office out of my mind. So I borrowed the doc's stethoscope and went to crack that safe. It was late, I didn't expect him to be there, but when he was, I didn't hesitate to put a hole in the center of his chest."

"What was in the safe?" Hattie asked.

Ruby and I exchanged a shocked expression. *What was in the safe?* That was Hattie's question?

"Nothing of monetary value. Ledgers, papers."

"Then you killed him for nothing," Joan said.

She rounded on Joan. "I killed him because he threatened Hattie. He wasn't going to let any of you be, and I couldn't let that stand. No. That would *not* fucking stand. So yes, I killed that bastard and enjoyed watching him die, hearing his death rattle. I don't regret it for one second. Callum being in that office merely saved me the trouble of hunting him down to do it."

Everyone in the room save Hattie wore shocked expressions. Not at what she'd done, I think every one of us would have done the same, but that she seemed to relish it, take pleasure in it. Newt's eyes were as wide as dinner plates, and I think he switched from boy to man in that moment, hearing the things we said. There was no fear in that room, but astonishment and, in some quarters, grudging admiration.

Garet held up her hands to Rhodes. "So, how about it, Sheriff? You going to turn me in?"

Hattie moved between her friend and the sheriff and put her hand on her gun. "You'll have to go through me first." Everyone else in the room tensed up and put their hands on their weapons.

"No need to bow up, Hattie. Out of my jurisdiction. Hell, I fear for my life being in the same room as you all."

"That's probably wise," Hattie said.

"You're never going to forgive me."

"I wouldn't tell you even if I did," Hattie said.

"Where's Spooner, Luke?" Garet said.

"Why, are you going to kill him, too?"

"Not unless I have to."

"Garet…"

"Shut up, Luke," Garet said. "We appreciate your help breaking Jehu out, but none of this is your fight, and none of this is your place to judge, or to offer your opinion. If you want to help us get Spooner out of the Hole for good, we could use you. If not, there's the door."

Luke studied Garet with narrowed eyes. He clicked his tongue, leaned against the door, and said, "You're just itching to get rid of me, aren't you? Well, it ain't gonna work. Not this time, Duchess. What's your plan?"

"Rob the bank, just like we originally planned, and lead the posse straight to the Hole."

"Dorcas knows you've tried to blame Spooner for your jobs before," I said. "She'll know it's you."

"Even though I'm dead?"

"Dorcas isn't as easily fooled as Callum. I guarantee you the first name that came into her head when she found Callum murdered was Margaret Parker. She was on the platform today with the sheriff. Dorcas suspected you of all the heists, with very little evidence, I might add. She sent me on the stage instead of the train, because she knew it was a better mark. I'm not trying to tell you what to do or not do, but if Dorcas is leading the chase, I think you're taking a pretty big risk."

"No one's caught us yet," Stella said.

"Because no man thinks you're a worthy opponent," Ruby said, surprising everyone. "They think you'll do the obvious thing, because women don't know better. They can't give you credit for being cleverer than them because that would be an admission that they've been bested by women."

"Every newspaper and sheriff I asked about you before the stage job dismissed the idea outright. Dorcas *knows* it's you, and that gives her an edge."

"Let's just go back to the ranch," Jehu said. "Drive Spooner off and get on with our lives."

"The only way to get rid of Spooner and his guys for good is to kill them all. You willing to do that?" Hattie asked.

Jehu shook his head, turned away from everyone, and stared out the window.

"Ought-Not, Jack, and Domino are nice," Newt said. "I heard them talking, they aren't helping Spooner in this bet. They don't want to outlaw anymore."

"They're safe if they're not against us," Hattie said.

Garet started pacing, which was difficult in the crowded room. "No. I'm not going to let some bloody man reap the benefits of our hard work again." She stopped and shook her head. "After everything you all went through to get free of what or whomever was holding you down, there's no way I'm leaving this earth without making sure none of you get trapped in a life you don't want. I wish I had more time."

"We can't ever go back, can we?" Jehu asked, his back still to us.

"To where, baby?" Hattie asked.

"You know where. If we go back, we'll be lucky if Spooner turns us in. He'll probably kill us."

"I won't let that happen," Rhodes said.

"I'm not going back to the cooler," Jehu said, "and I'm not killing anyone. But I want to make that son of a bitch Spooner pay for having me thrown in jail. He knew about me, and he did it anyways. Did you tell him, Joan?"

"Why would Joan tell Spooner anything?" Stella said.

"For someone who likes to think they're observant, you're a blind woman when it comes to your sister," Jehu said. "Spooner's been fucking her ever since Garet and Hattie left."

Stella lunged for Jehu, who stepped forward to meet her. Hattie got in front of Jehu, Luke grabbed Stella, picking her up off the floor, and Ruby went to Joan and stood a little in front of her, as if protecting her. Stella's arms and legs were windmilling and she was yelling for Jehu to take it back. Garet slapped her hand over Stella's mouth and told her to shut up. "In case you haven't noticed, this place is lousy with curly wolves. If you want to bring them down on us, keep up your caterwauling."

Newt watched it all with a stunned expression on his face. Joan reached out and said his name, but Newt turned around and walked out the door. Ruby said she'd watch him, and she left, too.

Stella glared at Jehu.

"Why are you mad at him?" Hattie said. "He's just the messenger."

"Is it true?" Stella asked Joan.

The poor girl was crying too hard to answer, so she just nodded.

"I'm gonna kill that bastard."

Joan found her voice at that threat. "No, you're not. He said we'd get married."

No one could look at Joan, the embarrassment was too great. Garet went up to her and put her hands on her shoulders. "Joanie, sweetheart. Spooner isn't the marrying kind. Even if he did marry you, he'd never be faithful. Jed doesn't have that in him."

"I'm having his baby."

"Oh, Lord," Hattie said under her breath.

"Now I'm definitely killing the bastard."

"No, you aren't, Stella Elbee. I won't allow it," Joan said.

"I'd like to see you stop me."

"OK, OK," Garet said, putting her hands out to separate the sisters. Luke was still leaning against the door, but now he had a smirk on his face. "We aren't killing Spooner, and you're not marrying him."

"If he'll have me I will."

"Fine. You go to Spooner and you tell him you've got his bastard in your belly and see what he says."

"Don't talk to my sister that way," Stella said.

"You know what, I've had it with you two. Hattie, hand me my gun."

"Enough, all of you," Jehu said. "I just spent the last week in a jail, not able to shit or piss for fear of people mocking me or beating me. I'm tired, I'm hungry, and I am not sure if I'll ever not be thirsty again. So would you all just please get the hell out of here so I can lay down with my wife and feel like a whole person again? Is that too goddamn much to ask?"

That shocked everyone into silence, even the bickering sisters. Though I haven't been around the gang for long, I'd seen enough to know Jehu was a man of few words, or at least that when he did have words, he said them in private. And I'd never heard him swear. After what he'd been through, I guess I can't blame him. The way Hattie looked at Jehu in that moment…I hope to have someone look at me that way one day.

She shooed everyone out the door, and the five of us joined Ruby and Newt in the hall.

"This is awkward," Garet said. "That's my room, after all."

Ruby suggested we would stand out less as a group if we split up to different boardinghouses. Newt wanted to come with me and Ruby. We left with the promise to return after breakfast in the morning, that is, if Joan and Stella don't kill each other first. When I turned the corner for the stairs, I saw Garet knock on the door and go back into the room.

32

Margaret Parker's Journal

Tuesday, August 28, 1877
Denver, Colorado

I hope you got a good night's sleep last night, Grace, because I didn't, for various reasons. Hattie, Jehu, and I stayed up late, planning the job. Luke sat in the room, one leg crossed over the other, his Stetson using his foot as a hat rack. I expected him to try to take charge, but he didn't. He offered a suggestion here and there, which we almost always used, but he remained the taciturn man I'd always known.

I hope you aren't offended we didn't include you. It isn't because we don't trust you, or Ruby for that matter. We don't trust Joan not to tell our plans to Spooner. She's stupid and in love and would most likely do anything to convince Jed of her loyalty. Stella is always a wild card and works better the less she knows. Of course, letting Newt in on the plan is ridiculous.

Jehu's plan is simple, and he held firm when I wanted to try to complicate it by hitting multiple Connolly businesses and leading the resulting posse into the Hole to catch Spooner. We are going to Timberline, stealing thirty or forty horses (we can't drive our whole herd through Lodore Canyon), scattering the remainder across the valley, and setting fire to the house and outbuildings. I think Spooner and his gang are too lazy to rebuild the ranch, or even round up the horses. But so what if they do? They won't be benefiting from our hard work, and that's all I care about.

Jehu and Hattie can start over somewhere, the sisters with them. Again. Unless, of course, Spooner declares his undying love for Joan. Ruby can go back to the Blue Diamond with Opal, and you can go start your detective agency somewhere. I'll forge a recommendation from Dorcas Connolly for you. I hear San Francisco is a bustling town with a fair amount of nefarious goings-on.

As for me, I'm going to the Grand Canyon to die. If there happen to be a couple of ripe banks to rob along the way, I might just try my hand at going it alone. Though I'm not sure Luke will give me that chance.

He snores, by the way. Like a locomotive.

After Jehu kicked us out of their room, there was nothing for it but to share the room Luke had taken at the hotel next door. We've been lovers for months, and, back in the Hole, he proposed to me in a very unromantic way. He claims to love me, that he has since the moment we met, and if he hadn't told me after we lay together, I wouldn't have believed him. But it's easy to love a dead woman. There will be no long-term commitment on his part, and he is a tender and considerate lover. Best of both worlds.

He said he would stand by me, stay with me, to the bitter end. I'm not entirely sure how I feel about that. I kept my distance for a year because I didn't want to be that woman who jumped from man to man depending on who was near at the time. But Luke wore me down. He charmed me, if you can believe it. Now I'm dying and there's no future. I told him that Ruby would make him a good wife, and at one time I thought they might make a life together, but I don't think so anymore. They've barely looked at or talked to each other lately. I suspect she has another future in mind than being married to a pickle farmer in the middle of nowhere.

Someone is awake and beckoning me, enticing me with the thought this may be the last time we share a real bed. I intend to take advantage of his eagerness while I am still well enough to enjoy it myself.

Judge me as you will.

33

WPA Slave Narrative Collection

Interview with Henrietta Lee

September 17, 1936 cont

We made if off the train and to Garet's boardinghouse in Denver. We'd solved the Jehu problem, so now we were back to the original problem: Spooner. He had taken over the Heresy Ranch, and Garet was bound and determined to root him out of there. We planned to leave Denver the next day, in groups of two since we weren't sure that Dorcas didn't have Pinkertons on the lookout for us.

"I wish I could say we had a nice little homecoming in that dingy little room, but we didn't. When Luke and Garet finally left, Jehu crumbled right in front of my eyes. But I was there to catch him, I sure was. I led him to the bed and held him while he cried and told me about the terror he lived with those days he was in jail. My heart shattered into a million pieces and I wanted him to stop talking, oh, how I wanted him to. It dredged up my past, the terror I felt every time the master rode his horse by me in the cane fields, the way he looked at me, knowing what he was going to do to me that night.

"Jehu had always felt comfortable in his disguise. He was a good teamster, and there wasn't ever a need for anyone to see him undressed. In jail, that possibility became a reality, and it had taken some ingenuity on his part to avoid being seen relieving himself the first couple of days. He stopped eating and drinking to limit the need, but the fear was always there, because there was nothing he could do about not growing facial hair. He kept his face averted as best he could and smudged dirt across his cheeks and lips in hopes of fooling them.

"He made me swear on his life that I wouldn't ever pull another job. It was the straight and narrow for us, or he would have to go out on his own. I didn't hesitate. I promised on his life and my own, and I kept that promise. For sixty years I've kept that promise.

"He cried when I made love to him that night. I offered to stop, but he said no, that I was the only person who had ever loved him for himself, for everything he was, and that no one or nothing was going to ever take that away from us. We spoke vows to each other that night, and from then on we considered ourselves married, even if society and the government didn't. When we woke, we made love again, and I told him he was the best man I'd ever known. I told him that every day for the rest of his life, every morning when we woke up, and even now, alone in bed, those are the first words out of my mouth of a morning."

34

Claire Hamilton's Case Notes

Wednesday, August 28, 1877
Idaho Springs, Colorado

My first thought when Jehu told us we were leaving Denver and not returning was, *We sewed all those damn purple sashes for nothing.* We were to meet in Idaho Springs, a gold town on Clear Creek west of Golden, in two days, and travel north to the Yampa River to follow it to the Green and Brown's Hole. It was going to be hard riding, cold camp most nights. Hattie gave us a list of supplies to buy and some money and told us Luke was buying us horses and tack at four different stables. He would tell us where to go when he got back.

"Ruby and I are going together?"

"Just as far as Idaho Springs. Is that a problem?"

"Um, no. Of course not. It's just…I don't know how to get to Idaho Springs. Do you, Ruby?"

She took the list from Hattie. "We'll figure it out."

"There's a little extra in there so you can get some riding clothes. Men's clothes would be a good idea. Hat and a coat. It gets chilly at night up at altitude."

"Where did you get all this money?"

"Me," Garet said. "I lied when I said Connolly didn't have any money in the safe. I wanted to keep it back for Hattie and Jehu to start over. But we need it now."

"Don't go throwing it around. Ain't bottomless."

We left not long after Luke arrived. Ruby led the way, and we kept going deeper and deeper into the tenderloin district. "Where are we going?"

"To get clothes."

"Here?"

"The vice districts have some of the best secondhand shops. Men lose their money and have to sell their coats, hats, boots. Sometimes even their guns. But that's always a last resort. But the best reason to go here? No one asks questions, and you and me going into a reputable shop to buy men's clothes? Would cause questions."

"I thought *lost the shirt off his back* was an idiom."

"Doesn't mean it's not true."

To my surprise a Chinaman greeted us when we walked into the store Ruby chose. Ruby spoke to him in Chinese and he looked us up and down and started picking clothes off the racks and handing them to us. He glanced at my gloved hands and came back with a pair of sturdy leather gloves. He motioned for the back room, and we went to change. Everything fit perfectly.

"How did he do that?" I marveled, looking at myself in the mirror. I was dressed all in black, with tall brown boots, a waxed brown leather coat, and a buff John Bull hat.

"Yung Su was a tailor in San Francisco before he came to Colorado during the gold rush."

I caught Ruby's gaze in the mirror. She wore tan pants, a white shirt, and a dark-green wool short coat. A red bandanna was tied around her long neck, and she held a navy slouch hat in one hand.

We complimented each other on our transformation and left the room, avoiding each other's eyes. Yung Su nodded his appreciation, and when Ruby tried to pay him, he shooed the money away. She argued with him, but his round face had a determined set to it. She hugged him and kissed him on the cheek. Yung Su handed us both thick wool overcoats, and he gave Ruby a pair of dark-green-tinted glasses. When she put them on, my stomach fluttered.

When we were outside she answered my question before I had the courage to ask it. "He's my uncle. Did you leave anything of value at the boardinghouse? Anything you can sell one day?"

"No."

"Are you sure? You understand you can never come back to Denver. Not as long as Dorcas Connolly is alive."

"Yes. There's nothing I need."

"Then let's get our horses and get out of here."

"Why do I get the feeling you've done this before?"

Ruby laughed and didn't answer.

We were confident enough in our disguises that we didn't bother going a circuitous route to Idaho Springs. The road to Idaho Springs was well traveled, and we made good time, arriving at the end of the day. It hardly seemed as if it had been less than eight hours since we left Garet and the gang. We rode through the main part of town and stabled our horses at a smithy run by a large black man with a voice that sounded like falling rocks. He told us the price, which was fair, and didn't ask questions about why two women dressed as men were riding alone into a town like Idaho Springs. He said that if we were looking for a place to stay, the cooper along the way a bit would rent us a room, no questions asked. We thanked him and procured the room. When the door was closed behind us, we smiled at each other and let out sighs of relief.

"Did that seem too easy?" Ruby asked.

"Yes. I'll take first watch."

"No, you sleep. I'm used to staying up all night."

Instead of sleeping, I decided to update my notes. It was quite the production, removing my journal from where I'd taken to secreting it, down the back of my corset. Ruby asked me what I was doing at the same time the journal fell to the floor. I was pulling my corset together when Ruby picked it up off the ground and asked me what it was. I told her it had started as case notes, evolved into a journal, and was now more like a novel.

She raised her eyebrows. "Am I in it?"

"A little."

"Only a little. That's disappointing."

"I've only just gotten to know you."

"May I r—"

"No." Of course, that piqued her curiosity. "One day."

My hands shake recording the encounter. Ruby discombobulates me, and I'm not sure why. That's a lie. I know why. I have always been drawn to women, more so than men, especially women who are gifted in ways I am not. With Garet it is her bravery. With Ruby it's her dignity. With Hattie it's her discernment. With Kate it was her determination. I try to soak up as much from these magnificent women as I can, learn, become a better person, a better detective, a better friend and, maybe, a better companion.

There are times I think Ruby is flirting with me, but most times I think that's ridiculous. I remember what Garet told me about her once, that Ruby is cunning and can adjust her personality to fit whom she's with. Is she doing that with me, now? Does she think she knows me, knows what kind of friendship I respond to, and want to manipulate me? Or is this blossoming friendship I sense between us real? I'm afraid to ask.

She sits by the window still, watching the street. I stare at her profile for I don't know how long, memorize its curves, the way her cheekbones define her face, the way her eyes narrow slightly at the corners, the dark eyelashes that contrast with her pale brown skin. Last night I saw her hair loose around her shoulders, and it is long and looks like spun silk. Newt had been as mesmerized as I. He'd blushed, wrapped himself in a blanket, and slept in the corner.

I put my journal aside and looked over her shoulder out the window. Though it was nearly midnight, the town was still alive. Barrels of fire dotted the streets, lighting the way for the men to go from saloon to saloon, brothel to brothel. An occasional gunshot broke through the air. Men laughed. A piano played in the distance. I wanted to release Ruby's hair from its western twist, but I didn't have the courage. Instead I rested a hand on her shoulder and offered to relieve her watch.

"Opal is going to be furious." Ruby's voice was quiet. I gently squeezed her shoulder, and she placed her small hand over my gloved one. "I've been gone for weeks. We argued about who should go to Rock Springs. I won, of course. She's a horrible judge of flesh." I shifted my hand as if to remove it, but caught myself. Ruby noticed and met my gaze. "That's what we are, you know. To the men. Merely flesh. Something to take their pleasure with."

"Don't say that."

"Is the truth too difficult to hear, Claire?" When I remained silent, she removed her hand. "I wasn't going back. To Timberline. I would put a few girls on the wagon with Jehu for Opal and go my own way. I've been putting money back for months. I just couldn't do it anymore. If I had to spread my legs one more time, I was going to kill myself. The thing is, there's nothing else for me to do."

"That's not true."

"What's true is I'll always be a half-breed, too white for the Celestials and too yellow for white men to marry. Johns, for the most part, don't care as long as you're warm and willing."

"Ruby..."

"My name is Mingzhu."

"Mingzhu. That's a beautiful name."

"I haven't heard it in a long time."

"Would you like for me to call you by that name?"

"Yes. But only in private. Opal doesn't know my true name."

"Thank you for trusting me with it."

"I'm not going back."

"What?"

"To Timberline. I should have left when I brought the news about Jehu, but...it is easy to get drawn into their world, isn't it?"

"Yes, it is."

"Come with me."

"What? Now?"

"Yes. This isn't our fight. They don't need us. We will probably just get in the way. Let's take the money and go."

"Mingzhu, I..."

"We could start a detective agency in San Francisco. You could work the Anglo cases, and I would work the Chinese cases."

"Chinese cases?"

"Lord, yes. Chinatown is corrupted to the bone."

"I wouldn't want you to be in danger."

She laughed. "I *hope* to be. I haven't felt alive in years."

"You've really thought about this."

She looked away. "I have. The idea came to me sitting next to you on the train from Cheyenne. The thrill I felt with just the little bit I did to help."

"But that was outlawing. Detective work is inside the law."

"Two sides of the same coin, and you know it."

"You're right." I paced the floor. "I have to admit, I like the idea. It's always better to have a partner to bounce ideas off of. And we would be our own bosses."

"I've run my own business for a while. I can show you how to keep books and such."

"This might really work."

"It will."

She grasped my hands, her eyes shining with excitement to match my own. Slowly the smiles left our faces, and the air in the room thickened with a tension I'd never known. Mingzhu's gaze dropped to my gloved hands, and slowly she removed one glove and then the other. My bare hands rested gently on her upturned palms. She traced one scar, then the other, and I trembled, feeling sensation in areas I'd long thought dead. I wanted to tell her to stop, that I could not survive the disappointment sure to come, but the words ricocheting so clearly through my mind could not find their way to my tongue.

"You've been hurt," she whispered.

Still I couldn't speak, my hands alive with a feeling so exquisite it was almost painful. Mingzhu lifted my hands and kissed each one. She held them close to her heart and said, "I will never hurt you, Claire. That is my vow to you."

"I vow the same."

I steeled myself for what I had to say, fear no easy foe to vanquish, even now. "There's just one thing. I have to see this through with Garet and Hattie. I've worked so long to gain their trust, I can't just disappear. And I truly want to write their story. I can't do that if I don't know how it ends."

She smiled and stroked my cheek. "I know. I confess to being insatiably curious as to how this all ends, too. So we help our friends, then we start over in San Francisco."

I embraced her to seal our agreement and to capture this feeling of pure companionship, friendship, and belonging. Finally.

Events of September 4, 1877
Written September 7, 1877
Heresy Ranch
Timberline, Colorado

We rode down into Brown's Hole from Cold Spring Mountain, me, Luke, Mingzhu, Joan, and Stella. We were to reconnoiter Timberline and the Heresy Ranch, discover if Spooner was in town, talk to Rebecca Reynolds, and in Mingzhu's case, return to the Blue Diamond to smooth things over with Opal. Garet had pulled me aside the night before and told me not to leave Joan's side, to be there when Spooner rejected her, and to keep Stella from killing him for violating Joan. No small task, I knew.

She checked my gun and said, "I have faith in you," which is the only reason I agreed to do it.

Her faith was misplaced.

Luke and Mingzhu rode into Timberline while I rode to the ranch with the sisters. Joan and Stella had been quieter than normal on the journey here. We'd passed five days and nights together and I don't think they'd spoken one word to each other. I understood Stella's silence all too well. Stella's threat from the night of Spooner's bet hung in the air between them. Stella couldn't believe her sister would betray her like that, that Joan would choose the warmth of a man over her sister's love and loyalty. The baby in Joan's belly was incontrovertible proof that Stella wasn't the center of Joan's universe, as Joan was the center of hers. She had been supplanted by a man, and in nine months she would be forever supplanted by a child. Stella wasn't the nurturing type, and Joan's description of Stella drowning her babies in the water barrel played over and over in my mind. Part of me hoped that Spooner would do right by Joan, if only to protect the unborn baby from Stella.

Someone was in residence. Men worked around the barns. They were too far away for us to see their faces, but there were more men than had arrived with Spooner a few months ago. Garet said the gang's members ebbed and flowed, but as we rode closer, and they came into clearer view, they didn't look like cowboys or bandits to me. Their clothes were too well fitted, and they almost looked like uniforms.

"We should turn around," I said, but it was too late. If we turned and ran now, we would have the whole posse on us, and they would know our arrival was more than just a homecoming. Two men waiting on the front porch came to meet us, the preacher and Valentine. They grabbed my and Stella's horses' bridles by the shank. My horse tossed her head, but the preacher held firm.

"We wondered when you might be back," Deacon said.

"This is our home," Stella said.

"Not anymore," Valentine said. "You brought the wrong Pinkerton back."

"I'm not a Pinkerton."

"Salter said you were."

"Is Jed here?" Joan asked.

"Inside. Waiting for you," Deacon said.

Joan was off her horse, and Valentine held out his arm to stop her. "Give me your gun."

Her hesitation gave me a glimmer of hope she wasn't as lost to us as I'd feared. "Is he afraid I'll shoot him, Val? The father of my child?"

Val pulled the gun from her holster and pushed her toward the door. Stella flinched, but the blacksmith aimed her sister's gun at her. "You, too. Both of you."

They took our rifles and our pistols, and I'd never felt so vulnerable. I'd long since lost track of my own Peacemaker, but having a gun on my person had become a comfort I'd never expected. Once they had our guns they lost interest in us. We went into the house unabated.

"Keep your head, Stella," I said.

"Not taking orders from the likes of you."

I pulled on her arm to stop her. "Do you really think Spooner is going to marry her? Or to even keep her as a mistress? No. She's a child. If you keep your mouth shut, she'll realize it soon enough."

Stella jerked her chin down once and barreled through the door. The inside of the house hadn't changed, other than smelling of sweat, piss, and tobacco instead of fresh-baked bread and saddle leather. Footprints of dried mud crisscrossed the floor, and there were open jugs of whiskey and tin mugs stale with beer littering the tables and the floors.

"Love what you've done with the place," I said.

Spooner sat at the kitchen table with Joan in his lap. From her body language, she didn't sit there of her own free will. Her eyes were darting to her right, and I think she would have silently signaled more to me if Deacon and Valentine hadn't walked in.

"Well, well, if it isn't the lady detective. I felt sure Hattie or Garet would have killed you by now."

"They have not, though every one of them has threatened it. Except Joan."

"Joanie is a sweetheart." He nuzzled the girl's neck, but kept his eyes on Stella. "Inside and out."

Stella inhaled, but didn't move or say anything. I took the opportunity to glance over to my left. The door to Hattie and Jehu's room was slightly ajar.

"Joanie says y'all've come to live with us. We could use a feminine touch around here, as you can see."

"She tell you she's pregnant?" Deacon asked.

"She did not. Is that true?"

"Yes."

"You sure it's mine?"

"Jed, of course it is."

"Right. I took your maidenhead."

"Jed," Joan said.

"When did you become so disgusting?" Stella asked.

"Listen to that, boys! Stella used a four-dollar word!"

"You used to be a nice man, Spooner. But you came back from Mexico with a mean streak as wide as the Mississippi."

"Well, I'll tell you. We got hired on by the Texas Rangers, not officially, you see. Our job was to raid and kill Mexicans on the border. I never liked killing, as you know, but we were low on funds and we didn't know the country well enough to make an escape after a job. Besides, the terrain out there is about as unforgiving as you can imagine. Hell, there weren't no places to hide. So we did one job for the Rangers, and I got a taste for it, to be honest. Those Texas businessmen pay damn good money to kill Mexicans. More money than we make up here, and we're protected from the law."

I glanced at the bedroom door. It had opened a fraction more, and a shadow moved in the gap between the door and the floor.

"Should've just stayed down there," Stella said.

"I would've, but I heard the Spooner Gang was pulling some lucrative jobs up here and didn't like the idea of a gang using my name. Then when I heard it was a bunch of women…"

"Well, you'll be happy to know Garet's dead," Stella said. "Died in Black Hawk about a week back. Hattie sprung Jehu from jail and they took off to I don't know where, left me and Joanie by ourselves, but told us the ranch is ours. So we're back, and you and your gang can get on back to murdering Mexicans. We ain't gonna be pulling any more jobs, what with Joanie being in the family way. We'll even give you some horses for your string, as a peace offering."

"You know, I don't think I've ever heard Stella say so many words in a row. She can talk in complete sentences, and even make a coherent argument."

"There's no need to be cruel," I said.

"So why are you here?"

"To live, of course. They'll need an extra pair of hands when the baby comes, and I loved it here."

"That's awfully nice of you, to live in the middle of nowhere to help out two ignorant girls who you barely know. I guess your dream of opening your own detective agency is shattered, what with you helping Hattie break Jehu out of jail. It was a ballsy plan, but I expect nothing less from Hattie. That's one smart nigger."

That's when I knew who was behind the door. I tried to keep my expression neutral as Dorcas Connolly walked out of Jehu and Hattie's room.

Everything about Dorcas was different, save her appearance. She wore the same simple black dress unadorned with lace or frills and the cameo brooch at her neck, her salt-and-pepper hair was pulled into a tight bun, her face plain and unremarkable. But the air around her shimmered with self-confidence and power. I'd seen the longing for it during our meeting in May, but it had been tempered by the reality of a patriarchal world. The power she'd longed for suited her, made her plain face somehow more handsome, her dull brown eyes spark with intelligence and cunning. Her lips were curled into a self-satisfied half smile. Everything that had led to her being there, in that ranch house, on the trail of her family's nemesis, had been down to her and her alone. She was delusional, in a way, and I felt sorry for her. Society wouldn't make it easy for her, most like. She would have to struggle to keep her power for the rest of her life. I knew that now she had tasted it, even for a few days, Dorcas Connolly would do anything to keep it. I suppose she was like a man in that way. Was there so little that separated the sexes, after all?

"I am so glad to see you, Claire."

"Dorcas. I should have known you wouldn't waste your time looking for us in Denver. You came straight to their North Star, their home."

"And I was right. Here you are."

"The men outside are Pinkertons?"

"Yes. Allan Pinkerton is on his way to Denver. He said he will take care of you himself. I'm not sure what that means. It's so difficult to interpret nuance in a telegram."

"I'm shocked you came all this way to apprehend me. I felt sure you'd be swamped running your new business. My condolences for your loss."

"Don't flatter yourself. I'll admit that seeing you ride up was a bonus. I felt sure you would have left town after you helped spring Jehu from the cooler. Yet here you are. You have turned outlaw, completely. No, I'm not here for you. I'm here for Garet."

"She's dead," Joan said.

"How many times do we have to say it?" Stella said.

"She died in Black Hawk, Dorcas. I was there."

"Yes, Callum told me about the whole bloody affair in Black Hawk. He can't stand the sight of blood, a remnant of the war, which is why he left. I knew as soon as he told me he left the transportation of Garet's body to other people that she wasn't dead."

"Are you actually implying she arranged for the shootout in the kitchen, while in a *coma* upstairs, so she could mastermind an escape? You really do admire her; otherwise why would you concoct such an absurd fantasy?"

"No, I believe Margaret Parker is eighty percent lucky, twenty percent intelligent."

"She's a lot fucking smarter than you are, grandma," Stella said.

"I have no idea who you are, and I don't care. But if you don't shut up, I'll have Deacon here take you outside and do whatever it is he likes to do."

"Spooner, you're awfully quiet," I said. "Letting a woman take charge isn't like you, from what I've heard."

"She pays me enough, I'll do whatever she wants."

"Yes, Jed Spooner is on the Connolly payroll now, thanks to Salter, may he rest in peace. I believe you said in our first meeting, hire a woman to catch a woman. Well, who better to be in charge of my company's security than a man who thinks like a crook? He will spot the weaknesses, and I will keep him so well compensated with money and whores, he will never feel the need to stray."

"How could I turn that offer down?" Spooner said.

"Jed, what about me? Our baby? We're getting married. You said so."

"You can have it if you want, but there's ways to take care of it. I don't care one way or the other. But we aren't getting married, sweetheart."

Poor Joanie. I'll never forget her expression, and I'll never forget the growl of anger that emanated from Stella.

"You bastard," Stella said. "You take her maidenhead, get her hard up, and toss her aside like she's some whore?"

"Stella, I hate to ruin your rose-colored opinion of your little sister, but she wanted it. Practically begged me for it. There ain't no man alive that would turn this down. Not even Luke Rhodes, that holier-than-thou hypocrite."

"Enough about the farm girl. Where's Garet?" Dorcas said.

"She's dead."

Dorcas nodded, and something hard hit me on the back of the head. I dropped to my hands and knees, my eyes going in and out of focus. The ground swayed beneath me and I fell onto my side. Joan was trying to get to me, but Spooner held her fast. Deacon had Stella's arms behind her back, but her face was red with anger. Her mouth was open as if she was screaming. I heard only the ringing in my ears.

Valentine kicked me onto my stomach and pulled my hands behind my back. With one hand in a viselike grip on my wrists and the other in my hair, he jerked me up off the floor. My feet dangled in the air for a moment before he set me on the ground with a knee-jarring thud. Through my swimming vision, I saw a moment of doubt in Dorcas's expression before she pushed it away.

"Two men were found murdered, shot in the back, down a ravine near Black Hawk. One of them had a telegram from Allan Pinkerton in his pocket, addressed to Salter. There were five people and one dead woman in that wagon. None of them made it back to Denver. I know, because I waited at the graveyard. I wouldn't believe Margaret Parker was dead until I saw her."

My stomach roiled with fear and nausea. My vision swam, and two shaky versions of Dorcas stood close before me. "Why do you hate her so much?"

"She murdered my nephew."

My voice was hoarse, and all I wanted to do was curl up and sleep. "You have a vendetta against her, have from the beginning. Why?"

"She humiliated my brother, my family, stole from his bank, his businesses, and continued to do so even after he was dead. The vendetta is *hers*. Now she is reaping what she sowed."

She nodded again, and I knew something was coming, but was still stunned when Valentine's fist connected with my side. My shaky vision went dark, and I lurched to the side protectively, opening myself up to another fist, this one to the side of my head. I fell into a heap on the floor, unconscious. I don't know how long I was out, not long I think. Stella and Joan were shouting and struggling against their captors, and through narrowed eyes I saw Spooner talking to Dorcas, but what they said was lost beneath the sisters' yelling and the loud hum in my head.

When I woke up, the three of us were in Jehu and Hattie's room. Joan sat on the edge of the bed, dabbing my head with a wet cloth. Stella stood next to the window. It was dark outside, but the moon showed a man standing outside the window easy enough. They filled me in on what had happened when I was unconscious. Spooner had convinced Dorcas that beating me, as enjoyable as it was to watch, was a waste of time. Garet, if she was alive, Jehu, and Hattie would be coming along soon enough if we didn't return.

"Spooner said we're the scouts," Joan said, "and that the cavalry would be along tonight."

"Is he right?" I asked, and immediately wanted to vomit. Joan put a glass of water to my lips and I took a tentative sip.

"Yep," Stella said.

"And here we are with no weapons to help."

Stella said that wasn't entirely true and was about to say more when the door opened and Mingzhu was pushed into the room. The door slammed, and a board scraped across the door, locking us in.

Mingzhu saw me and came to my bedside. "Claire, what did they do to you?"

"What does it look like?" Stella said. "They beat her almost to death."

Mingzhu held my hand and pushed my sweaty hair out of my face. "No, it wasn't that bad," I said.

"You sure looked dead for a bit," Stella said. "Put a mirror up to your nose just to make sure."

Mingzhu swore in Chinese.

"Why are you here?" I asked.

"Opal," she said. "She resented that I went off on an adventure without her. To appease her, I made the mistake of telling her a little of what happened, nothing about Jehu's plan, but I did tell her about helping Jehu escape. Opal's a shallow, vain person. I should have known she would take revenge, especially when I came back without extra whores."

"Did they hurt you?" I asked. I hated that my voice was weak, that I was laid up in bed like an invalid.

"No. Opal isn't cruel, just selfish." Mingzhu's small hand still held mine, and I squeezed it. She covered my hand with her other one and looked to Stella when she started speaking.

"Hattie is a distrustful person, and she's never far from a weapon. She has them stashed all over the ranch." Stella leaned forward and whispered, "When we made this bed, we chiseled out spaces for rifles and shells on the platform. Lift up this mattress and there will be three guns hidden there."

"There's four of us."

"Can you shoot, Ruby? I know Grace is terrible," Joan said.

"I'm not a good shot, but I know how to," Mingzhu said.

"I'm not terrible," I said.

"Hattie said you were."

"You two can fight over the shotgun," Stella said. "Buckshot will scatter and give you a better chance of hitting something."

"Just don't hit us," Joan said.

"You need to be at the back, Joanie," Stella said.

"Why? I'm as good a shot as you are."

"You got a baby in there, or have you forgotten?"

"What do you care? You hate babies."

A muscle in Stella's jaw pulsed, but not from anger, from hurt. "I loved *you* even though you were a red-faced screaming pain in my ass until you could crawl. Then you got into everything. You were a lot to handle for a seven-year-old," she said. "But I did it, because I love you. Always have, since I set eyes on you. It was the damnedest thing. So if you want to keep some crying, shitting baby, I'll damn well make sure you're both taken care of."

Joan leaped off the bed and hugged her sister. "I knew you'd come around. You're a big boll of cotton beneath that crusty shell. You're like a turtle."

"I see that look on your face, Joan Jennifer Elbee. Don't you even think about calling me Turtle."

"That's a great idea."

"No, it ain't. And I ain't changing no diapers, so get that straight out of your mind. I did my time with the nappies. Thank God I'm not going to have to live with the bastard Jed Spooner."

"If y'all get a clear shot, aim that shotgun at his pecker," Joan said.

The guns were under the mattress, and all the guard had to do was look over his shoulder and he would see we were up to something. Stella opened the window, and the man leveled his rifle at her. She held up her hands. "I ain't trying to escape. My friend here is hurt, and there's a tin of salve in the tack room over there that will help ease her pain. I can't get it, for obvious reasons. Will you get it for us?"

"You're trying to trick me."

"No, I'm not. We can't get no one's attention in the front room there. Maybe they've gone outside since we're so good and locked in." Stella leaned forward a bit and stage-whispered, "Look, I'm tired and want to get some rest, but she's groaning and it's gonna keep me up all night, I just know it. That salve will help her."

"How?"

"How would I fucking know? I ain't no doctor. We aren't going anywhere. She can't be moved and we aren't going to leave her."

"Move aside so I can see her."

Stella did and I closed my eyes and tried to look as miserable as I felt. I groaned loudly for good effect. Mingzhu stroked my arm, and I shivered.

"See that guy by the barn? Tell him to keep an eye on me. I'll stand right in this window, with my hands up the whole time," Stella said.

"All right. What does the tin look like?"

Stella went into a detailed description of it and sent the guy off, blocking most of the window with her body. I moved as quickly as I could, and Mingzhu and Joan got the guns and ammunition and hid them in the wardrobe. When the man came back with the ointment, we were back in our positions, thinking of what lay ahead.

35

Margaret Parker's Journal

Events of September 4, 1877
Written October 2, 1877
Heresy Ranch
Timberline, Colorado

It wasn't easy for me and Hattie to stay up on Cold Spring Mountain while all of you went down to scout. We were used to making the plans, being in charge, and to lose that control was a tax on our patience. Jehu and Newt sat on a rock whittling, while Newt told him about his time in Cheyenne and learning photography from Rosie.

—Hope she ain't sore I left without a word. She'd said I could be her apprentice. Learn the business.

I asked him if that was what he wanted and he said maybe, that it was a damn sight better than blacksmithing.

I knew something was wrong before Luke rode up the coulee to our camp. When I saw the expression on his face I knew it was bad.

—Dorcas Connolly has them.

—Bloody hell.

—Ruby, too? Hattie asked.

—Yep. It would seem Opal's in with them.

—Where's my dad? Newt asked.

—Thrown in with Spooner, they say.

—He won't last long with them. He's too drunk to be any help outlawing.

—You're with us now, whether you like it or not, Jehu said.

Newt grinned.

—Change of plans, I said.

Luke removed his bedroll and tossed it on the ground along with his saddlebags.

—Got us some supplies.

The saddlebag was filled with bullets and shells, the bedroll revealed a shotgun and a rifle, and there were gun holsters on both sides of his saddle.

—Four guns along with what we already have gets us to seven rifles and six pistols, Luke said.

—We're just gonna go in with guns blazing? Is that our plan? Jehu said.

—No. The plan is to get our friends out alive, no matter what.

—Which means killing. You OK with this, Sheriff?

—I don't see any other way. This Connolly woman is going to take Garet in, and I'm not going to let that happen.

—Not concerned about her taking us in, I see, Hattie said.

—I guess it's easy to let your morals and standards go when you're getting snatch on the regular.

—Jehu! My God, what has gotten into you? I said.

—I'll tell you what's gotten into me. You're gonna be dead soon, so you aren't gonna get any blowback if we go down there and murder a bunch of men. Me and Hattie and the sisters and everyone else, though, we'll be on the run from it forever. So you can talk all you want about wanting to leave us with a stake to start over, but it's looking more and more like you want to have a final adventure before you turn to dust. Maybe sate your bloodlust while you're at it.

I half expected Hattie or Luke to stand up for me, but everyone remained silent, except Newt, who came to stand next to me.

—You take that back, Jehu. Miss Margaret wouldn't do anything to put y'all in danger. You're family. Family is thicker than blood, ain't that right, Miss Margaret?

Jehu was the only one looking at me, with a defiant expression I rarely saw. His plain talk about my mortality cut me deeper than I would have expected. The past few weeks I've made my imminent death something of a badge of honor, a joke even, to avoid the reality of it. Standing on the top of Cold Spring Mountain, I faced a beautiful sunset I would soon never see again, I felt a cool breeze on my face that portended a winter I wouldn't experience, I looked at friends I wouldn't watch grow old, and I thought a little goddamn selfishness on my part was in order.

But Jehu was partly right, and I didn't want to part ways with him on bad terms. We'd been together too long, had meant too much to each other, for me to dismiss what he said. I don't know what he went through in jail, but I suspect that was the source of his anger, and for that I couldn't blame him. What kind of friend was I if I didn't respect my friends and their opinions and feelings? I figured this would end in bloodshed, but I had to at least give the other option a try.

—That's right, Newt. Which is why we'll try reason first.

—See? What'd I tell you?

Jehu nodded, but Hattie's gaze was questioning.

—First thing in the morning, we need to reconnoiter the ranch, see how many men they have. Then we'll make our plan. One we all agree on. Deal?

—Deal, Jehu said.

Of course, I had no intention of waiting around. Dorcas wanted me, and I figured that if she got me, she'd let my family be.

It was a weak, optimistic plan, and Hattie let me know as much when she caught me trying to sneak away around midnight. Specifically, she called it the stupidest damn fool plan she'd ever heard.

—You won't walk out of there alive.

—Dorcas isn't a killer, and neither is Jed.

—Jed was hired on by the Rangers at the border. He's a killer.

—He won't kill me.

—What's your plan? Walk in there with a white flag, chat a little, win Dorcas over, and walk out with our folks?

—When you put it like that, it sounds so stupid.

—It is stupid.

—Give me a better one.

There wasn't one, and she knew it. I expected her to offer to go with me, to have my back, but she didn't, and I knew then that something had changed with her and Jehu, that her loyalty was to him first. It stung, but also felt right. Luke walked up and past us to saddle his horse, and that felt right, too.

—What if Dorcas isn't reasonable?

—Then it probably won't be a lie that I'm dead. You make sure that boy doesn't come down there, understand?

—I do.

Hattie hugged me, and it felt like goodbye. Like when all was said and done, if I made it back up to Cold Spring Mountain, she and Jehu and Newt would be long gone.

36

Claire Hamilton's Case Notes

Events of September 4–5, 1877
Written September 12, 1877
Heresy Ranch
Timberline, Colorado

We didn't know what Garet, Jehu, and Hattie would do to free us, but we had no doubt they would do something. Stella came into her own that night, shed the brooding, angry follower, and became a leader—organizing, taking charge, planning for a couple of different possibilities. Joan listened to her sister with a rapt expression, one where surprise lingered around the edges. It's said that there is always one who loves more, in marriage, family, friendship, and I'd always had the impression that it was Stella in the case of the sisters. I'd been wrong, and it was a little bit of grace to see this relationship blossoming into one of equals.

I was happy to let Stella take the lead. I tried not to show how much pain I was in, how my vision was hazy, my stomach constantly on the verge of rebelling, the effort it took to keep the bile down. I gained a new appreciation of Garet's ruse, though I am in no way comparing my fleeting injuries to her terminal sickness. I didn't have the energy to move and had even less energy to exert the mental capacity necessary to plan our escape.

Mingzhu stayed by me, playing devil's advocate to Stella. Stella from a few weeks ago would have yelled at her, shut her down immediately. Tonight she took Mingzhu's suggestions to heart and was willing to adjust the plans if necessary.

Unfortunately, it all boiled down to one thing: we couldn't get out of this room without someone else's help. The best plan we had was to disable the guard at the window when Garet and Hattie made their move. We didn't know when that would be, where they would hit, but we never doubted they would come.

It was well past midnight when we heard movement outside. There was an energy about it, but not an urgency or a panic. We'd dimmed the lamps earlier so the guard couldn't see what we were doing, and Stella had kept the window raised slightly to eavesdrop on him. The guard was talking to another man, asking what was going on.

"Someone's riding up under a white flag."

We heard the guard curse under his breath at being left at the back of the house, out of the action. Mingzhu and I were on the bed, feigning sleep. Stella sat on the floor, her back against a wall, doing the same. And Joan sat in a chair in the corner. There was a rustling outside and then silence. Stella lifted the window and leaned out to check the area. "He's gone," she whispered.

We all moved to leave, but Stella stopped us. "I'll go."

"We all have to go," Joan said.

"No. The four of us would never make it past the guards. Grace can't move fast, and we can't walk our way out. There would be lots of shooting, and that's not a fight we would win. I'm going out there to see what's going on, try to figure what Garet's play here is." Stella got a gun from the wardrobe.

"I don't think we should split up," Joan said.

"I don't, either," Mingzhu said.

"I'll be back in five, ten minutes."

She was out the window before we could say another word, and Joan was reaching for a gun to follow. I got up and stopped her. "She's right, Joan. We can't shoot our way out of here. What if someone walks through that door and we're not here? The alarm will go up, and that ruins whatever plan Garet has."

"You two can stay here and be cowards, but I'm going to help my sister."

The telltale sound of someone opening the bedroom door stopped her. I grabbed the gun, put it back, and managed to close the wardrobe before the door opened. Opal looked around the room until her eyes fell on Mingzhu. Any hope that she was here to free us was dashed when I saw her expression and the holster around her waist.

"Did you turn outlaw?" Mingzhu asked.

"You did."

"Not really. Only helping out our friends. Unlike you. What did they promise you?"

"Nothing." Her gaze shifted to me. "Valentine really did a number on you."

"What do you want, Opal?" Mingzhu asked. "Are you here to gloat? To kill us? To try to make me feel guilty again? Or are you here to help us?"

"Garet's here. As soon as that Connolly woman has Garet in custody, she'll let y'all go."

"No, she won't," Joan said.

"Oh, have you been having breakfast with the sheriff?"

"What the hell does that mean?" Joan asked.

Mingzhu explained. "It means you're privy to private conversations." When Joan and I still looked puzzled, she said, "It's a private expression. One of many things Opal and I have shared over the years. Does none of that matter to you? Everything we've been through?"

"It didn't seem to matter to you," Opal said. "You've been trying to leave me for years. Now, with her, you have your chance." Opal threw me a nasty look, and I wondered how close their relationship had been and what the true motivation for this betrayal was.

"And you have the chance to get out of this life, too. If you hadn't been so eager to take your revenge on me, I would have told you."

I knew it was a lie; Mingzhu and I had talked about Opal, and she'd made it clear that the accordion-playing whore didn't figure into her future. But Mingzhu was inching closer to Opal, keeping her voice low and soothing. She had managed to keep the whore's attention distracted from the fact that Stella wasn't in the room.

"Of course, you were always in my plans. We're sisters, remember?"

Mingzhu was stroking Opal's cheek, and Opal's naked expression of hope and longing made my stomach twist.

"You promise?"

"Who would play the accordion for me?"

Opal hugged Mingzhu, and I caught her eye over Opal's shoulder. She cut her eyes down to Opal's holster, and I moved as quickly as possible and stole her gun. When she tried to pull away from Mingzhu's embrace, Mingzhu held her tighter. Joan took the gun from my hand and hit Opal in the back of the head with the handle. Mingzhu let go, and Opal stared at her sister in astonishment.

"Ruby?"

"You shouldn't have betrayed me, Opal."

Joan hit her again, and Opal crumpled to the floor. "Get the guns," Joan said.

We followed Joan out the window and crouched in the dark next to the house. "We need horses," Joan said. "Can you two get four horses saddled?"

"Yes," Mingzhu said.

"Don't shoot anyone if you can help it. Hit them over the head. There's knives in the tack room. I'm going to find Stella."

We went our separate ways, Mingzhu and I crouched in the shadows. Pain burned through every part of my torso, but I gritted my teeth and stifled the groan that I wanted to make. Deacon stood in the yawning doorway of the barn, smoking. Mingzhu watched him with an expression of pure hatred. I motioned for her to follow me around to the back, remembering my failed attempt at eavesdropping all too well. I picked up a nearby stone and threw it far to the right of where we were, hitting a horse in the corral. I cried out in pain this time, and Mingzhu helped me run across the open yard when the guards were distracted by the bucking horse. We made it to the back of the barn and rested against the wall. Sweat poured down my temples, and my breaths came in gasps. Mingzhu squeezed my hand. "Stay here."

"No. We go together."

"You're in no condition to take on a man. I have to take care of this myself." She embraced me. "Wait here. I mean it." She peeked around the wall again, took a deep breath, and entered the barn.

I realized too late she'd left her gun.

When I looked around the wall, the barn was empty. There was no sign of Mingzhu anywhere. I crept into the barn and whispered her name. Besides the soft nicker of a horse in the stall next to me, the barn was quiet. In the distance I heard a shout, the jingling of tack, and soft footsteps on the dirt-packed floor of the barn. Before I could turn, I felt the cold steel of a gun press against the base of my skull just below my right ear.

"I guess Valentine didn't do a good enough job on you if you've managed to escape."

"I'm tougher than I look."

"Not tough enough to stop a bullet to the back of the head. Drop your guns."

There was nothing for it but to obey. I bent down to place the guns on the floor and was standing up when the man kicked me in the back. I fell forward, eating a big helping of dirt that tasted of horse manure. I tried to crawl away, but Deacon kicked me in the side, precisely where Valentine had earlier. I screamed and curled into a protective ball.

Deacon let loose a string of fire-and-brimstone warnings that morphed into gibberish, a language only he and his Creator could understand.

I'll never forget the crazed look in his eyes. He wasn't seeing me, or the present, but some far-off memory, or maybe a vision of the future. A vision that was cut short by an ax to his neck. Blood spurted from it in a steady rhythm, arcing through the air and hitting the stall doors. The horses smelled the blood and grew restless, stamping their feet, nickering, a couple kicking the walls. "Dead-Eye" Deacon Dobbs grasped at the wound, but managed only to redirect the blood down his chest, a bright red streak across the starched white front of his shirt. He turned enough that I could see who wielded the ax: Mingzhu. He was a dead man standing, but she pulled the bloody ax back like a baseball player and drove it into his abdomen. He curled forward over it and tipped onto his face, dead.

She came to me and helped me stand on shaky legs. I was thankful for her embrace, to help me steady my wobbling knees and racing heart.

"Did he hurt you?"

"No worse than Valentine. We need to hurry."

"Wait. Claire, we can saddle two horses and be on our way."

"We've been through this."

"All I care about is me and you making it out of here alive. I want that life in San Francisco with you."

"Do you know how to ride us out of this valley? In the dark? Because I don't."

Her silence was her answer.

"I understand if you don't want to, none of this is your fight. But I have to see this through."

"This isn't your fight, either."

"You're right. But they're... my family. I'm not going to abandon them."

"I want to be your family."

"You barely know me."

"You know that's not true."

I blushed, thinking of our nights alone. "I didn't know if..."

"It was genuine on my part? It was. It is. I told you last night."

"I know, but it's difficult for me to believe, to trust..."

"I'm not perfect. I've told hundreds of men what they wanted to hear, what they paid to hear. But I've never lied to a friend, or a lover."

She cradled my face, and our lips had barely touched when the gunshot rang out.

37

Margaret Parker's Journal

Events of September 5, 1877
Written October 2, 1877 cont
Heresy Ranch
Timberline, Colorado

I rode up to my ranch alone, with a white handkerchief tied to the end of a stick. Lamplight shone from the windows, bringing to mind days past when we would have been snug inside, sitting around the fire: me settling the books, Hattie sewing, Jehu and Stella repairing a piece of tack or mending a saddle blanket, Joan playing with her dog on the floor. We'd had a good life, a simple one, a life that had deserved to be lived in peace. I rode down the lane with one intention: to make sure my family could live in peace again.

A dog barked nearby, and a man came out from behind a tree. His hat was pulled low and all I could see was a cigar glowing in the corner of his mouth. He came forward out of the darkness, his rifle barrel resting on his shoulder. In a hoarse whisper he said, —That you, Garet?

—Yes, Ought-Not. It's me.

He looked around before coming closer.

—What the hell are you doing? Get out of here. They're gonna kill you.

—Is Dorcas in there?

—Yes, and Spooner and Valentine. He jumped at the chance to catch you. Thinks you stole his son. He also said something about you killing his wife, but he's loaded to the gunwales and not making a lot of sense. He did a number on that Grace woman, warming up for the main event, he said.

—He hurt Grace?

—Beat her up some. She'll be fine.

—What are you doing here helping them?

—I'm not. I'm waiting on Opal. She's in there to see her sister.

—Why is Ruby in there?

—I tried to convince Opal to leave with me, to get the hell out of here before something happens we regret. But she couldn't help herself. She had to see Ruby brought low.

—I know you've had a thing for her for a long time, Ought-Not, but Opal's going to be nothing but trouble.

—I'm starting to think you're right.

—Help me.

Ought-Not stared at the cabin for a long time before looking back up at me.

—I did like working on those cattle ranches in Texas. Think you might be interested in expanding your outfit?

—I might be, but right now I have to get my family to safety. Tell me what I'm up against.

—Deacon's here, Spooner, Valentine, and about four or five Pinkertons that Connolly woman brought.

—About eight, then?

—Not counting me or Opal.

—Jack and Domino? Scab?

—In town. Scab said he don't mind killing Mexicans but he ain't killing white women. Jack and Domino ain't got no complaint with you, neither, like me. We all liked working out here for you. You're a fair boss, and a dang sight prettier than the jefe we worked for in Texas.

—Would they help me?

He shook his head.

—They ain't gonna go against you, but they ain't gonna go against Spooner, either.

Ought-Not spit on the ground.

—He's a killer now. It's why the three of us want out.

I'd resisted the idea that Jed could have changed so much, but if Ought-Not said it, I believed him.

—What's your plan anyways? Ought-Not said.

—Ride up under this flag and talk to Dorcas.

Ought-Not waited for more, and when it didn't come, he shook his head.

—That's a damn fool plan.

—Not if I have you on the porch, watching my back.

Ought-Not stared off in the darkness, worrying the chaw of tobacco he had in his cheek. He spit again.

—Hell, why not? You're saner than Spooner is.

I waited down the road a piece while Ought-Not went to the house to tell them I was here. It didn't take long for the Pinkertons to show themselves, dark coats and hats, double-holstered pistols, bandoliers full of bullets, and shotguns held in two hands across their bodies, ready for action. Luke's single rifle covering me somewhere in the dark sure did seem weak in the face of all that firepower.

Opal, Valentine, Spooner, and finally Dorcas came out of my ranch house. Damn if I didn't admire Dorcas in that moment. There was no doubt in my mind she was in charge, and, well, it gave me a new line of argument for when we finally did talk. All the Pinkertons aimed their rifles at me and chambered a bullet.

—She's under a damn flag, Ought-Not said.

—That sure is a lot of muscle for an unarmed woman. I appreciate the compliment more than you know, I said.

—Check her, Dorcas said.

I took my coat off, tossed it on the ground, and held my arms out.

—See? Unarmed. Where is my family?

—Family? I don't have your family. I have two stupid farm girls, a Celestial, and a traitor. Turn yourself over to me and I'll let them go.

—OK.

—What?

—That's why I'm here, to turn myself in. But I want to make sure you truly let them go before I do.

—You don't trust me?

—Nope. Or Spooner and definitely not that son of a bitch Valentine.

The blacksmith moved as if to come drag me off my horse. Dorcas stopped him.

—Opal, get the women.

She looked irritated at the order, but followed it easy enough when Spooner told her to do as Dorcas said.

—Before we make the exchange, I'd like to talk to you for a minute. Alone.

Spooner started down the steps, and I laughed.

—Not you, you traitorous rip. Dorcas.

—Just shoot her, Spooner said.

—Unarmed doesn't mean unprotected. There's a gun trained on you, Dorcas. If anyone shoots me, you're the first to die. I hope you've promised Spooner and Valentine enough to want you to live.

She held up her hand, said something to Spooner in a low voice, and came toward me. I dismounted and waited by my horse's head. When she caught clear sight of me, her expression changed.

—Oh, now, I don't look that bad, do I? You don't have to answer. Do you mind if I smoke? It helps with the pain.

She shook her head slightly and waited while I lit my rolled cigarette. I offered it to her after I'd inhaled a lungful.

—No, thank you.

—It'll take the edge off, and, I have to be blunt, you look like you're on the edge.

—Are you going to try to convince me to let you go?

—Would you?

—No.

—Not even a dying woman. That's a little surprising. I thought you had more compassion than that.

—You blew a hole the size of a dinner plate in my nephew's chest.

—The papers said you found him.

—Yes.

—I'm sorry about that. Truly. It is difficult to see violence on a body like that. I guess thanking me is too much to ask.

—Thank you? For killing my last remaining family member?

—Well, yes.

I took another drag.

—Power looks good on you, Dorcas. Don't try to act modest. You're reveling in it, as you should be. Never know how long you'll have it, do you? You had it for a bit after the colonel died, didn't you? Until Callum showed up to claim his birthright?

Her nostrils flared, and the tip of her nose went white.

—I saw how your brother treated you, and I don't imagine Callum treated you much different. Did he? You don't have to answer. I could tell from our conversations that he held little regard for you, your opinions, or your business acumen. But now you're back in charge, and, unless Callum or your brother has some by-blow no one knows about, the company is yours. Last remaining relative and all. Correct?

—That doesn't absolve you of killing my nephew.

—Not asking for absolution. Just for a little bit of grace.

—Grace?

—Let me and my family go. They're all going to have to leave the territory, so you won't have to worry about them stealing from you. I'm closer to hell than I've admitted to them. I only have a couple of weeks to get where I need to go, where I want to die. I would rather be surrounded by my friends, and the beauty of God's creation, than in a cell.

—I'm sorry, but no. You've stolen from us for years, you killed my nephew. I'm not going to let you die on your own terms. I won't let that happen. I won't make you die in a cell, but I will make you die in chains. I know you, Margaret, and—

I never got to hear the rest, because all hell broke loose. Spooner was on the ground, holding his leg and screaming. The Pinkerton to my left unloaded his gun into the dark, and the other Pinkertons turned their guns toward us.

My horse screamed, and warm blood splattered on my sleeve. The horse reared and almost ran me over trying to get away. A shot whizzed by my head. I shoved Dorcas out of the way and told her to run. I pulled the sawed-off shotgun I'd hidden down the back of my vest and laid out as much fire as I could to get me and Dorcas safely to the bent cottonwood tree. I pushed Dorcas down and behind me for safety. Another whiz and the tree splintered next to my head, and I felt a sharp pain like a bee sting on my cheek. I wiped at it with my hand and saw blood.

—Bloody hell.

—So you were armed.

I rolled my eyes at Dorcas and reloaded my shotgun. —Of course I was.

—Why are they shooting?

—Hell if I know. I'm assuming you didn't tell them to shower me with lead while you stood two feet away.

—No.

—Stay down.

I peeked around the tree. A haze of gun smoke and dust hovered over the ground, but it didn't blot out the bodies lying between me and the house. Smoke drifted from Ought-Not's rifle, and his expression was one of bewilderment and shame. Spooner still writhed on the ground, and I saw a knife sticking up from the meaty part of his thigh.

—Don't move, Dorcas.

Using the shadows as cover, I ran toward the keening, half expecting to be shot down, and sure enough I heard the shot at the same time that my upper right arm exploded in pain. It knocked me down to the ground, and I crawled behind a woodpile, bullets kicking up puffs of dirt around me.

I leaned against the wood Stella and Jehu had been chopping and hauling since the spring to stock us up for the upcoming winter. In the dim light of the moon, I saw blood blooming on my sleeve. I checked the wound; as much as it hurt, it was only a graze.

I heard the steady footfalls of a heavy man at the same time that I realized I'd dropped my gun. The only weapon at hand was a stick of wood. What the hell was Ought-Not doing? And where the bloody hell was Luke Rhodes?

Valentine emerged from behind the woodpile, blotting out the moon. I couldn't see his face, but I imagined his expression of superiority easy enough. The moon rays did manage to glint off the honed blade of an ax on Valentine's shoulder, and the bravado I was preparing to hurl at the blacksmith died on my tongue. I'd always imagined dying in a blaze of gunfire, not being hacked to pieces with an ax. It looked sharp, at least.

—Not so high and mighty now, are you, Duchess?

The smell of whisky oozed from him, and his speech was slurred. He was big, slow, and drunk. I thought I could best him, and the urge to needle this man was just too great. If I couldn't die looking at a beautiful view, I might as well die taking the piss out of Ulysses Valentine. I waved my hand in front of my nose.

—A little early to be toasting my demise, isn't it, Val?

—In a minute it won't be.

—Go ahead, Valentine. Kill me. But it'll never change the fact that for two years, it was a woman's generosity that kept a drunken coward like you alive.

Growling, he raised the heavy ax over his head.

—Get away from her, Pa.

Jehu, Hattie, and Newt were all in a line, staring down the barrels of their rifles, advancing toward Ulysses Valentine.

—You OK, Garet? Hattie called.

—Never better.

Valentine looked at Newt and laughed.

—I guess I shouldn't be surprised you threw in with a bunch of women. You always were a gal-boy, clinging to your mother's skirt.

—This gal-boy's got a gun on you, and I know how to shoot, thanks to Garet.

I was not going to let Newt have killing his pa on his conscience for the rest of his life, and I'd made a promise to myself I'd make Valentine pay for the damage he'd done. I pulled my knife from my boot, lunged forward, and jabbed the long, sharp blade into his leg. Valentine screamed and dropped the ax behind his back, thank God. I managed to roll away as a gunshot rent the air and the side of Valentine's head exploded. Chunks of flesh and blood hit me in the face.

I crawled away and vomited by the picnic table under the tree. When I sat up, Jehu and Luke looked down on me. Luke's rifle was smoking and he was breathing heavy. Jehu held out his hand to help me stand.

—You came.

—You've never let me down. I couldn't very well not return the favor, Jehu said.

He pulled out his handkerchief and wiped my cheeks. I stared into his lovely little face, my throat constricting from emotion, tears blurring my vision. I blinked them away, not wanting to lose a moment of seeing him clearly, this tenderhearted man who'd been with me through so much, his quiet strength always propping me up, his love a constant for a quarter of my life. The closest thing to a son I'd ever had. For the first time I truly felt the impending loss, *my loss* of their future, seeing Jehu and Hattie happy and in love. They would grow old without me, achieve without me, cobble together a new family without me. Love others. Their memory of me would fade, and I would be a footnote in their lives, taking up a few years, hopefully fondly remembered.

Where would I be? Watching from heaven or hell? Or would I merely cease to exist? I hoped the latter; I'm not sure my spirit could take watching my family move on without me.

Shaking from everything that had happened, I pulled Jehu to me, wrapped my arms around his shoulders, and whispered in his ear that I loved him. His arms tightened around me, and he told me the same. We pulled apart, and he looked down at the ground, face red.

I turned to Luke to give Jehu time to compose himself and said, —It's about goddamn time you showed up.

—My horse fell in a hole. Broke his leg. I just ran half a mile in a few minutes, woman. Have you ever tried to run in boots and spurs?

—I've never had to. Proof positive I'm the better horsewoman.

I was still shaky, and thought Luke was moving forward to embrace me, maybe kiss me, and was disappointed when he touched my arm and said I was shot.

Someone screamed my name, and I picked up my shotgun and ran toward the sound.

I stopped when I came upon Joan cradling Stella's head in her lap. Stella's guts were spilling out of her stomach.

I knelt down beside the sisters and took Stella's hand. Hattie, Jehu, and Newt surrounded the sisters. A quick glance at Stella's stomach and we all knew how this would end. When she spoke and asked if she'd hit Spooner, her voice was hoarse.

—Yes. In the leg, I said.

—Shit…I was…aiming for his…cock.

We laughed, but there was no humor in it, no energy. Stella's life was ebbing away and Joan was comforting her, telling her Hattie would fix her right up. Grace and Ruby came running up and stopped when they saw us all staring down at a broken woman. A note of desperation came into Joanie's voice when no one moved, and she started to order people around, for bandages, hot water, my laudanum.

Stella's body jerked, and a trickle of blood oozed from the corner of her mouth. Joan tried to lift her, asking us to help take Stella inside.

Hattie reached out and grasped Joanie's arm, telling her it was time to say her goodbyes. Stella's face had relaxed and her eyes had taken on a faraway expression. Joanie sobbed, thinking Stella was gone, but her sister's eyes refocused. Her face relaxed and she looked up into Joanie's eyes.

—Joanie, be...

She never finished.

Joan stood and grabbed Stella under the arms to pull her up.

—You aren't going to die on me, Stella. We have a baby to raise. You promised you'd take care of us! Help me get her inside, goddamn it!

Her frantic entreaties washed over us. We couldn't move, couldn't hear, all we could do was stare as Stella's indomitable spirit was defeated at last.

Joanie went completely still, stopped breathing. Her hair was disheveled around her tear-streaked, red face, and her blue eyes shone with pooled tears. She screamed, fell to her knees, and pulled her sister's body closer to her.

I stood on wobbly legs and went to Spooner, who'd pulled the knife from his thigh and was tying a kerchief around it. Luke held a rifle on him. Newt stood nearby, staring at Joan and Stella.

Spooner looked genuinely shocked, remorseful, about what had happened, as if it finally, after all these years, had dawned on him that his actions hurt others.

—I didn't mean for any of this to happen, Duchess.

—Kill him if he says another word.

I walked into the house and went to the water pump. I rinsed my face off with the cold water and scrubbed it with a wet rag. I could hear Joan sobbing outside and wanted to scream, *Shut up, shut up, shut up*. I kept scrubbing my face until it felt raw, and leaned over the washbasin and cried.

That's how Opal found me. Dazed and rubbing the back of her head, she asked what she'd missed. I told her Stella was dead and the whore didn't have the grace to look sad. She asked about Ruby, and I told her in no uncertain language to get out of my house. Opal started in with her ignorant, fun-loving, harmless whore routine, and I picked up the closest item and threw it at her. Turned out it was a coffeepot with hot coffee in it. She screamed at the same time the gunshot rang out.

I went to the front door and saw Spooner dead on my porch, blood pooling beneath him before oozing slowly between the cracks and dripping down onto the dusty ground below.

38

Claire Hamilton's Case Notes

Events of Wednesday, September 5, 1877 cont
Written on Friday, September 7, 1877
Heresy Ranch
Timberline, Colorado

No one will ever know why Stella chose a knife instead of a gun, but it was a fatal decision. No one is even sure who shot her. Spooner was dead before the question could be asked.

Mingzhu and I gently took Stella out of Joan's arms. I lay my coat over Stella. All the while, Mingzhu knelt next to Joan and held her hand and rubbed small, comforting circles on her back.

I looked around the yard. Four dead Pinkertons, Stella, and Spooner being guarded by Luke. Newt. A pair of legs stuck out from behind the woodpile, but I didn't have the stomach to see who or what it was. I still wasn't over Deacon lying dead in the barn.

Dorcas stood near a tree, in a trance. I went to her.

"Was it worth it?"

"What?"

"Your revenge on Garet. Was it worth it?" I motioned to the yard.

"You're blaming this on me?"

"Who else?"

"I'm sorry your friend is dead, truly. But no one was shooting until she came around the corner."

"Joan, stop!" Mingzhu called out.

We turned and saw Joan walking toward Spooner with her pistol out. Spooner started to rise, but Joan put a bullet in his heart before he'd straightened his legs. He dropped like a sack of potatoes at Luke Rhodes's feet.

"My God, these women are crazy," Dorcas said.

I moved in front of Dorcas, cutting off her view of the carnage in the yard. "What about earlier? Inside. You enjoyed watching Valentine beat me, didn't you?"

Dorcas's nostrils flared. "No, I did not."

"You didn't try to stop him."

"Sometimes, the lengths you have to go to..."

"Have you ever seen that before? Someone being beaten? Or been on the receiving end?"

"No, of course not."

I took my gloves off and threw them on the ground. I lifted my hands, showing my scars. "I have. It isn't something I want to relive, and I would never take joy on inflicting pain on the weak."

Dorcas's eyes stayed on my hands.

"Dorcas, you had it all figured out. From the beginning. You know that, but I want to tell you how much I admired you for it. A rare intelligence. I hope it's more of a benefit than a hindrance for you."

"What do you mean?"

"Is the company yours?"

"As far as I know. Unless Callum made someone else his heir, I'm the last family member."

"It's exciting, isn't it? The power of being in command. I saw it on your face inside. You are in your element. I have no doubt you would be a brilliant businesswoman. You're intelligent and ruthless. I look forward to reading your marriage announcement."

"What? That's absurd."

"With a company as valuable as yours? With all of the different types of businesses? I imagine you'll have a marriage proposal within six months. Maybe less."

"I'm not getting married."

"Ironic, that. Think of all the reasons why not, and then think back on your brother and what he did to Garet. What he took from her. You remember that when you're running Connolly Enterprises, remember that your success was built by ruining people like Margaret Parker."

The sun was rising behind Heresy Ranch as I walked back to my family, my gloves abandoned at Dorcas's feet.

PART SIX

THE AFTERCLAPS

39

Margaret Parker's Final Journal Entry

Tuesday, October 2, 1877
The Owlhoot Trail, Utah

Today is the referendum on suffrage. I hope it passes, but, well, it won't. Men aren't ready for it, and we live in a man's world.

Luke and Dorcas smoothed out the story about the shoot-out, since a report would have to go back to Pinkerton about his dead agents. We buried them in a mass grave in the town graveyard. Out of consideration for Newt we gave Valentine his own grave, right next to Lou's. We did the same for Spooner, but no one really cared. Joan didn't come to the service, and Ought-Not, Domino, and Sly Jack didn't step up to say anything. It was left to Ruby to say something over the grave.

—His breath smelled better than most men's. Like mint.

I felt a tad sorry for Spooner right then, this outlaw who was once a good man, as outlaws go, that his eulogy complimented his minty breath. But I didn't speak up for him. I couldn't. I was too busy cataloguing my sins.

Since that night, I've tried to figure where everything went wrong. What was the decision I made that ended there, at our ranch, with dead Pinkertons littering the ground and a young woman and her unborn baby orphaned? For I had no doubt then, and I believe it even more today, that I was the cause of all of the pain and death we suffered. In my effort to take care of my family after I'm gone, I'd been the instrument of its destruction.

It won't bother me for too much longer. I feel the end, and it's a relief.

Newt moved out to the ranch and became Joan's protector. She sat on the gallery and stared into the distance most of the day. She disappeared from time to time, and Newt would ride out to Stella's grave with an extra horse and they would ride down to the river. Newt fished and Joan lay on the ground, staring at the clouds through her tears. I know this because Newt came to me, asking what to do, how he could fix it. I asked him if he still grieved for his mother. He thought for a bit and said that he did more lately than when his pa was alive.

—I was too afraid of him to miss her. Seeing Joan brings it back, though.

—Grief isn't something that you can fix for someone. They have to work through it on their own. Some people like to talk through their sadness, and I think after the shock wears off, Joanie will be that person. Remember, don't try to fix it, just listen.

—Listen. That ain't very manly advice.

I laughed so long and hard that my scar started throbbing. Newt looked alarmed. I told him I was fine.

—I'm not going to be around to help you, Newt, but I will give you one piece of advice. You ready?

—Yes, ma'am.

—Whenever you're faced with a tough situation, think of what your father would do, and do the opposite. Except for blacksmithing. Your father was a damn fine blacksmith when he was sober. But when it comes to women, well, I consider Sheriff Rhodes and Jehu as fine examples of good men.

My failure was weighing on me. I saw disappointment in everyone's eyes, blame, embarrassment, because they'd trusted me, followed me, believed in me, in my promises of protection, of providing for the future. I couldn't stand their solicitousness about my illness, their wanting to take care of me. Taking care of the family was my job. My responsibility. My reason for staying.

The truth of it is I wanted to be alone. I wanted to die alone. I didn't want anyone to have to see me like that, I didn't want it to feel like a responsibility to be borne. I'd hoped to be able to sneak away as a success, a champion, and ride south with a jaunty lift in my step, treating my death journey as an adventure. The night I decided to leave, there was none of that, only a profound sense of failure and the almost unbearable need to get away. To free my family from their burden. Me.

Horse saddled and one ponied behind, with enough supplies to get me two hundred miles south to a wide spot in the road named Owlhoot, I mounted, adjusted my sawed-off shotgun in its holster (I'd become partial to it), and clicked my horse. It was well past midnight, and everyone should have been asleep.

They weren't.

There they were, all clumped in the road, blocking my path, seven of the best people I'd ever known.

—Did you really think we were gonna let you go without us? Hattie asked.

—Go where?

Hattie looked at the gang, the family, with an expression of "Can you believe this woman?" Hattie's a born leader, and it's only right that she take my place as head of the family. As such, she stepped forward. She held my horse's reins as if I were going to bolt (an impossibility with a pack horse, of course) and met my gaze with her beautiful copper eyes. My throat constricted.

—Garet, come on down. Come on. I want to talk to you.

I dismounted.

—I know why you're doing this, leaving like this, and I'm here to tell you you're wrong. No one here blames you for what happened. Look at those troublemakers and think of what you did for all of them. You took us all in, treated us with respect, took care of us, and loved us. Ain't none of us been loved for us until we met you. That's a rare gift, Margaret, and you gave it to all of us, and more besides.

—I failed you, Hattie.

—You might have failed yourself, but that's just because your goal was too ambitious this time. No crime in aiming high, just got to be prepared to fail, is all. You're not used to failure, and, well, it don't look good on you, neither. But you didn't fail me, or them. Don't you ever think that. Ever, you hear? You could never fail me, Margaret Parker. I love you, just as I know you love me. You've been a true friend, one I won't see the likes of again, I suspect. More than that, you're my sister, and you always will be.

She embraced me, and I buried my face in her shoulder and sobbed. Why did I ever think it was hard and bony? My face notched perfectly into her neck. She smelled of sweet sage and lemongrass, comfort, family, home. When she spoke, I heard the tears in her voice.

—I wish it could be just you and me riding south. I want you to myself a little while, to tell you all the things I've held back over the years, to take care of you, and maybe rob a little bank or two along the way, Hattie said.

I laughed and we pulled apart, and I saw she was smiling through her tears as well.

—These yahoos won't let me out of their sight, though.

My smile dipped a little.

—Hattie?

—Yeah, Duchess?

—I don't want to go.

—We can stay here, then.

—No, I don't want to die. To leave you, and Jehu, and this world. I thought I was ready, but seeing all of you, feeling…I'm going to miss so much.

—I know. I don't want you to go, either. It's tearing my heart apart, the knowledge of it. But you were right. Staying here and waiting for it will be torture for everyone. Best we ride, give us something to do. Keep us occupied. Maybe get into a tiny bit of trouble.

She pulled a slip of paper from her breast pocket and waved it in front of me. It was the notes I'd jotted down from Callum's office after I killed him. A list of businesses to hit. Hattie grinned and said that there were quite a few near enough the Owlhoot Trail that we might make a couple of detours.

—What will Jehu say?

—Well, I guess we're gonna find out.

We left two days later. We rode down through Timberline and picked up Rebecca and Harvey along the way. They had two wagons, one loaded down with their possessions and the other with enough stock to start a general store in Oro City, or Leadville, as it had been renamed. The silver strike was real, and it was a lode.

Opal drove one of the Reynoldses' wagons, and Eli sat beside her. They were going to Oro City as well, to open up a brothel. Opal and Ruby had come to some sort of truce, but all during our ride so far, they've avoided each other and have rarely spoken. Tonight Opal played a little on her squeezebox, and I think I saw a smile pass between the Gem Sisters.

It will take two weeks or more to get to the canyon, and I don't know if it's the promise of adventure or the easy camaraderie between everyone, but I feel better than I have in months. I am…content.

40

WPA Slave Narrative Collection

Final Interview with Henrietta Lee

September 20, 1936

I'm finishing my story today, Grace. Don't look sad, though it does an old woman's heart good to see it. I'll tell you, it's been nice having your visits to look forward to. I sure do, and that's a fact. It's been a real blessing to be able to relive all of my adventures. The sixty years since? Well, those were good years, too. I was with my family. We were safe, and together. Jehu, Joan, Newt, and that rascal son of theirs, Win. Win Valentine. Have you ever heard of a more ridiculous name? He had a little too much Spooner in him, if you ask me. Turned out all right, I suppose.

"But I'm getting ahead of myself. I left you up on Cold Spring Mountain, didn't I?

"Garet and Luke had ridden off to their deaths, I figured. I stared out across the valley for a long time, thinking I probably wouldn't ever get to see it again. Mourning my best friend. I did a lot of that over those last few weeks. Couldn't let it show, least of all to Garet. She was done being the strong one, it was down to me to do it. I was up for it, and that's a fact, but when you're always the strong one there ain't ever anyone there to comfort you. Jehu was too upset himself. He made himself scarce…I'm getting ahead of myself again.

"I'd practiced what I was going to tell you, to make sure I told you everything. Didn't do me much good, though. I've almost lost the thread.

"I stood on that mountain for I don't know how long. When I finally returned to the campsite, Jehu was awake, poking the fire. Newt was asleep. 'You didn't go,' he said. I didn't answer him because it made me mad that he thought I might. I made a promise, and by God if you can't say anything else about Henrietta LaCour you can say she's a woman of her word.

"'She's riding down there to die.'

"I agreed with him, said, 'To save her family, she sure is. It's up to us to honor her, to keep the family together.' Jehu nodded his head real firm like, like he'd come to a decision. He stood and nudged Newt awake with his boot, told the boy to go saddle his horse, that we were going down to watch Garet's back. I asked him what he was doing, and he said, 'It's about time I started acting like the man in this family.'

"The three of us rode down to the ranch as quick as we could, telling Newt the entire way to do what we said and stay back out of trouble. I figured his dad was down there, and I figured he wouldn't stay back out of the way. Newt was on fire to impress Joan. Jehu and I didn't even need to say it aloud: he would be in charge of keeping Newt safe and I would watch Garet's back.

"We rode up right as the shooting started. We dismounted and got our guns and approached real slow like, rifles shouldered, in a line. I turned around and walked backward behind Jehu and Newt to cover our backs. Didn't think no one was back there, but you had to play it safe. Checked in with Newt and his voice trembled when he said OK.

"The gunfire'd stopped when we dismounted, so we were walking up to a dusty scene. Gun smoke, dust kicked up, moaning men, and then a couple of extra gunshots. I heard Garet curse, and that was it; didn't care about our back none. We picked up our pace and who do we find standing over Garet but Valentine. Raised ax, ready to kill her. I was pulling the trigger when Newt hollered at his dad. Val barely registered his son was holding a gun on him when his head exploded like a watermelon. I've never seen anything like that, before or since. I wasn't looking at Salter when he got his noggin blown off. The aftermath was bad enough. But there ain't nothing like seeing a man's head burst like that. I've carried that with me my whole life. Thought of it every day. Don't get me wrong. I didn't mourn Ulysses Valentine for one day, but I did mourn Newt's loss of innocence. I pulled him to me, covered his eyes, as soon as I could, but it wasn't soon enough. He was shaking like a leaf, but we went over to Garet, to see how she was. Luke Rhodes came loping up. He's the one who shot Valentine. Garet had a flesh wound on her arm and one on her cheek, but she was fine.

"Then we heard Joan screaming out for help. Stella'd gotten gut shot, never found out who did it. She lived maybe three, four minutes when we got there. She'd gone after Spooner. Threw a damn knife at him instead of shooting him. Stupid, stupid girl. Why? Why would she do that? Oh, I understand wanting to cut Spooner's pecker off; he got her sister in the family way, and like I said before, Stella hated men. But goddamn, if you're going after someone you make sure you kill 'em. You don't throw a knife at them from thirty feet away.

"Joan didn't. She picked up Garet's shotgun from where she dropped it, stepped over her sister's dead body, and pumped Jed full of lead. Died right there on our porch, with Luke Rhodes, our "no killing" sheriff, standing over him. That girl tossed the gun at Luke's feet, daring him to do something about it. He never did.

"It was a mess. There were dead bodies everywhere. Dorcas, that bitch, lived. She was there, and, well, I guess I should thank her for making up some story about the shoot-out that didn't involve us. She saw how broken Garet was and figured she would suffer enough from guilt in the little time she had left.

"Next morning, I had Jack escort Dorcas to Rock Springs and sent Domino on an errand for me. They were going to come right back, though. They wanted to stay on at the ranch, and that was just fine with us. Domino and Jack were good workers. Ought-Not, too. They all turned straight after that, as far as I know. Don't know what happened to them after we left the Hole.

"That night that Stella died, that broke Garet. I'm surprised it took so long. I'd been expecting it to come earlier, but she was so focused on taking care of all of us…well, she thought she failed us."

Mrs. Lee is quiet for some time, and I can see tears leaking from her eyes.

"I said she didn't, of course I did. We had our ranch, and only one of us dying, with all we went through those couple of months? That's a goddamn miracle. But we did go through all of it, and I've wondered over the years if we really had to. At the time I thought we'd had no choice, that Garet hadn't had a choice but to take that bet. But you've always got choices, Grace. And every single choice you make ripples out through your life and every other person you meet. The people you love. The people you hate. Remember that, but don't let it paralyze you, neither.

"I don't regret those months because that was the last bit of hell-raising we got to do, me and Jehu. Not that he ever raised hell. No, we moved on. Became respectable. Started a freight business. First one in Northern California to switch to automobiles. Made a good living. Sold the business for a pretty penny, and that's a fact.

"It would've broke Garet's heart to know we left the ranch that she'd worked so hard to save for us. It was too remote, and once the town died…Joan wanted her son to go to school. I taught her to read and do her numbers, but she wanted her son to have real schooling. I couldn't blame her. About that same time Newt came back from Cheyenne, a man and a professional. He'd been traveling around the West in a mobile photography studio, taking photos of Indians. It was a good line. Well, when Joanie saw him for the first time in five years? She fell instantly in love, much to Newt's relief.

"So we did what was best for our family and moved to California. Claire and Ruby'd moved to San Francisco back in '77 and had nice things to say about it. We didn't move into the city. Could you imagine going from the Hole to that ruckus? No, we moved to a small town outside the city called Monterey. Started our freight business, Newt and Joanie ran a photography studio, and we lived our lives. Good lives. Full ones. A few ups and downs, but nothing we couldn't meet. Joan and Newt got married, raised Win, had a couple children who didn't survive the cradle. They died in the influenza, Joan and Newt. Took 'em fast. Win, he disappeared, oh, I guess about fifteen years or so ago. Just stopped coming around, writing letters. He was a bit of a scoundrel, but he was loyal, and he loved me and Jehu like we were his grandparents. I suspect he met a violent end, and Lord only knows where his remains are.

"Claire and Ruby? They moved to San Francisco, like I said, and opened up a detective agency. It was pretty successful for a few years. Did she try to write Garet's story? She sure did. Nobody would buy it. Just like I told Garet in that cabin. Well, Claire and Ruby came on hard times, and Claire decided to make it an adventure story in hopes it would sell for a penny a page. You heard of those penny dreadfuls? Problem was two-fold: One, by the time Claire did it, they'd fallen out of fashion. Two, those dreadfuls were read mostly by young boys and men. They weren't interested in a female gang fighting the men. She gave me a copy and I read it. No idea where it ended up. The trash is where it belonged.

"Claire and Ruby were hard up, and our business was growing, so they came to work for us. Ran our office in the city. Both died in the big earthquake. Nineteen-oh-six.

"I know that's a lot of death. I'm ninety-two years old, child. I'm the last one left. Jehu died in his sleep in '31. Prepared his body for viewing myself. I didn't want him to have any humiliation after he died, didn't want people making fun of him. Of us.

"Oh, I'm not completely alone. I have some young women from my church who check on me regular, bring me groceries and a casserole once a week. Good girls, those. I've made arrangements. They know what to do. I'll be taken care of when I pass, don't you worry. It's sweet of you to, though. It nice to have someone worrying over me.

"What happened to Garet? I was afraid you were going to ask me that.

"Garet wanted to see the Grand Canyon, she wanted to die there. That had been the next stop on her honeymoon back in '64, but first they wanted to see Colorado. Thomas wanted to try his hand at mining, and when Garet saw that first herd of wild mustangs? She was in love. So they never made it to the Grand Canyon, but they always talked about going. Then you had the outlaws stopping in and telling stories about how it had to be seen to believed and how words didn't do it justice.

"I wanted to see it, too. We all did. We'd all heard the stories at one time or another. More than that, I wanted to be with

Garet when she died. I owed her that much, at least. I owed her more. My life. Jehu. Our family. No matter what we went through, right or wrong, should we have done this or that or the other, didn't matter. All that mattered to me was that I was losing my best friend. I could see it, death coming for her. I asked him to wait, and he did. But he followed us every step of the way down the Owlhoot Trail.

"She tried to leave without us. She'd gone around and said goodbye without really saying goodbye. Trying to be sly about it. We all knew what she was doing. We let her make her plans, pack Ole Pete with supplies, saddle Rebel, and met her at the front of the house when she rode up well past midnight. I told her she was crazy if she thought I'd let her go off to die by herself.

"We left two days later. Luke had pulled me aside and told me it would take us a month to ride there, at the least, and that was going at a good clip. 'She can't go at a good clip,' he said. I told him that knowledge was not to leave his mouth again, especially in front of everyone else. Garet wasn't stupid; she knew how far away the canyon was. The journey wasn't about the canyon, but about letting her die on her terms, in the saddle, with her family around her. By God, after everything Garet had given me, I was going to give her that.

"The day before we left, Domino returned from the errand I sent him on the day after the shoot-out. He came trotting up the lane ponying Old Blue behind him. I don't know who was happier in that reunion, Garet or Old Blue. She hugged me so tight she almost cut off my breath. Didn't say a word, just let her sob into my shoulder and told her I loved her.

"When I think of Garet too long, the grief,' cause there's still grief there, after sixty years, it changes to anger. She died too damn young. All that lost possibility. She could have been a great woman, greater in the eyes of the world, if she hadn't been brought low by the colonel. Well, I blame him, but he was just being a man of his times. Of these times, too, if you want to know the truth of it.

"No, I'm not talking about her outlawing, I'm talking about her capacity for love and empathy, how she pretty much always put others before herself. She was driven by love, that woman. Love of horses is what gave us the ranch and allowed women to find us when they were brought low. The love of her family is what led her to pull that first bank job. She took that bet with Spooner for the possible glory, I'll give you that. But underneath it she was driven by the responsibility of being the head of the household, taking care of her family after she was gone. If that ain't love, I don't know what is.

"We left on a Wednesday. Don't ask me how I remember that. We took our time. It was a pretty ride. The trail hugged this wall of red cliffs to the east, and the plains we rode on for the first little bit were grassy. Prime grazing land. I saw Luke eyeing it with interest. Further south, it turned scrubbier, more desert-like, but the view. Lord have mercy, the desert can be a beautiful place. Utah has some of the nicest scenery in the West, and I've been all over it.

"Garet was well enough to ride on her own for about ten days, then we took turns riding double with her. Claire suggested we get a wagon for her comfort, I told her Garet wouldn't want it, but she asked anyways. I was right. So we kept riding. We saw some Utes one day, riding the ridge of the cliffs. There were a few tense hours, but they eventually decided that a band of a bunch of women and two men wasn't worth their time.

"There wasn't a lot of civilization, to be honest. That's why the outlaws used it to travel. The trail extended from way up in

Montana to Mexico, and I'd be surprised if a thousand people lived on the whole of it. But the people we did run across were nice enough, for outlaws. Listen to me, judging outlaws when we were recently retired. We were able to buy some cannabis off of a cowboy for Garet's pain.

"We'd been following the Green River for some time, knowing it joined up with the Colorado, which would lead us into the canyon. The further south we went, the fewer people we saw and the more beautiful it got. The last day we came to a dead end. We were high up on a mesa that narrowed into a point. Just below, the Green flowed into the Colorado. Green and red water ran alongside each other for a bit till they mixed together off in the distance.

"I was riding with Garet at the time. She sat in front of me, and she'd fallen asleep on my shoulder. I nudged her awake and told her we were here. She opened her eyes and I could see the confusion in them. It took her longer and longer to come to herself. When she finally did she gave me a heartbreaking smile. Her lips were dry and cracked, her eyes were circled with bruises, and her breath was coming in short little gasps.

"'You're my hero,' she said. I told her to look at the view, partly because I didn't want her to see me cry. She let out a little sigh and said it was just as beautiful as she expected. We all sat on our horses for a while, enjoying the beauty, coming to terms that this was the end of our journey. Garet inhaled deeply and whispered to me, 'I better say my goodbyes.'

"I had my arms around her, to keep her upright on the horse, and I tightened my grip and told her I wasn't ready. That it wasn't fair, she had so much life left, so much more to give, and that I didn't know if I could be the full me without her there, believing in me, respecting me, teasing me. She said I had Jehu, and I did, but it's not the same, lovers and friends. You need both kinds of closeness to be whole, and I was losing that. It really did feel like someone was scooping my heart out of my chest.

"What I really wished was that it was just me and her. I wanted all of her at the end. I didn't want to share her goodbyes. I'm a possessive and jealous person. Always have been. But Garet wasn't, and I knew saying goodbye was important to her. She had messages to give everyone, and who was I to deny them the last little bit of her wisdom and love?

"Luke helped her down, and she held on to his arms to hold herself up. She leaned into him, and he held her like she was as delicate as an eggshell. She whispered into his ear, and they talked like that for a minute. We all looked away, not listening, to give them privacy. She ended with an admonishment to never shave his magnificent mustache. He laughed, but when he turned away from her, he was wiping tears from his eyes.

"She went to Claire next, who wasn't trying to hide her grief, and you know what, I loved her for it. Garet asked her if she'd had fun these past few months, and Claire nodded and cried harder. Garet gave Claire her journal and said she hoped Claire still liked her after she read it.

"Joan and Newt had stayed at the ranch. Joanie told Garet she couldn't go on a death march like that, not so soon after Stella. None of us could blame her, and Newt staying with her seemed the natural thing. He was the only one who could tease a smile out of her.

"She asked Jehu to escort her to the edge, help her sit down. Ruby wrapped a blanket around her shoulders and they said their silent goodbyes.

"She and Jehu sat for a good while on the edge of that canyon. I don't know what they said, or if they said much of anything. We never shared our goodbyes with Garet to each other.

I wanted to keep mine close, private, something to pull out on a bad day, something that would make me smile. I think Jehu wanted to do the same.

"The sun was starting to set when he got up. He walked straight past the fire and over to the picketed horses. I saw his eyes when he did. He couldn't share his grief right then. I rose and went to Garet.

"I've seen a lot of sunsets, but nothing like that one. The colors in the sky were magnificent. The sky was aflame, the dark sky butting right up against it, pushing it below the horizon. When the sun finally dipped out of sight, the sky turned purple, and that's a fact. Every color purple you can imagine. The underside of the clouds was lavender; closer to the ground was a deep, almost black purple. The dark blue sky lightened, if you can believe it, to a color I've never seen again. It wasn't purple, but it wasn't blue.

"We'd been silent; there was nothing left to say and too much to say. It was beyond us. Beyond me, at least. But that beauty, sharing it with Garet as her last moments on earth?

"She leaned her head on my shoulder, and I put my arm around her to hold her up. She felt light as a feather; she'd lost considerable weight on the trail, and I knew she'd been in a lot of pain, but she never complained. Not once.

"She exhaled so completely I thought that was it, but she spoke and told me this was what she wanted. She was right to come, it was beautiful. 'Even if it's not the Grand Canyon?' She smiled up at me and told me she'd suspected she wouldn't make it, but this was a wonderful substitute. She took my hand and it felt as fragile as bird bones, like it was hollow and would crumble at the slightest pressure. The important thing, she said, was that we were together, that she was with me. 'You're my favorite, you know.' I teased her and said she probably told every one of us the same thing. She admitted it, but said she meant it with me.

"'I knew you would be my confidante, my challenger, my one true equal and friend from the moment I saw you.' I asked her how she could have known that. 'You looked me straight in the eye. Never flinched. Never backed down. Don't you ever lose that, Hatt. But be careful. I worry about you the most.'

"It took me aback, I have to admit. Before I could argue with her, she said, 'We both know how cruel people can be, especially to women they don't understand. I want you to live a long, long life. Promise me?'

"She didn't need to spell it out for me. I understood. But I didn't want our last moments to be so solemn. I asked her, my parting wisdom was 'Don't die' and Luke's was 'Don't shave your mustache'?

"That put a smile on her face. She closed her eyes and nestled closer to me. 'It is a magnificent mustache. Very soft. Tickles in all the right places.'

"I laughed long and hard, and eventually my laughter turned to tears, and I told her what I felt. The words poured out of me, and I don't know if she heard a one. When the sun finally set, and I saw that purple sky for the last time, Garet had gone limp. Her breath still came, but there were longer pauses between them. She was still in there, and I had to believe she could hear me. I said, 'I love you, Margaret Parker, and I'll never stop.'

"She breathed in one last time and exhaled her spirit to the heavens, and there was a smile on her face. I stayed there with her for a long, long time. I cried so many tears, took me forty years to cry again. Nothing could ever match the loss I felt that day. Jehu died in his sleep, which was a blessing. I didn't want to watch him die like I did with Garet. I grieved for Jehu, of course

I did, but he was an old man and we'd had a good life. Garet's death was a tragedy.

"Garet gave each of us what we wanted, even if we didn't know it ourselves. She gave Jehu a home. She gave Joan and Stella a mother figure. She gave Claire the adventure of a lifetime. She gave Newt safety and Luke genuine affection, if not love. Hell, she even gave Dorcas something. Dorcas went on to turn Connolly Enterprises into one of the biggest companies in the West, until she finally sold out to Hearst at the turn of the century. Retired as the richest woman in Colorado.

"What did Garet give me? If you don't have an inkling after hearing me talk for all these hours, well…you haven't been listening."

Forgotten Women Podcast (Transcript) Hosted by Krys Chestnut

Episode 5.17

Guest: Historian Stephanie Bailey, Western American History professor, University of Colorado Boulder

In this episode, historian Stephanie Bailey, a professor of western American history at the University of Colorado Boulder, will talk about her new book, Heresy, *an account of a gang of female outlaws in Colorado during the late 1870s and the long, winding road to discovering the story.*

Krys Chestnut: Welcome to the *Forgotten Women* podcast, I'm Krys Chestnut and today we are talking to Stephanie Bailey, author of the recently released book *Heresy*, a nonfiction book about a gang of female outlaws in 1877 Colorado. Thanks for joining me.

Stephanie Bailey: Thank you for having me. I've been a listener since episode one. I think you're doing important work, highlighting women who have been lost to history, bringing them to a wider audience. A younger audience.

KC: Thank you, and it should be disclosed that Professor Bailey and I are friends. I was her TA when I was working on my master's in women in history, and we have remained friends. I've contacted Professor Bailey many times to confirm a fact that I thought was too fantastic to believe.

SB: There are quite a few of those in history, aren't there?

KC: Yes, and I have to confess to you, Professor: I found myself doubting this book many, many times as I read it.

SB: I don't hold that against you, because I had much the same reaction when I started focusing in on the research. European historians seem to come across scandalous women buried in letters and archives all the time, but to discover these women who were so outside of the norms of the time in the American West? Well, I went back and forth between thinking I'd hit the mother lode of forgotten women, or the whole story would fall apart with the next found document.

KC: Tall tales were common then.

SB: Yes, they were, and if any story is ripe to be accused of being a tall tale, it's the story of the Parker Gang.

KC: Briefly, for our listeners who aren't familiar with the story or the book, tell us about the Parker Gang.

SB: As you know, the story is anything but brief. My children tease me that I've finally made it as a historian because I've published a doorstop. But I'll give it a go. The Parker Gang was a group of women, numbering anywhere from four up to seven, who worked during the years 1873 to 1877. There are six confirmed robberies they did, seven if you include one Margaret Parker did when she killed Callum Connolly. They were never officially caught, and they definitely were never convicted, though one member spent about a week in jail. Before they busted him out.

KC: I can't believe they walked in and walked out with him.

SB: I couldn't, either.

KC: That's a great outline of the story. Before we talk about the story and the characters, I want you to tell our listeners how you discovered the Parker Gang.

SB: By accident, as most good stories are. As you know, I have friends across the country, the world really, who I exchange finds with. We all have our areas of expertise, and when we run across something that isn't our specialty but might be of interest to someone else, we send it to them. About ten years ago a friend of mine found a penny dreadful at a flea market. The owner knew what he had, and she paid a pretty penny for it. But it was an American penny dreadful, and those are all but lost to history. She sent the original to one of our literature professor friends who specializes in nineteenth-century American literature and folklore, and sent me copies because of the subject matter: a gang of female outlaws.

I read it and dismissed it as fiction, wholly fabricated, immediately. I'm an expert on Colorado history and I'd never heard about or read about a band of female outlaws. It was an interesting premise, no doubt. But as a historical document to benefit my area of research, it was useless. But historians are pack rats, so I dutifully filed it away.

Five years or so later, I came across a book about prostitutes in the Old West. It was a book written in the early twentieth century by amateur historians who seemed more interested in confirming their rose-colored ideas of the West than any actual historical accuracy. One chapter was dedicated to Opal Steele Driscoll, a prostitute turned miner's wife turned society lady when her husband hit a lode. I'd known of Opal and of her claim to ride with the Spooner Gang, but she was considered an unreliable narrator.

KC: She was a liar.

SB: For the most part, though I've come to give her more of the benefit of the doubt as I researched this book. It was just a little piece of information in that book, a throwaway line that sounded like the least plausible part of her story, to be honest, that Opal Steele had played the accordion. There had been an accordion-playing prostitute in the penny dreadful, so I pulled it back out and looked at it a little closer, and with the assumption it was based on fact.

KC: How do you even begin to research something based on a tiny bit of information like that? It seems an impossible task.

SB: That's what historians live for. But yes. It was one of the more difficult investigations, for reasons I'll get into later. I had three avenues I could pursue: the accordion-playing prostitute, Opal Steele; the author of the penny dreadful; or Margaret Parker, the outlaw heroine in the story. I ruled Opal out as a good avenue immediately. She didn't exist until the 1880 census, which meant she moved to Colorado from somewhere the previous decade, or she'd changed her name along the way. The author of the penny dreadful was another dead end. So I turned to Margaret Parker. When you read the penny dreadful, you'll see that the names of the characters are dramatic and ridiculous, so *Margaret Parker* stood out for its blandness. I didn't find her on the *census rolls*, but I did find her obituary in the *Rocky Mountain News* in 1877.

KC: And then it's just a matter of following the threads.

SB: Exactly. I was working on another project at the time, so I did this in my spare time, which there wasn't much of. I was getting discouraged, too. The real Margaret Parker I found was a widow who'd lost her horse ranch after her husband died. And she dropped off the record from '73 to '77, when her obituary ran.

I was in DC at a conference and went to the Library of Congress during a free afternoon I had. I'd decided I was going to have a shot at finding the former slave that was in the penny dreadful. Henrietta LaCour, a French Creole who had an affinity for head scarves and voodoo. The librarian chuckled when I asked her if she'd ever run across a former female slave turned outlaw. She said no, but that the LoC had just finished digitizing the WPA Slave Narrative Collection, and I could look through that. It wasn't public yet, so of course I jumped at the chance. What do you know, there was a Henrietta Lee with a short entry, which ended with her teasing a more interesting story to come. The interviewer never followed up.

KC: You're kidding.

SB: The WPA writers weren't historians, and they probably didn't really care about the subjects or their stories. This particular interviewer was especially racist in his transcriptions, including extreme vernacular, making every slave sound ignorant. Of course, we understand now that many if not all of the slaves told those white writers what they wanted to hear instead of the truth.

KC: What a lost opportunity, and not just losing the story that Henrietta Lee alluded to, but the lost opportunity to get in-depth, real accounts of slavery experiences before it left living history.

SB: That is one of the frustrations of being a historian, as you know. But it's the frustration of never having the complete story that makes the things you do find all the more exciting. In this case, I thought I would go back to Boulder, start working on another project I was interested in, and put the Parker Gang back in the filing cabinet.

Two days later the LoC librarian called me, said she couldn't stop thinking about my inquiry, so she went into the archives for the original transcriptions and notes. The woman who assisted the original interviewer, Gerald Coleman, was named Grace Williams, and she kept a file of all his notes and the carbon copies of the interviews she typed up. In that file was the rest of Henrietta Lee's story. Grace had gone back herself, over a month and a half, and taken down Mrs. Lee's story. It was all there. Every bit of it. Talk about a gold mine.

KC: Why was it not included in the archives?

SB: Because of where it was filed. But then the question became, why was it filed there? Did she not turn it in to her boss? There's no record or mention of the interviews in the WPA Writers' Project paperwork, so we have no idea. We're lucky it wasn't thrown away.

KC: Henrietta Lee's narrative then gave you the names and clues to discover the rest of the story.

SB: Yes, but again, we had the amazing good fortune to find Margaret Parker's and Claire Hamilton's journals, and in such good condition. Henrietta said that Claire Hamilton and Ruby Steele moved to San Francisco and died in the 1906 earthquake. I contacted the San Francisco city archivist, gave her their names, and asked if they had information about them. As part of the San Francisco Museum's earthquake section, there are saved everyday items, some with earthquake damage, others just as examples of the times.

In 2006, the San Francisco National Bank donated two or three trunks of items that had been left in their safe-deposit boxes, never claimed by the owner or their family or descendants. The trunks had been in storage and forgotten. When they were discovered, the board decided to donate the items, some quite valuable, to the museum, figuring if they hadn't been claimed in one hundred years they weren't likely to be. Claire Hamilton had a safe-deposit box. Inside were a dozen journals spanning from 1877 to 1905. The museum started digitizing the most recent journals, as they had the most connection to the era of the earthquake, and as with so many projects, money ran out.

KC: Always the first cut, art and history.

SB: Yes. The last two journals were bundled together, and were Margaret's and Claire's accounts of those five months.

KC: That is amazing.

SB: Yes, once word got out, I had colleagues from around the world wanting to take me gambling because I was obviously on a lucky streak!

KC: That's one way to look at it. Another is that this story wanted to be told.

SB: Yes. A thousand times, yes. It is heartbreaking that these women were forgotten. Not even forgotten, but ignored even during their time. I'm not going to get on my soapbox here, but this story isn't just an exciting, real-life action adventure, but also a lesson in the power of the press to shape history, of people in power to shape what we know so that it fits a certain narrative and preserves their influence. People think that fake news and propaganda are serious threats to our democracy, and they're not wrong. The difference is that now the counterpoint, or the truth, according to some people, is available. At everyone's fingertips. That is a very, very recent phenomenon. Today's historians suffer from a lack of information, large gaps, and downright holes. Future historians will suffer from too much information, and such conflicting accounts it will be difficult to parse it.

KC: But the winners will always write the history.

SB: They always have, with the exception of the South and the Civil War. It will be interesting to see who writes the history, and if it will even be possible to quash opposing, losing perspectives. I don't think it will, and it remains to be seen if that's a good thing or not. I tend to think so. Our history has been one-sided for too long.

KC: The white male perspective.

SB: Mostly, yes.

KC: But that's changing.

SB: It is. There has been an increased interest in these lost women of history, thanks in part to podcasts like yours, and I hope that *Heresy* inspires more historians to focus on women in history, and inspires nonhistorians to think about history in a different light, not as something that doesn't impact us, but as a living, breathing part of everything we experience. Women will read this book, and too much of it will be familiar to them. Maybe they'll stop and think, 'You know, we haven't made as much progress as we should have in a hundred and forty years.'

KC: What is next? Surely this isn't the end of this story.

SB: I'm not sure what contemporaneous information is left to be found. There's always the possibility that Luke Rhodes will turn up in the historical record sometime. But who knows.

KC: Is it true that Hollywood has come calling?

SB: Yes, and a New York City publisher has approached me about writing a novel about the Parker Gang.

KC: As in fiction?

SB: Yes.

KC: Don't they know historians don't do fiction, only facts?

SB: They say the story is so outlandish it might as well be fiction, and I don't disagree with them. I'm halfway tempted to do it.

KC: Professor!

SB: Margaret Parker wanted her story to be told, and through a set of crazy coincidences and a huge dose of good luck, I'm the one who has been entrusted with it. I want Margaret and Hattie and Claire and Stella and Joan to have their stories told, to get their due finally, one hundred and forty years later. If that means a movie, a novel, a graphic novel—hell, skywriting, I'm going to do it. I love these women, their resilience, their spirit. The world needs to know that these women were real, and they were magnificent.

Acknowledgments

It's nothing short of a miracle that you find this book in your hands and are reading these acknowledgments. This was a difficult book to write, for many reasons, some of which have to do with writing, some of which do not. There were many times I thought about quitting, about giving back my advance and admitting the story was too big for me, that I wasn't good enough, that I was beaten. Basically, I suffered from imposter syndrome for most of the year I spent writing *Heresy*.

Well, guess what? I won. This book is a big middle finger to imposter syndrome, among other things, and, in the end, it's my best work to date.

I didn't do it alone.

Thanks to my agent, Alice Speilburg, for being my biggest champion.

Thanks to Lindsey Hall, Anne Clarke, Tim Holman, and the Orbit/Redhook team for having faith in me that I could deliver this book based on a very thin idea. I can admit now how very thin this idea was. Razor thin. Almost nonexistent. Hence the Year of Difficulties. Their belief in me, not wanting to let them down, is what made me keep going.

Thanks to Bradley Englert for picking up my little orphan and offering wonderful editorial insight, and for loving it as much as I do. Thanks also to Ellen Wright for being the best publicist in the world. Also thanks to Gleni Bartels, S. B. Kleinman, Jenna Dutton, and Crystal Benn, as well as the designers at Jouve.

Thanks to my tribe of writers and pub professionals, who pick up the phone and answer my calls and texts and listen to everything from my "I don't have a process! Why don't I have a process yet!" rants (Brooke Fossey) to all my crazy plot ideas (Jenny Martin) to "This book is going to kill me. Will you be sad?" (Mark Hoover) to "Remind me when I have a Great Idea to keep it to myself" (Kendel Lynn/Lindsey Hall/Alice Speilburg). Thanks, too, to everyone at DFW Writers' Workshop and Sisters in Crime North Dallas for keeping me motivated.

Thanks to historian Laura Ruttum Senturia for your invaluable help with Colorado history, to Ashlee Clark Thompson for help with the representation of Hattie LaCour, to Mark Hoover for your constant love and support and being the best mentor a writer could ask for.

Thank you to all the readers who have reached out to me, excited about my work and eager for this book. I hope the wait has been worth it! To Suehyla El-Attar, Suzanne Owen, Christy Ramirez, Diane Fenci, Jennifer Mason-Black, Blake Leyers, Carin Thrum, Heather Wheat, Terry Matthews, the Winnsboro Book Club, and all of my other friends who have offered support in various ways in the last year.

To my extended family for loving me, believing in me, and looking past my faults and our differences to the soul beneath.

Last, but never, ever least, to Jay, Ryan, and Jack. Whenever things are darkest, I look to you three—my beacons, my true north—on the other side of the doubt, the challenges and the setbacks, and know that your love is there, waiting to embrace me.

Cast of Characters

WPA Slave Narrative Collection (1936)

Henrietta Lee—Ninety-two-year-old former slave

Grace Williams—Interviewer

Marshall Pass Stage Robbery

Grace Trumbull—A bluestocking from Chicago traveling the West to write her memoirs

Emily Butler—Margaret Parker's alias during the Marshall Pass stage robbery

Benjamin Adamson—Callum Connolly's clerk

Stella Elbee—Member of the Parker Gang; Joan's older sister

Joan Jennifer Elbee—Youngest member of the Parker Gang; Stella's younger sister

Toddy—Wells Fargo stagecoach guard

Jehu Lee—Wells Fargo teamster

Hattie LaCour—Former slave and Buffalo Soldier; co-leader of the Parker Gang (Henrietta Lee)

Margaret Elizabeth Standridge Parker, Duchess of Parkerton—British widow; co-leader of the Parker Gang

Thomas Parker, Duke of Parkerton (deceased)—Margaret's husband; hero of the Charge of the Light Brigade

Horace Whatley—Miner

Timberline

Newt Valentine—Twelve-year-old son of Timberline's blacksmith

Ulysses Valentine—Blacksmith; alcoholic and violent man

Lou Valentine (deceased)—Ulysses Valentine's wife

Sheriff Luke Rhodes—Timberline sheriff who enforces one law: no killing

Rebecca and Harvey Reynolds—Owners of the Timberline general store

Opal Steele—One of two whores in Timberline

Ruby Steele—The other whore; Opal's "sister"; half-Chinese

Eli—Bartender/bouncer at the Blue Diamond Saloon

Salter—Stranger

The Spooner Gang

Jed Spooner—Outlaw; Margaret Parker's former lover

Hank "Ought-Not" Henry—Jed Spooner's lieutenant; safecracker

Domino Jones—Cardsharp

"Sly" Jack Fox—Pickpocket

Maurice "Scab" Williams—Explosives expert

"Dead-Eye" Deacon Jones—Religious fanatic

The Connolly Family

Colonel Louis Connolly (deceased)—Colorado militiaman during the Civil War; cattleman; owner of Connolly Enterprises

Dorcas Connolly—Colonel Connolly's sister; Callum's aunt
Callum Connolly—Colonel Connolly's son; Dorcas's nephew

Poudre River Ranch and Dinner Party

Zhu Li—Connolly's Chinese cook; formerly worked for Margaret
Bohai—Her husband
Zeke—Cowboy
Governor John Routt and his wife, Eliza—First governor of Colorado
Nathaniel P. Hill—A gold smelter
Lewis and Dorothy Wilson—A dry goods proprietor with stores in Cheyenne, Denver, Golden
Alexander Bisson—Callum Connolly's lawyer; helped Colonel Connolly steal Margaret's ranch
Evangeline White—His paid companion

Denver/Colorado Springs/Cheyenne/Black Hawk

Claire Hamilton—Female detective hunting the female gang; former Pinkerton, hired by Dorcas Connolly
Dr. Alida Avery—First female physician in Colorado; president of the Colorado Woman Suffrage Association
Kaye Hunter—Suffragist
Ashley Perkins—Suffragist
Sally Dove—Colorado Springs prostitute
Rosemond—Photographer and portraitist
Portia Bright—Rosemond's partner
Clay Cooper—Cheyenne sheriff
Frank Chambers—Owner of the Chambers Lodge in Black Hawk, Colorado

Lana Chambers—His wife; Margaret took Lana and her son, Zeke, in when they ran away from her abusive former husband
George—Pinkerton
Wilson—Pinkerton
Mingzhu—Ruby Steele's given name
Yung Su—Denver tailor; Mingzhu's uncle

Glossary

Afterclaps—Unexpected happenings after an event is supposed to be over

Arbuckle's—Coffee; taken from a popular brand of the time

Blue belly—Yankee

Bluestocking—An epithet for literary ladies

Bow up—puffing up as if preparing to fight someone

Buffalo Soldiers—Black soldiers of the U.S. Army who fought Native Americans and policed the frontier in the years following the Civil War

Calico queen—Prostitute

California collar—A hangman's noose

California widow—A woman separated from her husband, but not divorced; from when men went west, leaving their wives to follow later

Cracker—A poor southern white person, named after the cracking whips used by rural southerners

Celestial—Derogatory term for a Chinese person

Coulee—a deep ravine

Curly wolf—Mean fellow; tough guy; sometimes a bit of a bastard

Hemp—Marijuana

Filling the blanket—Rolling a cigarette

Fingersmith—Pickpocket

Granger—A derogatory term for a farmer

Laudanum—An alcoholic solution containing morphine, prepared from opium, and used as a narcotic painkiller

Lynching bee—A hanging

Owlhoot—Outlaw

Pancake—English saddle

Peacemaker—Colt .45; the "Gun that Won the West"

Penny dreadful—A cheap, sensational novel of adventure, crime and violence; dime novel; pulp fiction

Pert near—Pretty near

Peterman—Safecracker

Pinkerton—a detective working for Pinkerton National Detective Agency

Poke bonnet—A long, straight bonnet, worn by Quakers and Methodists

Powder monkey—Explosions expert

Six-shooter coffee—Strong coffee

Sodbuster—Farmer

Soroche—Mountain sickness

Shebang—General store

Smock-faced boy—Smooth-faced man; white man

Sutler store—General store on an army fort

Throw up the sponge—Give up

Tignon—A piece of cloth worn as a turban by Creole women of Louisiana

meet the author

Photo Credit: Amy Freshwater

MELISSA LENHARDT lives in Texas with her husband, two sons, and two golden retrievers. For more information about her, visit melissalenhardt.com.